H.H. Wilson

Vishnu Purana

A system of Hindu mythology and tradition. Vol.5, Pt. 2

H.H. Wilson

Vishnu Purana
A system of Hindu mythology and tradition. Vol.5, Pt. 2

ISBN/EAN: 9783337385453

Printed in Europe, USA, Canada, Australia, Japan

Cover: Foto ©Andreas Hilbeck / pixelio.de

More available books at **www.hansebooks.com**

THE

VISHNU PURÁŃA:

A SYSTEM

OF

HINDU MYTHOLOGY AND TRADITION.

TRANSLATED FROM

THE ORIGINAL SANSKRIT,

AND ILLUSTRATED BY NOTES DERIVED CHIEFLY FROM OTHER PURÁŃAS

BY THE LATE

H. H. WILSON, M.A., F.R.S.,

BODEN PROFESSOR OF SANSKRIT IN THE UNIVERSITY OF OXFORD, ETC. ETC.

EDITED BY

FITZEDWARD HALL.

VOL. V., PART II. INDEX.

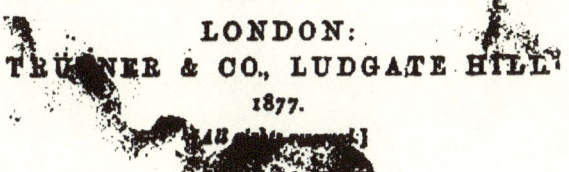
LONDON:

TRÜBNER & CO., LUDGATE HILL.

1877.

[All rights reserved.]

THE circumstances which have operated to retard the appearance of the following pages are such as hardly to admit, in this place, of any statement except that, if my pleasure had been consulted, the publication of this Index would have followed immediately that of the volumes to which it relates.

That it is free from mistakes is very much more than I venture to suppose. Beyond question, if I had enjoyed access to books and manuscripts additional to those in my own limited collection, I might often have done otherwise than simply repeat that which I strongly suspected, and still so suspect, of being erroneous.

To the fourteen pages with which the Index concludes, the attention of the inspector is particularly invited. With much else that concerns him, he will there find materials for occasional emendation of the admirable Sanskrit lexicon for which we are indebted to the unrivalled research of the learned Messrs. Böhtlingk and Roth.

F. H.

MARLESFORD, WICKHAM MARKET,
November 1, 1876.

CORRECTIONS.

Page.	Col.	Line.			
10	1	40, 41	*See*	Vijaya, son of Jaya or Vijaya.	
17	1	16	*For*	Aśrutavraña	*read* Aśrutabraña.
34	2	14	,,	135	,, 136.
35	1	13	*Insert*	1. 174.	
51	2	16	*For*	Vámadevn	*read* Dhṛitavrata.
55	2	33	,,	Páṅdu	,, Páṅdu.
58	1	39	,,	Gañeśa	,, Gañeśa.
63	1	41	,,	Gúnas	,, Guṇas.
63	2	21	,,	-vyákhya	,, -vyákhyá.
64	1	14	,,	Haimavati	,, Haimavatí.
68	2	21	,,	Mánasarovara	,, Mánasasarovara.
71	2	9	,,	Íśwara	,, Íśwara.
75	1	7, 11	*See*	Vijaya, son of Jaya or Vijaya.	
80	2	22	*For*	Kámarúpiní	*read* Kámarúpíñí.
87	2	28	,,	Keśin	,, Keśin.
89	1	8	,,	Urú	,, Úru.
95	1	3	,,	Rádika	,, Rádhika.
100	1	34	,,	Kuśanára	,, Kuśanárá.
100	2	11	,,	Kuśasthalí	,, Kuśasthalí.
105	1	3	,,	Váruśí	,, Várusí.
120	2	28	*Insert*	Nabhaga.	
122	1	18	*For*	Ayus	,, Áyus.
122	2	6	*Read*	N., or R., his city, where.	
123	1	14	,,	Nalopákhyana	*read* Nalopákhyáina.
124	1	1	,,	Nandiyaśis	,, Nandiyaśes.
127	2	40	,,	Suśrama	,, Suśrama.
130	1	20	*For*	Brahmá	,, Brahma.
135	1	17	,,	Pariśáśa	,, Pariśáśá.
141	2	27, 31	,,	Pránśu	,, Pránśu.
149	1	36	,,	Budhá	,, Budha.
149	2	26	,,	Budhá	,, Budha.
154	1	12	,,	Suvárna	,, Suvárná.
154	1	17	,,	Ramánas	,, Ramañas.
158	2	36	,,	Ṛishyaśringa	,, Ṛishyaśringa.
160	1	5	,,	-pa	,, -dwípa.

CORRECTIONS.

Page.	Col.	Line.					
160	2	17	*For*	Viswajit	*read*	Viśwajit.
161	1	36	„	Śri-	„	Śri-.
161	2	9	„	Bhishmaka	„	Bhishmaka.
162	1	21	„	Sabda-	„	Sabda.
164	2	21	„	Sisunága	„	Śiśunága.
168	2	25	„	Santatateyu	„	Santateyu.
170	2	24	„	Śaura	„	Saura.
174	1	3	„	Saraswatí	„	Saraswatí.
177	1	4	„	Sataprasúti	„	Sataprasúti.
180	2	28	„	Sauśratas	„	Sauśrutas.
184	1	18	Sishṭi *is a better reading than* Slishṭi.				
187	2	30	*For*	Srénta	*read*	Srénta.
190	2	18	„	Strirájya	„	Strirájya.
193	2	13	„	Sudhárá	„	Sudhárá.
199	2	3	„	Súnyabindu	„	Śúnyabindu.
211	1	32, 34	„	Tirthankara	„	Tirthaṅkara.
216	1	31	„	Ugrampaśyá	„	Ugraṁpaśyá.
219	2	32	„	Vyasa	„	Vyása.
230	2	26	„	Puráravas	„	Purúravas.
233	2	18	„	Prána	„	Práṇa.
234	1	9	„	Vedavit	„	Vedavid.
237	2	14	„	Vikrishna	„	Vikrishṇa.
240	1	18	„	Virankará	„	Viraṁkará.
242	2	37	„	Viswadhara	„	Viśwadhára.
245	2	40	„	Havirdhaúa	„	Havirdhánn.
248	1	39	„	Dwapara	„	Dwápara.
249	1	8	„	an	„	on.
253	1	19	„	Bharatavarsha	„	Bháratavarsha.
261		19	„	Uchchaihśravas	„	Uchchaiḥśravas.
265	2	23	„	Pánina	„	Pánine.
267	2	33-35	*Expunge* See . . . . . explaining.				

It will have been observed that most of the errors here corrected pertain to accents and diacritical marks. Others similar have, probably, eluded notice.

INDEX.

—◦◦—

.˙. The abbreviation P. denotes the Preface to the work here indexed. The volumes of the work are denoted by larger Arabic numerals; their pages, and likewise those of the Preface, by smaller.

Abala, variant of Sunítá, 4. 176.

Abhaya, 'fearlessness,' son of Dharma, 1. 111.

Abhaya, son of Idhmajihwa, king of Plaksha-dwípa, 2. 193.

Abhaya, a region in Plaksha-dwípa, 2. 193.

Abhayá, a river in Krauncha-dwípa, 2. 198.

Abhayada, son of Manasyu, 4. 127

Abhidhána, the term explained, 5. 14.

Abhidhána-chintámani, a vocabulary, referred to, 3. 122, 246.

Abhidhána-ratna-málá, a vocabulary, referred to, 2. 160.

Abhijana, what, 3. 143.

Abhijit, son of Vyoman, 4. 68.

Abhijit, variously genealogized, 4. 98.

Abhijit, a certain asterism, 2. 264, &c., 308.

Abhijita, variant of Abhijit, 4. 98.

Abhijnáta, son of Yajnabáhu, king of Sálmalá-dwípa, 2. 195.

Abhijnáta, a region in Sálmalá-dwípa, 2. 195.

Abhimána, a Rishi in the sixth Manwantara, 3. 12.

Abhimána, the term, 1. 33; 5. 198 (note §§).

Abhimánin, an Agni, eldest son of Brahmá, 1. 155 (where correct the spelling); 5. 387.

Abhimanyu, son of Chákshusha, the Manu, 1. 177.

Abhimanyu, son of Arjuna, son of Pándu, 3. 321, 326; 4. 159, 160, 163.

Abhináman (?), variant of Atináman, 3. 12.

Abhinámin, a Rishi in the sixth Manwantara, 3. 13.

Abhiniveśa, what, 1. 69.

Abhíras, Ábhíras, peoples, 2. 133, 134, 167, 168, 184, 185; 4. 222, 224; 5. 157-159, 162, 164.

Ábhíras, a race of kings, 4. 202, 205-208.

Abhisáras, a people, 2. 174, 175.

Abhishava, what, 3. 196.

Abhiyukta, a caste in Kuśa-dwípa, 2. 197.

Abhrayantí, a Kṛittiká, 2. 337.

A

Abhúmi, son of Chitraka, 4. 96.

A'bhútanayas, variant of A'bhú-tarajas, 3. 9.

A'bhútarajas, a class of gods in the fifth Manwantara, 3. 9, 10.

A'bhútarajases, variant of A'bhú-tarajas, 3 9, 10.

A'bhútaramas, variant of A'bhú-tarajas, 3. 9

A'bhúturayas, variant of A'bhú-tarajas, 3. 9.

Abhyudaya-śráddha, a certain mortuary rite, 3. 99, 338.

Abiria, the classical name of the country of the Abhíras, 2. 185.

Abjá, daughter of Bhárgava, 3. 238.

Abjabhava, the same as Abjayoni, 4. 111.

A'bjayoni, an epithet of Brahmá, 1. 17; 3. 150, 251; 4. 2; 5. 196, 250.

A'bu, a mountain in Central India, 4. 225. See Arbuda.

Achala, a Devarshi, son of Pratyú-sha, 3. 68.

Achala, variant of Suníta, 4. 176.

A'chára, the term defined, &c., 3. 85, 107, 338.

A'chára-chandriká, a law-book, referred to, 3. 198.

Achchhodá, daughter of the Ag-nishwáttas, 3. 160.

Achyuta, a name of Vishńu or Krishńa, its etymology, &c., 1. 15, 162, et passim.

Adbhuta, an Iudra in the ninth Manwantara, 3. 25.

Adbhaĺśiras, a hell, 2. 215.

Adharma, 'vice,' son of Brahmá, 1 101, 111, 112.

A'dhi-bhautika, what, 5. 60, 203.

A'dhi-daivika, what, 5. 60, 203.

Adhikánga, adhikángí, what, 3. 104.

Adhi-purusha, 'supreme spirit,' 1. 170.

Adhirájya (?), a country, 2. 165.

Adhiráshtra (?), a country, 2. 165.

Adhiratha, son of Satyakarman, 4. 126

Adhikámakrishńa (?), variant of Adhisímakrishńa, 4. 163.

Adhisímakrishńa, son of Aśwa-medhadatta, 4. 163.

Adhisomakrishńa, variant of Adhi-símakrishńa, 4. 163.

Adhiváhana, variant of Pára, 4. 123.

Adhivájya (??), a country, 2, 165.

Adhivájyakuládya (??), a country, 2. 165.

Adhokshaja, an epithet of Vishńu or Krishńa, 1. 28; 4. 252; 5. 11.

Adhomukha = Adhaĺśiras, a hell, 2. 218.

Adbrishťa, variant of Anádbrishți, son of Súra, 4. 101.

Adhrishyá, a river, 2, 149.

Adhwaryu, a sort of priest, 3. 43, 343.

Adhyas, variant of Andhas, 2. 170.

Adhyátma-rámáyaṅa, a part of the Brahmáńḍa-puráńa, P. 84.

A'dhyátmika, what, 5. 60, 202, 203.

A'di-bhúta, what, 3. 230.

A'di-kŕit, what, 5. 195.

Adína, son of Sahadeva, 4. 44.

A'di-puráńa = Brahma-puráńa, P 27.

A'díra (?), A'díra, variants of An-dída, 4. 117.

Adîti, daughter of Daksha, and wife of Kaśyapa, 1. 147, 151; 2. 26, 27, 259; 3. 18-20, 230; 4. 265, 318; 5. 88, 90, 92, 93, 96, 97.

Aditi, one of the Viśwe devas, 3. 179.

Áditya, the sun, P. 3; 3. 56, 117; 4. 74, 75, 103; 5. 382.

Ádityas, certain gods, twelve in number, 1. 121, 123, 125; 2. 27, 285, 286, &c.; 3. 3, 13, 15, 18; 4. 249, 272, 293; 5. 2, 143, 247. Their chief, Vishńu, 2. 85.

Áditya, Á'dityá. Punarvasu, an asterism, 2. 266, 276.

Áditya-upapuráńa. P. 87.

Ádi-upapuráńa, P. 91.

Adrava (?), variant of Amavat, 3. 191.

Ádravas (?), variant of Amavat, 3. 190, 191.

Adriká, an Apsaras, mistress of Vasu, 2. 81-83; 4. 149.

Adfiśyantí, wife of Śakti, and mother of Paráśara, 1. 8.

Adwaita, what, 2. 90.

Adwija, what, 4. 222.

Ádyas, a class of gods in the sixth Manwantara, 3. 12.

Adya, variant of Apas, the Rakshasa, 2. 293.

Agada, 'alexipharmacy,' 4. 33.

Agada-tantra = Agada, 4. 33.

Agasti, the same as the next, (?) 3. 128.

Agastya, son of Pulastya, P. 72, 86; 1. 154; 5. 387.

Agastya, or Canopus, an asterism, 2. 263, 268, 308.

Agha, an Asura, Kamsa's generalissimo, 5. 11.

Aghora, a Kalpa, P. 62.

Aghorástra, a weapon borne by Śiva, 5. 118.

Ágneya, a kind of cloud, 2. 279.

Ágneya = Kŕittiká, an asterism, 2. 277; 4. 235.

Ágneya - puráńa = Agni - puráńa, P. 23, 58; 3. 65, 67 (where correct the spelling), 338.

Ágneyástra, 'a fiery weapon,' 3. 81.

Ágneyí, wife of Úru, 1. 177.

Agni, god of fire, son of Angiras, P. 3, 21, 58; 1. 154, 155, 192; 2. 306, 307; 3. 2, 28, 128, 162, 166; 4. 235, 249, 254; 5. 100, 158, 382. King of the Pitŕis, 2. 86. His city, 2. 112, 118.

Agni, the Vaidik, 2. 79.

Agnis, forty-nine in number, 1. 141, 156; 4. 249, 258, 272; 5. 143.

Agni, a Ŕishi in the fourth Manwantara, 3. 8.

Agni, a star so called, 2. 306.

Agni, a Kalpa, P. 67.

Agni (?), variant of Nimi, 4. 72.

Agnibáhu, son of Priyavrata and Kámyá, 2. 100, 101.

Agnibáhu, a Rishi in the fourteenth Manwantara, 3. 28.

Agnidagdhas, certain Pitŕis so called, 1. 156; 3. 166, 339.

Agnídhra, son of Priyavrata and Kámyá, and king of Jambú. dwípa, 2. 100, &c.; 3. 2.

Agnídhra, variant of Ghídhra Rishi, 3. 28.

Ágnídhraka, a Rishi in the t[...] Manwantara, 3. 27

Agni-hotra, a sort of sacrifice, 3. 40, 113, 117, 213.

Agni-kárya, a particular ceremony, 3. 189.

Agni-linga, an epiphany of Śiva, as a fiery phallus, P. 67.

Agnimáchara, variant of Agnimáṭhara, 3. 45.

Agnimáṭhara, disciple of Báshkali, and teacher of the Rig-veda, 3. 44, 45.

Agnimátura, variant of Agnimáṭhara, 3. 45.

Agnimitra, disciple of Báshkali, and teacher of the Rig-veda, 3. 44.

Agnimitra, son of Pushpamitra, 4. 172, 190, 191.

Agninévara (?), disciple of Báshkali, and teacher of the Rig-veda, 3. 44.

Agni-puráṇa, analysis of it, &c., P. 20, 24, 58, &c.; 3. 190; 5. 315, 337, 381. See Vahni-puráṇa.

Agnishṭoma, son of Chákshusha, Manu of the sixth Manwantara, 1. 177-179.

Agnishṭoma, a kind of sacrifice, its origin, &c., 1. 84, 85; 3. 113

Agnishṭut, variant of Agnishṭoma, son of Chákshusha, 1. 179.

Agnishṭut = Agnishṭoma, the sacrifice, 1. 85.

Agnishwáttas, a class of Pitris, variously genealogized, 1, 156; 2. 303, 343; 3. 159, 160, 163, 339.

Agnítejas, a Rishi in the eleventh Manwantara, 3. 26.

Agnivarchas, descended from Bharadwája, and disciple of Romaharshaṇa, 3. 64-66.

Agnivarṇa, son of Sudarśana, 3. 314, 321, 325.

Agniváyu, variant of Agnibáhu, the Rishi, 3. 28.

Agniveśya, a form of Agni, and son of Devadatta, 3. 336.

Agniveśyáyanas, certain Bráhmans, 3. 336.

Agnyádheya, a particular sacrifice, 3. 113.

Agrahára, what, P. 105.

Ágraháyaṇa = Márgaśírsha, a month, Nov.-Dec., 2. 261; 3. 114, 168.

Ágraháyaṇí, a particular sacrifice, 3. 113.

Ágrayaṇeshṭí, a particular sacrifice, 3. 113.

Ahalyá, daughter of Badhryaswa, and wife of Śaradwat or Gautama, 3. 316; 4. 146.

Ahaṁkára, particulars touching, 1. 33-35, &c., 76, 140, 169, 172; 2. 94, 232; 5. 94, 199.

Ahaṁmána, what, 5. 223, 225.

Ahaṁyáti, son of Samyáti, 4. 128.

Ahan, 'day,' a body of Brahmá, 1. 81.

Ahárya, variant of Mahávírya, 4. 137.

Áhavaníya, a certain holy fire, 3. 175; 4. 11; 5. 114.

Ahi, 'serpent,' whence the term, 1. 83.

Ahi, variant of Swáhi, 4. 61.

Ahichchhatra, two regions so called, 2. 161.

Ahichchhatrá, a city, 2. 161.

Ahikshátra, a region, 2. 161 ; 4. 145.

Ahiṃsá, what, 3. 77 ; 4. 294 ; 5. 229.

Ahína, variant of Adína, 4. 44.

Ahínagu, son of Devánika, 3. 320, 321, 323.

Ahínara, son of Udayana, 4. 165, 166.

Ahínara, variant of Ahínagu, 3. 321.

Ahíra, the vernacular corruption of Ábhíras, 2. 208.

Ahirbudhna, a Rudra, 2. 24, 25, 337.

Ahirbudhna = Uttara-bhádrapadá, an asterism, 2. 277.

Ahirbudhnya = Abirbudhna, the Rudra, 2. 24, 25, 337.

Ahirvradhna, corrupted from Ahir-budhnya, 2. 24, 25.

Ahitá, variant of Mahitá, 2. 148.

Ahorátra, the term explained, 5. 47.

Áhuka, variously genealogized, 4. 98, 99, 114 ; 5. 150.

Áhukí, variously genealogized, 4. 98.

Áhútas, a class of Apsarasas, 2. 75.

Áhuti, variant of Dhṛiti, son of Babhru, 4. 67.

Áhuti, what, 3. 181.

Aidas, certain Rájarshis, 3. 70.

Aiḍaviḍa, variant of Ilavila, 3. 311.

Aiḍiviḍa, variant of Ilavila, 3. 311.

Aikshwákas, certain Rájarshis, 3. 70.

Aikshwákas, a dynasty, 4. 171, 181, 184.

Ailá, metronym of Purúravas, 3. 168.

Ailavila, variant of Ilavila, 3. 311.

Ailina, son of Taṃsu, 4. 130, 131.

Aindras (?), a people, 2. 341.

Aindra = Indra-dwípa, a portion of Bháratavarsha, 2. 112

Aindra = Jyeshṭhá, an asterism, 2. 265.

Aindriyaka, what, 1. 74.

Ainila, variant of Ailina, 4. 130.

Air, presiding over the skin, 1. 38.

Airávata, king of elephants, produced. by churning the ocean, and appropriated by Indra, 1. 136, 147 ; 2. 85 ; 4. 317, 319, 321 ; 5. 87, 89, 101.

Airávata, a serpent, son of Kaśyapa, 2. 74, 285, &c.

Airávata, three certain triads of asterisms, 2. 265, 267.

Airávatá = Airávatí, a certain triad of asterisms, 2. 276, 277.

Airávatí, a certain triad of asterisms, 2. 265, &c., 277.

Airávatí = Irávatí, a river, 4. 118.

Aishíkas, variant of Ishíkas, 2. 173.

Aitareya-bráhmaṇa, the, or its commentary, referred to, 2. 135, 170, 339, 342, 343 ; 3. 231, 244, 248, 256, 257, 338, 340 ; 4. 27 ; 5. 81.

Aja, a Rudra, 2. 25.

Aja, same as the last, (?) 2. 16, 65.

Aja, son of Auttami, the third Manu, 3. 6.

Aja, variously genealogized, 3. 313, 314, 316 ; 4. 124.

Aja, son of Urdhwaketu, 3. 334.

Aja = Púrva-bhádrapadá, an aster-ism, 2. 276. 277.

Ajagava, the bow of Siva, 1. 183, 186.

Ajagava, variant of Jaradgava, 2. 267.

Ajaikapád, a Rudra, 2. 24, 25.

Ajaikapád = Púrva-bhádrapadá, an asterism, 3. 167.

Ajaka, variously genealogized, 4. 14, 15.

Ajaka, son of Yadu, 4. 53.

Ajaka, variant of Janaka, 4. 179.

Ajamídha, variously genealogized, 4. 138–140, 142, 144, 145, 147, 148, 153.

Ajapála = Aja, 3. 314.

Ajaśyáma, son of Sukumára, 4. 163.

Ajátaśatru, variously genealogized, 4. 181, 182, 186.

Ájava (?), variant of Kathájava, 3. 50.

Ajavíthi, a certain triad of asterisms, 2. 263, &c., 308.

Ajaya, variant of Udayáśwa, 4. 182.

Ajígarta, father of Sunaḥśepha, 4. 25-27.

Ajika, son of Yadu, 4. 53.

Ajina, son of Havirdhána, 1. 193.

Ajitas, a class of gods in the first Manwantara, 2. 26; 3. 2.

Ajita, a form of Vishńu in the second Manwantara, 3. 17.

Ajita, a Ŕishi in the fourteenth Manwantara, 3. 29.

Ajita, son of Yadu, 4. 53.

Ajita, son of Punarvasu, 4. 98.

Ajyapas, a class of Pitŕis, variously genealogized, 1. 123, 157; 3. 160, 164, 339.

Akapi, a Ŕishi in the fourth Manwantara, 3. 8.

Akapívat, a Ŕishi in the fourth Manwantara, 3. 8.

Ákaśa, particulars regarding. 1. 34, 36; 2. 232, 235; 5 198, 254

Ákáśagangá a river, 2. 280, 281.

Ákhyána, Ákhyánaka, defined. 2. 95; 3. 63, 66 (note §).

Akrúra (?), variant of Andíáa, 4. 117.

Akrísáswa, son of Samhatáswa, 3. 265, 266.

Akŕitabraṅa, sprung from Kaśyapa, and disciple of Romaharshaṅa, P. 19; 3. 64-66

Akŕitavrata, variant of Akŕitabraṅa, 3. 66.

Akriya, sprung from Rambha, son of Áyus, 4. 43.

Akrodhana, son of Ayutanáyin. 4 128.

Akrodhana, son of Ayutáyus, son of Árávin, 4. 153.

Akrúra, son of Swaphalka. 4. 80, 82, 84, 86, &c., 94, 96, 335, 336, 338; 5. 3, 4, 5, 8-13 16–18, 23, 26, 148.

Akshagandhá, an Apsaras, 2. 82.

Akshara, what, 5. 211.

Aksha-sútraka, ᵃrosary, 5. 239.

Akshauhiní, the term explained, 4. 250; 5. 50, 140.

Aksha-valaya = Aksha-sútraka. 5 239.

Aksha-váťa, what, 5. 26.

Akshaya, what, 5. 51.

Ákshepa, variant of Upekaha, 4. 96.

Ákúti, daughter of Swáyambhuva Manu, and wife of Ruchi, 1. 108; 3. 16 (where correct the spelling); 5 390.

A'kúti, wife of Chakshus, son of Vyusht'a, 1. 178.

Alaká, the capital of Kubera, and city of the Gandharvas, 4. 6; 5. 386.

Alakanandá, a river, 2. 112, 120, 122, 272.

Alakshmí, goddess of misfortune, daughter of Lakshmi, 1. 147. Is called offspring of Adharma, 1. 112.

A'lambana, what, 5. 231.

A'lambi, disciple of Vaiśampáyana, and teacher of the Yajur-veda, 3. 52.

Alambushá, an Apsaras, mistress of Triñabindu, 2. 81, 82; 3. 246.

Alarka, variously genealogized, 4. 36-39.

A'layá (?), a river, 2. 146.

Alindas, a people, 2. 180.

Alpá (?), a river, 2. 196.

A'ma, son of Kŕishńa and Satyá, 5. 79.

A'ma, son of Ghŕitapŕishťha, king of Krauncha-dwípa, 2. 198.

A'ma, a region in Krauncha-dwípa, 2. 198.

Amá, a ray of the sun, 2. 301.

Amáhaka = Avyanga, 5. 383.

Amalajá, daughter of Raudráśwa, and wife of Prabhakara, 4. 129.

Amantravit (?), variant of Amitrajit 4 169.

Amaras, the gods,' 5. 252.

Amarakańťaka, a mountain so called, 5. 118.

Amara-kośa, a vocabulary, referred to, 2. 22, 54, 142, 147, 149, 160; 3. 73, 102, 318; 5. 50, 51, 300. See Amarasińha

Amara-loka = Deva-loka, 5. 145.

Amarasińha, an author, P. 7, 10, &c.; 3. 73, 207; 5. 259, 266, 274, 324, 332. See Amara-kośa.

Amarávatí, the city of Indra, 1. 137; 2. 240; 3. 253; 5. 57.

Amarávatí, a city in Berar, 5. 69

Amarsha, son of Susandhi, 3. 325

Amarshańa, variant of Amarsha, 3. 325.

Amávasu, son of Purúravas, 4 13, 14, 138, 139.

Amávasu, son of Kusa, 4. 15.

Amávásyá, etymology of, &c., 2. 260, 301.

Amavat (?) one of the Viśwe devas, 3. 191.

Amáyus, son of Purúravas, 4. 13.

Ambas, a people, 2. 136.

Ambá, a Kŕittiká, 2. 337.

Ambáliká, daughter of a king of the Káśis, 4. 158.

Ambarísha, son of Pulaha, 1. 155

Ambarísha, son of Nábhága. 3. 238, 239, 256, 257.

Ambarísha, on of Mándhátŕi, 3 268, 280, 281; 5. 391.

Ambarísha, variously genealogized, 3. 303, 314, 315.

Ambarísha, king of Ayodhyá (which of the Ambaríshas named above?), 4. 25, 26.

Ambarísha (who?), P. 49, 68.

Ambashťhas, Ambashťhas, a people, 2. 133, 135, 136, 340; 4. 121

Ambashťhá, a city, 4. 122

Ambashťhya, a king named in the Aitareya-brahmańa, 2. 135

Ambhánsi, four classes of beings so called, 1. 80.

Ambhogiri, variant of Asta, 2. 199.

Ambiká, an Apsaras, 2. 81.

Ambíká, wife of Bhava, the Rudra, I. 117; 4. 262.

Ambiká, daughter of a king of the Kásis, 4. 158.

Ambiká = Indráni, (?) 5. 70.

Ámbikera (?), variant of Ámbikeya, 2. 199.

Ámbikeya, a mountain-range in Sáka-dwípa, 2. 199.

Ambupa = Varuna, 2. 112.

Ambuváhiní, variant of Madhu-váhiní, 2. 150.

Ameya, what, 5. 4.

Ameyátman, what, 3. 206; 4. 304.

Amitábhas, two classes of gods, so called, 3. 9, 23.

Amitrajit, son of Suvarna, 4. 169.

Amnáya = Veda, 5. 9.

Amritás, a class of Apsarases, 2. 82.

Amrita, father of the Amritás, 2. 82.

Amrita, son of Idhmajihwa, king of Plaksha-dwípa, 2. 193.

Amrita, a region in Plaksha-dwípa, 2. 193.

Amrita, the ocean churned for it, 1. 142, &c. Drunk by the gods, 1. 145. Stored in the moon, 2. 300. Drunk by the Pitris, 2. 302. Its character, 2. 300.

Amrita, a river in Plaksha-dwípa, 2. 192.

Amritábhas, a class of gods in the fifth Manwantara, 3. 10.

Amritaprabhas, a class of gods in the eighth Manwantara, 3. 24.

Amritaughá, a river in Kraunchadwípa, 2. 198.

Amsa, an Áditya, 2. 27, 286, 291, &c.

Amsa, variously genealogized, 4. 69.

Amsa, what, 4. 234.

Amsaka, what, 4. 66.

Amsámsa, what, 4. 240.

Amsámsávatára, what, 4. 247.

Amahaspands, the, referred to, 2. 230.

Amsu, variant of Amsá, the Áditya, 2. 27, 285, 286, &c.

Amsu, variant of Amsa, 4. 69, 70.

Amsudatta, an author, referred to the court of King Vikramáditya, P. 9.

Amsumat, son of Asamanja, 3. 298, 301-303.

Amúrta, what, 5. 232, 236.

Amúrtarajas, son of Kusa, 4. 15.

Amúrtárajasa (?), son of Kusa, 4. 15.

Amúrtaraya, son of Kusa, 4. 15.

Amúrtarayasa (correct the spelling), variant of Amúrtárajasa (?), 4. 15.

Amúrtimat, son of Kusa, 4. 15.

Amúrtirajas, son of Antinára, 4. 130.

Amúrtiraya, variant of Amúrtaraya, 4. 15.

Anadhita, variant of Áravin, 4. 153.

Anádrishi (?), variant of Anádhrishti, 4. 101.

Anádhrishti, son of Súra, 4. 101, 113.

Anádhrishti = Matinára, 4. 130.

Anagá, variant of Maningá, 2. 154.

Anagha, son of Vasishtha, 1. 155.

Anagha, a Rishi in the eleventh Manwantara, 3. 26.

Anagha, variously genealogized, 4. 132.

Anaghá (?), an Apsaras, 2. 81.

Anaghá, a river in S'áka-dwípa, 2. 200.

Anagnidagdhas, certain Pitṛis so called, 1. 156; 3. 166, 339.

Ánaka, son of S'úra, 4. 101.

Ánakadundubhi = Vasudeva, father of Kṛishṇa, 4. 79, 101, 108, 110, 268, 269; 5. 8, 154.

Ánakadundubhi = Tamas, &c., 4. 98.

Anala, a Vasu, 2. 23.

Anala (the same as the last?), 4. 111.

Ánalavi (?), variant of Álambi, 3. 52.

Anamitra, father of Chákshusha, the Manu, 3. 11.

Anamitra, son of Nighna, 3. 305, 314.

Anamitra, variously genealogized, 4. 73, 74, 93, 94, 100.

Anámnáya, what, 4. 251.

Ánanda, son of Medhátithi, king of Plaksha-dwípa, 2. 191.

Ánanda, a region in Plaksha-dwípa, 2. 191.

Ánandagiri, a commentator, referred to, 3. 175.

Ananga = Káma, P. 65; 4. 107; 5. 72, 76.

Ananta = Vishṇu, 2. 313; 3. 78; 5. 15, 214.

Ananta = S'esha, a form of Vishṇu, 2. 211-213; 3. 152; 5. 3, 65.

Ananta, one of the Viśwe devas, 5. 192.

Ananta, variant of Ánanda, the region so called, 2. 191.

Anauta, variant of Bharata, 4. 57.

Anantaka, son of S'aśabindu, 4. 63.

Auapána, Anápána, Anapánga, variants of Pára, 4. 123.

Anaraṇya, father of Pushkariṇí, wife of Chakshusha, 1. 177; 5. 388.

Anaraṇya, variously genealogized, slain by Rávaṇa, 3. 283, 284, 297.

Anaraṇya, son of Sarvakarman, 3. 305, 314.

Ánartas, a people descended from Ánarta, next named, 2. 171.

Ánarta, son of Saryáti, 2. 172; 3. 248, 249; 5. 390.

Ánarta, son of Vibhu, 4. 37.

Ánarta, a country, 3. 249.

Anarta (??), variant of Bharata, 4. 57.

Anárya, what, 5. 178.

Anasúyá, ' good-will,' daughter of Daksha, and wife of Atri, 1. 109, 135, 153. In 1. 110, she is called daughter of Kardama.

Anavadyá, an Apsaras, 2. 81, 82.

Anavaratha, son of Madhu, 4. 69.

Anavaśá, an Apsaras, 2. 82.

Anávṛishṭi, what, 3. 285; 4. 87.

Anávṛishṭi, variant of Anádhṛishṭi, son of S'úra, 4. 101.

Anaya, variant of Anagha, the Rishi, 3. 26.

Anáyus, daughter of Daksha, and wife of Kaśyapa, 2. 26, 73, 74.

Áṇḍa-kaṭáhs, what, 2. 204, 231.

Andhas, a people, 2. 170.

Andhakas, a people, 2. 159; 5. 143, 147, 148, 150, 159.

Andhaka, an Asura, P. 79, 82.

Andhaka, a Nága, 3. 38

Andhaka, son of Nahusha, 4. 46.

Andhaka, variously genealogized, 4. 71, 87, 88, 96, 99; 5: 110, 132, 163.

Andhaka (??), son of Aihsu, 4. 69.

Andhaka, variant of Mahídhraka, 3. 332.

Andhaka (?), variant of Dhanaka, 4. 54.

Andhakáraka, son of Dyutimat, king of Krauncha-dwípa, 2. 197.

Andhakáraka, a region in Krauncha-dwípa, 2. 197.

Andhakáraka, a mountain-range in Krauncha-dwípa, 2. 197.

Andhakúpa, a hell, 2. 215.

Andhatámisra, a hell, 2. 215.

Andhatámisra, what, in philosophy, 1. 69.

Andhras, a people, P. 109, 112; 2. 170, 184; 4. 194, 195, 203–205, 207, 208, 210, 216, 220, 221, 231, 232, 234–236.

Andhra, variant of Puñdra, 4. 122.

Andhra, variant of Odra (?), 4. 221.

Ándhra, variant of Árdra, son of Viéwagaéwa, 3. 263.

Andbrabhŕityas, a dynasty, 4. 194, 195, 199, 201, 202.

Andhrajátiyas, a dynasty, 4. 194.

Ándíd'a, son of Karúttháma, 4. 117.

Ándíra, variant of Ándíd'a, 4. 117.

Andras (?), a people, 2. 184.

Andraka, variant of Árdraka, son of Vasumitra, 4. 191.

Anenas, son of Kakutstha or Puranjaya, 3. 263

Anenas, son of Kshemári, 3. 334.

Anenas, son of Áyus, 4. 30, 43.

Angas, a people, 2. 166, 170.

Anga, son of Uru, 1. 177. He is son of Uhnaka, 1. 178; and is descended from Atri, 1 179.

Anga, son of Bali, 3. 289, 4. 122, 123, 126.

Anga, a country, 2. 166; 4. 125, 126, 162; 5. 161.

Angas, six supplements to the Veda, 3. 67, 174.

Angada, son of Lakshmaña, 3. 318.

Angada, a country, 3. 319.

Ángadí, a city in Kárapatha, 3. 319.

Anga-dwípa, a certain island, 2. 129.

Angaja, sprung from Brahmá, 1. 102.

Angáras, a people, 2. 178.

Angáraka, a Rudra, 2. 25.

Angáraka = Lohitanga, or Mars, 2. 226, 308.

Angárasetu, variant of Setu, 4. 118.

Angárasetu, variant of Áradwat, 4. 118.

Angiras, variously genealogized, 1. 100, 122, 153, 158, &c.; 2. 285, &c.; 3. 68, 163, 245; 257–259, 280, 281, 297, 342; 4. 2, 39, 145. His wife, 1. 109, 110. His offspring, 1. 153; 2. 259.

Angiras, son of Daksha, 1. 103, 122; 3. 2, 3, 8, 11, 15, 28. For wives and offspring of some Angiras, see 2. 21, 28.

Angiras, son of Uru, 1. 177 He is said to be son of Ulmnaka, 1. 178.

Angiras, a lawgiver, 3. 148.

Angiras (apparently another), 3.
62. (Some of the references
under the Angirases are very
likely misplaced. To discri-
minate these persons seems all
but impracticable.)
Angiras = Mandhátrí (?), 3. 281.
Angirases, descendants of Angiras,
3. 341 ; 4. 31.
Angirases, certain Bráhmans rank-
ing as Kshattriyas, 3. 258, 259,
280.
Ángirasas, a class of Pitris, 3. 159.
Angirasa (?), a Veda of the Magas,
5. 383.
Ángirasí, a river in Plaksha-dwípa,
2. 193.
Angula = Angulí, 4. 10.
Angulí, finger-breadth,' 2. 204.
Aníha, variant of Ahínagu, 3. 323.
Anila, a Vasu, 2. 23; 5. 387.
Anila, son of Krishna and Mitra-
vindá, 5. 79.
Anila = Váyu, 2. 112; 4. 102; 5.
391.
Anila, variant of Ailina, 4. 130,131.
Anilátmaja = Hanumat, 1. 117.
Animals, creation and classification
of, 1. 84.
Anindas, variant of Alindas, 2. 180.
Aniruddha, son of Pradyumna, 3.
166; 4. 112; 5. 16, 83, 84,
86, 108, 111, 112, 120, 141,
148, 150.
Anishtakarman, variant of Arish-
takarman, 4. 197.
Anjaka, son of Viprachitti, 2. 71.
Anjala, sprung from Brahmá, 1.
102.
Anjana, a serpent, son of Kasyapa,
2. 74.

Anjana, son of Kuni, 3. 334.
Anjana, father of Buddha, 5. 178.
Anjika, son of Yadu, 4. 53.
Anjika, variant of Anjaka, 2. 71.
Anjita, son of Yadu, 4 53.
Annáda, son of Krishna and
Mitravindá, 5. 79.
Annapána, variant of Pára, 4. 123.
Antiná, variant of Anúchána, 2. 81.
Antita, 'untruth,' son of Adhaima,
and husband of Nikriti, 1. 111.
Antacháras, a people, 2. 185.
Antachárá, an Apsaras, 2. 82.
Antahkarana, what, 3. 202.
Antahpránin, what, 3. 110 (where
correct the spelling).
Antahsilá, variant of Antrasilá, 2.
151.
Antaka = Yama, 2. 112 ; 4. 241 ;
5. 15, 207.
Antaka, differenced from Yama,
1. 188.
Antaka, variant of Ardraka, son of
Vasumitra, 4. 191.
Antara = Manwantara, 3. 40.
Antardháua, 'disappearance,' a
form of Brahmá, 1. 82.
Antardhána = Antardhi, son of
Prithu, 1. 192.
Antardhi, son of Prithu, 1. 192.
Antariksha, the Vyása of the thir-
teenth Dwápara age, 3. 34.
Antariksha, son of Kinnara, 4. 168.
Antáyus, son of Purúravas, 4. 13.
Antinára, variant of Rantinára, 4.
129.
Antrasilá, a river, 2. 151, 340.
Antyas, variant of Andhas, 2. 170.
Anu, Aitu (?), son of Yayáti, 3.
289; 4. 46, 48, 50, 119, 120,
123, 129.

Anu, variously genealogized, 4. 69, 70, 99.

Anu, variant of Bhava, son of Viloman, 4. 97.

Antichâná, an Apsaras, 2. 81.

Anugá, an Apsaras, 2. 81.

Anugangá, a certain tract of country, 4. 219.

Anugraha, a Sarga so called, 1. 75, 76.

Anuha, Anuha, son of Vibhrája, 4. 141.

Anubláda = Anuhráda, 2. 30.

Anuhotra, variant of Suhotri, 4. 136.

Anuhráda, son of Hiranyakaśipu, 2. 30, 69.

Anúká, an Apsaras, 2. 81.

Anukalpa, what, in ritual matters, 3. 175.

Anukramanîká, or Index, to the Rig-veda, referred to, 3. 242, 284; 4. 31.

Anumati, daughter of Angiras, 1. 153; 2. 261, 342; 3. 117.

Anumati, a river in S'álmalá-dwípa, 2. 195.

Anumati, the first day of the moon's wane, 2. 261.

Anumitra, variant of Anamitra, 4. 73, 100.

Anumlochá, an Apsaras, 2. 81, 83, 285, 288, 291, 293.

Anumlochantí, an Apsaras, 2. 81, 82, 83.

Anúná, an Apsaras, 2. 81.

Anupadeva, variant of Upadeva, 4. 96.

Anupadeva, variant of Upadeva (another), 4. 98.

Anupavrittas, a people, 2. 169.

Anupráśin, what, 3. 110.

Anurádhá, an asterism, 2. 265, &c.; 3. 132.

Anurata, variant of Anuratha, 4. 69.

Anuratha, son of Kuruvatsa, 4. 69.

Anúru = Aruna, 2. 28.

Anuruddhako, Páli name of a king, 4. 182.

Anushanga-páda, a part of the Váyu-puráña, P. 37, 38.

Anushñá, a river, 2. 149.

Anushñá, variant of Anumlochá, 2. 293.

Anushtubh, a metre, its origin, 1. 85, 86. It is identified with a horse of the Sun, 2. 239.

Anuta, son of Anu, 4. 69.

Anutápana, son of Kaśyapa, 2. 70.

Anutaptá, a river in Plaksha dwípa, 2. 192.

Anuváda, what, 2. 95.

Anuvatsara, a kind of year, 2. 255.

Anuvinda, son of Jayasena, 4. 103; 5. 82.

Anuvrata, a caste in S'áka-dwípa, 2. 200.

Anuvrata, variant of Suvrata, 4. 175.

Anwagbhánu, son of Raudráswa, 4. 127.

Anwáháryapachana, a specific holy fire, 3. 175.

Anwíkshikí, what, 1. 148; 4. 310.

Anyá (?), a river in Kuśa-dwípa, 2. 196.

Ap, variant of Apas, the Rákshasa, 2. 288, 292, 293.

Ápa, a Vasu, 2. 23.

Apachiti, daughter of Paurñamasa, 1. 153.

Apakshaya, what, 5. 254.

Apámmúrti, a Rishi in the tenth Manwantara, 3. 26.

Apána, what, 5. 231.

Apara, what, 4. 252 ; 5. 232.

Aparachínas, a people, 2. 176.

Aparáditya, a commentator, referred to, 2. 343 : 3. 102, 173, 187.

Aparájita, a Rudra, 2. 24, 25.

Aparájita, son of Kŕishńa and Lakshmańá, 5. 81 (where Parájita is to be corrected).

Aparájitá, a river in Śáka-dwípa, 2. 200.

Aparakáśis, a people, 2. 161.

Aparakuntis, a people, 2. 163.

Aparamatsyas, a people, 2. 158.

Aparántas, a people, 2. 168.

Apárapára, what, 2. 6.

Aparavallabhas, a people, 2. 180.

Aparigraha, what, 3. 77; 5. 229.

Aparimeya, what, 5. 139.

Aparińámin, what, 1. 27.

Aparítas, variant of Aparántas, 2. 168.

Apas, a Prajápati in the second Manwantara, son of Vasishťha, 3. 5.

Apas, a Rákshasa, 2. 285, 288, 292.

Apasarpińí, variant of Avasarpińí, 2. 192.

Apaspati, son of Uttánapáda, 1. 159.

Ápastamba, an ancient lawgiver, referred to, 3. 113, 114.

Apátra, what, 3. 120.

Ápava, a name of Vasishťha, 1. 106; 4. 56.

Apavábas, a people, 2. 165.

Apílaka, Ápílaka, variants of Ivílaka, 4. 196, 202.

Apítaka, variant of Ivílaka, 4. 196, 200.

Apomúrti, son of Atri, 1. 154.

Appayya Díkshita, a modern author, quoted, 5. 391.

Aprakáśa, what, 1. 139.

Apramada, 'heedfulness,' son of Dharma, 1. 111.

Aprameya, what, 4. 249 ; 5. 153.

Apraśasta, what, 3. 132.

Apratápin, variant of Ayutáyus, 4. 173.

Apratimaujas, a Rishi in the tenth Manwantara, 3. 26.

Apratípa (?), variant of Ayutáyus, son of Śrutavat, 4. 173.

Apratíratha, son of Rantinára, 4. 129, 130, 140.

Apratishťha, a hell, 2. 215.

Apsarases, 'nymphs,' their origin, &c., 1. 87, 144, 147 ; 2. 75, 81, &c. ; 3. 281; 4. 59; 5. 83, 92, 165, 246, 247. Classed and named, 2. 75, 80, &c. Their chief, 2. 86, 285, &c. Cursed by Ashťávakra, 5. 166.

Aptoryáma, a certain sacrifice, its origin, &c. 1. 85 ; 3. 113.

Áptoryáman = Aptoryáma, 1. 85.

Ápúraňa, a Yaksha, 2. 285, 288, 292; 5. 251.

Ápúrayat, variant of Ápúraňa, 2. 289.

Apúrva, what, 2. 273.

Ápyas, variant of Ádyas, 3. 12.

Ápyáyana, son of Yajnabáhu, king of Sálmala-dwípa, 2. 195.

Ápyáyana, a division of Sálmala-dwípa, 2. 105.

Árabdha, variant of Áradwat, 4. 118.

Arada, variant of Aradwat, 4. 118.

Áraddha, variant of Áradwat, 4. 118.

Árádhin, variant of Árávin, 4. 153.

Áradwat, son of Setu, 4. 118.

Aráhu, Áráhu, variants of Ráhu, 4. 30.

Araṇi, the term explained, &c., 3. 330; 4. 265; 5. 96.

Aranya, variant of Anaranya, father of Pushkarinî, 1. 179; 5. 388.

Aratni, the ulnar side of the hand, 5. 37.

Árattas, a people, 2. 339.

Áratta, a country, 4. 118.

Áratta, variant of Áradwat, 4. 118.

Árávali, a certain mountain-range, 2. 141.

Árávin, son of Jayasena, 4. 153.

Arbudas, a people, 2. 133, 134; 4. 224.

Arbuda, Mount Aboo, 2. 132, 142; 4. 222; 5. 248.

Archis, wife of Kríśáśwa, 2. 29.

Ardhaketu, a Rudra 2. 25.

Ardhaganga = Káverí, 2. 148.

Ardhajáhnavî = Káverí, 2. 148.

Ardra, son of Viśwagaśwa, 3. 263.

Árdrá, an asterism, 2. 265, &c., 308; 3. 167, 169.

Árdraka, son of Vasumitra, 4. 191.

Árdraka, variant of Árdra, 3. 263.

Árdrava (?), variant of Amavat, 3. 190, 191.

Argala, a hell, 2. 215.

Arghya, what, 3. 269.

Arhat, a certain Buddha, 5. 376.

Arhat = Jina, P. 80; 5. 364, 375, 376. 388.

Arhat, a king of the Konkas, &c., 2. 104, &c.

Árhatas = Bauddhas, or else Jainas, P. 79; 3. 209 (where correct the spelling); 5. 286, 287, 322, &c., 350, &c., 360, &c., 370, 388, 390.

Aridyota, son of Dundubhi, 4. 99.

Ariha, son of Devátithi, 4. 128.

Ariha, son of Aváchína, 4. 128.

Arijit, son of Kríshṇa and Bhadrá, 5. 82.

Arijit (?), variant of Aridyota, 4. 99.

Arikshipa, son of Swaphalka, 4. 96.

Arimardana, son of Swaphalka, 4. 95, 96.

Arimardana, son of Kuru, 4. 148.

Arimejaya, son of Swaphalka, 4. 94, 95, 96.

Arimajaya (correct Animejaya), son of Kuru, 4. 148; 5. 391.

Arinjaya, variant of Ripunjaya, 4. 176.

Arishta, a king, son of Vaivaswata, the reigning Manu, 3. 13, 231, 256, 342.

Arishta, a Daitya, son of Kasyapa, 2. 70; 4. 250, 272, 320, 333, 335; 5. 34, 87. Slain by Kríshna, 4. 334.

Arishtá, daughter of Daksha, wife of Kaśyapa, and mother of the Gandharvas, 2. 26, 75; 3. 281. Her eight daughters, 2. 82.

Arishṭakarman, son of Patumat, 4. 197.

Arishṭakarṇis, Arishṭakarṇí, variants of Arishṭakarman, 4. 197.

Arishṭanemi, a Prajápati, 1. 102.

Arishťanemi = Kaśyapa, 2. 28; 3. 297. His wives, 2. 21. His offspring, 2. 28.

Arishťanemi, a Yaksha, 2. -285, &c.

Arishťanemi, variously genealogized, 3. 334.

Arishťanemi, son of Chitraka, 4. 96.

Arjava, disciple of Báahkali, and teacher of the Ŕig-veda, 3. 50.

Arjikiyá = Vipaś, the river, 2. 121.

Arjita, variant of Ajita, the Ŕishi, 3 29.

Arjuna, son of Kŕitavírya, 4. 2, 22, 55. 56. See Kártavírya.

Arjuna, son of Páňďu and Pŕithá, P. 40, 55; 2. 72; 3. 83, 84, 326; 4. 102, 159, 160, 163, 246. 247, 320, 321; 5. 62, 134, 140, 149-151, 154-163, 166, 167, 226.

Arjuna, son of Raivata, 3. 11.

Arjuna, variant of Anjana, son of Kuňi, 3. 334.

Arjuna Miśra, commentator on the Mahábhárata and Harivaṁśa, referred to, 1. 5; 3. 265; 4. 39.

Arjuní = Báhudá, the river, 2. 142.

Arka, variant of Chakshus, 4. 144.

Ároga, a certain sun, 5. 191.

Ársha, a form of marriage, 3. 105.

Árshabhí, a certain triad of asterisms, 2. 265, &c.

Arshiňeśwa, son of Śala, 4. 31.

Árshťishena, variously genealogized, 4. 30, 31.

Árisparňa = Sudáaa, 3. 303.

Artha, son of Dharma, 1. 111

Artha, the pin of the Sun's yoke. 2. 238.

Artha-śástra, defined, &c., 3. 68, 338.

Arthasiddhi, variant of Dhruvasandhi, 3. 325.

Aruddha, Á'ruddha, variants of Á radwat, 4. 118.

Aruňa, son of Kaśyapa and Kadrú, 2. 28. His mother is Danu, 2. 70; Vinatá, 2. 73. An Aruňa is named in 5. 383.

Aruňa, a Yaksha, 2. 288, 292.

Aruňa, father of Uddálaka, 3. 49.

Aruňa, son of Haryaśwa, 3. 284.

Aruňa, a caste in S'álmala-dwípa, 2. 194.

Aruňa, a lake in Chaitraratha, Kubera's grove, 2. 112.

Aruňa, variant of A'ruňi, the Ŕishi, 3. 26.

Aruňá, a river in Plaksha-dwípa, 2. 193.

Aruňá, variant of Anúná, 2. 81.

Aruňapriyá, an Apsaras, 2. 81.

Arundhatí, daughter of Kardama, and wife of Vasishťha, 1. 110, 200. She is said to be daughter of Daksha, and wife of Dharma, 2. 21, 23.

Aruňi, a Ŕishi in the eleventh Manwantara, 3. 26.

Aruňi (?), a Sádhya, 2. 22.

Aruňi, disciple of Vaiśampáyana, and teacher of the Yajur-veda, 3. 52.

Aruňi, variant of Traiyáruňi (?), 3. 37.

Aruňoda = Aruňa, the lake, 2. 117.

Árushí, daughter of Manu, and wife of Chyavana, 3. 80. The same as Sukanyá. (?)

Arvágwasu = Parjanya, 2. 83.

Arváksrotas, what, 1. 73-75, 89.

Arvarívat, a Rishi in the second Manwantara, variously genealogized, 1. 154; 3. 5, 8.

Arvarívat, son of Sávarñi, Manu of the eighth Manwantara, 3. 24.

Arvaríyat, variant of Arvarívat, both first and second, 1. 154; 3. 24.

Arvávasu, variant of Sarvávasu, 2. 297, 298.

Áryas, a people, 4. 225.

Áryas, variant of Ádyas, 3. 12.

Áryá = Yoganidrá, 4. 262.

Árya, the word, and its cognates, &c., 2. 141; 5. 132.

Áryaka, a caste in Plaksha-dwípa, 2. 193.

Áryaká, a river in Krauncha-dwípa, 2. 198.

Áryakulyá, a river, 2. 130, 154.

Aryaman, an Áditya, 2. 27, 285, &c., 306; 5. 15. An Arya-man is named in 1. 190

Aryaman, one of the Viśwe devas, 3. 179.

Áśáditya, a writer on law, referred to, 3. 40, 111.

Asamanja, son of Sagara, 3. 298, 299, 301.

Asamanjas, Asamanjasa, variants of Asamanja, 3. 298.

Asamaújas, son of Kambalabar-hisha, 4. 100.

Ásana, what, 5. 240.

Ásandí, what, 3. 125.

Asanga, son of Yuyudháua, 4. 93.

Ásanga, son of Swaphalka, 4. 96.

Aśaucha, the term defined, 3. 130.

Áshádba, a month, June–July, 2. 261, &c.

Ashta, variant of Ashtaka, 4. 27.

Ashtaka, variously genealogized, 4. 27, 28.

Ashtaká, a certain sacrifice, 3. 113, 260. The four great Ash-takás, 3. 168.

Ashtakarñakas (?), a people, 2. 162.

Ashtáratha, son of Bhímaratha, 4. 36.

Ashtávakra, son of Kahoda, 5. 164-166.

Así, a small stream near Benares, 2. 152.

Asikní, daughter of Vírana, and wife of Daksha, &c., 2. 12, 19.

Asikní, a river, 2. 121, 131, 149.

Asíma, variant of Asanga, 4. 93.

Asímakrishña, son of Aśwame dhaka (Aśwamedhaja?), 4. 163

Asipatravana, a hell, 2. 214, 215, 219.

Asita, son of Bharata, son of Dhru-vasandhi, 3. 297; 4. 238.

Asita, a Muni, 4. 238.

Asitá, an Apsaras, 2. 82, 83.

Asitoda, a lake, 2. 117 (where correct the spelling), 339. See Swetajala.

Áśleshá, an asterism, 2. 159, &c., 308.

Áśmakas, a dynasty, 4. 184.

Áśmakas, variant of Áśwakas, 2. 164.

Áśmaka, son of Saudása, 3. 310, 314. An Áśmaka is named in 4. 162.

Áśmaka, a country, 2. 164.

Áśmakí, wife of Śúra, or else of Devamídhusha, 4. 100.

Áśmalas, variant of Áśwakas, 2. 164.

Aśma-nirghâta, what, 5. 37.

Aśmasârin, minister of King Devâpi, 4. 155, 156.

Aamitâ, what, 1. 69.

Aśoka, variant of Aśokavardhana, 4. 188, 189, 205.

Aśoka, variant of Suyaśas, 4. 188.

Aśokavardhana, son of Bindusâra, 4. 187.

Asoko, Pâli for Aśoka, 4. 188.

Aśrama, what, P. 63, 104 ; 3. 91.

Asridh, one of the Viśwe devas, 3. 179.

Aśruta, variant of Aśrutavraña, 1. 152.

Aśrutavraña, son of Dyutimat, 1. 152.

Asta, a mountain-range in S'âka-dwîpa, 2. 199.

Asta-dosha, what, 5. 215.

Astagiri, variant of Asta, 2. 199.

Astaraña, what, 5. 33.

Asterisms, daughters of Daksha, and wives of Soma, 2. 10, 21, 265, &c.

Asteya, what, 3. 77 ; 5. 229.

Asti, daughter of Jarâsandha, and wife of Kaṁsa, 5. 50.

Astra, what kind of weapon, 5. 147.

Astra-prayoga, the term explained, 5. 47.

Asumati, son of Rantinâra, 4. 129.

Asuras, the, P. 56, 110 ; 1. 80, 82, 142, 147 ; 3. 311 ; 4. 82, 272 ; 5. 58, 110, 118-120, &c., &c. Their origin, 1. 80.

Asura, a form of marriage, 3. 105.

Asurasûdana, an epithet of Kṛishṇa, 5. 48.

Asurendra, ' great Asura,' 5. 136.

Aśwa, son of Daksha, 1. 103.

Aśwa, son of Chitraka, 4. 96.

Aśwabâhu, son of Chitraka, 4. 96.

Aśwagrîva, son of Chitraka, 4. 96.

Aśwagrîva = Hayagrîva, 5. 3.

Aśwuhanu, son of Gṛinjima (?), 4. 113.

Aśwajit, variant of Viśwajit, 4. 140.

Aśwakas, a people, 2. 164.

Aśwalâyanas, of the Ṛig-veda, 3. 51.

Aśwalâyana, compiler of a Sâkhâ, 3. 48, 50.

Aśwalâyana, author of a Gṛihya-sútra, 3. 112, 114, 168, 281, 338 ; 5. 386.

Aśwamedha, ' a horse-sacrifice,' P. 32 ; 3. 40, 213, 234 ; 4. 162 ; 5. 248, 249, 252.

Aśwamedhadatta, son of Satânîka, 4. 163.

Aśwamedhaja (Aśwamedhaka better ?), son of Sahasrânîka, 4. 163.

Aśwasena, son of Kṛishṇa and Satyâ, 5. 79.

Aśwaśiras, an epithet of Nârâyaña, 5. 3.

Aśwaśiras, a demon so called, 5. 3.

Aśwatara, a serpent, son of Kaśyapa and Kadrú, 2. 74, 285, &c. ; 5. 251.

Aśwatîrtha, a certain holy place, 4. 16.

Aśwatthâman, son of Droña, 3. 23 ; 4. 147, 160 ; 5. 148.

Aśwavatí, an Apsaras, 2. 82.

Aśwavatí, a river, 2. 339.

Aśwayuja = Aświna, the month, 2. 285, 288.

Áswayují, a certain sacrifice, 3. 113.

Aswáyus, son of Purúravas, 4. 13.

Aswins, son of Vivaswat and Sanjná, 1. 122, 123, 141 ; 2. 306, 308, 343 ; 3. 15, 21, 248, 322, 342, 343 ;. 4. 249, 258, 293 ; 5. 2, 43, 143, 247. They preside over the nose, 1. 38.

Aswins, two of the Viswe devas, 3. 179.

Aswin = Aswini, the asterism, 2. 277.

Áswina, a month, Sept.-Oct., 2. 261, &c. ; 3. 114.

Aswina-graha, what, 3. 343.

Aswini, an asterism, 1. 122, 141 ; 2. 265, &c. ; 3. 132. An Aswini is named in 4. 159.

Aswini Kumáras (?) = Aswins, 1. 141 ; 3. 248.

Atala, a Pátála, 2. 209.

Asamána, variant of Patumat, 4. 196.

Atavin, Átavin, variants of Atevin, 3. 57.

Atavisikharas, a people, 2. 169.

Átavya, variant of Atevin, 3. 57.

Atevin, a teacher of the Yajurveda, 3. 57.

Atharvan, his wives, 1. 110, 200.

Atharvángirasí, a Samhitá so called, 3. 42.

Atharva-veda, its origin and its divisions, &c., 1. 85 ; 2. 338 ; 3. 61, 62 ; 5. 210, 388. Offspring of Satí, 2. 29.

Atibhánu, son of Krishńa and Satyabhámá, 5. 81.

Atibhára (?), variant of Rantinára, 4. 129.

Atikriahná, variant of Anushná, 2. 149.

Atimára (?), variant of Rantinára, 4. 129.

Atináman, a Rishi in the sixth Manwantara, 3. 12, 13.

Atinára, variant of Rantinára, 4. 129.

Atiratha, variant of Apratiratha, 4. 129, 130.

Atirátra, Atirátra, son of Chákshusha, Manu of the sixth Manwantara, 1. 177, 178 (where read Atírátra).

Atirátra, a kind of sacrifice, its origin, &c., 1. 85 , 3. 113.

Ati-sankírńa, what, 3 125.

Ati-tána, what, 3. 249.

Atitára, variant of Rantinára, 4. 129.

Atithi, son of Kusa, 3. 320.

Atithi-bhojana, a kind of sacrifice, 3. 114.

Ativibhúti, son of Khaninetra, 3. 243.

Átman, what, 1. 3 ; 5. 14, 91, 201, 212, 242.

Átma-prakása, a commentary on the Vishńu-puráńa, P. 115.

Átma-prayatna, what, 5. 227.

Átma-vidyá, what, 1. 148.

Átreyas, a people, 2. 187.

Átreya, a medical authority, 4. 33.

Atri, son of Brahmá, 1. 8, 100, 135, &c.; 2. 113, 285, &c.; 3. 3, 4, 8, 11, 13, 15, 16, 23, 68, 161 ; 4. 2, 55. 129, 249. His wife, 1. 109, 110. His offspring, 1. 153.

Attiká, variant of Adriká, 2. 81.

Atyagnishťoma, a sort of sacrifice, 3. 113.

Atyantamadanapriya, an Apsaras, 2. 82.

 Átyantika, what, 1. 113.

Átyantika-laya, what, 5. 169, 186.

Auďras, a people, 2. 177, 184; 4. 220, 221.

Aukn (?), variant of Uktha, 3. 321.

Aupásana-homa, a sort of sacrifice, 3. 114.

Aurńavabha Áchárya, his opinion referred to, 3. 19

Aurva, a Rishi of the second Man-wantara, &c., variously genealo-gized, 3. 3. 4, 80, 81, 84, &c., 290, 291, 298.

Auśanasa-upapuráńa, P. 87.

Auttama, variant of Auttami, 3. 5.

Auttami, Manu of the third Mun-wantara, son of Priyavrata, 3. 1, 5, 11.

Avabhŕiti, a city, 4. 205.

Avabhrityas, a branch of the Ábhíras, 4. 205.

Avabodha, what, 4. 265.

Avabŕitha, what, 3. 220.

Aváchína, son of Jayatsena, 4. 128.

Avadańśa, what, 5. 33.

Avadhúta, what, 5. 36.

Áváha, son of S'waphalka, 4. 95 (where correct the spelling), 96; 5. 391.

Avákstinjima (?), variant of Stin-jaya, 4. 113.

Avákstrotas, the word suggested, 1. 73.

Avanta, son of Nirvŕiti, 4. 68.

Avantis, a people, 2. 162, 4. 222, 224. See also 4. 58, 59.

Avanti, a country, 4. 57, 103, 141.

Avanti, a city, 2. 145, 171, 3. 246; 4. 59; 5. 46, 82.

Avanti, a river, 2. 155.

Ávantya (?), disciple of Sukar-man, and teacher of the Sáma-veda, 5. 59-61.

Ávantyas = Avantis, 4. 58, 103 (note **), 344.

Ávarańa, what, 1. 36.

Avarivat (?), variant of Arvarívat, the Rishi, 1. 154.

Ávartana, an island, 2. 129 (where correct the spelling), 339.

Ávartis, variant of Avantis, 4. 58.

Ávartyas, variant of Ávantyas, 4. 103 (note **).

Avasarpiń, a period of time, 2. 192.

Ávasathya, a certain holy fire, 3. 175; 5. 114, 115.

Avastha, what, 1. 13.

Avasthánas of the sun, what, 2. 267.

Avasyáya, 'hoar-frost,' 5. 35.

Avatańsaka, what, 4. 283; 5. 12, 13.

Avaťanirodhana, a hell, 2. 215.

Avatáras, 'epiphanies.' Alluded to in the Vedas, P. 3. Twenty-eight of S'iva, and twenty-four of Vishńu, P. 68. See also Kúrma-puráńa, Matsya-puráńa, Vámana-puráńa, Varáha-puráńa, Kŕishńa, Nŕisińha, Ráma, &c.

Avayava, what, 4. 66.

Ávi (??), son of Sátakarńi, 4. 202.

Ávi (??), variant of Saudása, 4. 202.

Avichi, two hells so called, 2. 215.

Avidyá = Yoganidrá, 4. 260.

Avidyá, what, 1. 69.

Avijnátagati, son of Anila, 2. 23; 5. 387.

Avikára, what, 1. 14; 3. 279.

Avikshi, Avikshit, Avikshita, son of Karandhama, 3. 243, 244; 4. 240.

Avikshita, Ávíkshita, = Marutta, 3. 244; 4. 240, 241.

Avimardana, variant of Arimardana, son of S'waphalka, 4. 95.

Avimukta = Váráṇasí, or Banares, 5. 126, 129.

Avyákŕita, what, 5. 59.

Avyakta, what, 1. 15, 38, 39.

Avyakta-karaṇa, what, 1. 22.

Avyanga, what, 5. 383, 384.

Avyaya, a Ŕishi in the thirteenth Manwantara, 3. 28.

vyaya, what, 1. 17, 27; 3. 78, 205; 5. 90, 191, 201, 211; 225, 254.

Avyáyátman, what, 3. 183, 252.

Aya, a Prajápati in the second Manwantara, son of Vasishṭha, 3. 5.

Ayaḣpána, a hell, 2. 215.

Ayana, what, 1. 48, 49.

Ŕyása, what, 5. 172.

Ayátayámas, certain texts of the Yajur-veda, 3. 57.

Ayati, son of Nahusha, 4. 45.

Ŕyáti, son of Nahusha, 4. 45, 46.

Ayati, daughter of Meru, and wife of Vidhátŕi, 1. 152, 157.

Ayodhyá, a city, P. 106, 107; 2. 172, 173; 3. 261, 297, 304, 317, 320; 4. 25, 26, 168, 170; 5. 82.

Ŕyogava, a caste sprung from S'údra males and Vaiśye females, 4. 216.

Ŕyogava, the name of a bow snapped by Kŕishṇa, 5. 23.

Ayomukha, son of Kaśyapa, 2. 70.

Ayonija, Ayonijá, what, 2. 8; 3. 316.

Áyu, son of Puruhotra, 4. 69.

Áyu, variant of Ŕrdra, 3. 263.

Áyu, variant of Áyus, son of Puráravas, 4. 13.

Áyurdá, a river in S'áka-dwípa, 2. 200.

Áyur-veda, defined, 1. 148, 3. 67.

Áyus, son of Pururavas, 4. 9, 13, 30, 43, 137, 138, 139.

Áyus, son of Kŕishṇa and Rohiṇí, 5. 79.

Áyushmat, son of Uttánapáda, 1. 159; 5. 387.

Áyushmat, son of Saṃhráda, or else of Anuhráda, 2. 69.

Ayuta, son of Rádhika, 4. 153.

Ayutájit, son of Bhajamána, 4. 72.

Ayutájit, variant of Ayutáśwa, 3. 303.

Ayutanáyin, son of Mahábhauma, 4. 128.

Ayutáśwa, son of Sindhudwípa, 3. 303, 315.

Ayutáyus, son of Bhajamána, 4. 72.

Ayutáyus, son of Ŕrávin, 4. 153.

Ayutáyus, son of S'rutavat, 4. 173.

Ayutáyus, variant of Ayutáśwa, 3. 303.

Ŕyuvatyas, a class of Apsarases, 2. 82.

Babhravya, son of some Babhru, 3. 239.

Babhrus, Kauśika Bráhmana, 4. 28.

Babhru, son of Angiras, disciple of S'aunaka, &c., and teacher of the Atharva-veda, 3. 62.

Babhru, son of Romapáda, 4. 67.

Babhru, son of Devávridha, 4. 72, 73, 84; 5. 142, 148, 149.

Babhru, son of Druhyu, 4. 118.

Babhru (who?), 4. 84 (note ‡).

Babhru, variant of Andhaka, 4. 97, 99.

Babhrusena, variant of Babhru, son of Druhyu, 4. 118.

Babhrusetu, variant of Babhru, son of Druhyu, 4. 118.

Babhruváhana, son of Arjuna, son of Páńd'u, 4. 160.

Bádaráńyas(?), Kaućika Bráhmans, 4. 29.

Bádaráyańa = Vyása, 3. 23.

Bádaráyańa, an astronomer, referred to the court of King Vikramáditya, P. 9.

Badari = Badarikáśrama, 5. 146.

Badariká = Badarikáśrama, 5. 146.

Badarikáśrama, a certain place of pilgrimage, P. 75; 5. 146.

Baddha-pála, what, 2. 217.

Badhas, 'imperfections,' of twenty-eight kinds, 1. 71.

Badhnas, a people, 2. 175.

Badhryaśwa, variously genealogized, 4. 145, 146, 343 (where it is once misspelt Bhadryaśwa).

Bahanakas, certain barbarians, their origin, 1. 182.

Bahlkas, a people, 2. 167, 175, 339, 340.

Báhlka, a country, 2. 167, 175.

Bahishpavamána, a certain text of the Rig-veda, 3. 343.

Báhlikas, Báhlkas, a people, 2. 167, 175, 181; 4. 212-215, 345.

Báhlika, Báhlka, father of Pau-

ravi, 4. 108, 109; 5. 131, 134. See Váhlka, the less correct form.

Báhu, son of Vríka, 3. 289, 290.

Báhubádhas, a people, 2. 175.

Babubhúmi, son of Chitraka, 4.96.

Báhudá, two rivers so called, 2. 142, 151, 340; 3. 266.

Bahugava, son of Sudyumna, 4. 128.

Báhuka, variant of Báhu, 3. 289.

Bahula, a Prajápati, 1. 102.

Bahulá, a river, 2. 150.

Báhula, variant of Bŕihadbala, 3. 321.

Báhula, variant of Rátula, 4. 169.

Bahuláśwa, son of Dhŕiti, 3. 335.

Báhu-nighatťana (?), what, 5. 37.

Bahuputra, a Prajápati, 1. 102. His wives, 2. 21. His daughters, 2. 28.

Bahuradas (?), variant of Báhubádhas, 2. 175.

Bahuratha, son of Nŕipanjaya, 4. 144.

Bahurúpa, a Rudra, 2. 24, 25.

Bahurúpa, son of Medhátithi, king of Sáka-dwípa, 2. 200.

Bahurúpa, a region of Sáka-dwípa, 2. 200.

Bahurúpaka, variant of Bahurúpa, the Rudra, 2. 25.

Bahuvádin, variant of Abamyáti, 4. 128.

Bahuvádyas (?), variant of Báhubádhas, 2. 175.

Báhuvat, son of Punarvasu, 4. 98.

Bahuvidha, variant of Bahugava, 4. 128.

Bahwŕichas, promulgators of the Bahwŕichá, 3. 50, 268.

Bahwrichá, a Saṁhitá of the Rig-
veda, 3. 42.

Bahwricha-bráhmaṅa, the, referred
to, 4. 26.

Báhyá, a river, 2. 156.

Báhyas, variant of Bodhas, 2. 156.

Báhyáswa, variant of Haryaswa,
4. 144.

Baid'ála-vratika, what, 3. 222.

Bakas, a people, 2. 179.

Bala = Balabhadra, 4. 91, 109, 285,
297, 300, 304, 305, 316 ; 5. 8,
13, 84-86, 113, 116, 130-132,
135-138.

Bala, son of Krishṅa and Laksh-
maṅá, 5. 81.

Bala, a demon so called, 4. 316,
334.

Bala, a horse of the Moon, 2. 299.

Bulá, daughter of Raudráswa, and
wife of Prabhákara, 4. 129.

Bála, variant of Vúta, a Rákshasa,
2. 293.

Bala, variant of Chhala, 3. 321.

Bala, variant of Dala, 3. 321, 323.

Bala (?), variant of Bhava, son of
Viloman, 4. 97, 98

Balabandhu, son of Raivata, Manu
of the fifth Manwantara, 3. 11.

Balabhadra, son of Vasudeva and
Devaki, 4. 111, 260. An epiphany of Sesha, 2. 211, 212 ;
4. 260 ; 5. 12, 139. Marries
Revati, daughter of Raivata, 3.
254 ; 4. 109. His sons by her,
4. 109. Is brought up by
Nanda, 4. 275, &c. Is offended
with Krishṅa, 4. 83. Silays
Dhenuka, a Dánava, 4. 297, &c.
Slays Pralamba, an Asura, 4.
300, &c. Slays Mushtika, a

pancrakiast, 5. 39. Repairs to
Vraja, 5. 63. Compels the
river Yamuná to attend him, 5.
66. &c. Slays Prince Rukmin
and others, 5. 86. Rescues
Samba, 5. 134. Slays Dwivida,
an Asura, 5. 138. Resumes the
form of Sesha, 5. 150. See also
4. 84, &c. ; 5. 5, 9, 30, 32, 35,
36, 41, 42, 51, 70, 116, 130,
131,344. See, further, Bala, Baladeva, Balaráma, Haláyuda, San-
karshaṅa, Sirin, Tálaketu, &c.

Balabhadra, a mountain in Sáka-
dwípa, 2. 200.

Balabhid, an epithet of Indra, 4.
316.

Baladá, daughter of Raudráswa.
and wife of Prabhákara, 4. 129.

Baladeva = Balabhadra, P. 55, 56 ;
3. 253 ; 4. 81, 82, &c., 109,
296, 304 ; 5. 20, 23, 39, 48,
63, 65, 67, 85, 86, 113, 131,
134, 137, 139, 140.

Bála-gopála = Krishṅa, as a child,
P. 22 ; 5. 284, 285, 342, 345.

Baláhaka, a serpent, son of Kaśyapa
and Kadrú, 2. 74.

Baláhaka a horse of Krishṅa, 4. 83.

Baláhaka, a mountain-range in
Sálmala-dwípa, 2. 194.

Balaja, a river, P. 29.

Baláka, disciple of Sákapúṅi, &c.,
3. 48, 50.

Baláka, son of Púru, 4. 15.

Bálaka, son of Pulika, 4. 178.

Balákáswa, son of Ajaka, 4. 15.

Balakáswa, variant of Baláswn, 3.
243.

Balakrama, a mountain, 2. 142
(where correct Valakrama), 340.

Bálam Bhatťa, a commentator, referred to. P. 36, 48.

Balandhará, wife of Bhímasena, 4. 159, 345.

Balaráma = Balabhadra, P. 12; 3. 254; 4. 81, 108, 250, 258, 285, 289, 300, 301, 305; 5. 12, 13, 16, 64, 65, 68, 70, 71, 84, 85, 123, 130, 132, 135–137, 139.

Balasani (??), son of Yadu, 4. 53.

Baláśwa = Karandhama, 3. 243.

Báláyani (?), disciple of Báshkali, and teacher of the Ŕig-veda, 3. 49.

Báleyas, certain Bráhmans named from Bali, 4. 123.

Bali, a Daitya, and also an Indra in the eighth Manwantara, son of Virochana, P. 76; 2. 55, 69; 3. 19, 23; 4. 123, 250; 5. 6, 108, 115. His abode, 2. 211.

Bali, son of Sutapas, 4. 122.

Báli, variant of Bálin, the monkey, 3. 316 (where correct the spelling), 343.

Bali, a certain offering, 3. 118, 220; 5. 290.

Bali = Vali, 5. 32.

Bali-karman, a certain sacrifice, 3. 93, 114.

Bálin, a monkey-chieftain slain by Ráma, 3. 316.

Balin, variant of Sindhuka, 4. 195.

Balivindhya, son of Raivata, Manu of the fifth Manwantara, 3. 11.

Balivŕishahan, son of Nirvŕiti, 4. 68.

Bali-yajna, a certain sacrifice, 3. 93, 118.

Báluváhini, a river, 2. 155.

Balwalas, variant of Kalkalas, 2. 180.

Báña, son of Bali, and slain by Kŕishña, 2. 69; 4. 250; 5. 108, 109, 111–119.

Báña, son of Vikukshi, 3. 297.

Báñapura = Soñitapura, 5. 112.

Bandha, variant of Budha, son of Vegavat, 3. 245.

Bandhavat (??), variant of Bandhumat, 3. 245.

Bandhu, variant of Budha, son of Vegavat, 3. 245.

Bandhu, the term defined, 3. 155.

Bandhumat, son of Kevala, 3. 245.

Bandhupalita, son of Kuśála, 4. 189.

Bandhyáśwa, son of Indrasena, 4. 145, 146.

Bangas = Vangas, 3. 293.

Banga, son of Bali, son of Sutapas, 4. 122.

Bángangá, the popular name of the Sarávatí, a river, 2. 147.

Banjula, a river, 2. 155.

Baujulá, a river, 2. 155.

Barbaras, a people, 2. 176; 3. 292.

Barbara, a country, 2. 179.

Barbará, a river, 2. 341.

Barbarí, a river, 2. 341.

Bárhadrathas, descendants of Bŕihadratha, 4. 177, 184, 231.

Barhañáśwa, variant of Samhatáśwa, 3. 265.

Bárhaspatyas, sectators of Bŕihaspati, 3. 212.

Barhis, variant of Dharmin, 4. 169.

Barhishads, a class of Pitŕis, variously genealogized, 1. 156; 2. 303; 3. 159, 160, 161, 163, 339.

Barhishad, son of Havirdhána, 1. 193.

Barhishmatí, daughter of Viśwakarman, and wife of Priyavrata, eldest son of Swáyambhuva, 2. 100.

Barsam or Barsom, identified with Varama, 5. 384.

Báshkalas, Kauśika Bráhmans, 4. 28.

Báshkalas, of the Rig-veda, 3. 51.

Báshkala, son of Saṁhráda, 2. 69, where he is also called son of Anuhráda.

Báshkala, two or more persons, one a disciple of Paila, another a son of Bharadwája and disciple of Satyaśrí, &c.. 3. 44, 337. And see Báshkali.

Báshkali, variant of Báshkala (the last named), 3. 44, 45, 47–50.

Bathing, rules of, 8. 113, &c.

Bauddhas, religionists, P. xii ; 3. 201, 207, 210, 211, 223 ; 4. 225 ; 5. 359, 361–363, &c.

Baudháyanas, of the Yajur-veda, 3. 57.

Baudháyana, a lawgiver, 3. 96, 113.

Baudhya, disciple of Báshkali, 3. 44.

Benares, burnt by the discus of Krishńa, 5. 128.

Bhadras, a people, 2. 185.

Bhadras, a class of gods in the third Manwantara, 3. 6.

Bhadras, variant of Madras, 2. 133.

Bhadra, son of Vasudeva and Devakí, 4. 110.

Bhadra, son of Krishńa and Kálindí, 5. 79.

Bhadra, variant of Madraka, son of Sibi, 4. 122.

Bhadrá, wife of Vasudeva, 4. 109, 110.

Bhadrá, daughter of Srutakírtti, and wife of Krishńa, 5. 82, 83.

Bhadrá, daughter of Raudráśwa, and also called daughter of Prabhákara, 4. 129.

Bhadra = Yoganidrá, 4. 262.

Bhadrá, a river, 2. 112, 120, 122, 272.

Bhadrá, variant of Chandrá, a river in Sálmala-dwípa, 2. 194.

Bhadrabáhu, son of Vasudeva, 4. 109.

Bhadrachárn, son of Krishńa and Rukminí, 5. 78.

Bhadradeha, son of Vasudeva and Devakí, 4. 110.

Bhadradeva, variant of Bhadradeha, 4. 110.

Bhadraka, variant of Madraka, son of Sibi, 4. 122.

Bhadrakn, variant of Árdraka, 4. 191.

Bhadrakálí, a form of Párvatí, P. 89 ; 1. 133 ; 4. 262.

Bhadramanda, variant of Bhadravinda, 5. 107.

Bhádrapada, a month, August-September, 2. 261, &c.; 3. 197.

Bhadraratha, son of Haryanga, 4. 125.

Bhadrásana, what, 5. 230.

Bhadrasára, variant of Bindusára, 4. 188.

Bhadrasena, son of Vasudeva and Devakí, 4. 110.

Bhadrasena, variant of Bhadraśreńya, 4. 54.

Bhadrásraiya, son of Mahishmat. 4. 34-36. 54.

Bhadráswa, son of Agnídhra, and king of a region, 2. 102.

Bhadráswa, son of Vasudeva, 4. 109.

Bhadráswa, a region to the east of Mount Meru, 2. 112, 116, 120, 123, 125, 126, 207; 5. 3.

Bhadráswa, variant of Chandráswa, 3. 265.

Bhadráswa, variant of Raudráswa, 4. 128.

Bhadráswa, variant of Haryaáswa, 4. 144.

Bhadraturaga, a country lying between Mályavat and the sea, 2. 111.

Bhadravinda, son of Krishńa and Nagnajití, 5. 107.

Bhaga, an Áditya, 1. 131; 2. 27, 285, &c.

Bhaga, one of the Viswe devas, 3. 179.

Bhaga (?), variant of Bharga, son of Vahni, 4. 116.

Bhága, variant of Bhágavata, son of Vajramitra, 4. 192.

Bhagadatta, a king, 5. 54, 55.

Bhagadheya, variant of Nábhánedishtha, 3. 227.

Bhaganetra, an epithet of Indra, 1. 134.

Bhagavad-gítá, or its commentary, referred to, or quoted, P. 15, 33; 2. 49, 86; 3. 65, 126, 253; 5. 126, 389.

Bhagavad-gítá-máhátmya, a composition, referred to, P. 33.

Bhagavat = Vishńu or Krishńa, P. 40; 1. 45, 46; 2. 63, 65, &c.;

3. 17, 83, 279; 4. 77, 79, 80, 92, &c., 101, 259, 269, 320; 5. 1, 2, 146, 152, 185, 209, 212, 213, 234, 239, 244, 246. The word etymologized, 5. 212.

Bhágavata, son of Vajramitra, 4. 192.

Bhágavata = Bhágavata-puráńa, 3. 67.

Bhágavatas, an heretical sect, 5. 379.

Bhágavata-kathá-sangraha, a composition, quoted, or referred to, P. 49; 3. 62, 66.

Bhágavata-puráńa, analysis of it, &c., P. 17, 20, 22-24, 26, 32, 34-36, 39, &c., 53, 57. 58, 67, 68, 80, 88, 110, 114; 5. 264, 277, 278, 284, 322, 327, 332, 343, 358, 389. Its probable age, 2. 106.

Bhágavata-upapuráńa, P. 87.

Bhágavatí-saṁhitá, a part of the Kúrma-puráńa, P. 77.

Bhagíratha, son of Dilípa, 2. 119; 3. 303, 315; 4. 241.

Bhágírathí, the Ganges proper, 2. 120. 121; 3. 217, 303, 343; 5. 134.

Bháguri, an ancient writer, 2. 113; 5. 250.

Bhailla = Súrya, 3. 150.

Bhalmarika, son of Krishńa and Satyabhámá, 5. 107.

Bhairava, a god, P. 79, 90.

Bhairavas, an heretical sect, P. 79, 80; 5. 286, 287. 375, 380.

Bhairavás, a class of Apsarasas, 2. 82.

Bhajamána, son of Satwata, 4. 71, 72.

Bhajamáua, variously genealogized, 4. 97, 99.

Bhajamáua, variant of S'amin, 4. 99, 100.

Bhajana, variant of Bhajin, 4. 72.

Bhájaras (?), variant of Bhrájiras, 3. 28.

Bhájeratha, a country, 3. 343.

Bhaji, variant of Bhajin, 4. 71.

Bhajin, son of Satwata, 4. 71; 72.

Bhájiras (?), variant of Bhrájiras, 3. 28.

Bhajya, disciple of Baahkali, 3. 49.

Bhakta, 'rice,' 3. 150.

Bhakti, what, P. 32, 52 ; 5. 244, 247.

Bhaktichchheda, the term explained, 5. 22.

Bhakti-yogya, what, 2. 336.

Bhalaudana, variously genealogized. 3. 240, 242.

Bhalláda, variant of Bhallára, 4. 142.

Bhalláka, variant of Bhallára, 4. 142.

Bhallára (?), variant of Bhallára, 4. 142.

Bhallára, son of Udaksena, 4. 142, 143.

Bhanandana (?), variant of Bhalandana, 3. 241.

Bhánda, an Asura, P. 86.

Bhándíra, a sort of tree, 4. 299, 301.

Bhánus, a class of gods in the third Manwantara, 3. 6. Sons of Dharma and Bhánu, 2. 22.

Bhánu, daughter of Daksha, and wife of Dharma, 2. 21, 22.

Bhánu, variously genealogized, 4. 116

Bhánu, son of Divárka, 4. 168.

Bhánu, son of Krishńa and Satya bhámá, 5. 81, 107.

Bhánuchandra, variant of Bhánuratha, son of Chandragiri, 3. 321.

Bhánula, variant of Rátula, 4. 169.

Bhánumat, variously genealogised, 3. 333.

Bhánumat, son of Bharga, son of Vahni, 4. 116.

Bhánumat, son of Krishńa and Satyabhámá, 5. 81.

Bhánumat, variant of Bhánuratha, 4. 168.

Bhánumitra, variant of Bhánuratha, son of Chandragiri, 3. 321.

Bhánuratha, son of Chandragiri, 3. 321.

Bhánuratha, son of Bŕihadaśwa, 4. 168.

Bhára, what, 4. 76.

Bhára, variant of Nabhíra, 4. 214.

Bharadwájas, a people, 2. 187.

Bharadwája, a Rishi, son of Bŕihaspati, 2. 285 &c. ; 3., 13, 15, 16, 23, 48, 66 ; 4. 134–136.

Bharadwája, a medical authority, 4. 33, 40.

Bharadwája, the Vyása of the twelfth Dwápara age, 3. 34.

Bharadwája, the Vyása of the nineteenth Dwápara age, 3. 35, 37.

Bharadwája, variant of Bháradwája, the Vyása, 3. 34.

Bháradwája, variant of Bharadwája, the Vyása, 3. 35.

Bharadwája, variant of Satyadhwaja, 3. 333.

Bharadwája, variant of Bŕihadrája, 4. 169.

Bháradwájí, a river, 2. 151.

Bharaṇí, an asterism, 2. 259. &c., 337.

Bharatas, a tribe, 4. 59.

Bharata. a Muni, author of the Gándharva-veda, 3. 68 ; 4. 324, 346.

Bharata, son of Ŕishabha, and a king in the first Manwantara, P. 97 ; 2. 103, 105, 106, 127 ; 4. 38. India is called, from him,- Bharatavarsha.

Bharata, son of Dushyanta, 4. 117, 132-136, 320.

Bharata, son of Daśaratha, 3. 315, 318.

Bharata. king of Aśmaka, 2. 164.

Bharata, son of Tálajangha, 4. 57, 59

Bharata, son of Dhruvasandhi, 3. 297 ; 4. 338.

Bharata (who ?), P. 42. See also 2. 312, &c.

Bharatá, an Apsaras, 2. 81.

Bhárata = Bháratavarsha, or India, P. 97 ; 2. 105, 114, 115, 120, 123, 125-127, 129, 132, 136-138, 154, 207.

Bhárata = Máhábhárata, P. 46, 50, 54.

Bharatamalla, a modern commentator, referred to, 3. 22.

Bháratavarsha, India, P. 97 ; 2. 107, 111. 112, 127, 133, 135, 137.

Bhárata-yuddha, what, 3. 326 ; 4. 321.

Bháratí = Bháratavarsha, India, 2. 107.

Bharatí. variant of Gabhastí, 2. 199.

Bhargas, a people, 2. 170, 171. .

Bharga, variously genealogized, 4. 37, 39.

Bharga, son of Vahni, 4. 116.

Bhárga, variously genealogized, 4. 38.

Bharga, variant of Garga, son of Pratardana, 4. 36.

Bhárgabhúmi, variously genealogized, 4. 37-39.

Bhárgavas, a people, 2. 170.

Bhárgava, a descendant of Bhŕigu, 1. 152 ; 5. 218. Applied to various persons, 2. 39 ; 3. 23, 238 ; 4. 39.

Bhárgava, son of Vahni, 4. 116.

Bhárgava = Paraśuráma, 4. 22.

Bhárgava, variant of Bhárga, 4. 38.

Bhárgavabhúmi, variant of Bhárgabhúmi, 4. 38.

Bhárgava-puráṇa, P. 90.

Bhármyas, who, 4. 146.

Bhármya, patronym of Mudgala, 4. 146.

Bharmyáśwa, variant of Haryaśwa, 4. 144, 146.

Bháru, variant of Bhánu, son of Kŕishṇa, 5. 107.

Bharuka, variant of Kuruka, 3. 289.

Bhásí, daughter of Kaśyapa, and wife of Garuḍa, 2. 73.

Bhásí, an Apsaras, 2. 82.

Bháskara, the Sun, 3. 56 ; 4. 192

Bháskara Áchárya, an astronomer, quoted, 2. 110, 129. . .

Bháswat, variant of Bháskara, 4 102.

Bhaṭṭa, the title, 5. 385.

Bhaṭṭáchárya, the title, 5. 385.

Bhaṭṭa Utpala, an astronomer, referred to 2. 275, 277
Bhauma = Lohitánga. 2. 304.
Bhauma (?), a country, 4. 220.
Bhautyas, a dynasty, 4. 93.
Bhautya, the Manu of the fourteenth Manwantara, variously genealogized, 3. 28, 29. He is called Manu of the tenth Manwantara, 3. 25.
Bhautya (?), son of Bhautya, 3. 29.
Bhauvana, son of Manthu. 2. 107.
Bhava, a Rudra, or form of Siva, 1. 116, 117, 126, 157 ; 2. 25 ; 4. 251 ; 5. 386.
Bhava, a Sádhya, 2. 22.
Bhava, a Muni, 1. 109.
Bhava, son of Viloman, 4. 97.
Bhava, variant of Bhuva, 2. 106.
Bhavás (?), a class of Apsarases, 2. 82.
Bháva, one with Mahat, in philosophy, 1. 32.
Bháva-bhávaná, what, 5. 233, 237.
Bhávaka, son of Skandaswáti, 4. 202.
Bhávana, son of Swárochisha, and a Rishi in the second Manwantara, 3. 5.
Bhávaná, what, 5. 222, 233, 240, 245.
Bhavanmanyu, son of Vitatha, 4. 135.
Bháva-pushpas, the, enumerated, 4. 294.
Bháva-sára = Avyanga, 5. 383.
Bhávin, a caste in Plaksha-dwípa, 2. 193.
Bhavishya-puráńa, analysis of it, &c., P. 20, 23, 24, 62, &c. ; 5. 319, 365, 381, 383, 384.

Bhavishyat = Bhavishya-puráńa, 3. 67.
Bhavishya-upapuráńa, P. 87.
Bhavishyottara-puráńa, P. 63, 64.
Bhavyas, a class of gods in the sixth Manwantara, 3. 12.
Bhavya, son of Dhruva, 1. 177.
Bhavya, a Rishi in the ninth Manwantara, 3. 25.
Bhavya, son of Priyavrata, and king of Sáka-dwípa, 2. 100, &c., 198.
Bhárya, variant of Bhánuratha, son of Bṛihadaswa, 4. 168.
Bhávyaratha, variant of Bhánuratha, son of Bṛihadaswa, 4. 168.
Bhaya, 'fear,' son of Antita, 1. 111, 112.
Bheda, what, 5. 52.
Bhakurayas (?), a class of Apsarases, 2. 82.
Bhí, 'fear,' daughter of Kali, and wife of Mṛityu, 1. 111.
Bhikshu = Parivráj, 3. 279.
Bhillas, a wild race, their origin, 1. 182.
Bhíma, a Rudra, 1. 116; 2. 25; 5. 386.
Bhíma, son of Páńḍu and Pṛithá, 4. 102; 5. 134, 159, 167. In a former birth, son of Anila or Váyu, 4. 102, 132; 5. 391.
Bhíma, variously genealogized, 4. 14.
Bhíma, variant of Urukshaya, 4. 137.
Bhímá = Bhímarathí, 2. 148.
Bhímaratha, son of Ketumat, 4. 33. 36, 343.
Bhímaratha, son of Vikriti, 4. 68.

Bhimaratha, variant of Bhima-
rathí, 2. 130.

Bhímarathí, the river now called
Beema, 2. 130, 132, 147, 148.

Bhímasena, variously genealogized,
4. 152, 162.

Bhímasena, son of Ríksha, 4. 153.

Bhímasena = Bhíma, son of Pándu,
4. 102, 159, 345.

Bhíshma, son of Sántanu, P. 30;
3. 75, 201; 4. 144, 157; 5.
130, 131, 134, 135. Slain by
Arjuna, 5. 157, 161, 163.

Bhíshma, king of the Vidarbhas,
5. 69.

Bhíshmaka = Bhíshma, king of the
Vidarbhas, 4. 112; 5. 69.

Bhogavatí, a city in Rasátala, an
underworld, 2. 211.

Bhogin, son of Seshanága, (?) 4.
212.

Bhogin, variant of Bhajin, 4. 72.

Bhojas, a people, or peoples, 2. 158,
159; 4. 58, 59, 73, 86, 260,
271; 5. 148, 382, 392.

Bhojas, certain kings, 2 159.

Bhoja, king of Dhárá, 4. 59.

Bhoja, variant of Swayambhoja, 4.
99, 113, 248.

Bhoja = Bhojakata, 2. 159.

Bhojakas, certain descendants of
the Bhojas of Dwáraká, 5. 382.

Bhojaka, variant of Swayambhoja,
4. 99.

Bhojakata, a city founded by
Rukmin, 2. 159; 5. 71, 84.

Bhojana, a mountain in Kraunche-
dwipa, 2. 198.

Bhojapurís, a tribe in Western
Behar, 2. 159.

Bhojarája = Kamsa, 4. 260, 271.

Bhojyá, variant of Márishá, 4. 100.

Bhokhyaka (??), variant of Múshika,
4. 222.

Bhokshyaka, variant of Múshika,
4. 222.

Bhrája, a sun, 5. 191.

Bhrájiras, a class of gods in the
fourteenth Manwantara, 3. 28,

Bhrájishtha, son of Ghritaprishtha,
king of Kraunche-dwipa, 2.
198.

Bhrájishtha, a region in Kraunche-
dwipa, 2. 198.

Bhramaras, their origin, 1. 182
(where correct the spelling); 5.
388.

Bhrami, 'revolution,' daughter of
Siśumára, and wife of Dhruva,
1. 178.

Bhrigu, son of Brahma, P. 88;
1 100, 125, 131, 150-152; 2.
113, 259, 285, &c.; 3. 3, 8,
11, 14-16, 23, 35, 68, 80-82,
98, 162, 291, 338, 342; 4. 16,
17, 19, 23, 25, 31, 39, 40; 5.
76, 218, 250. His wife, 1.
109, 110, 118. His offspring,
1 152, 2 276. Lord of Lakshmípura, 1. 150. Teacher of
the Dhanur-veda, 3. 67.

Bhrigu, variant of Ribhu, 2. 330.

Bhrigubhúmi, variant of Bhargu-
bhúmi, 4. 39.

Bhrigukshetra, a holy spot on the
river Narmadá, 2. 151.

Bhrigutunga, a certain forest, 4. 49.

Bhringaríti, an attendant of Síva,
P. 89.

Bhrinjin (?), son of Súra, 4. 101.

Bhriti (?), variant of Dhriti, 4. 67.

Bhujingas (?), a people, 2. 163.

Bhúman, son of Pratihartri, 2.107.

Bhumanyu, son of Bharata, son of Dushyanta, 4. 136, 138.

Bhumanyu, variant of Bhuvan-manyu, 4. 136.

Bhúmi, wife of Vishńu as Para-śurama, 5. 87, 88, 90. See Dharańí.

Bhúmi, variant of Túńi, 4. 93.

Bhúmi - khańďa, a part of the Padma-puráńa, P. 30.

Bhúmimitra, son of Kańwáyana, 4. 181.

Bhúmimitra, son of Vasudeva, 4. 193, 194.

Bhúminanda, son of Vangava (?), 4. 212.

Bhúmiputra, variant of Bhúmi-mitra, 4. 181.

Bhúmitra, variant of Bhúmimitra, 4. 193.

Bhúpatis, variant of A'bhútarajas, 3. 9.

Bhúrbhúra, variant of Jharjhara, 2. 69.

Bhúrbhúva, variant of Jharjhara, 2. 69.

Bhúri, son of Somadatta, 4. 157; 5. 134.

Bhúri, variant of Dhuni, 2. 23.

Bhúrijyeshťha, variant of Ushńa, 4. 164.

Bhúrisheńa, son of Brahma-sávarńi, 3. 26.

Bhúrishena, son of Saryáti, 3. 249.

Bhúriśravas, son of Somadatta, 4. 157; 5. 134.

Bhúr-loka, the earth, 2. 113, 225.

Bhúshikas, variant of Múshikas, 4. 222.

Bhútas, certain evil spirits, their

origin. &c., 1. 82, 83; 2. 74, 75; 3 120, 216; 5. 127, 144. Their king, S'úlapáńi, 2. 86.

Bhúts, a patriarch, 2. 25. His wives, 2. 21.

Bhúta, son of Vasudeva, 4. 109.

Bhúta, what, in philosophy, 1. 140.

Bhúta-bhávana, what, 5. 91, 386.

Bhútádi, what, 1. 33, 34, 169; 2 232; 5. 94, 198, 199.

Bhútajyotis, son of Sumati, 3. 335.

Bhrttaketu, son of Dakshasávarńa, 3. 25.

Bhútananda, a Yavana king, 4. 211, 213.

Bhútanayas (??), variant of A'bhú-tarajas, 3. 9.

Bhútaruyas (??), variant of A'bhú-tarajas. 3. 9, 10.

Bhútasantapana, son of Hirań-yaksha. 2. 69.

Bhuta-sarga, what, in philosophy, 1. 74

Bhútátman, what, 1. 3; 5. 91.

Bhúta-vidya, what, 4. 33.

Bhúta-yajna. a certain sacrifice, 3. 40, 118.

Bhúteśa, an epithet of Viahńu, 1. 42.

Bhúti, son of Angiras, 3. 28, 29.

Bhuti = Lakshmí, 1. 119; 3. 28 (where correct the spelling Bhúti).

Bhúti, variant of Túńi, 4. 93.

Bhúti, what, in philosophy, 1. 148

Bhútigauri, variant of Gaurí, 5. 387.

Bhútimitra, variant of Bhúmimi-tra, 4. 193.

Bhútinauda, a king, 4. 212.

Bhuva, son of Pratihartri, 2. 106.

Bhuvana, a Rudra, 2. 25.

Bhuvaneśwara, an epithet of Śiva, P. 73.

Bhuvanmanyu (?), variant of Bhavanmanyu, 4. 136.

Bhuva-loka = Bhuvar-loka, 2. 113.

Bhuvar-loka, the space between the earth and the sun, 2. 225; 5. 192. See Bhuvo-loka.

Bhuvo-loka = Bhuvar-loka, 2. 230; 5. 192, 194.

Bíja, what, in the Yoga philosophy, 5. 230, 231.

Bimbasára, variant of Bimbisára, 4. 171, 181.

Bimbisára, king of Rájagṛiha in Magadha, variously genealogized, 4. 171, 180, 181, 186.

Bindumat, son of Marichi, 2. 107.

Bindumatí, daughter of S'asabindu, and wife of Mándhátṛi, 3. 268.

Bindumatí, wife of Viduratha, 3. 268; 4. 153.

Bindusára, king of Pátaliputra, variously genealogized, 4. 181, 186, 187, 188.

Bindusena (?), variant of Bimbisára, 4. 180, 181.

Birth, ceremonies ordained at, 3. 98, 99.

Bodhaa, a people, 2. 156.

Bodha, son of Dharma, 1. 110.

Bodha, variant of Rodha, 2. 214.

Bodhaa, variant of Sodhas, 2. 163.

Bodhana, a hill, 2. 142.

Bodhya, disciple of Báshkali, and promulgator of the Ṛig-veda, 3. 44.

Bopadeva, an author, his time, &c., P. 44, 48, 50, 51, 88; 5. 277, 278, 327.

Bopadeva (another?), 3. 174.

Bradhna, son of Bhautya, Manu of the fourteenth Manwantara, 3. 29.

Brahmás = Brahmarshis, 1. 100. &c.

Brahma, the supreme nonentity, unthinking thought and what not. Typified by Om, 1. 1. One with Vishńu, &c., 1. 3. Possessed of properties, and the source of creation, 1. 44. Two states of, 2. 92. Endowed with form, and formless, 5. 232. Etymology of the word, 1. 30; 3. 37, 38. See also 1. 3, 18, 21, &c., 45; 4. 293 (misprinted Brahmá), 326, 346; 5. 12, 15, &c., &c.

Brahmá, the first hypostasis of Brahma. The same as Vishńu in his character of creator, 1. 41. The duration of his life, 1. 46. His various creations, 1. 68, &c. The four castes proceed from him, 1. 89, &c. His mind-born sons, 1. 100, &c. Parent of the Rudras, 1. 115, &c. The same as Mahat, 1. 29, &c. The first teacher of the Vishńu-puráńa, 1. 5. He arranges the Veda, 3. 34. His city, 2. 112, 118. He praises Vishńu, 4. 251, &c. See also P. 4, 21, &c., &c.; 1. 13, 22, 30, 39, 40, &c.; 3. 11, 37, 38, 297; 4. 266, 292, 293, 319, 346; 5. 2, 3, 11, 14, 15, 43, 59, 94, 95, 114, 118, &c., &c.

Brahmá, a Kalpa so called, 1. 53; 3. 66.

Bráhma, a Pralaya so called, 1. 113, &c.

Bráhma, a form of marriage, 3. 105.

Bráhma, 'sacred philosophy,' 1. 85.

Brahmabáli, disciple of Devadarśa, &c., and teacher of the Atharva-veda, 3. 61, 62.

Brahma-bhúta, what, 2. 89; 5. 17, 153.

Brahmabodhyá, a river, 2. 151, 152, 340.

Brahmachárin, what, 3. 101.

Brahmacharya, what, 3. 77; 5. 181.

Brahmadaṇḍa, son of Naravâhana, 4. 166.

Brahmadatta, variously genealogized, 4. 142.

Brahmaja, a kind of cloud, 2. 279.

Bráhma-khaṇḍa, a part of the Brahma-vaivarta-purâṇa, P. 65, 67.

Brahmakośa = Atri, 3. 16.

Brahma-loka = Satya-loka, P. 66; 1. 98; 2. 227-230; 3. 198; 4. 266; 5. 193, 195.

Brahma-maya, what, 5. 253.

Brahmamedhyá, a river, 2. 152, 340.

Bráhmana. Produced from the mouth of Brahmá, 1. 89. Their duties, 3. 86. Families of, 4. 28. Early settlements of them in India, P. 102.

Brahman, a sort of priest, 3. 43, 44.

Brahmáṇḍa, what, 1. 170.

Brahmáṇḍa-purâṇa, analysis of it, &c., P. 20, 23, 24, 84, &c.;

3. 67, 187 (where correct the spelling); 5. 308, 319 (where correct the spelling), 390, 392.

Brahmáṇḍa-upapurâṇa, P. 87.

Brahmáṇí, a river, 2. 153.

Bráhmaṇí, a sacred spot named in the Mahábhárata, 2. 153.

Brahmaṇya-deva, what, 2. 57.

Brahmápeta, a Rákshasa, 2. 285, &c.

Brahmapura, the city of Brahmá, situated on a peak of Mount Meru, 2. 112.

Brahma-purâṇa, analysis of it, &c., P. 20, 21, 24, 26, 27, &c., 58, 110; 5. 282, 284, 292, 298, 305-314, 317, 319, 320, 325, 327, 344, 351.

Bráhma-purâṇa = Brahma-purâṇa, P. 23, 27; 3. 66.

Brahmaputras, what, 1. 100.

Brahmaputra, a river, 2. 154.

Brahmaráta, father of Yájnavalkya, 3. 53.

Brahmarshis, 'Bráhman saints,' their abode, &c., 1. 100; 5. 69, 271; 4. 52, 246; 5. 121.

Brahmarshideśa, a region in Central India, 2. 143.

Brahmasávarṇa, Brahmasávarṇi, the Manu of the tenth Manwantara, and son of Upaśloka, 3. 25. He is called son of Brahmá, 3. 24.

Brahma-śiras, a fiery weapon so called, 3. 83, 84.

Brahmástra, a fiery weapon so called, 3. 84, 338; 4. 160.

Brahma-varáha, P. 65.

Brahmávarta, a district in Central India, P. 105; 2. 143.

Brahma-vaivarta-puráña, analysis
of it, &c., P. 20, 21, 23, 24,
65, &c., 110; 3. 67; 5. 264,
269, 270, 282, 284, 298, 316,
319, 321, 327, 342, 343.

Brahma-yajna, a sort of sacrament,
3. 40, 93.

Bráhmí Samhitá, a part of the
Kúrma-puráña, P. 77, 78.

Brahmishṭha, son of Kauśalya, 3
324.

Brahmopeta, variant of Brahmápeta, 2. 292, 293.

Brahmottara-khañḍa, a part of the
Skanda-puráña, P. 27, 73.

Brahmottara-puráña, P. 27.

Bṛihad-árañyaka-upanishad, the,
or its commentary, referred to,
3. 113, 122, 191, 338; 5. 388.

Bṛihadaśwa, a Sádhya, son of
Sádbyá, 2. 22.

Bṛihadaśwa, son of Śrávasta, 3.
264.

Bṛihadaśwa, son of Sahadeva, 4.
168.

Bṛihadaśwa, son of Satadhara, 4.
189.

Bṛihadaśwa, variant of Pṛishad-
aśwa, 3. 284.

Bṛihadbala, variously genealogized,
3. 321, 325; 4. 167, 172.

Bṛihadbhánu, variously genealogized, 4. 125.

Bṛihadbhánu, son of Krishña and
Satyabhámá, 5. 81.

Bṛihaddarbha, variant of Bṛihadbhánu, 4. 125.

Bṛihad-devatá, an ancient composition, referred to, 3. 48.

Bṛihaddhanus, variant of Bṛihadishu, son of Ajamíḍha, 4. 140.

Bṛihaddhanus, variant of Bṛihadvasu. 4. 140.

Bṛihaddharman, variant of Bṛihadvasu, 4 140.

Bṛihaddhwaja, variant of Vṛijini-
vat, 4 61

Bṛihadishu, son of Ajamíḍha, 4.
140.

Bṛihadishu, son of Haryaśwa, 4.
144.

Bṛihadraja, variously genealogized,
4. 169.

Bṛihadraśa, variant of Bṛihatkshaña, 4. 167.

Bṛihadrathas = Bárhadrathas, 4.
178.

Bṛihadrathá, variously genealogized, 4. 125. A Bṛihadratha
is named in 4. 24.

Bṛihadratha, son of Vasu, and
king of Magadha, 4. 149, 150,
173, 177, 344, 345.

Bṛihadratha, son of Tigma, 4. 165.

Bṛihadratha, son of Bṛihatkshaña,
4. 167.

Bṛihadratha, son of Satadhanwan,
4 189, 190.

Brihadratha, variant of Bṛihaduktha, 3. 331.

Bṛihadratha, variant of Dṛiḍharatha, 4. 126.

Bṛihadratha, variant of Jayadratha,
4. 140.

Bṛihadratha, variant of Aśokavardhana, 4. 187.

Bṛihaduktha, son of Devaráta, 3.
331.

Bṛihadvasu, son of Bṛihadishu, 4.
140.

Bṛihadvishñu (??), variant of Bṛi
hadvasu, 4. 140.

C

Brihadwati, one or more rivers, 2. 151, 152.

Brihanmanas, son of Brihadbhánu, 4. 125. ·

Brihanmanas (?), a king between Nanda and Chandragupta, 4. 345.

Brihan-Manu, an ancient lawgiver, quoted, 3. 151.

Brihan - náradíya - puráña, P. 51, &c.

Brihaspati, son of Angiras, P. 38 ; 1. 141, 188, 190; 2. 84; 3. 16, 244, 245 ; 4. 2-4, 42, 123, 134, 135. Author of the Arthasástra, 3. 68. Identified, as a planet, with Jupiter, 2. 226, 259, 308. His cycle, 2. 255.

Brihaspati, the Vyása of the fourth Dwápara age, 3. 34, 36. ·

Brihaspati, a Rishi in the second Manwantara, 3. 4.

Brihaspati, founder of an heretical sect, 3. 213.

Brihaspati-smriti, an ancient code of law, referred to, 3. 189-191.

Brihat, a portion of the Sáma-veda, 2. 295, 343.

Brihat, a Kalpa, P. 51, 52.

Brihat (?), variant of Brihatkshattra, 4. 137, 139.

Brihatí, wife of Ripu, són of Sliahti, 1. 177.

Brihatí, daughter of Sibi, and wife of Krishña, 5. 83.

Brihatí, a metre, its origin from Brahmá, 1. 86. Identified with a horse of the Sun's car, 2. 239.

Brihatkarman, variously genealogized, 4. 125.

Brihatkarman, son of Brihadvasu, 4. 140.

Brihatkarman, son of Sukshattra, 4. 174.

Brihat-kathá, a composition, 2. 177, 211. See Kathá-sarit-ságara.

Brihatkáya, variant of Brihatkarman, 4. 140.

Brihatkshaña, son of Brihadbala, 4. 167.

Brihatkshattra, son of Dhritishta-ketu, 4. 103.

Brihatkshattra, son of Bhavanmanyu, 4. 135, 138, 139.

Brihatkshaya, variant of Brihatkshaña, 4. 167.

Brihatkshetra, variant of Brihatkshaña, 4. 167.

Brihat-Parásara, an ancient lawgiver, quoted, 3. 180.

Brihat-sámán, a portion of the Sáma-veda, its origin from Brahmá, 1. 84.

Brihat-samhitá, an astronomical work, referred to, 2. 190, 275 ; 4. 153.

Brihatsena, son of Krishña and Bhadrá, 5. 82.

Brihatsena, variant of Brihatkarman, 4. 174.

Brihatsena, variant of Dridhasena, 4. 175, 176.

Brihattajas, a name of Brihaspati, son of Angiras, 2. 259.

Brishadaswa (?), variant of Prihadaswa, 3. 284.

Buddha, founder of a religion, P. 72; 3. 235, 236; 4. 170, 187, 188; 5. 322, &c., 375. Fanciful etymology of his name, 3. 210, 211; 4. 5; 5. 350, 361,

368. A form of Vishńu, 5. 178, 323, 378. And see Anjana.

Buddhi, 'intellect,' daughter of Daksha, and wife of Dharma, 1. 109, 110.

Buddhi, what, in philosophy, 1. 4, 32; 5. 198.

Buddhism, 5. 177, 178. And see Buddha.

Budha, or Mercury, son of Siva, 1. 117; 2. 225, 258, 304, 308; 8. 236; 4. 5, 60. He is also said to be son of Soma, 2. 259; 4. 4.

Budha, son of Vegavat, 3. 245.

Budha, variant of Vadha, a Rákshasa, 2. 287.

Budha, 'wise man,' 5. 239.

Budhna, variant of Bradhna, 3. 29.

Budhnya, variant of Bradhna, 3. 29.

Bukháras (?), a people, 2. 186.

Castes, four, their origin from Brahmá, 1. 89, 171. Their primal state, 1. 90. Divided by occupations, 1. 96, 97. Their future abodes, 1. 97, &c. Their duties, 3. 85, &c. Instituted by different kings, 4. 31, 32, 38, 123.

Cathaei, the, a tribe of Kshattriyas, 2. 184.

Caumojees, a tribe, 3. 292. See Kámbojas.

Ceremonies, at birth, &c., 3. 98, &c.

Chaidyas, a people, 4. 65.

Chaidyas, certain kings, 4. 67.

Chaidyoparichara, an epithet of Vasu, son of Kritaka, 4. 149.

Chaitanya, founder of a sect, P. 22; 5. 318, 343, 345.

Chaitra, two Rishis, of the second and fourth Manwantaras, variously genealogized, 3. 5, 8.

Chaitra, a month. March–April, 2. 261, &c.; 3. 114.

Chaitra (?), a mountain-range in Krauncha-dwípa, 2. 197.

Chaitraratha, Kubera's grove on Mount Mandara, 2. 111, 116; 4. 6; 5. 137.

Chaitravatí, variant of Chandrabhagá, 2. 147.

Chaitrí, a certain sacrifice, 3. 113.

Chakora, a city, 3. 318.

Chakora (?), a hill, 2. 142. See Kora.

Chakora, variant of Chakora Sátakarńin, 4. 197, 198.

Chakora Sátakarńin, Chakoraswátikarńa, &c., son of Sundara Sátakarńin, &c., 4. 197, 201, 202.

Chakras, a people, 2. 165.

Chakra, a mountain in Kusadwípa, 2. 197.

Chakravartin, what, 1. 183; 3. 31, 267, 290; 4. 60.

Chakrin, an epithet of Krishńa, from his chakra, 'discus,' 4. 82; 5. 1, 69, 70, 82, 107, 108, 116, 127, 149, 161.

Chakshu, the river Oxus, 2. 112, 120–122, 272.

Chakshu, variant of Chákshusha, son of Anu, 4. 120.

Chakshus, son of Vyushta, 1. 178.

Chakshus, son of Purujánu, 4. 144.

Chákshushas, a class of gods in the fourteenth Manwantara, 3. 28.

Chakshusha, son of Ripu, 1. 177.

Chákshusha, Manu of the sixth Manwantara, variously genealogized, 1. 177, 178; 2. 26, 27; 3. 2, 11, 12, 14, 17, 18, 192; 4. 5.

Chákshusha, son of Anu, 4. 120.

Chákshusha, the sixth Manwantara, 2. 9, 11; 27, 258. 259, et passim.

Chalá = Lakshmí, 1. 110.

Champa, son of Prithulaksha, 4. 125.

Champa, variant of Chunchu, 3. 289.

Champá, a city, the ancient capital of Anga, 2. 166; 4. 124, 125, 221.

Champápuri = Champá, 3. 289; 4. 125.

Champávatí = Champá, the city so called, 4. 218, 219.

Chánuko, Páli for Chánakya, 4. 185.

Chánakya = Kautilya, 4. 186.

Chanchu, variant of Chunchu, 3. 289.

Chandagutto, Páli for Chandragupta, 4. 185.

Chandála, what, 3. 120.

Chandana, a certain mountain, 2. 155.

Chandana, a species of tree, 2. 200.

Chandaná, a river, 2. 155.

Chándaní, a river, 2. 155.

Chandanodakadundubhi, &c., variously genealogized. 4. 97.

Chandapradyota(?), a king, 5. 391.

Chandasrisátakarní (?), variant of Chandrasrí, 4. 201.

Chandí = Kálí, a Sakti, P. 56; 1. 104.

Chandí, ruled over by Kákavarna, 4. 180.

Chandí - pátha, a part of the Márkandeya-puráña, P. 56; 3. 22.

Chandra = Soma, 1.. 131; 2. 304; 4. 293.

Chandra, son of Krishna and Satyá, 5. 79.

Chandra, a mountain - range in Plaksha-dwípa, 2. 191.

Chandrá, a river, 2. 194.

Chandra, Chándra, variants of Árdra, son of Viswagaswa, 3. 263.

Chandra, variant of Cháru, 5. 78.

Chandrabhágá, the river Chenab, 2. 130, 131, 142, 144, 147; 4. 118, 223 (where correct the spelling), 224; 5. 381, 385, 392.

Chandrabhánu, son of Krishna and Satyabhámá, 5. 81.

Chandragiri, son of Tárápída, 3. 321.

Chandragupta, son of Nanda (?), P. 109; 4. 186–188, 203, 205, 219, 232, 345; 5. 313.

Chandraketu, son of Lakshmaña, 3. 318.

Chandraketu, king of Chakora, 3. 318.

Chandraketu, a country near the Himálayas, 3. 319.

Chandramá, a river, 2. 151.

Chandrápída, son of Súryápída. 4. 163.

Chandrápída, king of Cashmere, 4. 223.

Chandrasrí, son of Vijaya, son of Yajnasrí, 4. 199.

Chandraśukla, an island, perhaps fabulous, 2. 129.

Chandráśwa, son of Kuvalayáśwa, 3. 265.

Chandravaktrá, a city near the Himálayas, 3. 319.

Chandrávaloka, son of Sahasráśwa, 3. 321.

Chandravijna, variant of Chandraśrí, 4. 199.

Chángerí, what, 5. 33.

Chándra, a famous pancratinst, slain by Kríshńa, 4. 335, 337; 5. 23, 28, 35. 36, 38-40, 87.

Chapa (?), variant of Apus, a Rákshasa, 2. 288.

Charáchara, what, 5. 385.

Charakas. = Charakádhwaryus, 3. 54, 55.

Charaka, a teacher of the Yajurveda, 3. 55.

Charaku, an ancient medical authority, 4. 33.

Charakádhwaryus, of the Yajurveda, 3. 54.

Chárańas, 'panegyrists of the gods,' 2. 124, 213; 4. 266.

Charańa, a technicality, explained. 3. 121.

Charańa-vyúha, a composition. referred to, 3. 51.

Charanta, son of Árshťishena, 4. 31.

Chariots. Of the Sun, 2. 237. Of the Moon, 2. 299. Of Mars, Jupiter, Saturn, Ráhu. and Ketu, 2. 304, 305.

Charishńu, son of Kírttimat, 1. 154.

Charma, a country in the north of India, 2. 169.

Charmakháńďikas, variant of Charmamańďalas, 2. 169.

Charmamańďulas, a people. 2. 169.

Charmańwatí, the river Chumbul, 2. 131 (where correct the spelling), 147, 339; 4. 137.

Cháru, son of Kríshńa and Rukmińí, 5. 78, 148.

Cháruchandra, variant of Charuvinda, 5. 78.

Chárudeha, son of Kríshńa and Rukmińí, 5. 78.

Cháruadeshńa, son of Kríshńa and Rukmińí. 4. 112, 113; 5. 78.

Chárudharman, variant of Cháruvarman, 5. 148.

Cháringupta, son of Kríshńa and Rukmińí, 5. 78.

Cháruhásiní, wife of Kríshńa, 4. 112; 5. 69, 79. The same as Lakshmańá, (?) 5. 81.

Cháruka -- Cháru, 5. 148.

Chárumatí, daughter of Kríshńa and Rukmińí, 5. 78.

Chárupada, variant of Abhayada. 4. 127.

Cháruśravas, son of Kríshńa and Rukmińí, 4. 112.

Charuvarman, associated with Samba, Akrúra, and others. 5. 148.

Cháruvesha, son of Kríshńa and Rukmińí, 4. 112.

Cháruvinda, son of Kríshńa and Rukmińí, 5. 78.

Cháruyaśas, son of Krishńa and Rukmińí, 4. 112.

Charakas, of the Yajur-veda, 3. 55.

Chatuh'śringa, a mountain in Kuśa dwípa. 2. 197.

Chaturanga, son of Romapáda, 4. 124, 125.

Chaturhotra, variant of Anuha, 4. 141.

Cháturmásyas, certain sacrifices, 3. 40, 113.

Chaturvedas, a class of Pitris, 3. 339.

Chaulas (??) = Cholas, 3. 292.

Chaulimaheswara, a town on the river Narmadá, 2. 167.

Chayana, a certain ceremony, 3. 174.

Chedis, a people, 2. 157; 5. 118.

Chedi, variously genealogized, 4. 67.

Chedi, a country in Central India, 2. 132, 157; 3. 157; 4. 65, 104, 107, 149, 150, 159.

Chedipa, son of Vasu, son of Kritaka, 4. 150.

Chekitána, son of Dhrishtaketu, 4. 103.

Cheshtita, what, 5. 206.

Chhala, variously genealogized, 3. 321.

Chhampaña, variant of Saukhanábha, 3. 322.

Chhandajas, certain classes of deities so called, 2. 29.

Chhandas, 'metre,' an Anga of the Veda, 3. 67.

Chhandoga, a Samhitá of the Sáma-veda, 3. 42.

Chhándogya-upanishad, the, referred to, 3. 175; 5. 345.

Chhanna, what, 5. 31.

Chháyá, daughter of Viswakarman, and mistress of Vivaswat, 3. 20, &c.

Chhesmaka (??), variant of Chhismaka, 4. 195.

Chhismaka, a king, 4. 195, 201.

Chidi (??), variant of Chedi, 4. 67.

Chikitsá, 'the practice of medicine,' 4. 33.

Chínas, a people, the Chinese, 2. 176, 181, 183, 184; 3. 293, 295.

Chiti, the same as Mahat, 1. 32.

Chit-para, what, 1. 31.

Chitrá, an Apsaras, 2. 81.

Chitra, an asterism, 2. 265, &c.

Chitrabhánu, or Fire, 4. 56.

Chitrabhánu, variant of Traisámba, 4. 116.

Chitragu, son of Krishña and Satyá, 5. 79.

Chitragupta, recorder of hell, 2. 216.

Chitraka, variously genealogized, 4. 94, 96.

Chitraketu, son of Vasishtha, 1. 155.

Chitraketu, son of Krishña and Jámbavatí, 5. 79.

Chitraketu, variant of Chandraketu, the region so called, 3. 319.

Chitráksha (??), variant of Nrichakshus, 4. 164.

Chitrakúta, a hill in Bundelkhand, 2. 141, 153, 155.

Chitrakúta, a mountain in Kusadwípa, 2. 197.

Chitrakúta, a river, 2. 155.

Chitralekhá, an Apsaras, 2. 82, 286.

Chitralekhá, daughter of Kumbhañda, 5. 109-111.

Chitramanas, a horse of the Moon, 2. 299.

Chitranátha, son of Dhṛíshṭa, 3. 255.

Chitrángada, a Gandharva, 4. 158.

Chitrángada, son of Sántanu, 4. 157.

Chitraratha, chief of the Gandharvas, 1. 188; 2. 86; 5. 66.

Chitraratha, son of Gaya, 2. 107.

Chitraratha, son of Rushadgu, 4. 61.

Chitraratha, son of Dharmaratha, 4. 124.

Chitraratha, variously genealogized, 4. 163, 164.

Chitraratha, king of Mṛittikávatí (identifiable with some preceding Chitraratha?), 4. 19.

Chitraratha, a river, 2. 153.

Chitraratha, variant of Sanjaya, 3. 334.

Chitraratha, variant of Chitraka, 4. 94.

Chitrarepha, son of Medhátithi, king of Sáka-dwípa, 2 200.

Chitrarepha, a region in Sáka-dwípa, 2. 200.

Chitrasena, a Gandharva, 2. 285, &c.; 3. 281.

Chitrasena, son of Rauchya, Manu of the thirteenth Manwantara, 3. 28.

Chitrasena, son of Narishyanta, 3. 335.

Chitrasená, a river, 2. 146.

Chitravahá, a river, 2. 145.

Chitropalá, a river, 2. 153.

Chitrotpalá, a river, 2. 153.

Chitsukha (same as the next?), author of the Bhágavata-kathá-sangraha, P. 49.

Chitsukha Yogin, commentator on

the Vishṇu-puráṇa, P. 115; 5. 385.

Chitti, daughter of Kardama, and wife of Atharvan, 1. 110.

Chivilika, variant of Iviláka, 4. 196.

Cholas, a people, 2. 178; 3. 292.

Chola, sprung from Turvasu, 4. 117.

Cholamaṅḍala, the country on the Coromandel coast, 2. 178.

Chronology, system of, 1. 46, &c. That of the kings of the Kali age, 4. 229, &c.

Chúḍákarmádika, what, 3. 149.

Chulaká, a river, 2. 148.

Chulí Maheśwar, a place, 2. 167.

Chuluká, variant of Chulaká, 2. 148.

Chunchu, son of Harita, 3. 289.

Chunchulas, Kauśika Bráhmans, 4. 29.

Chupuṅíká, a Kṛittiká, 2. 337.

Chyavana, a Ṛishi, P. 64; 3. 80, 239, 248, 282, 342. Referred to the second Manwantara, 3. 4.

Chyavana, son of Mitráyu, 4. 147.

Chyavana, son of Suhotra, 4. 149.

Cities of the gods, 2. 112, 118, 239, 240.

Cleanliness, rules of, 3. 109, &c.

Clepsydra, the, described, 5. 189.

Clouds, how formed, classes of them, &c., 2. 279, &c.

Colonization of India, P. 102, &c.

Cooay, popular name of the Koál.

Cosmogony of the Hindus, 1. 20, &c. Its analogies to ancient cosmogonies, 1. 27.

Countries and kingdoms, how named in pure Sanskrit, 5. 80.

Creation. Accounts of it, 1. 23, 68, &c., 79. Of nine kinds, 1. 69, &c. In three divisions, 1. 76, &c. Mode of primary creation, 1. 27. Course of, 1. 29, &c. Various kinds of, 1. 72, &c. Periods of secondary creation, 1. 55, &c. Kinds of, 1. 70, &c. Of the .immortals, 1. 72. Of mankind, 1. 73. Of properties, 1. 75, &c. A property of Brahma, 1. 44. A function of Vishńu as Brahmá, 1. 41, &c.

Dadátivádaras, Kaúsika Bráhmans, 4. 28.

Dadhícha, a sage. 1. 124, 125; 5. 250.

Dadhífchi = Dadhícha, P. 68, 69.

Dadhimafufa, a sea of whey, around Krauncha-dwípa, 2. 198.

Dadhivähana, king of Champá, 4. 124.

Dadhivähana, variant of Pára, son of Anga, 4. 124

Dadhividarbhas, variant of Daśi-vidarbhas, 2. 181.

Dáhas, variant of Vaidehas, 2. 177.

Dahana, a Rudra, 2. 25.

Dahaná = Vaiśwánarí, 2. 276, 277.

Dahrágni = Agastya, 1. 154

Daigambaras, an heretical sect, 5. 379, 380 See Digambaras.

Daihitra (?), variant of Dauhitra, the king so called, 4. 213.

Daiteyas = Daityas, 3. 211; 4. 114; 5. 115.

Daityas, eldest sons of Kaśyapa by Diti, 2. 30. Their chief. Prahláda, 2. 85. Defeated by

the gods, 1. 145. Obtain the sovereignty of the earth, 2. 34. Overcome the gods, 3. 201, &c. Fall into heresy, and are subdued, 3. 207, &c. Oppress the earth, 4. 250. See also P. 76; 82; 1. 142, 143, 190; 2. 70; 4. 265, 266, 273, 339; 5. 94, 109, 113, 115-117, 119, &c.; 234, 246, 247.

Daiva, a form of marriage, 3. 105.

Daivarakshitas, sprung from Deva-rakshita, king of the Kośalas, 4. 220.

Daivaráti = Janaka, 3. 53.

Daivata, variant of Devaja, 3. 247.

Daiva-tírtha, what, 3. 99, 148.

Daivika-śráddha, a particular ceremony, 3. 147.

Daksha, a Prajápati, 1. 100. Chief of the Prajápatis, 2. 85. Born from Brahma's thumb, 1. 102; 2. 10; 3. 230. Marries Prasúti, and has twenty-four daughters by her, 1. 108, 109. His sacrifice, 1. 120, &c.; 4. 262. It is spoiled by Vírabhadra, 1. 130. He propitiates Śiva, 1. 133. See also P. 28; 1. 31, 37, 38, 75, 89, 96, 108, 117, 122, 126; 2. 2, &c., 108; 3. 24, 162; 4. 339; 5. 48, 77, 386, 387.

Daksha, son of the Prachetases, 2. 9. Marries Asikní, 2. 12. His offspring, 2. 10, 13, 20.

Daksha, an Áditya, 2. 27, 286.

Daksha, one of the Viśwe devas, 3. 179, 189-192.

Daksha, a lawgiver. 3. 111.

Daksha. son of Chitrasena, 3. 335.

Daksha, variant of Háhá, a Gandharva, 2. 288.

Daksha, variant of Ratheswana, a Yaksha, 2. 289.

Daksha, variant of Riksha, Vyása of the twenty-fourth Dwápara age, 3. 35.

Daksha, variant of Darva, 4. 121.

Dakshaputra, according to one account, the Manu of the ninth Manwantara, 3. 337. See Dakshasávarna.

Dakshasávarna, the Manu of the ninth Manwantara, son of Varuña, 3. 24.

Dakshasávarñi (?), variant of Dakshasávarña, 3. 24.

Daksha-smriti, a code of law, quoted, 3. 111.

Dakshiña = Dakshiñagui, 3. 175; 4. 11; 5. 114.

Dakshiña, 'honorarium,' daughter of Ruchi, 1. 108.

Dakshinábdhi, 'the southern sea,' 5. 53.

Dakshinágni = Anwáhárya-pachana, 3. 175; 5. 126.

Dakshiñápatha, Southern India, 2. 145; 3. 240; 4. 205; 5. 53.

Dala, son of Páripátra, 3. 321.

Dálaki, disciple of Sákapúni, and teacher of the Rig-veda, 3. 49.

Dálbhya, a Rishi in the third Manwantara, 3. 7.

Dama, son of Brahmá, 1. 103.

Dama, son of Narishyanta, P. 57; 3. 245, 336.

Damabhúta (?), son of Vasudeva, 4. 109.

Damaghosha, a Chaidya king, 4. 67, 104.

Dámalipta, a city in Suhma, 2. 177.

Dámaliptas, variant of Támraliptakas, 2. 177.

Damayantí, daughter of Bhíma, king of Vidarbha, 2. 171.

Dambha, 'hypocrisy,' son of Adharma, 1. 111.

Dambha, variant of Rambha, son of Ayus, 4. 30.

Dambhobhi, variant of Dattoli, 1. 154

Dambholi, variant of Dattoli, 1. 154; 3. 4.

Damin, a caste in Kusá-dwípa, 2. 195.

Dámodara, an epithet of Krishña, 4. 281, 283, 310, 317, 326; 5. 64, 120.

Damshtrin, 'fanged,' a term applied to the progeny of Krodhavasá, 2. 74.

Dánavas, enemies of the gods. Sons of Kasyapa and Danu, 2. 70. Their chief, Prahláda, 2. 85, 86. See also 1. 138, 143, 144, 190; 2. 71; 4. 261, 323; 5. 115, 247, 387.

Dáhavrata, a caste in Sáka-dwípa, 2. 250.

Danáyus, variant of Anáyus, 2. 26, 73.

Dańda, 'punishment,' son of Dharma, 1. 110; 5. 386.

Dańda, son of Ikshwáku, 3. 239, 259, 260. Slain by Sudyumna, 3. 238.

Dańda, a measure of time, variously estimated, 1. 48, 49.

Dańda, variant of Prámsu, 3. 232.

Dańdaka, variant of Dańda, son of Ikshwáku, 3. 238, 260.

Daṅḍaka, a certain forest, 2. 144; 3. 238.

Daṅḍanaya (?), son of Dharma, 1. 111; 5. 368. See Daṅḍa-níti.

Daṅḍa-níti, what, 1. 149; 2. 202; 4. 310.

Daṅḍa - páda - nipátana = Daṅḍa-páta, 4. 291.

Daṅḍapáṅi, variously genealogized, 4. 165.

Daṅḍapáṅi, son of a king of the Káśis, 5. 126.

Daṅḍa-páta, a disposition of the feet in dancing, 4. 291.

Daṅḍa-páta (another), what, 5. 52.

Daṅḍásana, what, 5. 230.

Daṅḍaseha, variant of Udaksena, 4. 142.

Daṅḍaśrí, variant of Chandraśrí, 4. 199.

Daṅḍaśrí Sátakarṅi, variant of Chandraśrí, 4. 199.

Dandaśúka, a hell, 2. 215.

Daṅḍin, a modern author, his relative age, 4. 347.

Dantavaktra, son of Vṛiddhaśarman, 4. 103, 104; 5. 70 (where correct the spelling).

Dantobhi, variant of Dattoli, 3. 4.

Dantoli, variant of Dattoli, 3. 4.

Danu, daughter of Daksha, and wife of Kaśyapa, 1. 144; 2. 26, 55, 70; 4. 250; 5. 87, 387.

Dara, variant of Hari, a mountain in Kuśa-dwípa, 2. 196.

Daradas, a people, 2. 181, 184–186; 3. 295.

Darbha, variant of Rambha, son of Áyus, 4. 30.

Darbha, variant of Darva, 4. 121.

Darbhaka, son of Ajátaśatru, 4. 181.

Darpa, 'pride,' son of Dharma, 1. 110, 111.

Darśa, son of Kṛishṅa and Kálindí, 5. 79.

Darśa, a Sádhya, 2. 22.

Darśakas, a people, 2. 174.

Darśaka, variant of Darbhaka, 4. 182.

Darśa-paurṅa-mása = Darśa-púrṅa-mása, 3. 40.

Darśa-púrṅa-mása, a fortnightly sacrifice, 3. 113.

Darśa-śrāddha, worship of one's ancestors' manes, 3. 160.

Dáruka, Kṛishṅa's charioteer, 5. 148-151.

Dáruṅa (?), a hell, 2. 215.

Darvas, a people, 2. 175.

Dárvas a people, 2. 174, 175; 3. 292.

Darva, son of Uśínara, 4. 121.

Darvá, wife of Uśínara, 4. 121.

Dárvábhisáras, a people, 2. 174.

Darvakas, a people, 2. 174.

Darví (?), a country, 2. 175.

Darví, variant of Darva, 4. 121.

Darvíchas (?), a people, 2. 175.

Dárvika = Devíká, a river, 4. 223.

Dása, a name appropriate to a S'údra, 3. 99.

Daśagríva = Rávaṅa, 4. 104.

Daśahará, an autumnal festival in honour of Durgá, 4. 336.

Dáśaka, son of Bhajamána, 4. 72.

Daśaka (?), variant of Darbhaka, 4. 182.

Dáśaketu, variant of Díptiketu, 3. 25.

Daśa-kumára-charita, a modern work, referred to, 2. 157, 177.

Daśnmálikas, a people, 2. 183.

Dásamánas, a people, 2. 183.

Dasánana = Rávaña, 4. 104, 107, 241.

Dasáparswaa, variant of Dasárñas, 2 176.

Dasaratha, son of Aja, and father of Ráma, 3. 313, 314, 316 ; 4. 124.

Dasaratha, son of Múlaka, 3. 310, 314.

Dasaratha, son of Navaratha, 4. 68.

Dasaratha, son of Romapáda, 4. 124.

Dasaratha, son of Suyasa, 4. 188-190.

Dasarathi, patronym of Ráma, 4. 107.

Dasárhas, a people, 2. 176, 178.

Dasárha, son of Nirvriti, 4. 68.

Dasárha (?), a country, 4. 65.

Dasárñas, peoples, 2. 159, 162, 176, 178.

Dasárña, a country, 2. 159, 160; 3. 245 ; 4. 65.

Dasárñá, a river, 2. 155, 160.

Dasa-rúpa, the, a modern drama-turgical work, referred to, 3. 301.

Dasavadyá (?), an Apsaras, 2. 82.

Dasavarman, variant of Devavar-man, 4. 189.

Dásí, a river, 2. 151.

Dasívidarbhas, a people, 2. 181.

Daara, son of Áditya, 4. 103, 358.

Dasyu, what, 5. 166.

Datta = Dattátreya, son of Atri, 1. 154.

Dattáli, variant of Dattoli, 1. 154.

Dattátreya, son of Atri, 1. 154 ; 3. 96 ; 4. 21, 55.

Dattátreya, variant of Dattoli, 3. 4.

Dattátri, variant of Dattoli, 3. 3.

Dattobhi, variant of Dattoli, 3. 4.

Dattobhri, variant of Dattoli, 1. 154.

Dattokti, variant of Dattoli, 3. 4.

Dattoli = Agastya, 1. 154, 155. He appears as a Rishi in the first Manwantara, 3. 3-5.

Dattoni, variant of Dattoli, 3. 4.

Dattori, variant of Dattoli, 3. 4.

Dattolti, variant of Dattoli, 1. 154.

Dattotri, variant of Dattoli, 1. 154; 3. 4.

Dauhitra, a king, 4. 212, 213.

Dauhitra, the term explained, &c., 3. 186, 187.

Dauhitrya, variant of Dauhitra, the king so called, 4. 213.

Daurvásasa-upapuráña, P. 87.

Day. Of the gods, 1. 49. Of Brahma, 1. 52. Of a Manu, 1. 54. Divisions of the day, &c., 2. 253, &c.

Dayá, 'clemency,' daughter of Daksha, and wife of Dharma, 1. 110.

Dáya-bhága, a celebrated work on inheritance, quoted, or referred to, 3. 102.

Deities, thirty-three in number, 2. 29.

Desamánikas, a people, 2. 183.

Devas = Ádityas, 2. 284, 292.

Deva = Indra, 2. 125.

Deva, son of Viswámitra, 4. 27, 28.

Devá = Deviká, the river, 2. 144, 147.

Deva, variant of Devavat, son of Akrúra, 4. 96.

Deva, variant of Devavat, son of Devaka, 4. 98.

Devabáhu, variant of Vedabábu,
1. 155; 3. 10, 11.

Devabhága, son of Súra, 4. 101,
113.

Devabhúmi, variant of Devabhúti,
4. 192.

Devabhúri, variant of Devabhúti,
4. 192.

Devabhúti, son of Bhágavata, son
of Vajramitra, 4. 192.

Devadarsá, disciple of Kabandha,
and teacher of the Atharva-veda,
3. 61.

Devadatta, son of Urusravas, 3.
336.

Devadeva (?), son of Viswámitra,
4. 27, 28.

Devadbání, Indra's city, according
to the Bhágavata - puráñu, 2.
240.

Devadharman, variant of Suma-
śarman, 4. 190.

Devadyumna, son of Devatájit, 2.
107.

Devagarbhá, a river in Kuśa-
dwípa, 2. 197.

Devagiri, popularly called Deogur,
a monntain, 2. 141.

Devahúti, daughter of Swáyambhuva Manu, P. 42; 1. 108,
110.

Devaja, son of Samyama, 3. 247.

Devaka, son of Áhuka, 4. 98, 111,
248.

Devaka, son of Yudhishthira, 4.
159.

Devaka, a caste in Krauncha-
dwípa, 2. 198.

Devaka, variant of Devaja, 3. 247.

Deva-khála-jala, what, 3. 113.

Devakí, daughter of Devoka, wife

of Vasudeva, and mother of
Krishñá, 4. 98, 109, 110, &c.;
248, 259-261, 264, 268-270,
273, 329, 335; 5. 8, 26, 27,
35, 42, 44, 89, 100, 154, 345.
Called an incarnation of Aditi.
4. 318.

Devakshattra, son of Devaráta, 4.
68, 69.

Devakulyá, daughter of Paurña-
mása, 1. 153.

Devakúta, a monntain-range con-
necting Níla and Nishadha, 2.
123, 124.

Devalas, Kausíka Bráhmans, 4.
28.

Devala, a Rishi, son of Pratyúsha,
the Vasu, 2. 23.

Devala, son of Krisáswa, 2. 29.

Devala, author of an ancient code
of law, 2. 276, 343.

Devala, son of Reñu, 4. 27, 28.

Devalaka, a Bráhman who ministers
to idols, 3. 176.

Devamídha, variant of Kriti, son
of Kritaratha, 3. 331.

Devamídha, variant of Devami-
dhusha, son of Hridika, 4. 100.

Devamídhaka, variant of the same
Devamídhusha, 4. 100

Devamídhusha, son of Vrishñí, 4.
73, 74, 94.

Devamídhusha, son of Hridika,
4. 99, 100.

Devamídhusha, son of Súra, 4.
100.

Devamídhushá, daughter of Súra,
4. 100.

Devamitra = Sákalya, 3. 45.

Devana (?), son of Devakshattra (?).
4. 69.

Devánakshatra, variant of Devak-shattra, 4. 68.

Devanáman, a ruler in Kuśa-dwípa, 2. 197.

Devanáman, a region in Kusa dwípa, 2. 197.

Devánika, a king, son of Dhar-masávarnika, 3. 27.

Devánika, son of Kshemadhanwan, 3. 320, 321.

Devánika, a mountain in Kusa-dwípa, 2. 197.

Devapála, a mountain in Saka-dwípa, 2. 200.

Devápi, variously genealogized, 4. 153-157. He is still living, through force of devotion. 4. 237.

Devápi, variant of Devátithi, 4. 153.

Devaráj, a title of Indra, 3. 259.

Devaraj, variant of Devaráta, son of Karambhi, 4. 68.

Devárája, a title of Indra, 4. 321; 5. 97.

Devarakshita, son of Devaka, son of Áhuka, 4. 98.

Devarakshita, king of the Ko-śalas, 4. 218, 220.

Devarakshitá, daughter of Devaka, and wife of Vasudeva. 4. 98, 110, 111.

Devarátas, Kanńka Bráhmana, 4. 28.

Devaráta = Sunaḥśepha, son of Viśwámitra, 4. 25, 26 (where correct the spelling), 27, 28, 343.

Devaráta, son of Saketu, 3. 331.

Devaráta, son of Karambhi, 4. 68

Devaráta, variant of Brahmaráta, 3. 53.

Devaráta (?), variant of Daśaratha, son of Navaratha, 4. 68.

Devárha, variant of Devamídhusha, son of Hridika, 4. 100.

Devárhana, variant of the same Devamídhusha, 4. 100.

Devarshis, 'divine sages,' their abode, &c., 3. 69; 4. 52.

Devasávarni, Manu of the thir-teenth Manwantara, 3. 25, 27.

Devaśravas, son of Śálávatí, 4. 28.

Devaśravas, son of Śúra, 4. 101, 113.

Devaśreshtha, son of Sávarna, Manu of the twelfth Manwan-tara, 3. 27.

Devaśrí, variant of Vedaśrí, a Rishi in the fifth Manwantara, 3. 10.

Devastava, variant of Devaśravas, son of Śúra, 4. 101.

Devatójit, son of Sumati 2. 107.

Devátithi, son of Akrodhana, 4. 128.

Devátithi, variously genealogized, 4. 153.

Devavardhana, variant of Deva-rakshita, son of Devaka, 4. 98.

Devavarman, son of Indrapálita, 4. 189.

Devavarsha, son of Yajnabáhu, king of Sálmala-dwípa, 2. 195.

Devavarsha, a region in Sálmala-dwípa, 2. 195.

Devavat, son of Sávarna, Manu of the twelfth Manwantara, 3. 27.

Devavat, son of Akrúra, 4. 96.

Devavat, son of Devaka, son of Áhuka, 4. 98.

Devávṛidha, son of Satwata, 4. 71–73, 84.

Devávṛit, a limitary mountain range in Krauncha-dwípa, 2. 197.

Deva-yajna, a particular sacrifice, 3. 40; 93.

Devayáni, daughter of Uśanas, and wife of Yayáti, 4. 46, 47.

Devendra = Indra, 1. 119; 4. 316, 320; 5. 104, 247.

Deví = Umá, Durgá, Párvatí, &c., P. 60, 61, 65, 89, 90; 1. 126, 128, 130, 133; 3. 22; 4. 260, 262; 5. 88, 261, 263, &c., 310, 347.

Deví (?), an Apsaras, 2. 81, 82.

Deví = Saraswatí, or Sávitrí (?), 2. 21.

Deví, wife of Kṛishṇa (??), 5. 79.

Deví-bhágavata-puráṇa, P. 24, 45, &c., 47–50, 80, 86–88; 5. 332.

Deviká, daughter of Govásana, and wife of Yudhishṭhira, 4. 159.

Deviká, a river, the Deva or Goggra, 2. 144, 147, 330; 4. 223.

Devíkoṭa = Soṇitapura, 5. 112. Supposed to be Devicotta.

Devíratha (who ?), 4. 24.

Deví-máhátmya = Durgá - máhátmya, 3. 22; 5. 311.

Devotion of contemplation, 5. 225, &c.

Dhairya, what, 1. 138; 4. 265.

Dhámaṇ (?), variant of Dhátṛi, a Ṛishi in the fourth Manwantara, 3. 8.

Dhamani, wife of Hráda, 2. 69.

Dhammásoko, Páli for Aśoka, 4. 188.

Dhana, variant of Vadha, a Rákshasa, 2. 289.

Dhanada, an epithet of Kubera, 3. 22, 246.

Dhanadhamita (?), variant of Dhanadharman, 4. 212.

Dhanadharma, variant of Dhanadharman, 4 212.

Dhanadharman, a king, 4. 212.

Dhanaka, son of Durdama, 4. 54.

Dhanakapívat, variant of Vanakapívat, 1. 155.

Dhananando, Páli for Dhanananda, a king, 4. 185.

Dhananjaya = Arjuna, son of Páṇḍu, 5. 158, 226.

Dhananjaya, a serpent, son of Kaśyapa and Kadrú, 2. 74, 285, &c.

Dhananjaya, Vyása of the sixteenth Dwápara age, 3. 35, 37.

Dhananjaya, named in the Káśí-khaṇḍa, 3. 329.

Dhanapati, an epithet of Kubera, 5. 15.

Dhanáyus, son of Purúravas, 4. 13.

Dhaneśwara.= Kubera. So, for "Kubera," has the original of 1. 119; 5. 387.

Dhaneyu, son of Raudráśwa, 4. 128, 129.

Dhanishṭhá, a certain asterism, 2. 259, &c., 308; 3. 167, 169.

Dhanur-veda, 'military science,' 3. 67; 4. 71; 5. 47.

Dhaunaha, son of Satyadhṛita, 4. 150.

Dhanwantari, instructor in medical science, 3. 67; 4. 32. Produced from the ocean, when it was

churned, I. 144. Born as son of Dírghatamas, 4. 32. See also 1. 145, 147; 3. 118; 4. 33.

Dhanwantari, an author referred to the court of King Vikramáditya, P. 8.

Dhanyá, wife of Dhruva, 1. 178.

Dhanya, a caste in Krauncha-dwípa, 2. 197.

Dhánya-mána, what, 3. 171.

Dhara, one of the Vasus, son of Dharma and Vasu, 2. 23.

Dhárá, now Dhár, a city in Central India, 4..59, 209.

Dháraná, Dháraná, what, in the Yoga philosophy, 1. 164, 200; 5. 237, 238, 240, 241.

Dháraná, a certain mystical symbol, 2. 308.

Dharaní = Bhúmi, consort of Vishnu as Parasuráma, 1. 151; 5. 91.

Dháraní, daughter of the Pitris, and wife of Meru, 1. 157.

Dharma, a Prajápati, and son of Brahmá, 1. 101, &c. Marries thirteen daughters of Daksha, 1. 109. Their children, 1. 110, &c. Marries ten daughters of Daksha, 2. 10, 20. Their children, 2. 21, &c. See also 1. 111 (where correct the spelling); 2. 200, 259, 306, 307; 3. 24, 68, 191; 4. 102, 111, 159, 234; 5. 387, &c.

Dharma, according to one account, the Vyása of the thirteenth Dwápara age, 3. 37.

Dharma, son of Dírghatapas, 4. 32.

Dharma, son of Haihaya, 4. 54.

Dharma, son of Chitraka, 4. 96.

Dharma, son of Gandhára, 4. 119.

Dharma, son of Suvrata, 4. 175.

Dharma, son of Rámachandra, 4. 210.

Dharma, variant of Dharmanetra, 4. 54.

Dharma, variant of Tamas, 4. 63.

Dharma, the Sun's flag, 2. 238.

Dharma, 'law,' an Anga of the Veda, 3. 67.

Dharmabhrit, son of Chitraka, 4. 96.

Dharmabhrit, variant of Dharma-dhrík, 4. 95, 96.

Dharma-dhenu, what, 5. 218, 220.

Dharmadhrík, son of Swaphalka, 4. 95, 96.

Dharmadhwaja, or Janaka, son of Kusadhwaja, 3. 333; 5. 217.

Dharma dogdhrí, variant of Dharma-dhenu, 5. 218.

Dharmaketu, variously genealogized, 4. 37.

Dharmakshetra, variant of Dharma, son of Suvrata, 4. 175.

Dharmanetra, variously genealogized, 4. 54.

Dharmanetra, variant of Ailina, 4. 130, 132.

Dharmanetra, variant of Dharma, son of Suvrata, 4. 175.

Dharmapattana = Srávastí, a city, 3. 264.

Dharmaputra, according to one account, the Manu of the eleventh Manwantara, 3. 337. See Dharmasávarnika.

Dharmarája, an epithet of Yama, 3. 118; 5. 167.

Dharmarája, an epithet of Yudhishthira, 5. 167.

Dharmáraṅya, a city founded by
Amúrtarajas, 4. 15.

Dharmaratha, son of Diviratha, 4.
124.

Dharma-saṁhitá, the, a metrical
law-book, quoted, 4. 62.

Dharmasáruthi, son of Auenas, 4.
43.

Dharmasávarṅika, Manu of the
eleventh Munwantara, 3. 26.

Dharmasena, variant of Ambarísha,
son of Mándhátri, 3. 268.

Dharmasútra, variant of Dharma,
son of Suvrata, 4. 175.

Dharmatantra, variant of Dharmanetra, 4. 54.

Dharmavatí, daughter of Ugrasena,
4. 99.

Dharmavṛiddha, son of Swaphalka, 4. 96.

Dharmavṛiddha, variant of Kshattravṛiddha, 4. 30.

Dharmeyu, son of Raudráśwa, 4.
127-129.

Dharmin, son of Bṛihadrája, 4.
169.

Dharmin, variant of Yatidharman,
4. 96.

Dhárshṭaka, in place of Dhárshṭaka
elsewhere, 3. 255.

Dhárshṭaka, a race descended from
Dhṛishṭa, 3. 255, 256.

Dhátaki, son of Savana, king of
Pushkara-dwípa, 2. 201.

Dhátaki, son of Vítihotra, king of
Pushkara-dwípa, according to
one account, 2. 203.

Dhátaki, a region in Pushkara-
dwípa, 2. 201.

Dhátri, an aspect of Brahmá, 1.
87; 2. 88; 3. 75, 123; 5.
15.

Dhátri, son of Bhṛigu and Khyáti,
1. 118, 152, 157; 2. 307; 3.
118.

Dhátri (?), a Rishi in the fourth
Manwantara, 3. 8.

Dhátri, an Áditya, 2. 27, 284, &c.

Dhátri, an epithet applied to
Vishṇu, 5. 15, 214.

Dhavalí, a river, 2. 142.

Dhavat, variant of Arvarívat, 3. 3.

Dhenuka, a Dánava, slain by
Balabhadra, 4. 250, 272, 297,
298, 325, 335; 5. 34, 87.

Dhenuká, wife of Kírttimat, 1.
154.

Dhenuká, a river in Sáka-dwípa,
2. 199.

Dhenuka, variant of Dhanaka, 4.
54.

Dhí, wife of Manyu, a Rudra, 1.
117.

Dhímat, a Rishi in the fourth
Manwantara, according to one
account, 3. 8.

Dhímat, son of Viráj, 2. 107.

Dhímat, son of Purúravas, 4. 13.

Dhishaná, descendant of Agni, and
wife of Havirdhana, 1. 192.

Dhishaná, wife of Kṛiśáśwa, 2. 29.

Dhisháya, what, 2. 305.

Dhishṇyádhipati = Dikpála, 5.
247.

Dhṛishaṇa, variant of Vṛishaṇa, 4.
57.

Dhṛishṇa (?), variant of Vṛishaṇa,
4. 57.

Dhṛishṇokta (?), variant of Vṛishaṇa, 4. 57.

Dhríshńu (?), in place of Dhríshťa, son of Vaivaswata, 3. 13 (where correct Dhríshťu), 3. 232, 233, 255, 337, 342.

Dhríshńu (?), variant of Vríshťa, 4. 97.

Dhríshťa, son of Vaivaswata, Manu of the current Manwantara, 3. 13, 14, 232, 233, 239, 255, 256, 335, 342.

Dhríshťa, son of Nríga, 3. 335.

Dhríshťa, son of Buváśa, 4. 100.

Dhríshťa, variant of Vríshaňa, 4. 57.

Dhríshťa, variant of Vríshńi, son of Kunti, 4. 68.

Dhríshťa, variant of Vríshńi, son of Bhajamána, 4. 72, 74.

Dhríshťa (correct the spelling), variant of Vríshťa, 4. 97; 5. 391.

Dhríshťadyumna, son of Drupada, 4. 148.

Dhríshťaka, variant of Dhríshťaketu, son of Nríga, 3. 335.

Dhríshťaketu, son of Dhríshťa, son of Vaivaswata, 3. 255.

Dhríshťaketu, son of Satyadhríti, 3. 331.

Dhríshťaketu, son of Nríga, 3. 335.

Dhríshťaketu, variously genealogized, 4. 37, 38.

Dhríshťaketu, son of Dhríshťadyumna, 4. 148.

Dhríshťaketu, a Kaikeya king (different from any preceding Dhríshťaketu?), 4. 103.

Dhríshťhi (??), variant of Vríshńi, son of Bhajamána, 4. 72.

Dhríshťi, variant of Vríshńi, son of Kunti, 4. 68.

Dhríshťokta, variant of Vríshaňa, 4. 57.

Dhríta, son of Dharma, son of Gándhára, 4. 119.

Dhríta, variant of Rita, son of Chákshusha, the Manu, 1. 178.

Dhrítadevá, daughter of Devaka, and wife of Vasudeva, 4. 98, 110, 111.

Dhrítadeví, variant of Dhrítadevá, 4. 110.

Dhrítahavya, variant of Vítahavya, 3. 335.

Dhrítaka, variant of Vríka, son of Ruruka, 3. 289.

Dhrítaketu, son of Dakshasávarńa, Manu of the ninth Manwantara, 3. 25.

Dhrítaráshťra, a king, son of Kríshńa-dwaipáyana, by Vichitravírya's widow, 4. 84, 142, 158, 232; 5. 391.

Dhrítaráshťra, a serpent, son of Kaśyapa and Kadrú, 1. 188; 2. 74; 5. 250.

Dhrítaráshťra, a Gandharva, 2. 285, &c.

Dhrítaráshťrí, daughter of Kaśyapa, wife of Garuďa, and mother of geese, ducks, &c., 2. 73.

Dhrítasandhi, variant of Dhruvasandhi, son of Susandhi, 3. 297.

Dhrítavatí, a river, 2. 149.

Dhrítavrata, a form of Rudra, 1. 117.

Dhrítavrata, son of Dhríti, son of Vijaya, 4. 126.

Dhríti, 'steadiness,' daughter of Daksha, and wife of Dharma, 1. 109, 110; 4. 265.

Dhríti, wife of Manu, the Rudra, 1. 117.

D

Dhṛiti, son of Jyotishmat, king of Kuśa-dwípa, 2. 195.

Dhṛiti, son of Vítabavya, 3. 335.

Dhṛiti, son of Yajna, son of Anantaka, 4. 63.

Dhṛiti, son of Babhru, son of Romapáda, 4. 67.

Dhṛiti, son of Áhuka, 4. 98.

Dhṛiti, son of Vijaya, son of Jayadratha, 4. 125.

Dhṛiti (?), son of Sáraña, 4. 109.

Dhṛiti, a region in Kuśa-dwípa, 2. 195.

Dhṛiti, a fabulous grove so called, 2. 112. See Gandhamádana.

Dhṛiti, variant of Vishńu, a Ṛishi in the eleventh Manwantara, 3. 26.

Dhṛiti, variant of Mahádhṛiti, 3. 332.

Dhṛitiketu, variant of Dhṛitaketu, 3. 25.

Dhṛitimat, a Ṛishi in the thirteenth Manwantara, 3. 28.

Dhṛitimat, son of Kírttimat, 1. 154.

Dhṛitimat, son of Purúravas, 4. 13.

Dhṛitimat, son of Yavínara, 4. 142.

Dhṛitimat, variant of Puruvat (?), 3. 190, 191.

Dhṛitimat, variant of Vṛishńimat, 4. 163.

Dhṛitimatí, a river, 2. 152.

Dhrutapápá (?), variant of Dhútapápá, 2. 196.

Dhruva, son of Uttánapáda and Suníti, 1. 161. Directed to worship Vishńu, 1. 162, &c. Performs penance, 1. 165, &c.

Legend of him, 1. 159, &c. Vishńu raises him to the pole-star, 1. 174. . As the pole-star, 2. 205, 225-227, 230, 239, 243, 270, 278, 298, 305, 306, &c. His year, 1. 49. See also P. 42, 52, 96; 1. 158, &c., 177; 2. 2, &c., 99; 3. 1, 11.

Dhruva, one of the Vasus, son of Dharma and Vasu, 2. 23.

Dhruva, son of Medhátithi, king of Plaksha-dwípa, 2. 191.

Dhruva, son of Viśwámitra, 4. 28.

Dhruva, son of Nahusha, 4. 45.

Dhruva, son of Vasudeva, 4. 109.

Dhruva, son of Rantinára, 4. 130.

Dhruva, a region in Plaksha-dwípa, 2. 191.

Dhruva, variant of Bhuva, 2. 106.

Dhruvasandhi, son of Susandhi, 3. 297.

Dhruvasandhi, son of Pushya, 3. 324.

Dhruváśwa, variant of Bṛihadaśwa, son of Sahadeva, 4. 168.

Dhúmaketu (?), variant of Dhúmraketu, 3. 246.

Dhúmapas, a class of Pitṛis, 1. 123.

Dhúminí, wife of Ajamídha, 4. 140.

Dhúmorńá, wife of Yama, 1. 119.

Dhúmrakeśa, son of Pṛithu, son of Vena, 1. 192.

Dhúmrakeśa, son of Kṛiśáśwa and Archis, 2. 29.

Dhúmrakeśa, son of Kaśyapa, 2. 70.

Dhúmraketu, son of Triñabindu, 3. 246.

Dhúmráksha, son of Hemachandra, 3. 247.

Dhûmrâksha, variant of Dhûmrâswa, 3. 247.

Dhûmrânîka, son of Medhâtithi, king of Sáka-dwípa, 2. 200.

Dhûmrânîka, a region in Sáka-dwípa, 2. 200.

Dhûmrâswa, son of Suchandra, and king of Vaiśálí, 3. 247.

Dhûmravarṇa, son of Ajamídba, 4. 143.

Dhunḍhirája, a modern author, quoted, 3. 136.

Dhundhu, an Asura, slain by Kuvalayáśwa, 3. 264, 265.

Dhundhu, variant of Chunchu, 3. 289.

Dhundhumára, an epithet of Kuvalayáśwa, 3. 264, 297.

Dhundu (?), variant of Sudyumna, 4. 128.

Dhuni, son of Ápa, 2. 23.

Dhuni (?), variant of Dhwani, 3. 191.

Dhur (??), son of Ápa, 2. 23.

Dhurandharas, a people, 2. 160.

Dhuri, variant of Dhuni, son of Ápa, 2. 23.

Dhuri (?), variant of Dhwani, 3. 189-191.

Dhuśulyá (?), variant of Purávatí, 2. 149.

Dhûtapápá, a river in India, 2. 146.

Dhûtapápá, a river in Kuśa-dwípa, 2. 196.

Dhwajinyutsavasanketas (??), a people, 2. 178.

Dhwani, one of the Viśwe devas, 3. 190, 191.

Dhwani, variant of Dhuni, 2. 23.

Dhyána, what, in the Yoga philosophy, &c., 1. 151, 164; 2. 94; 4. 294; 5. 12, 240, 241.

Dhyánajapyas (so correct the spelling), Kauśika Bráhmans, 4. 28.

Dhyushitáśwa, son of Sankhanábha, 3. 322-324.

Digambaras, religionists, 3. 201, 207. See Daigambaras.

Dikkaravásiní, an epithet of Deví, 5. 83.

Dikpálas, 'regents of the directions,' 3. 171; 5. 247. . See Directions, &c.

Díkshá, wife of Ugra, the Rudra, 1. 117. In the same page, she is called wife of the Rudra Vámadeva.

Díkshá, what, P. 59; 5. 315.

Dilípa, variously genealogized, 3. 311, 314, 316. He is called Khatwánga, also.

Dilípa, son of Amśumat, 3. 303.

Dilípa, son of Duliduha, 3. 305.

Dilípa, son of Bhímasena, 4. 153.

Dilípa, a king (different from any Dilípa named above?), P. 32.

Dípa-kaliká, the, a commentáry on the Yájnavalkya-smṛiti, quoted, 3. 90.

Dípawamso, the, a Singhalese work, referred to, 4. 185, 187, 189.

Díptaketu, variant of Díptiketu, 3. 25.

Díptiketu, son of Dakshasávarṇa, Manu of the ninth Manwantara, 3. 25.

Díptimat, a Ṛishi in the eighth Manwantara, sprung from Atri, 3. 23.

Díptimat, son of Kṛishṇa and Rohiṇí, 5. 79, 107.

Directions, regents of the, 2. 112, 118, 239. See Dikpálas.

Dírghabáhu, variously genealogized, 3. 313, 314.

Dírghasatra, what, 1. 179.

Dírghatamas, son of Uchathya or Utathya, 3. 16; 4. 122, 123, 134.

Dírghatamas, variously genealogized, 4. 32.

Dírghatapas, variant of Dírghatamas, 4. 32.

Diá, a river so called, 2. 147.

Diá, 'space,' presiding over the ear, 1. 38.

Diśas, wife of Bhíma, the Rudra, 1. 117.

Dishťa, a king, son of Vaivaswata, Manu of the current Manwantara, 3. 13, 14, 231, 232, 240, 241, 256, 336, 342.

Dissolution, four kinds of, 1. 113, &c.; 3. 72; 5. 186, 196. See Pralaya.

Diti, daughter of Daksha, and wife of Kaśyapa, 1. 62, 138, 144; 2. 26, 70, 77, 78, 80; 3. 211; 4. 265, 269. Mother of the Maruts, 2. 22, 78, 79. Mother of the Daityas, 2. 30.

Divákara, a Rákshasa, 2. 293.

Divákara, son of Prativyoma, 4. 168.

Divákírttyas, certain Bráhmans, 3. 343.

Diva-loka, one of the seven heavens, 1. 98.

Divárka, variant of Divákara, son of Prativyoma, 4. 168.

Divaspati, the Indra of the thirteenth Manwantara, 3. 28.

Divávŕit (?), variant of Devávŕit, 2. 197.

Divijáta (?), son of Parúravas, 4. 13.

Divílaka, variant of Ivílaka, 4. 196.

Divinities. Those who preside over the senses, 1. 38. Classes of them, 2. 29. Those of the various Manwantaras, 3. 2, &c.

Diviratha, son of Pára, 4. 123, 124.

Divodása, son of Bhímaratha, king of the Káśis, P. 72; 4. 33, &c.

Divodása, son of Badhryaśwa, 4. 145–147, 343.

Divya, son of Auttami, Manu of the third Manwantara, 3. 7.

Divya, son of Satwata, 4. 71.

Divyá (?), an Apsaras, 2. 83.

Dohadas, variant of Kálovas, 2. 180.

Doshá, wife of Pushpárńa, 1. 17?.

Dragons, offspring of Kaśyapa and Surasá, 2. 73.

Drakshalá, a river, 2. 146.

Draunáyani, patronym of Aśwattháman, 4. 147. (Note ‖ in 3. 23, perhaps is hasty.)

Drauńi, a Rishi in the eighth Manwantara, 3. 23.

Drauńi, the Vyása of the next Dwápara age to come, 3. 36.

Draupadí, wife of the five Páńḍus, P. 55; 3. 83; 4. 159.

Dravavasu, son of Madhu, son of Devakshattra, 4. 70.

Draviḍas, Dráviḍas, a people, 2. 177, 180, 184; 3. 295; 4. 117.

Draviḍa, son of Kŕishńa and Jámbavatí, 5. 79.

Dráviḍa, a country in the south of India, 2. 177.

Draviṅa, son of Pṛithu, son of Vena, 1. 192.

Draviṅa, son of Dhara, 2. 23.

Draviṅa, a caste in Krauncha-dwípa, 2. 198.

Draviṅa, a mountain in Kuśa-dwípa, 2. 197.

Dṛiḍhadhanus, son of Senajit, 4. 141.

Dṛiḍhabahu, variant of Dṛiḍha-dhanus, 4. 141.

Dṛiḍhamána(?). See 4. 197(note††).

Dṛiḍhanemi, son of Satyadhṛiti, 4. 142, 143.

Dṛiḍharatha, son of Jayadratha, son of Bṛihanmanas, 4. 126.

Dṛiḍharatha, variant of Daśaratha, son of Navaratha, 4. 68.

Dṛiḍharuchi, a ruler in Kuśa-dwípa, 2. 197.

Dṛiḍharuchi, a country in Kuśa-dwípa, 2. 197.

Dṛiḍhasena, son of Suśrama, 4. 175, 176.

Dṛiḍháśwa, son of Kuvalayáśwa, 3. 265.

Dṛiḍháśwa (correct the spelling), variant of Dṛiḍhadhanus, 4. 141; 5. 391.

Dṛiḍháyus, son of Purúravas, 4. 13.

Dṛishadáśwa (?), variant of Viśwagáśwa, 3. 263.

Dṛishadwatí, wife of Divodása, son of Bhímaratha, 4. 34.

Dṛishadwatí, wife of Uśínara, 4. 121.

Dṛishadwatí (different from any named above?), 4. 28.

Dṛishadwatí, a river, the Caggar, P. 104; 2. 142-144. Called daughter of Himavat, wife of Akṛiśáśwa, and mother of Prasenajit, &c., 3. 265, 266, 284.

Dṛishṭadharma, variant of Dṛish-ṭaśarman, 4. 95.

Dṛishṭaśarman, son of Swaphalka, 4. 95.

Droṇa, father of Aśwatthámán, 2. 160; 3. 23, 36, 83; 4. 147; 5. 130, 131, 134, 135. Slain by Arjuna, 5. 157, 161, 163.

Droṇa, a certain hill in India, 2. 141.

Droṇa, a mountain-range in Sálmala-dwípa, 2. 194.

Droṇa, variant of Práṇa, son of Bhṛigu, 3. 3.

Droṇakaa, variant of Proshakas, 2. 187.

Druhya, variant of Druhyu, son of Yayáti, 4. 46, 119.

Druhyu, son of Yayáti, 4. 46, 48, &c., 118.

Druhyu, son of Matinára, 4. 130.

Drumá, a river, 2. 155.

Drupada, king of Panchála, 2. 160.

Drupada, son of Pṛishata, 4. 144, 147, 148.

Duduha (?), son of Durgama, 4. 119.

Duḥkha, 'pain,' son of Naraka 1. 112.

Duḥsaha, P. 56. And see Dus-saha.

Duḥśalá, daughter of Dhṛitaráshṭra, 4. 158.

Duḥśásana, son of Dhṛitaráshṭra, 4. 158; 5. 134.

Dulá, a Kṛittiká, 2. 337.

Duliduha, son of Anamitra, son of Nighna, 3. 305.

Dumlánas, Kauśika Bráhmans, 4. 28.

Dundubhi, son of Dyutimat, king of Krauncha-dwípa, 2. 197.

Dundubhi, son of Andhaka, 4. 99.

Dundubhi, a region in Krauncha-dwípa; 2. 197.

Dundubhi, a mountain-range in Plaksha-dwípa, 2. 191.

Dundubhi, á mountain-range in Krauncha-dwípa, 2. 197.

Durbala, variant of Mŕidu, 4. 165.

Durbhakshaya (?), variant of Urukshaya, 4. 137.

Durdama, son of Bhadraśreńya, 4. 34–36, 54.

Durdama, variant of Durgama, son of Dhŕita, 4. 119.

Durdamana, variant of Udayana, 4. 165.

Durgá, a Śakti, P. 21, 56, 71, 78, 86, 90; 1. 1, 104; 3. 22, 288; 4. 260, 262, 336; 5. 117, 267. Her exploits alluded to, 4. 261. She is worshipped at Píṭha-sthánas, 4. 261.

Durgá, a river, 2. 151.

Durgá, a river (another), 2. 153.

Durga, 'stronghold,' 1. 94.

Durga Áchárya, a commentator, quoted, 3. 18.

Durgaha, father of the Purukutsa of the Ŕig-veda, 3. 268.

Durgalas, a people, 2. 172.

Durgama, a king, father of the Manu Raivata, according to one account, 3. 9.

Durgama, son of Vasudeva, 4. 109.

Durgama, son of Dhŕita, son of Dharma, 4. 119.

Durgá-mahátmya, a part of the Márkańdeya-puráńa, recounting the exploits of the goddess Durgá, P. 21, 56; 3. 22; 4. 260, 261.

Durgá-pújá, a festival in honour of the goddess Durgá, P. 57.

Duritakshaya, variant of Uru-kshaya, 4. 137.

Durjana-mukha-chapetiká, a controversial work on the Bhá-gavata-puráńa, P. 47.

Durjana-mukha-mahá-chapetiká, a controversial work like the last, P. 47.

Durjana-mukha-padua-páduká, another similar controversial work, P. 47, 88.

Durjaya, variant of Vŕisha and Sujáta conjointly, 4. 57.

Durjayanta, a certain hill in India, 2. 142.

Durmada, son of Vasudeva, 4. 109.

Durmada, variant of Durdama, 4. 54.

Durmada, variant of Durgama, son of Dhŕita, 4. 119.

Durmitra, son of Pushpamitra, 4. 213–215.

Durmukha, a serpent, son of Kaś-yapa and Kadrú, 2. 74.

Durukti, 'evil speech,' daughter of Krodha and Himsá, and wife of Kali, 1. 111.

Dúrva, variant of Mŕidu, 4. 165.

Durvá, what, 3. 112.

Durvásas, a sage, son of Atri, P. 32, 64, 68; 1. 135, &c., 146, 154; 3. 257; 4. 102; 5. 151, 381.

Durvi (?), variant of Mŕidu, 4. 165.

Duryodhana, son of Dhṛitarāshṭra, 1. 6; 4. 81, 84, 158; 5. 130, 131, 134. Slain by Kṛishṇa, 5. 161.

Dúshaṇa, a Rákshasa, slain by Ráma, 3. 316.

Dushmanta, variant of Dushyanta, 4. 116, 132.

Dushyanta, variously genealogized, 4. 116, 117, 130, 132, 133.

Duseaha, (Duḥsaha is better), variant of Trasadasyu, 3. 282; 5. 391.

Duties of castes and orders, 3. 85, &c.

Dwádaśákshara, a certain spell of twelve syllables, 1. 99.

Dwádaśárchis = Bṛihaspati, or Jupiter, 2. 257, 258.

Dwaipáyana, a Vyása, P. 38; 3. 23.

Dwáláki (?), variant of Dálaki, 3. 49.

Dwápara, an age of the world, 3. 31, 33, 34, 36, 40, 41, 254; 4. 237; 5. 58, 170, 181, 185, &c., &c. Its duration, 1. 50.

Dwáraká, a city, P. 107; 2. 135, 172; 3. 249, 253; 4. 75, 78, 79, 81, 84, 87, 88; 5. 63, 64, 68, 77, 86, 87, 89, 92, 97, 104, 105, 110, 111, 120, 123, 126, 127, 134, 140, 143-146, &c., &c., 381, 382, 384. Built by Kṛishṇa, 5. 56. Submerged by the sea, 5. 155.

Dwáravatí = Dwáraká, 5. 63, 77, 87, 104, 110, 112, 126, 127, 151, 155. The form Dwáravatí, 5. 151, is not without authority.

Dweaha, what, 1. 69.

Dwijarshi = Brahmarshi, 4. 52.

Dwijáti, the term explained, 3. 96.

Dwimíḍha, son of Hastin, 4. 140.

Dwimíḍha, son of Bhallátá, 4. 142.

Dwimúrdhan, a Dánava, son of Kaśyapa and Danu, 1. 188; 2. 70.

Dwípas, 'insular continents,' the seven principal named, viz., Jambu (or Jambú), Plaksha (or Gomedaka), Sálmali (or Sálmala), Kuśa, Krauncha, Sáka, Pushkara, 2. 101, 109, 110. Specifications of their sovereigns, divisions, inhabitants, &c., 2. 191, &c.

Dwivida, a certain powerful monkey, slain by Balabhadra, 5. 136-139.

Dynasties. Of the Sun, 3. 231. Of the Moon, 4. 13, &c. Of future kings, 4. 162, &c.

Dyumat, son of Vasishṭha, 1. 155.

Dyumat, another name of Pratardana, 4. 33.

Dyumatsena, variant of Dṛiḍhasena, 4. 175.

Dyumna, son of Chákshusha, the Manu, 1. 178.

Dyumni, variant of Túṇi, 4. 93.

Dyuti, variant of Dhṛiti, son of Babhru, 4. 67.

Dyutimat, son of Páṇḍu (or of Práṇa?), 1. 152.

Dyutimat, son of Priyavrata, and king of Krauncha-dwípa, 2. 100, &c., 197.

Dyutimat, a Rishi in the ninth Manwantara, 3. 25.

Dyutimat, a mountain in Kuśa-dwípa, 2. 196.

Earth. The element, 1. 35. Fabled as raised by the Varáha, 1. 57-61. Subdued by Pŕithu, 1. 186, &c. Milked by various beings, 1. 187, &c. Description of it, 2. 109, &c. Supported by S'esha, the serpent, 2. 213. Destruction of it, 5. 190, &c, Earth, the goddess, glorifies Vishńu as the Varáha, 1. 59, &c. Her song, 4. 238, 239. Oppressed by the Daityas, she applies to Brahmá, 4. 249. As mother of Naraka, she propitiates Kŕishńa, 5. 90, 91.

Egg of the world, how formed; a common symbol among the ancients; the abode of Vishńu as Brahmá; how composed; invested by the principles of creation, 1. 38, &c.

Eka, synonym of Mahat, 1. 32.

Ekachakra, a Dánava, son of Kaśyapa and Danu, 2. 70.

Ekachárin, what, 4. 272.

Ekalavya, son of Devaśravas, but brought up among the Nishádas, 4. 113; 5. 123.

Ekánekarúpa, what, 1. 15.

Ekapádakas, a people, 2. 162.

Ekapádukas (1), a people, 2. 162,

Ekaśŕingas, a class of Pitŕis, 3. 339.

Ekatwa, a kind of emancipation, 5. 242.

Ekavińśa, a collection of hymns, originated from Brahmá, 1. 85.

Ekoddishŕa, a particular S'ráddha, 3. 146, 153, 154, 156.

Elápatra, a serpent, son of Kaśyapa and Kadrú, 2. 74, 285, 287, &c.; 5. 251.

Elements. Evolution of them from primary matter; 1. 29. As subtile rudiments, how produced, 1. 34. Further particulars of them, 1. 35, &c. Disposition of them, 2. 232, &c. Successive resolution of them into their origin, 5. 196, &c.

Elina, variant of Ailina, 4. 130.

Eraká, what, 5. 142, 147.

Eshŕayas (1), a class of Apsarases, 2. 82.

Ether, the element. See Ákáśa.

Expiation, efficacy of, 2. 222, &c.

Faringí, 'Frank,' used as synonymous with Húńa, 2. 134.

Fever, its contention with Kŕishńa, 5. 113, 114.

Fire, as presiding over speech, 1. 38. The original fires forty-nine in number, 1. 156. The one original fire made threefold by Purúravas, 4. 11. Holy fires, 3. 175. Worship of fire referred to, 5. 384. See also Agni and Tejas.

Food, rules for taking, distributing, &c., &c., 3. 125, &c. Offered at Sráddhas, 3. 148.

Gabhastala, a Pátála or underworld, 2. 209.

Gabhastí, a river in S'áka-dwípa, 2. 199.

Gabhastimat, a portion of Bháratavarsha, 2. 112, 129.

Gabhastimat, a Pátála or underworld, 2. 209.

Gabhíra, son of Bhautya, Manu of

the fourteenth Manwantara, 3. 29.

Gabhíra, sprung from Rambha, 4. 43.

Gachchhas, variant of Kakshas, 2. 176.

Gada, sons of Vasudeva and Rohiṇí, 4. 109.

Gada, son of Vasudeva and Devarakshitá, 4. 111.

Gada, son of Vasudeva and Bhadrá, 4. 110.

Gadavarman, son of S'úra, 4. 99.

Gádhi, variously genealogized, 3. 16; 4. 16.

Gahlota, a tribe now in Central India, 4. 344.

Gajá = Gajavíthí, 2. 276.

Gajavíthí, a certain triad of asterisms, 2. 265. &c.

Gálavas, Kauśika Bráhmans, 4. 28.

Gálava, a Ŕishi in the eighth Manwantara, sprung from Ḳuśika, 2. 113; 3. 23.

Gálava, son of Reṇu, 4. 28, 39, 50,

Gálava, teacher of the White Yajurveda (different from Gálava the Ŕishi ?), 3. 57.

Gálava, variant of Gokhalu, 3. 46,

Gambhíra, the same as Gabhíra, son of Bhautya, the Manu, 3. 29,

Gambhírabuddhi, son of Indrasávarṇí, Manu, by one account, of the fourteenth Manwantara, 3. 29.

Games, public, celebrated, by Kaṁsa, 5. 24, &c.

Gaṇa-devas, certain classes of demigods, 2. 227,

Gáṇapatas (in correct spelling), a sect worshipping Gaṇeśa, 5. 280. See Gáṇapatyas.

Gaṇapati = Gaṇeśa, 5. 280.

Gáṇapatyas, a sect worshipping Gaṇeśa, P. 91. See Gáṇapatas.

Gaṇávará, variant of Guṇávará, 2. 81.

Gaṇd'aka (vulgarly, Gunduk) = Gaṇd'akí, 2. 103, 146, 149, 313; 3. 330. Its affluents, 2. 146.

Gaṇd'akí, a river, 2. 121 (where correct the spelling), 146, 313, 339. See Gaṇd'aka.

Gandha = Gandhamádana, the mountain-range extending from Mount Meru, so called, 2. 111.

Gandhakáraka (?), variant of Andhakáraka, son of Dyutimat, and also a region in Krauncha-dwípa, 2. 197.

Gandhamáda, son of S'waphalka, 4. 96.

Gandhamádana, a mountain-range extending from Mount Meru, 2. 117, 122, 123 (where once correct the spelling), 140, 141, 339, 340; 5. 388.

Gandhamádana, a mountain, 2. 111, 115; 4. 22; 5. 62, 146.

Gandhamádana, a forest to the east of Mount Meru, 2. 116, 117. (There is no little difficulty as to the various Gandhamádanas.)

Gandhamádana, a country, the same as Ketumála-varaha, 2. 102, 122.

Gandhamocha, son of S'waphalka, 4. 95.

Gándháras, a people, 2. 169, 174.

Gándhára, sprung from Turvasu, 4. 117.

Gándhára, son of Áradwat, 4. 118.

Gandhára (?),. Gándhára, a country, Candahar, 3. 319; 4. 118.

Gándhárí, wife of Vrishní, 4. 73, 74.

Gándhárí, wife of Dhritaráshtra, the king, 4. 158.

Gandharvas, celestial musicians, &c. Their origin from Brahmá, 1. 82, 83. Offspring of Kaśyapa and Arishtá, 2. 75. Still differently derived, 2. 27 (note 3). Their chief, Chitraratha, 2. 86. Those of the Veda, 2. 83. Twelve named, in connexion with the mouths of the year, 2. 285, &c. They assail the Nágas, 3. 281, 282. See also 1. 188; 2. 76, 77; 4. 266, 323; 5. 12, 14, 59, 94, 101, 102, 109, 234, 236, 246, 247, 386.

Gándharva, a portion of Bhárata-varsha, 2. 112, 129.

Gándharva, the heaven of Śúdras, 1. 97, 98.

Gándharva, a form of marriage, 3. 105.

Gándharva-veda, 'musical science,' 3. 67.

Gándharví, an Apsaras, 2. 82.

Gandharví, daughter of Kaśyapa and Surabhi, and mother of horses, 2. 75.

Gándiní, daughter of a king of the Káśis, 4. 88, 94.

Gándíva, Arjuna's bow, 5. 158, 161, 162.

Gandúsha, son of Śúra, 4. 101, 113.

Gaṇeśá, son of Śiva, P. 65, 89, 9?; 5. 118, 261, 263, 270, 321, 347.

Gaṇeśa-khanda, a part of Brahma-vaivarta-puráṇa, P. 65, 67.

Gaṇeśa-puráṇa, P. 90.

Gaṇeśa-upapuráṇa, P. 90; 5. 118.

Gaṇeyu, son of Raudráśwa, 4. 128.

Gangá, the river Ganges. Daughter of Himavat and Maná, 1. 157. Daughter of Daksha, and wife of Dharma, 2. 21. Regarded as daughter of Jahnu, 4. 14. Her descent from the foot of Vishńu, 2. 119, 272. Divides into four rivers, 2. 120. Divides into seven rivers, 2. 120 (note 1). A river in Bhárata-varsha, 2. 142. Its sanctity, 2. 273. Brought down to earth by Bhagíratha, 3. 301, &c. See also 1. 122, 145; 2. 121, 142, 271; 3. 303; 5. 164.

Gangádhara, a modern author, quoted, 1. 5.

Gangádwára, a town, 1. 122, 123; 4. 219.

Gangáságara, at the mouth of the Ganges, 5. 118.

Gángeya, a descendant of Gangá, 5. 164.

Gangú, the same as Kuhú, 2. 342.

Garbhasti (?), variant of Gabhasti, 2. 199.

Gardabhila, father of Vikramáditya, 5. 392.

Gardabhilas, variant of Gardabhins, 4. 202, 203, 205, 206.

Gardabhins, a people, 4. 203, 205, 209.

Garga, an ancient astronomer, 2. 113, 213, 276, 277, 343; 5. 58.

Garga, a priest of the Yádavas,

his offices for Kŕishńa and Balabhadra, 4. 279, 280.

Garga, variously genealogized, 4. 136, 137.

Garga, son of Bhuvanmanyu, 4. 136, 137.

Garga, son of Pratardana, 4. 36.

Garga, a Bráhman, father of Kálayavana, 5. 53, 54.

Gargas, variant of Gárgyas, &c., 4. 137, 138.

Gargabhúmi, son of Gárgya, son of Veńuhotra, 4. 38.

Garga-sańhitá, an ancient astronomical work, 2. 213.

Gárgyas, sprung from Garga, son of Bhuvanmanyu, and transformed from Kshattriyas into Bráhmans, 4. 137.

Gárgya, son of Baláka, disciple of Báshkali, and teacher of the Rig-veda, 3. 50.

Gárgya, son of Veńuhotra, 4. 38, 39.

Gárgya (?), variant of Garga, father of Kálayavana, 5. 53, 54.

Gárhapatyas, a class of Pitŕis, 3. 339.

Gárhapatya, a particular holy fire, 3. 175; 4. 11; 5. 114.

Garuda, son of Kaśyapa and Vinatá, 2. 73. King of birds, 1. 198; 2. 85. Ridden by Vishńu, 3. 205. His city, on Vaikanka, 2. 118. See also P. 83, 84; 2. 28, 66; 4. 251, 287, 295, 317; 5. 89, 92, 93, 98, 100, 101, 105, 113, 115, 120, 123-125, 382.

Gáruda, a Kalpa, P. 83.

Garuda-puráńa, Gáruda-puráńa,

analysis of it, &c., P. 20, 23, 24, 83, &c.; 3. 67; 5. 309, 316.

Garutmat = Garuda, son of Kaśyapa, 5. 101, 120, 123, 125.

Gáthá, defined, &c., 3. 66, 197, 338, 340.

Gáthin, old form of Gádhi, 4. 16.

Gati, daughter of Kardama, and wife of Pulaha, 1. 110.

Gátra, son of Vasishťha, 1. 155; 3. 8.

Gátravat, son of Kŕishńa and Lakshmańá, 5. 81, 107.

Gauda, countries so called, 3. 263.

Guura, 'the white deer,' 1. 72.

Gaurakŕishńa, son of Meghaswáti, 4. 200.

Gauramukha, family-priest of Ugrasena, 5. 382.

Gauri, a Śakti, wife of Śiva, 1. 104, 119; 5. 108. See also Párvatí and Bhútigaurí.

Gauri, wife of Virajas, 1. 153; 2. 262.

Gauri, variously genealogized, mother of Mándhátŕi, 3. 266; 4. 130. Changed into the river Báhudá, 3. 266.

Gauri, sister of Śiśiráyańa, and wife of Garga, 5. 53.

Gauri, a river in Bháratavarsha, 2. 149.

Gauri, a river in Krauncha-dwípa, 2. 198.

Gauri, the term, used of a girl, defined, 3. 102, 197, 198.

Gaurika, metronym of Mándhátŕi, 3. 266.

Gautama, a Prajápati, son of

Brahmá, 1. 101, 137; 2. 285, &c.; 3. 327; 4. 24. His hermitage, where, 3. 331.

Gautama, a Rishi in the current Manwantara, 3. 13.

Gautama, an ancient lawgiver, quoted, or referred to, 3. 89, 113, 114, 338.

Gautama, the Vyása of the twentieth Dwápara age, 3. 35, 37.

Gautama = Saradwat, 3. 16; 4. 146.

Gautama = Buddha, 4. 5, 325.

Gautama-smriti, the, an ancient code of law, quoted, or referred to, 3. 89, 113.

Gautamíputra, variant of Gotamíputra, 4. 198, 201.

Gavavartis (?), variant of Málavartis (?), 2. 157.

Gavavartilas, variant of Málavartis (?), 2. 157.

Gaveshaña, son of Chitraka, 4. 96.

Gavya, ' produce of kine,' offered to the Pitris, 3. 193.

Gaya, son of Ulmuka, 1. 178.

Gaya, son of Havirdhána, 1. 192.

Gaya, son of Nakta, 2. 107.

Gayá, son of Sudyumna, 3. 237.

Gaya, son of Vitatha, 4. 136.

Gayá, a town, P. 60; 3. 194, 197, 237; 4. 189.

Gaya, variant of Sala, 3. 321.

Gayá-máhátmya, a part of the Agni-puráña, P. 60.

Gáyatra metre = Gáyatrí, 1. 84.

Gáyatrí, the holiest verse of the Vedas, P. 39, 49; 2. 250, 251, 295; 3. 38; 4. 10; 5. 290, 308.

Gáyatrí, a metre so called. Its

.origin from Brahmá, 1. 86. Regarded as a horse of the Sun, 2. 239.

Gehlots = Gahlots, 4. 59, 344.

Gems, fourteen great, 4. 61, 62.

Gepa (?), variant of Sesha, 5. 383.

Gesha (?), variant of Sesha, 5. 383.

Ghanakapívat, variant of Vanakapívat, 1. 155.

Ghanasyáma, an epithet of Krishña, 5. 13.

Gharma, variant of Dharma, son of Gándhára, 4. 119.

Ghatakarpara, a poet, referred to the court of King Vikramáditya, P. 8.

Ghatasrinjayas, a people, 2. 180.

Ghatiká, a measure of time, 1. 47; 3. 120, 187 (note †).

Ghatotkacha, son of Bhímasena, son of Páñd'u, 4. 159.

Ghora, a hell (?, or the epithet of one ?), 2. 216.

Ghoratá, ' terror,' a property of sensible objects, 1. 37.

Ghosha, son of Dharma and Lambá, 2. 22.

Ghosha, variant of Ghoshavasu, 4. 192.

Ghoshavasu, son of Pulindaka, 4. 192.

Ghrita, the sea of boiled butter around Kusa-dwípa, 2. 197.

Ghrita, variant of Dhrita, son of Dharma, 4. 119.

Ghritáchí, an Apsaras, 1. 145; 2. 75, 81–83, 285, 288, 291, 293; 4. 128, 129.

Ghritachyutá, a river in Kusa-dwípa, 2. 197.

Ghritaprishtha, son of Priyavrata,

and king of Krauncha-dwípa,
2. 100, 198.

Ghŕitasthalá, an Apsaras, 2. 81.

Ghŕitavatí, variant of Dhŕitavatí,
2. 149.

Ghŕiteyu, son of Raudráśwa, 4.
128, 129.

Giri, son of S'waphalka, 4. 95, 96.

Girijá, a form of Párvatí, P. 89.

Giriká, wife of Vasu, son of Kŕitaka, 4. 149.

Girikshipa, variant of Arikshipa,
4. 96.

Girirakshas, son of S'waphalka, 4.
95, 96.

Girivraja = Rájagŕiha, a city in
Magadha, 2. 15, 180.

Girnar, the popular name of a
range of mountains in Western
India, 2. 141.

Gírváṇa-pada-manjari, the, a modern work, quoted, 3. 136, 222.

Gírváṇa-śabda-pada-manjari, the
same as the last, 3. 136.

Gírváṇa-vág-manjari, the same as
the last, 3. 136.

Gítá = Bhagavad-gítá, 5. 185.

Gnosticism, referred to, 4. 326.

Go, daughter of the Barhishads,
3. 161.

Go, daughter of Kákutstha, and
wife of Yati, 4. 45.

Go, wife of Brahmadatta, 4. 142.

Go = Govíthí, 2. 276.

Gobhánu, son of Vahni, son of
Turvasu, 4. 116.

Gobhila, eponymist of the tribe of
Gahlots, 4. 344.

Gochapalá, daughter of Raudráśwa, and wife of Prabhákara, 4.
129.

Goda, proceeded from Brahmá, 1.
79. They are overcome by the
demons, 1. 138. They churn
the ocean, 1. 143. Inferior
gods, offspring of Dharma and
of Daksha, 2. 21, &c., 26, &c.
Thirty-three in number, 2. 29.
Thirty-six thousand, three hundred, and thirty-three, in number, 2. 300.

Godávarí, a river, P. 76; 2. 130,
132, 142; 5. 1,12, 389.

Godhas, variant of Sodhas, 2. 163.

Godhana, son of S'waphalka, 4. 96.

Goghnatas, a people, 2. 163.

Gokámukha, a mountain in India,
2. 141.

Gokhala, variant of Gokhalu, 3. 46.

Gokhalu, disciple of S'ákalya, and
teacher of the Ŕig-veda, 3. 46.

Gokhalya (?), disciple of S'ákalya,
3. 46. See Gokhalu.

Gokula, a place, 4. 260, 275, 276,
279, 289, 290, 305, 315-317,
335, 342; 5. 1, 4, 9, 43.

Goládhyáya, the, an astronomical
work, referred to, 2. 113.

Golaka, disciple of S'ákalya, and
teacher of the Ŕig-veda, 3. 46.

Golava, variant of Gálava, teacher
of the White Yajur-veda, 3. 57.

Gold, soil of, 2. 204.

Goloka, a region, the heaven of
Kŕishṇa and of kine, P. 66; 1.
98; 2. 230; 4. 318, 319.

Gomanta, a hill in India, 2. 142;
5. 66.

Gomantas, variant of Goghnatas,
2. 164.

Gomatí, a river in Oude, 2. 2,
121, 146; 4. 34-36.

Gomatí, a river in Naimisha, P. 52; 3. 170.

Gomatí, a river affluent to the Sindhu, 3. 170.

Gómatíputra, variant of Gotamíputra, 4. 198.

Gomeda, a mountain-range in Plaksha-dwípa, 2. 191.

Gomedaka, a certain Dwípa or continent, 2. 110.

Gomukha, variant of Gokhalu, 3. 46.

Gopas, inhabitants of Gokula, 4. 279, &c. Associates of Kríshńa in his disports, 4. 285, &c.

Gopa (?), a country, 2. 164.

Gopajálá, daughter of Raudráswa, and wife of Prabhákara, 4. 129.

Gopála, an epithet of Vishńu or Kríshńa, 5. 34.

Gopála Bhatta, a modern mathematical writer, referred to, 1. 48.

Gopálaka, variant of Pálaka, 4. 178.

Gopálakachchhas, variant of Gopálakakshas, 2. 176.

Gopálakakshas, a people, 2. 176.

Goparáshtras, a people, 2. 164.

Gopati, son of Síbi, 4. 24.

Gopís, mistresses of Kríshńa, P. 66, &c. &c.; 4. 322, &c. Their grief at Kríshńa's departure, 5. 8, &c.

Goraksháswarí (?), variant of Gaurakríshńa, &c., 4. 200.

Gosava, a certain sacrifice, its origin, 1. 85.

Goshtí, a particular Sráddha, 3. 147.

Gotama, sprung from Utathya, 3. 16.

Gotama, an ancient lawgiver. See Gautama, the correct form.

Gotamíputra, Gotamíputra Srísátakarńi, son of Sívaswáti, 4. 198.

Gotra, what, 3. 121, 152, 196; 4. 28, 58.

Gova, a country in India, 2. 164.

Govaráshtra, now popularly called Goa, 2. 179.

Govardhana, a modern author, a work of his named, 5. 379.

Govardhana, a hill in India, 2. 141; 4. 313, 315-317, 322, 325, 335; 5. 34, 45. The Gopas worship it, 4. 312. It is lifted up by Kríshńa, 4. 315.

Govásana, king of the Síbis, 4. 159.

Govinda = Vishńu or Kríshńa, P. 22; 1. 60, 65, 119, 164; 3. 80; 4. 277, 295, 300, 301, 318, 324, 339, 340, 342; 5. 8-10, 22, 38, 41, 46, 56, 57, 64, 89, 90, 92, 97, 100, &c., &c. Fanciful etymology of the word, 4. 318.

Govíthí, a certain triad of asterisms, 2. 265, &c.

Grains, esculent and sacrificial, their names, 1. 94, &c.

Gráma, what, 1. 94.

Grámańí, the same as Yaksha, an attendant on the Sun, 2. 284, &c., 290, &c.; 5. 251.

Graphics, remarks on, 1. 94; 2. 100, 179, 187, 193, 195, 196; 3. 27, 46, 221, 241, 323; 4. 109, 112, 121, 141, 164, 203, 206; 5. 24, 39, 77, 83, 105, 115, 117, 247, 255.

Greeks, called Yavanas or Yonas, 2. 181.

Gŕidhra, son of Kŕishńa and Mitravindá, 5. 79.

Gŕidhra, a Ŕishi in the fourteenth Mauwantara, 3. 28.

Gŕidhrakúťa, a mountain in India, 4. 24.

Gŕidhramojáudhaka (?), son of Swaphalka, 4. 96.

Gŕidhrí = Gŕidhriká, 2. 73.

Gŕidhriká, daughter of Kaśyapa and Támrá, and mother of vultures, 2. 73.

Gŕihastha, 'householder' His duties, 3. 93. His fixed duties, 3. 107, &c. His miscellaneous duties, 3. 135, &c.

Gŕihya-sútras, various, referred to, 3. 112–114, 168, 338.

Gŕinjima (?), variant of Sŕinjaya, 4. 113.

Gŕitsamada, son of Śunahotra, &c., 4. 30–32, 40.

Gŕitsamati, variant of Gŕitsamada, 4. 136.

Gŕitsatamas, variant of Dírghatamas, 4. 32.

Guhas, a people, 4. 220.

Guha, a prince of the Nishádas, 4. 220.

Guha = Kárttikeya, 3. 22 ; 5. 115, 116.

Guhila = Gobhila, 4. 344.

Guhyakas, servants of Kubera, 1. 122 ; 3. 116 ; 4. 52, 266, 281 ; 5. 138.

Guhya-vidyá, 'knowledge of mystical prayers and incantations,' 1: 148.

Gúnas, 'qualities,' viz., goodness, foulness, and darkness, 1. 26, 68.

Guńamukhyá, an Apsaras, 2. 81.

Guńávará, an Apsaras, 2. 81.

Guptas, a dynasty, P. 109, 111 ; 4. 218, 219, 224.

Gupta, a name appropriate to a Vaiśya, 3. 99.

Gurgańas, variant of Tangańas, 2. 181.

Guru, variant of Ruchiradhí, 4. 137.

Guru, 'spiritual guide,' 3. 92, et passim.

Gurudhí, variant of Ruchiradhí, 4. 137.

Gurukshepa, son of Bŕihatkshańa, 4. 167.

Gurúńďas, a dynasty, 4. 206.

Guruvírya, variant of Ruchiradhí, 4. 137.

Guru-vyákhya, the, a metrical gloss, quoted, 5. 379.

Gwálpára, the popular name of a town in Assam, 5. 113.

Gypsies, speculations touching the, 4. 58.

Hálá, a Gandharva, 2. 285, &c. ; 3. 249.

Háháka, variant of Háhá, 2. 286.

Haihayas, a tribe. They conquer Báhu, 3. 289. They are conquered by Sagara, 3. 291, 292. Paraśuráma triumphs over them, 3. 316. They invade the king of the Káśis, 4. 40. Five divisions of them, 4. 58. Of Scythian origin, 4. 60. Began from Haihaya, father of a hundred sons, 4. 40. See also 4. 21, 24, 61.

Haihayas, a dynasty so called, 4. 184.

Haihaya, son of Vatsa, and father of the hundred Haihayas, 4. 40.

Haihaya, variously genealogized, 4. 53, 54.

Haima-koša, the, a vocabulary, referred to, 2. 148, 149, 154, 156, 157, 160, 167, 172–174, 177, 179. See Hemachandra, the name of its author.

Haimašaila, variant of Hemašaila, 2. 196.

Haimavati, a S'akti, P. 79.

Hair, how worn by ancient nations, 3. 294.

Haitukas, a sect, 3. 222.

Hála; variously genealogized, 4. 197, 201.

Hala, 'ploughshare,' 5. 51, 67, 134, 137. Compare Síra.

Hálahála, a specific poison, 1. 147.

Haláyudha, an epithet of Balabhadra, 5. 63, 85, 133, 135, 137.

Háleya, variant of Hála, 4. 197.

Halin, an epithet of Balabhadra, 5. 84, 135, 137.

Hamsa, son of Vasudeva, 4. 111 (where correct the spelling); 5. 391.

Hamsa, a caste in Plaksha-dwípa, 2. 193.

Hamsa, a horse of the Moon, 2. 299.

Hamsa, a mountain-range to the north of Mount Meru, 2. 117, 123 (where correct the spelling), 339.

Hamsamárgas, a people, 2. 187.

Hamsapádá, an Apsaras, 2. 82.

Hamsapadí, an Apsaras, 2. 83.

Hanta, a mystical exclamation, 3. 122, 123.

Hantakára = Hanta, 3. 122.

Hanuman-nátaka, a drama, referred to, 2. 231.

Hanumat, the monkey-god, names of, &c., P. 50; 1. 117; 5. 387.

Hara, a form of Rudra or Síva, 1. 134; 2. 24, 25; 4. 272; 5. 53, 108, 115, 386.

Harakeša, variant of Harikeša, 2. 297.

Haris, a class of gods in the fourth Manwantara, 3. 7, 17. Their origin, 2. 26.

Hari, or Kŕishńa, a form of Vishńu, and son of Vasudeva, P. 21, &c.; 1. 13, 41, 118, &c.; 3. 17, 75, &c.; 4. 106, 110, 251, 257, 259, 264, 272, 276, 289, 295, 315, 317, 322, 331; 5. 2–4, 8, 10, 11, 21, 22, 35, 36, 39, 44, 45, 50, 51, 58, 62, 64, 70, 76, 84, 87, 89, 90, 93, 98, 99, 102, &c. &c.

Hari, an author, referred to the court of King Vikramáditya, P. 9.

Hari, a mountain in Kuša-dwípa, 2. 196.

Hari, variant of Harita, 4. 64.

Haridwára, a town, now Hardwár, 1. 123; 3. 303.

Harikeša, a certain ray of the sun, 2. 297, 298; 5. 191.

Harimedhas, father of Hari, father of the Haris, 3. 17.

Hariní, mother of Hari, father of the Haris, 3. 17.

Haripura, a city, P. 34.

Harischandra, son of Triśanku, 3. 261, 287; 4. 25, 27. Elevated, with his subjects, to heaven, P. 56; 3. 288.

Harishéña, son of Brahmasávarñi, Manu of the tenth Manwantara, 3. 26.

Harisrává, a river, 2. 151.

Haritas, a class of gods in the twelfth Manwantara, 3. 27.

Háritas, Háritas, a race sprung from Harita, son of Yuvanáśwa, 3. 280, 281.

Háritas, a people (the same as the last?), 2. 186, 339.

Harita, son of Vapushmat, king of S'álmala-dwípa, 2. 193.

Hárita, disciple of Lomaharshaña, and teacher of the Puráñas, 3. 65.

Harita, Hárita, son of Yuvanáśwa, 3. 280, 281.

Harita, son of Rohitáśwa, 3. 288.

Harita, variously genealogized, king of Videha, 4. 63, 64.

Harita, a division of S'álmala-dwípa, 2. 193.

Hárita, variant of Háritaka, 4. 28.

Háritaka, variously genealogized, 4. 28.

Haritáśwa, son of Sudyumna, 3. 237.

Harivaṁśa, a mythological work, its character, P. 43, 92.

Harivarsha, son of Agnídhra, and king of Nishadha, 2. 102.

Harivarsha, a region far north of Bháratavarsha, 2. 111, 114.

Harsha, 'joy,' son of Káma, 1. 111.

Harsha, son of Krishña and Mitravindá, 5. 79.

Harsha, a king (one with Harshavardhana?), 2. 341.

Harsha, a king (different, perhaps), 4. 190.

Harsha-charita, the, a medieval chronicle, referred to, 2. 164; 3. 268, 318, 340; 4. 137, 172, 180, 191, 217; 5. 389.

Harshaka, variant of Darbhaka, 4. 182.

Harshakrit, son of Bhajamána, son of Satwata, 4. 72.

Harshaña, variant of Haryanga, 4. 125.

Harshavardhana, son of Yajnakrita, 4. 44.

Harshavardhana, a medieval king, 2. 341.

Haryá, mother of the gods called Haris, 3. 17.

Haryadwana, son of Jaya, 4. 44.

Haryaksha, son of Prithu, 1. 192.

Haryanga, son of Champa, son of Prithuláksha, 4. 125.

Haryaśwas, five or ten thousand, sons of Daksha, 2. 13, &c.

Haryaśwa, variously genealogized, 3. 265.

Haryaśwa (another), variously genealogized, 3. 284.

Haryaśwa, son of Dhrishtaketu, son of Satyadhriti, 3. 331.

Haryaśwa, king of the Káśis, 4. 40.

Haryaśwa, son of Chakshus, son of Purujánu, 4. 144.

Haryaśwa, variant of Harshavardhana, son of Yajnakrita, 4. 44.

E

Haryaśwata, variously genealogized, 4. 43, 44.

Haryátas, a tribe in Central India,
4. 58.

Haryátman = Uttama, the Vyása,
3. 35.

Haryavana, variant of Haryadwana, 4. 44.

Hasta, son of Vasishťha, 1. 155.

Hasta, a certain asterism, 2. 265,
&c.; 3. 132.

Hastin, variously genealogized, 4.
138–140.

Hastinápura, Hástinapura, a city.
Founded by King Hastin, 4.
139. Where situated, 4. 139.
Washed away by the Ganges, 4.
164. Undermined by Bala-
bhadra, 5. 134. See also P.
40, 107; 4. 145; 5. 131, 135,
160.

Hastisomá, a river, 2. 147.

Havihsaṁsthás, certain sacrifices,
3. 112, 113.

Havíndhra, a Prajápati in the
second Manwantara, son of
Vasishťha, 3. 5.

Havirbhú, daughter of Kardama,
and wife of Pulastya, 1. 110,
154.

Havirbhujes = Havishmata, 3. 162.

Havirdhána, son of Antardhána,
son of Prithu, 1. 192, 193.

Havishmats, a class of Pitris, sons
of Angiras, 3. 163.

Havishmat, a Rishi, or Rishis, in
the sixth and eleventh Manwantaras, 3. 12, 14, 26.

Havya, son of Atri, 1. 154.

Havya, 'boiled butter offered to
the gods,' 2. 58.

Havya, variant of Bhavya, the
Rishi so called, 3. 25.

Havyaváhana, son of Suchi, son
of Vahni, 1. 156.

Hayas (?), a tribe, 4. 60.

Haya, variously genealogized, 4.
53, 54.

Hayagríva, son of Kaśyapa, P. 49;
2. 70. His abode, 2. 211.
Slain by Vishńu, 5. 3, 90.

Hayagrívahan, an epithet of Vishńu, 5. 3.

Hayaśirá, daughter of Vaiswánara,
and wife of Kratu, 2. 71.

Hayaśiras, daughter of Vrishaparvan, 2. 70.

Hayaśiras = Hayaśirsha, 2. 125
(where correct the spelling),
339; 5. 3.

Hayaśirsha, a form of Vishńu, 5.
2, 3.

Hayaśirsha-pancharátra, a metrical
work, quoted, 3. 223.

Hells, different, &c., 2. 214, &c.;
5. 207, &c.

Hema, son of Ushadratha, 4.
122.

Hemá, an Apsaras, 2. 82, 83.

Hemá, a river, 2. 149.

Hemachandra, son of Viśála, 3.
247.

Hemachandra, author of a vocabulary, &c. &c., 2. 82, 141–
143; 3. 122, 246; 4. 171; 5.
364. See Haima-kośa.

Hemádri, titular author of the
Sráddha-kalpa, P. 50, 51; 3.
148, 166, 189–191, 198, 199,
339.

Hemaka, a Daitya (?), his abode,
2. 211.

Hemakúta, a mountain-range, 2. 102, 111, 114, 282.

Hemaśaila, a mountain in Kuśa-dwípa, 2. 196.

Hemaśringa, a mountain, on which stands the city of Brahmá, 2. 118.

Heretics. Sects of them, 1. 96. Jainas, Bauddhas, &c., 3. 206, &c. The sin of intercourse with them, 3. 225.

Hermit, the duties of a, 3. 94, 95.

Heti, a Rákshasa, presiding over the month of Madhu, &c., 2. 285, &c.

Hid'imbá, wife of Bhímasena, son of Pánd'u, 4. 159.

Hima, a country to the south of Himavat, 2. 102, 103.

Himáchala. = Himálaya, 3. 254; 4. 303, 304.

Himádri = Himálaya, 1. 129; 2. 127.

Himagiri, a mountain-range to the north of Lanká, 2. 111.

Himálaya, a range of mountains, 1. 8; 2. 130; 3. 254.

Himavat, husband of Mená, and father of Sati, 1. 118. See also 1. 157, 190; 3. 265. Identified with a mountain-range, 1. 122; 2. 86, 114, 118, 130, 282. King of mountains, 1. 188.

Himavat-khand'a, a part of the Skanda-purána, P. 73.

Himsá, 'violence,' wife of Adharma, 1. 111. Called daughter of Lobha, and wife of Krodha, 1. 111.

Hindus, their origin, and their first settlements in India, P. 101, &c.

Hirańmaya = Hirańwat, 2. 102.

Hirańmaya, a region lying to the north of Siddhapura, &c., 2. 111, 115.

Hirańwat, son of Agnídhra, king of Jambu-dwípa, himself ruling over S'weta, 2. 102 (where correct the spelling), 339.

Hirańwatí, a river, 2. 149, 339.

Hirańyagarbha, a form of Vishńu, 1. 13, 164.

Hirańyagarbha = Brahmá, 1. 106; 2. 229, 317; 3. 6, 121, 230; 5. 231, 233, 234, 236, 247.

Hirańyagarbha = Agni, 3. 162.

Hirańyakaśipu, son of Kaśyapa and Diti, and a king of the Daityas, 2. 30. His power, and his enmity to Vishńu, 2. 34, &c. Vishńu, as Narasimha, puts him to death, 2. 64, 65; 4. 104, 106. See also 2. 71; 3. 201; 4. 250, 259.

Hirańyákshas, Kauśika Bráhmans, 4. 28.

Hirańyáksha, a celebrated Daitya, son of Kaśyapa and Diti, 2. 30. His city, where, 2. 211. See also 1. 62; 2. 69–71; 4. 132.

Hirańyáksha, son of S'álávatí, 4. 28.

Hirańyaloman = Hirańyaroman, 2. 262.

Hirańyanábha, son of Viśwasaha, disciple of Jaimini, and teacher of the Sáma-veda, 3. 58–61, 323, 324; 4. 143.

Hirańyapura, a city floating in the air, inhabited by certain Daityas, 2. 72.

Hirańyaratha, variant of Dharmaratha, 4. 124.

Hiráńyaretas, son of Priyavrata, and king of Kuśa-dwípa, 2. 100, 197.

Hiráńyaroman, a Ŕishi in the fifth Manwantara, 3. 10.

Hiráńyaroman, a Lokapála, son of Parjanya and Márichi, 1. 154; 2. 263. Regent of the north, 2. 86. Dwells on the Lokáloka mountains, 2. 262.

Hiráńyashťhíva, a mountain in Plaksha-dwípa, 2. 193.

Hiráńyavatí, the Hirana or Little Gunduk river, 2. 149.

Hitáśwn, variant of Saṁbatáśwa, 3. 265.

Hláda = Hráda, 2. 30, 69.

Hládiní, a river, 2. 120, 121.

Homa-dhenu, what, 5. 218.

Horá, what, 4. 66.

Horse of Indra, and that of the Sun, produced at the churning of the ocean, 1, 147. Seven horses of the Sun, 2. 239. Horses of the Moon, 2. 299. Budha's eight horses, 2. 304. Śukra's ten horses, 2. 304. Bhauma's eight, 2. 304. Bŕihaspati's eight, 2. 304. Śanaiśchara's, the number unspecified, 2. 304. Ráhu's eight, 2. 304. Ketu's eight, 2. 305. Kŕishńa's four horses, Śaibya, Sugríva, Meghapushpa, and Baláhaka, 4. 83.

Hospitality, the duties of, 3. 120, 121.

Hotraka, son of Kánchana, 4. 14.

Hotŕi, a sort of priest who chants hymns of the Ŕig-veda, 3. 43, 327.

Householder, the duties of a, 3. 94, &c., 107, &c., 135, &c.

Hráda, son of Hiráńyakaśipu, 2. 30, 69; 3. 201; 5. 349

Hraswaroman, son of Suvarńaroman, 3. 332.

Hrí, 'modesty,' daughter of Daksha, and wife of Dharma, 1. 110.

Hŕidika, son of Swayaṁbhoja, 4. 99, 100.

Hŕidíka, variant of Hŕidika, 4. 99.

Hŕishíkeśa, a title of Vishńu, 1. 2, 3; 2. 8, 94; 4. 278; 5. 93.

Huhu, Húhú, Hóhu, or Huhú, a Gandharva, 2. 285, 286, &c.; 3. 249.

Húńas, a people, 2. 133-135, 182; 4. 60, 206, 209.

Húndes, the now current name of the country where Lake Mánasarovara is situated, 2. 340.

Hunus = Húńas, (?) 2. 340.

Hutabhuj = Agni, 1. 180.

Hutahavyavaha, son of Dhara, 2. 23.

Hutáśa, what, 4. 254.

Hutáśana, 'the god of flame,' 1. 138.

Hylozoism, as treated by Cudworth, 1. 66.

Hymns. To Vishńu, by Earth, 1. 59, &c. By Brahmá and the gods, 1. 139, &c. To Śrí, by Indra, 1. 148, &c. To Vishńu, by Dhruva, 1. 169, &c. By the Prachetasas, 1. 196, &c. By Prahláda, 2. 57, &c. By the Pitŕis, 3. 170, 197; 5. 249. By Brahmá, 4. 251, &c. To Kŕishńa, by Káliya, 4. 293, &c. By Akrúra, 5. 14, &c. By Aditi, 5. 93, &c.

Hypostases, three, of Vishńu, 1. 13.

Iďa = Ila, 3. 70, 234.
Iďá, variant of Irá, 2. 26.
Iďaspati, a title of Vishńu, 2. 17.
Iďaviďa, son of Daśaratha, son of
  Múlaka, 3. 311.
Iďaviďa, daughter of Tŕińabindu
  and Alambushá, and wife of
  Viśravas, 1. 154 ; 3. 246.
  Called wife of Pulastya, and
  mother of Viśravas, 3. 246.
  See Ilivilá and Iviďá.
Iďavila, variant of Iďaviďa, 3. 311.
Idhmajihwa, son of Priyavrata,
  and king of Plaksha-dwípa, 2.
  100, 193.
Iďiviďa, variant of Iďaviďa, 3. 311.
Idwatsara, a certain cyclic year,
  2. 255.
Ignorance, fivefold, and the origin
  of beings, 1. 69. The nature
  and cause of it, 5. 223, &c.
Íjikas, a people, 2. 173.
Ijyá, 'oblation,' an emanation
  from Brahmá, 1. 85.
Iksha (?), variant of Ikshu, a river
  in Śáka-dwípa, 2. 199.
Ikshu, a river in Bháratavarsha,
  2. 155.
Ikshu, a river in Śáka-dwípa, 2.
  199.
Ikshu, the name of a sea. See
  Ikshurasoda.
Ikshubudá, a river, 2. 146.
Ikshuká, a river, 2. 155.
Ikshubulá, a river, 2. 146.
Ikshumálavi, a river, 2. 145, 155.
Ikshumálini, variant of Ikshumá-
  lavi, 2. 146.
Ikshumati, a river, 2. 155, 318.

Ikshurasoda, Ikshurasodaka, a
  sea of molasses, surrounding
  Plaksha-dwípa, 2. 193, 194.
Ikshwákus (?), a people, 3. 343.
Ikshwáku, son of Vaivaswata, the
  Manu, 3. 13, 231–233, 297.
  Generated by a sneeze, 3. 259.
  In the Kŕíta age, son of Kshupa, 3. 243. A king in the
  current Manwantara, 3. 13, 14.
  A Rájarshi, 3. 68. A hymn
  of the Pitŕis, heard by him, 3.
  197. Performs an Aśwamedha,
  3. 234. Has a hundred sons,
  3. 259. His sons probably
  colonizers of various parts of
  India, 3. 260. First king of
  Ayodhyá, P. 106 ; 3. 261. See
  also P. 107.; 3. 238, 304, 309,
  326, 327, 343 ; 4. 18, 125,
  130, 167, 170, 171, 172, 237,
  240.
Il or Ilus of the Phœnicians, identified with Ila, 3. 235.
Ila, son of Vaivaswata, 3. 234–236.
Ilá, wife of Ugraretas, the Rudra,
  1. 117.
Ilá, daughter of Vaivaswata, wife
  of Budha, and mother of Purúravas, 3. 168, 232, 233, 236,
  237.; 4. 5, 11. Changed into
  a man, 3. 234, 235.
Ilá, wife of Vasudeva, 4, 110.
Ilá, variant of Irá, 2. 26.
Ilá, variant of Ilini, 4. 131.
Ilavila, variant of Iďaviďa, 3.
  311, 314.
Ilavilá, variant of Ilivilá, 3. 246.
  See Iďaviďa.
Ilávŕíta, son of Agnídhra, and
  king of Ilávŕíta, constituting

the circumjacencies of Mount Meru, 2. 102.

Ilávrita, a region, in the centre of which stands Mount Meru, 2. 111, 115, 116,122, 124; 3. 234.

Ilbana, variant of Ilvala, 2. 71.

Ilin, a king, 4. 131.

Ilina, variant of Ailina, 4. 131, 132.

Ilini, daughter of Medhátithi, or else of Yama, and wife of Tamsu, 4. 131.

Ilirila, variant of Ilivilá, 3. 246.

Ilivilá, daughter of Trińabindu, 3. 246. See Iḍavidá.

Ilivila, variant of Iḍavidá, 3. 311.

Ilus. See Il.

Ilwala, a celebrated demon, son of Hráda, 2. 69. Called son of Viprachitti, 2. 71.

Ilwańa, variant of Ilwala, 2. 71.

Immortals, creation of the, 1. 72.

Impurity, periods of, for the different castes, 3. 153.

India, civilization and colonization of, P. 102, &c.

Indras, deities present in the various Manwantaras, 3. 3, 6, 7, 9, 12, 13, 23–28.

Indras, gods attended by the winds, sons of Dharma and Marutwatí, 2. 22.

Indra, king of the gods, 2. 85. Presides over the hands, 1. 38. Husband of Indráńí or Sachí, 1. 119, 136; 5. 70. He slays the demon Vritra, 2. 79; 4. 258; 5. 354: and see Vritrahan and Vritraripu. Is cursed by Durvásas, 1. 136. Praises Srí, 1. 146, &c. Divides the embryo of Diti, 2. 78. The Vyása of the seventh Dwápara age, 3. 34, 37. Is born as Gádhi, 4. 16. Is vanquished by the sons of Raji, 4. 42. He recovers his power, 4.' 43. Is worshipped by the Gopas, 5. 308, &c. He rains angrily on Gokula, 5. 314, &c. He pays homage to Krishńa, &c., 5. 317, &c. He contends with Krishńa for the Párijáta-tree, 5. 97, &c. Is defeated in his attempt, 5. 102, &c. His city, Vaswaukńaśárá, its situation, &c., 2. 112, 118, 239, 240: and see Amarávatí. His sphere, 1. 97; 4. 217: and see Indra-loka. A personification of the firmament, P. 3. His bow, the rainbow, 4. 284, 299; 5. 13, 22. Is called Sahasráksha, with allusion to an unclean legend, according to the Puráńas, 4. 261, 321, 334. See also P. 84; 1. 50; 2. 307; 3. 118, &c.; 4. 102, 272, 293, 341; 5. 2, 15, 43, 45, 46, 87, 89, 93, 96, 99, 100, &c. &c. See also Maghavat, Sakra, Satakratu, Satamakha, &c.

Indra, an Áditya, 2. 27, 285, &c.

Indra-dhwaja-samutthána = Sakrotthána, 4. 308.

Indra-dwípa, a portion of Bhárata-varsha, 2. 129.

Indradyumna, associated with Vishńu incarnate as a tortoise, P. 76, 78.

Indradyumna, son of Sumati, 2. 106.

Indradyumna, a modern king, 5. 344.

Indragopa, an insect, 4. 284 ; 5. 194.

Indrakíla, a mountain in India, 2. 141.

Indra-loka, the same as Swarga, the heaven of Indra and of Kshattriyas, 1. 97, 98.

Indrání = Sachí, wife of Indra, 1. 119 ; 5. 70.

Indrapálita, son of Bandhupálita, 4. 189.

Indrapramati, disciple of Paila, and teacher of the Ṛig-veda, 3. 44-46, 49.

Indraprastha, a city on the Jumna, near Delhi, 3. 302 ; 5. 82, 150, 154, 160.

Indrasávarñi, Manu of the fourteenth Manwantara, 3. 25, 28.

Indrasena, son of Púrva, 3. 335.

Indrasena, son of Maudgalya, 4. 146.

Indrasená, wife of Maudgalya, 4. 146.

Indrasena, a mountain in Plaksha-dwípa, 2. 193.

Indravúha, another name of Puranjaya, 3. 263.

Indrávaraja, a name of Kṛishṇa, 4. 318.

Indriya, a species of creation, 1. 74. See Aindriyaka.

Indriya-nigraha, what, in philosophy, 4. 294.

Indriyátman, a name of Vishṇu, 1. 3.

Indu = Soma, 2. 21 ; 3. 118; 4. 4.

Irá, daughter of Daksha, and wife of Kaśyapa, 2. 26, 75.

Irávat, son of Arjuna, 4. 160.

Irávat, variant of Airávata, the serpent, 2. 293.

Irávatí, wife of Kála, the Rudra, 1. 117.

Irávatí, the river Rávi or Hydraotes, 2. 121, 144.

Íśa = Síva, 1, 124 ; 2. 112. See Íśwara.

Íśa, a Sádhya, 2. 22.

Íśa = Vishṇu, 5. 43.

Íśána, a form of Rudra or Síva, 1. 116; 4. 267 ; 5. 386, 387.

Íśána, a mountain in Sáka-dwípa, 2. 200.

Íśána, a Kalpa, P. 58, 67.

Íśána, a title of Vishṇu, 4. 267.

Íśána-bali, a certain sacrifice, 3. 114.

Isha, son of Vatsara, 1. 178.

Isha = Aświna, a month, Sept.-Oct., 2. 261.

Ishá-daṇḍa, what, 2. 237.

Ishaudhura, a caste in Sálmala-dwípa, 2. 195.

Ishíkas, a people, 2. 173.

Ishíká, what, 4. 4.

Ishíratha, ancestor of Kuśámba, son of Kuśa, 4. 15.

Ishṭí, what, 3. 233.

Ishṭi-śráddha, a certain mortuary ceremony, 3. 189, 190.

Ishuká, variant of Suchíká, 2. 81.

Íśwara, the same as Síva, 3. 235 ; 5. 307.

Íśwara, son of Brahmá, worshipped in Ketumála-var-ha, 2. 126.

Íśwara, a Rudra, 2. 25.

Íśwara, son of Púru, son of Yayáti, 4. 127.

Íswara, in theology, what, 1. 3. What, in philosophy, 1. 32.

Íswara-gítá, a part of the Kúrma-puráńa, P. 79; 2. 86.

Íswara-prańidháńa, what, in ethics, 3. 77.

Íswarasena, son of Śivadatta, 4. 208.

Iti, variant of Dhŕiti, son of Babhru, 4. 67.

Itihása, 'historical tradition,' a term for the Mahábhárata, &c., P. 45, 61, 98; 1. 85; 3. 42.

Itíkas, variant of Íjikas, 2. 173.

Itthana, variant of Ilwala, 2. 71.

Ividá (?), mother of Viśravas, 3. 246. See Iḍavidá and Ilivilá.

Ivílaka, son of Lambodara, 4. 196.

Jábálas, students of a branch of the White Yajur-veda, 3. 57.

Jagaddhátrí, a name of Saraswatí, 4. 264, 266.

Jagad-yoni, what, in cosmogony, 1. 21.

Jagannátha, a name of Vishńu or Kŕishńa, P. 22, 28, &c, &c.; 4. 315, 341; 5. 90, 282.

Jagannátha Tarkapanchánana, a modern legal writer, 3. 103, 142.

Jagatí, a metre, its origin, 1. 85, 86. Regarded as a horse of the Sun, 2. 239.

Jagatpati, variant of Yajnapati, 5. 177.

Jaghanjaya, son of Pradyota, 4. 178.

Jáhnaví, metaphorical patronym of Gangá, the Ganges, 1. 136; 3. 285; 4. 14, 157; 5. 180. Mistress of Śántanu, 4. 157.

Jahnu, a Ŕishi in the fourth Manwantara, 3. 8.

Jahnu, son of Suhotra, and drinker-up of the Ganges, 4. 14, 15, 138, 139, 343.

Jahnu, son of Kuru, 4. 148, 152, 153, 240.

Jahu, son of Pushpavat, 4. 150.

Jaimini, a Yogin, disciple of Vyása, and teacher of the Sáma-veda, P. 33, 54, 55; 3. 42, 58, 60, 323-325.

Jainas, religionists, P. 33, 79, III. 1. 96; 2. 159, 161, 165, 192; 3. 41, 196, 201, 207, 209, 340; 4. 225; 5. 286, 288, 299, 322, &c., &c., 359, &c., 388. Noticed, or alluded to, in the Bhágavata-puráńa, 3. 104, 105; 4. 43.

Jaitra, the name of Kŕishńa's chariot, 5. 149.

Jájali, disciple of Pathya, and teacher of the Atharva-veda, 3. 62.

Jalada, son of Bhavya, king of Sáka-dwípa, 2. 198.

Jalada, a region in Sáka-dwípa, 2. 198.

Jalédhára, a mountain-range in Sáka-dwípa, 2. 198.

Jalagambu, son of Súrya and Nishkumbhá, 5. 382.

Jálahásiní, variant of Chárubásiní, 4. 112. And see 5. 83, note §.

Jalaja, variant of Jalada, as doubly denotative, 2. 198.

Jalandhara, an Asura, the story of, P. 33.

Jálandhara, a name of Trigarta, 2. 179.

Jáleśwaratírtha, a place of pilgrimage on the river Narmadá, 5. 118.

Jaleyu, son of Raudráśwa, 4. 127, 128, 129.

Jalpa, a Ŕishi in the fourth Manwantara, 3. 8.

Jamadagni, a Ŕishi, son of Ŕichíka, and father of Paraśuráma, 2. 285, &c.; 3. 13, 15, 16, 80; 4. 18, 19, &c. Is slain by the sons of Kártavírya, 4. 22.

Jámadagnya, patronym of Paraśuráma, 3. 23; 4. 23.

Jámbavat, king of bears. He slays the lion that killed Prasena, 4. 76. He contends with, and is overcome by, Kŕishńa, 4. 78, 79. Kŕishńa accepts his daughter Jámbavatí as a bride, 4. 79.

Jámbavatí, daughter of Jámbavat, and wife of Kŕishńa, 4. 79, 112; 5. 78, 79, 82, 97, 107, 130, 142. Identified with Rohińí, 5. 79, 81.

Jambha, a demon slain by Indra, 4. 3, 334.

Jambu, a river so called, 2. 116. See Jambúnadí.

Jambu, Jambú, a certain tree. On Mounts Sugandha, Gandhamádana, and Merumandara, according to differing authorities, 2. 111, 116.

Jambu-dwípa, Jambú-dwípa, a continent so called, 2. 101, &c., 109, 110, &c.; 136, 138; 5. 382.

Jambúmárga, a forest so called, 2. 316; 5. 389.

Jámbunada, Jámbúnada, a sort of gold, used by the Siddhas, 2. 111, 116.

Jambúnadí, a river, 2. 111, 121.

Jámbúnadí (the same as Jambúnadí?), a river, 2. 151.

Jámi, Jámí, variant of Yámi or Yámí, 2. 21.

Janaka, or Dharmadhwaja, son of Kuśadhwaja, 5. 217.

Janaka, son of Nimi, 3. 45, 53, 316, 330, 331, 335.

Janaka, king of the Káśis, 3. 220.

Janaka, of Videha, father of Sítá, 3. 331; 4. 84, 146, 238.

Janaka, son of Viśákhayúpa, 4. 179.

Janaka, son of Mitadhwaja, or Khándika, 5. 214, 217.

Janaka (one of the Janakas already named ?), 5. 88.

Janaka, a title (?), 5. 217. (It may be added, that the persons named Janaka are not always easily distinguished.)

Jánakí, patronym of Sítá, 4. 107.

Janakpur, the popular name of a city now in ruins, 3. 331.

Jana-loka = Jano-loka, 1. 52, 59, 62, 98; 2. 113, 227, 228; 5. 193, 195.

Janamejaya, variously genealogized, 3. 247.

Janamejaya, son of Puranjaya, 4. 120.

Janamejaya, son of Dŕid'haratha, 4. 126.

Janamejaya, son of Púru, 4. 127, 128.

Janamejaya, son of Parikshit, P. 44; 4. 142, 152, 153, 162, 163.

Janamejaya, son of Chandrápída, son of Súryápída, 4. 163.

Janamejaya, variant of Arimejaya, son of Swaphalka, 4. 96.

Janárdana = Vishńu or Kŕishńa, P. 76; 1. 118, 151; 2. 198, 200; 3. 30, 76, 77, 85, 203, 204, 217; 4. 89, 268, 277, 320, 321, 333, 336, 340; 5. 13, 30, 42, 48, 50, 57, 97, 101, 105, &c. &c. Etymology of the term, 1. 41; 2. 198.

Janas = Jana-loka, 2. 231.

Jángalas, a people, 2. 156 (note †).

Janmáshṭamí, a particular festival, P. 71.

Jano-loka, a region inhabited by sons of Brahmá, 2. 226; 4. 266.

Jantu, variously genealogized, 4. 69, 70.

Jantu, son of Somaka, son of Sahadeva or Saudása, 4. 148.

Jantu, son of Sudhanwan, son of Satyadhŕita, 4. 150.

Jánujangha, son of Támasa, Manu of the fourth Manwantara, 3. 8.

Jánu-nirgháta (?), what, in the pancratium, 5. 37.

Janyu, variant of Jahnu, the Rishi, 3. 8.

Japa, what, 1. 164; 2. 93.

Jará, a certain ghouless, 4. 150, 344, 345.

Járadgava, three certain triads of asterisms, 2. 265, 267.

Járadgaví, a certain triad of asterisms, 2. 265, &c.

Jaras, a hunter so called, 5. 143, 152.

Jaras (?) (where correct Jará ?), son (?) of Mŕityu, 1. 112.

Jarásandha, king of Magadha, variously genealogized, 4. 150,

171, 173, 273, 344; 5. 54, 69, 70, 145. He besieges Mathurá, 5. 50, &c.

Jartikas, a people, 2. 339; 4. 58.

Járudhi, a mountain-range lying to the west of Mount Meru, 2. 117, 123.

Játs, speculations touching the tribe of, 4. 58.

Játas (?), a tribe, a branch of the Haihayas, 4. 59.

Játa, son of Brahmá, in S'weta-dwípa, 2. 200.

Játa-karman, a certain ceremony, 3. 146, 291, 338.

Játavedas, 'fire,' worshipped in Kuśa-dwípa, 2. 197.

Játáyu, son of Aruńa and S'yení, 2. 73.

Jaṭharas, a people, 2. 162.

Jaṭhara, a mountain-range connecting Níla and Nishadha, 2. 117 (note ||), 123, 124. Jaṭhara, where first named, is left unrendered by the Translator.

Jaṭharágni, a name of Agastya, 1. 154.

Játi = Rúpa, 2. 328; 5. 15, 200.

Jatu, what, 4. 80.

Játúkarńa, Vyása of the twenty-seventh Dwápara age, 3. 36, 37; 5. 25. See Játúkarńya.

Játukarńa, a name of Agniveśya, 3. 336.

Játúkarńya, disciple of S'ákalya, and teacher of the Rig-veda, 3. 48.

Játúkarńya (?), a Vyása, 3. 36; 5. 251. See Játúkarńa.

Javínara (?), variant of Praviíra, son of Haryaśwa, 4. 144.

Jayas, twelve gods so called, created by Brahmá, 2. 26.

Jaya, son of Vatsara, son of Dhruva, 1. 178.

Jaya, one of the Viśwe devas, 3. 190.

Jaya, variously genealogized, 3. 334, 335.

Jaya, son of Purúravas, 4. 13.

Jaya, son of Viśwámitra, 4. 27, 28.

Jaya, variously genealogized, 4. 43, 44.

Jaya, son of Bhavanmanyu, 4. 136.

Jaya, son of Kŕishńa and Bhadrá, 5. 82.

Jayá, daughter of Daksha, and wife of Kŕiśáśwa, 2. 29, 337; 3. 82.

Jayá, handmaid of Durgá, 3. 288.

Jayá; wife of Priyavrata, 3. 337.

Jaya, variant of Asanga, son of Yuyudhána, 4. 93.

Jaya, variant of Sŕinjaya, son of Haryaśwa, 4. 144.

Jayadhwaja, son of Arjuna, son of Kŕitavírya, 4. 57, 58.

Jayadratha, son of Bŕihanmanas, 4. 125, 126, Slain by Arjuna, 5. 157.

Jayadratha, son of Bŕihatkarman, 4. 140.

Jayadratha, king of the Saindhavas and Sauvíras, 5. 389.

Jayanta, a Rudra, 2. 25.

Jayanta, son of Indra, 2. 72.

Jayanta, ancestor of Yudhájit, 4. 94.

Jayanta, a city, founded by Nimi, 3. 331.

Jayasena, an Ávantya, 4. 103.

Jayasena, son of Sárvabhauma,

son of Vidúratha, 4. 153. See Jayatsena.

Jayasena, variant of Jayatsena, son of Adína, 4. 44.

Jayatsena, son of Adína, &c., 4. 43, 44.

Jayatsena, son of Sárvabhauma, 4. 128. See Jayasena.

Jayatsena, variant of Ugrasena, the Gandharva, 2. 293.

Jayatsena, variant of Jayasena, son of Sárvabhauma, 4. 153.

Jharjhara, son of Hirańyáksha, the Daitya, 2. 69.

Jillikas, a people, 2. 178.

Jímúta, son of Vapushmat, king of Sálmala-dwípa, 2. 193.

Jímúta, son of Vyoman. 4. 68.

Jímúta, a division of Sálmala-dwípa, 2. 193.

Jímúta, a kind of cloud, 2. 279.

Jímútaváhana, a writer on inheritance, quoted, 3. 102.

Jina, the god of the Jainas, P. 80; 5. 322, &c., 364, 367, 375, 376, 388.

Jina, a Buddha, 5. 376.

Jina, son of Yadu, 4. 53.

Jishńu, the same as Indra, (?) 1. 123.

Jishńu, the same as Arjuna, 5. 159, 160.

Jishńu, an author, referred to the court of King Vikramáditya, P. 9.

Jitáśwa, son of Sanjaya, 3. 335.

Jitavrata, son of Havirdhána, 1. 193.

Jívan-mŕitaka, what, 3. 293.

Jívátman, what, 2. 328; 4. 253; 5. 14, 228.

Jívaśwara, the term explained, 1. 172.

Jnána, 'wisdom,' epithets of it, according to the Yoga philosophy, 2. 90, 91.

Jnána-múrti, what, 5. 200.

Jnána-yoga, what, 5. 201.

Jŕimbhaṅa, 'yawning,' a form of Brahmá, 1. 82.

Junagur, the popular name of a town in Western India, 4. 198.

Jwálámukhí, a Píṭhasthána, 4. 262.

Jwalana, a name of Agni, 2. 112 (where correct the spelling), 339.

Jyaishṭha, the name of a month, May–June, 2. 261, &c.

Jyámagha, variously genealogized, 4. 63, 64, &c. Conquers Madhyadeśa, 4. 64.

Jyeshṭhá, the same as Alakshmí, a goddess churned from the ocean, 1. 147.

Jyeshṭhá, an asterism so called, 2. 265, &c., 308; 5. 248.

Jyeshṭhá-múla, what, 5. 248, 249.

Jyeshṭha-sáma-ga, a singer of the Jyeshṭha-sáman, 3. 175.

Jyeshṭha-sáman, a certain passage of the Veda, 3. 175.

Jyotirathá, a river, 2. 150.

Jyotirbhásin, a certain celestial region, 3. 161.

Jyotirdháman, a Rishi in the fourth Manwantara, 3. 8.

Jyotir-nibandha, the, a law-book, quoted, or referred to, 3. 103. 104.

Jyotirvidábharaṅa, the, an astrological work, quoted, or named, P. 8, 9; 5. 381.

Jyotis, a Prajápati in the second Manwantara, son of Vasishṭha, 3. 5.

Jyotis, 'astronomy,' an Anga of the Veda, 3. 67.

Jyotishímat, a sun, 5. 191.

Jyotishmat, son of Priyavrata, and king of Kuśa-dwípa, 2. 100, &c., 195.

Jyotishmat, a Rishi in the ninth Manwantara, 3. 25.

Jyotishmat, a mountain in Plaksha-dwípa, 2. 193.

Jyotishmat (?), variant of Jyotishímat, 5. 191.

Jyotishṭoma, a certain sacrifice, 1. 85; 3. 213.

Jyotis-tattwa, the, a modern law-book, referred to, 3. 328.

Jyotsná, 'dawn,' a body of Brahmá, 1. 81; 4. 265.

Ka = Prajápati or Brahmá, 2. 112; 3. 99. Presides over the generative organs, 1. 38.

Ka (?), a wind so called, 4. 304.

Kabandha, disciple of Sumantu, and teacher of the Atharva-veda, 3. 61.

Kabandha, a monster slain by Ráma, 3. 316.

Kachchha, a country, 2. 164.

Kachchhas, variant of Kakshas, 2. 169, 176.

Kachchhaníra, a serpent, presiding over the month of Mádhava, 2. 285, &c.

Kachchhapa, variously genealogized, 4. 27, 28.

Kachchhíyas, a people, 2. 169.

Kaḍa (?), son of Śúra, son of Vidúratha, 4. 101.

Kadamba, a certain tree. On Mount Mandara, 2. 116. Yields a spirituous extract, 5. 65.

Kádambarí, daughter of Chitraratha and Madirá, 5. 66.

Kádambarí, the, a medieval prose-composition, referred to, 2. 82.

Kadrú, daughter of Daksha, wife of Kaśyapa, and mother of the serpent-tribe, 2. 26, 28, 74.

Kahlá (?), daughter of Ugrasena, 4. 99.

Kahoda, father of Ashťávakra, 5. 164.

Kaichchhikilas, variant of Kailakilas, 4. 209.

Kaijava, variant of Kenava, 3. 49.

Kaikaya, a certain family, 3. 287.

Kaikaya, variant of Kaikeya, 4. 103.

Kaikeyas, a people, 2. 169; 4. 103. The five Kaikeyas, 4. 103. And see Kekayas.

Kaikeya, son of Śibi, son of Uśínara, 4. 121. See Kekaya.

Kaikeya, intended to designate the country of the Kaikeyas, 4. 103.

Kailakilas, a branch of the Yavanas, 4. 208, 211.

Kailása, a certain mountain-range, 1. 122, 129, 136; 2. 123, 124; 5. 5.

Kailása, the city of Śiva, or else of Kubera (?), situated on a peak of Mount Meru, 2. 112, 118, 230; 5. 123.

Kailása-yátrá, certain sections of the Harivaṁśa, 5. 123.

Kailikilas, variant of Kailakilas, 4. 209.

Kaiśika, variant of Kauśika, 4. 67.

Kaiśilya, variant of Kauśalya, 3. 58.

Kaiťabha, one of two demons that carried off the Vedas, 5. 3. The other was Madhu.

Kaivartas, a caste, sprung from Nisháda males and Áyogava females, 4. 216, 217.

Kajiṁkas (?), variant of Kalingas, 2. 187.

Kákas, variant of Kántíkas, 2. 181.

Kákaliká, an Apsaras, 2. 82.

Kákamukhas (?), a people, 2. 162.

Káka-paksha, what, 4. 283.

Kákavarṇa, son of Śiśunága, 4. 180.

Kákavarṇin, son of Muṇḍa, son of Udayibhadra, 4. 186.

Kákola, a hell, 2. 215.

Kakshas, a people, 2. 169, 176.

Kaksheyu, son of Raudráśwa, 4. 120, 127—129.

Kakubh, daughter of Daksha, and wife of Dharma, 2. 21; 5. 388.

Kakubha, a mountain, 2. 141.

Kakuda, variant of Kukura, 4. 97.

Kakudmat, a mountain-range in Sálmala-dwípa, 2. 194.

Kakudmatí, daughter of Rukmin, and wife of Pradyumna, 4. 112; 5. 83.

Kakudmin = Raivata, son of Revata, 3. 249, 255.

Kakutstha = Puranjaya, 3. 263, 260; 4. 241.

Kakutstha, son of Bhagíratha, 3. 315.

Kákutstha, father of Go, 4. 45.

Kálas, a class of Pitṛis, 3. 339.

Kála, a form of Rudra, 1. 117

Kála, son of Dhruva, the Vasu, 2. 23.

Kála, a Gandharva, 3. 2.

Kála, one of the Viṣwe devas, 3. 189, 190, 191.

Kalá, daughter of Kardama, and wife of Maríchi, 1, 110.

Kálá, daughter of Daksha, and wife of Kaśyapa, 2. 26.

Kála, 'time,' 'fate,' &c., P. 94, 1. 18, 19, 25, 27, 91, 96; 5. 133. 'Space,' 2. 247.

Kalá, a period of thirty Káshthás, 1. 47; 2. 253; 5. 189.

Kalá, a digit of the Moon, 2, 301, 302.

Kála, variant of Tála, a hell, 2. 216.

Káladas, variant of Kálavas, 2. 180.

Kálágni, what, 1. 128; 5, 192.

Kálajoshakas (?), variant of Kálatoyakas, 2. 168.

Kálakas, a dynasty, 4. 184.

Kálaká, daughter of Vaiśwánara, and wife of Kaśyapa, 2. 71, 72.

Kálakanjas, variant of Kálakhanjas, 2. 71, 72.

Kálakeyas, variant of Kálakhanjas, 2. 71, 72, 337.

Kálakhanjas, Dánavas, sons of Kaśyapa, 2. 71.

Kálakúṭa, a certain virulent poison, 1. 147.

Kálamukhas (?), a people, 2. 162.

Kálanábha, son of Hiraṇyáksha, 2. 70.

Kálanábha, son of Viprachitti, the Dánava, 2. 71.

Kálanadí, a river, 4. 16.

Kálánala, variant of Kálánara, 4. 120.

Kálanara, variant of Kálánara, 4. 120.

Kálánara, son of Sabhánara, 4. 120.

Kálanemi, an Asura, son of Virochana, 4. 250, 259. His abode, 2. 211.

Kálanjara, a mountain-range to the north of Mount Meru, 2. 117, 118.

Kálanjara, a mountain in Bundelkhand, 2. 316.

Kalápa, a certain village on the skirts of the Himálayas, 3. 197, 325; 4. 237. See Kalápadwípa, Kalápagráma, and Káliyadwípa.

Kalápadwípa, variant of Kalápa, 3. 325.

Kalápagráma = Kalápa, 4. 157.

Kálaśambara = Śambara, 5. 73, 75.

Kála-samyama, what, 2. 317.

Kála-sankalitá, the, an astronomical work, referred to, 2. 255, 302.

Kálásoko, the Pálí name of a certain king, 4. 185, 187.

Kálasútra, a hell, 2. 215 (where the spelling is once wrong), 219, 342.

Kálasútraka = Kálasútra, 2. 215.

Kálatoyas, a people, 4. 221. See the next.

Kálatoyakas = Kalatoyas, 2. 168; 4. 221.

Kálavas, a people, 2. 180.

Káláyani, disciple of Baahkali, and teacher of the Rig-veda, 3. 50.

Kálayavana, son of Garga, 5. 54. King of the Yavanas, 5. 54. Invades Mathurá, 5. 55, &c. Is slain by Muchukunda, 5. 57.

Káleyas, variant of Kálakas, 4. 184.

Kali, 'wickedness,' son of Krodha, 'wrath,' 1. 111.

Káli, a form of Párvatí, P. 21, 56, 89; 1. 104; 5. 267.

Kali, the last Yuga or age of the world. Its beginning, 4. 233, &c.; 5. 155. Its duration, 1. 50, &c. Kings of it, 4. 162, &c. Vices of it, 4. 234, &c.; 5. 171, &c. Redeeming traits of it, 5. 180, &c. See also P. 9, 17, 33, 44, 100, 102, 112; 3. 31; 4. 228-230, 232; 5. 62, 170, 247, 251, 252.

Káli = Satyavatí, wife of Sántanu, &c., 4. 150.

Kali (?), variant of Kála, a Gandharva, 3. 2.

Káli, variant of Kásí, wife of Bhímasena, 4. 159.

Kálidása, an author, referred to, P. 8. 31, 118; 2. 286; 3. 322, 323; 4. 5, 190.

Káligháť, the popular name of a village near Calcutta, 4. 262.

Káliká-upapuráña, P. 87, 89. The Káliká is erroneously called a Puráña in P. 89; 5. 316.

Kálikeyas, variant of Kálakhanjas, 2. 71.

Kalinda, the mountain where the river Yamuná rises, 4. 286.

Kálindí, daughter of the Sun, and a wife of Kŕishńa, 5. 78, 79 (where expunge the first sentence of note *), 107. One with Yamuná, 4. 286; 5. 12, 82, 249. Identified with Mitravindá, 5. 79.

Kalingas, a people, 2. 132, 156, 163, 166, 187.

Kalingas, a dynasty, 4. 184.

Kalinga, son of Bali, 4. 122.

Kalinga, a country, P. 107; 2. 134, 153, 156; 3. 75, 79; 4. 160, 220; 5. 84-86.

Kálingí, wife of Tamsu, 4. 131.

Káli Sindhu, a river, 2. 148.

Káliya, Kálíya, a huge serpent, son of Kaśyapa, 2. 74. His abode, 2. 211. Kŕishńa fights with and overcomes him, and orders him to depart from the river Yamuná to the sea, 4. 286, &c. See also 4. 292, 295, 298, 322, 325, 335; 5. 34.

Káñyadwípa, variant of Kálápadwípa, 3. 325.

Kalkalas, a people, 2. 179.

Kalki, the future epiphany of Vishńu, 3. 31; 4. 229.

Kalmáshánghri = Kalmáshapáda, 3. 305.

Kalmáshapáda, variously genealogized, 1. 8; 3. 304-306, 308, 313, 315.

Kalpa, son of Dhruva and Bhrami, 1. 178.

Kalpa, in chronology, calculation of, 1. 51, &c. Equivalent to a day of Brahmá, 1. 52. The past, or Pádma, Kalpa, 1. 53. The current, or Váráha, Kalpa, 1. 54. Kalpas innumerable, &c., 1. 53. Minor Kalpas, as Samvarta, &c., 1. 53. Duration of a Kalpa, 3. 30; 5. 190. See also P. 37, 52, 68, 80, 85, 93; 1. 41, 80, 88, 91, &c.; 3. 30; 5. 169, 170, 186, 193, 196.

Kalpas, digests of ceremonial rules, five, of the Atharva-veda, &c., 3. 63, 67. See Kalpa-sútra.

Kalpádhikárin, what, 2. 228.

Kalpadruma, a famous mythological tree, 5. 95.

Kalpa-druma-kaliká, the, a composition, referred to, 2. 163, 165 ; 4. 124, 171.

Kalpa-śuddhi, a technicality, defined, 3. 66.

Kalpa-sútra, what, 2. 95. See Kalpas.

Kalpataru, the, a law-book, referred to, 3. 187.

Kalpavaraha, son of Vasudeva and Upadeva, 4. 111.

Káma, the God of Love, 1. 102, 111 ; 3. 189, 190 ; 5. 72, 76, 77. Son of Dharma and Sraddhá, 1. 110. Son of Dharma and Lakshmí, 2. 21. Son of Dharma and Viśwá, and one of the Viśwe devas, 3. 191. See Ananga and Kámadeva.

Káma, the pin of the Sun's axle, 2. 238.

Kámadeva, son of Sahishńu and Yaśodhará, 1. 155. King of the Apsarasea, 2. 86. See also P. 75, 82, and Káma.

Kámadeva, a form of Vishńu, worshipped in Ketumála, 2. 126.

Kámadhenu, the fabulous Cow of Plenty, 2. 339 ; 4. 318.

Kámadugha = Kámaduha, 3. 164.

Kámaduha, a region tenanted by the Pitŕis called Ájyapas, 3. 164, 221.

Kámaga = Kámaduha, 3. 164.

Kámagamas, a class of gods in the eleventh Manwantara, 3. 26.

Kámagiri, a hill, 2. 142.

Kámajas, a class of gods in the eleventh Manwantara, 3. 26.

Kámákhyá = Kámákshí, P. 90 (where correct the spelling) ; 5. 88, 385.

Kámákshí, one with Durgá, as worshipped in Assam, P. 90. See Kámákhyá.

Kámalá, an Apsaras, 2. 83.

Kamalá = Lakshmí, 1. 151.

Kamaláchayá, an Apsaras, 2. 82.

Kamalákara Bhatťa, a modern author, referred to, 3. 89, 90, 103.

Kamalásana, what, in the Yoga philosophy, 5. 230.

Kamalodbhava, an epithet of Brahmá, 5 250. Compare Abjabhava and Abjayoni.

Kámarúpa, a country, 2. 132, 134, 5. 55, 88.

Kámarúpa-tírtha, a place of pilgrimage in Assam, P. 90.

Kámarúpiní, wife of Krishńa, (?) 5. 79.

Kambala, a Nága, son of Kaśyapa, 2. 74, 285, &c. ; 5. 251.

Kambala, variant of Kerala, 2. 165.

Kambalabarhia, son of Uśanas, &c., 4. 63, 64.

Kambalabarhisha, son of Andhraka, 4. 97, 100.

Kambojas, Kámbojas, a people, 2. 176, 181, 182, 184, 339 ; 3. 290, 294, 295. Conquered by Sagara, 3. 291. One with the Caumojees, (?) 3. 292.

Kámboja, a country, 5. 92.

Kampaná, a river, 2. 149.

Kámpilya, son of Haryaśwa, son of Chakshus, 4. 145.

Kámpilya, a city, 2. 161, 341 ; 4. 141, 144, 145.

Kańsa, a Dánava, son of Ugrasena, 4. 98. Is warned of his
own destruction, 4. 248. He
destroys the children of Vasudeva, 4. 259, &c. He sends
demons to discover and destroy
Krishńa, 4. 272, &c. He de-
spatches Akrúra to bring Krishńa to Mathurá, 4. 335, &c. He
holds public games, &c., 5. 23,.
&c., &c. Is slain by Krishńa,
5. 41. See also 4. 110, (where
correct the spelling), 249, 250,
258, 264, 269, 270 271, 320,
339, 341, 344; 5. 6, 9, 11, 18,
21, 43-45, 50, 87.

Kańsá, daughter of Ugrasena, 4.
99.

Kańsaavatí, daughter of Ugrasena,
4. 99.

Kámyá, mother of Uttánapáda,
&c., 1. 108.

Kámyá, daughter of Kardama, and
wife of Priyavrata, 1. 155; 2.
99, 100, 263.

Kámyá, an Apsaras, 2. 81.

Kámya, what, as regards ceremonies, 3. 160.

Kámya-karman, what, 4. 257.

Kámya-śráddha, defined, 3. 147,
189, 190.

Kánas (?), variant of Kanakas, 4.
221.

Kanakas, a people, 4. 221.

Kanaka, variant of Dhanaka, 4. 54.

Kanakhala, now Kankhal, a village near Hardwár, 1. 123.

Kanárka, 5. 312. See Koñárka,
the proper spelling.

Kanavaka, variant of Karandha-
ka, 4. 113.

Kánchana, son of Bhíma, 4. 14,
139.

Kánchanaká, a city, 4. 212. See
Káuchanapurí.

Kánchanaprabha, variant of Kánchana, 4. 14.

Kánchanapurí, a city, 4. 212. See
Kánchanaká.

Káuchí, a city, now popularly
called Conjeveram, P. 86.

Kańd́u, a Muni, the legend of
him, 2. 2, &c.

Kanganíla, variant of Kankańíka,
2. 293.

Kánína, a name of Agnivésya, 3.
336.

Kánína, the term, as used in law,
defined, 4. 102.

Kanishťhas, a class of gods in
the fourteenth Manwantara, 3.
28.

Kankas, a people, 2. 186.

Kankas, a dynasty, 4. 206.

Kanka, son of Ugrasena, 4. 98.

Kanka, son of Śúra, son of Deva-
míd́husha, 4. 101.

Kanka, a mountain-range in Śálmala-dwípa, 2. 194.

Kanká, variant of Kaukí, 4. 99.

Kaukańíka, a serpent, presiding
over the months of Madhu and
Mádhava, 2. 293.

Kankańíra, variant of Kankańíka,
2. 293.

Kankí, daughter of Ugrasena, 4.
99.

Kántápurí, variant of Kántípurí,
4. 217.

Kánti = Lakshmí, the goddess so
called, 5. 68.

Kántíkas, a people, 2. 181.

Kántipurí (correct the spelling), Kántipurí, a city, 4. 217, 219; 5. 392.

Kanurájadas (?), a people, 2. 178.

Káńwas, a race, 4. 145.

Káńwas, a dynasty, 4. 178, 192-194, 232. See Kańwáyanas, for which Kańwas seems to be an error.

Kańwa, disciple of Yájnavalkya, and teacher of the Yajur-veda, 3. 57.

Kańwa, son of Apratiratha, 4. 130; 5. 141.

Kańwa, son of Ajamídha, 4. 140.

Kańwáyanas, a dynasty, 4. 193, 194, 203. See Kańwas.

Kańwáyana, son of Ajátaśatru, 4. 181.

Kańwáyana Bráhmans, sprung from Kańwa, 4. 130, 140.

Kanyá (?), daughter of Kardama, &c., 2. 99, 100.

Kanyá, the term defined, 3. 103, 197, 198.

Kanyakágúńas, a people, 2. 173.

Kapálas, Kápálas, an heretical sect, 5. 287, 375, 380.

Kapálin, a Rudra, 2. 24, 25.

Kapardin, a Rudra, 2. 24.

Kapi, a Rishi in the fourth Manwantara, 3. 8.

Kapi, son of Urukshaya, 4. 137. Born a Kshattriya, he becomes a Bráhman.

Kápí, a river, 2. 149.

Kapila, a Rishi, portion of Vishńu, P. 42; 1. 5, 79; 2. 325; 3. 31, 299, 301, 302. His hermitage, 2, 318; 3. 302. He destroys the sixty thousand sons of Sagara, 3. 300.

Kapila, son of Kardama, son of Brahmá, 1. 108.

Kapila, a Dánava, son of Kaśyapa and Danu, 2. 70.

Kapila, son of Jyotishmat, king of Kuśa-dwípa, 2. 195.

Kapila, son of Vasudeva, 4. 110.

Kapila, son of Vitatha or Bharadwája, 4. 136.

Kapila, a serpent, son of Kaśyapa and Kadrú, 2. 74.

Kapila, a caste in Sálmala-dwípa, 2. 194.

Kapila, a city, 4. 170. See Kapilavastu.

Kapila, a region in Kuśa-dwípa, 2. 195.

Kapila, a mountain-range to the west of Mount Meru, 2. 117.

Kapila, a mountain in Kuśa-dwípa, 2. 197.

Kapilá, a river, 2. 151.

Kapilá, what, predicated of a cow, 5. 252.

Kapila, variant of Kapi, son of Urukshaya, 4. 138.

Kapila, variant of Kámpilya, son of Haryaśwa, 4. 145.

Kapila-samhitá, a part of the Skanda-puráńa, P. 73.

Kapiláśrama, 'Kapila's hermitage,' where, 3. 302.

Kapiláśwa, son of Kuvalayáśwa, 3. 265.

Kápila-upapuráńa, P. 87.

Kapilavastu, the capital of King Suddhódana, 4. 170.

Kapinjalá, a river, 2. 150.

Kapívat, a Rishi in the fourth Manwantara, 3. 8.

Kapotaróman, variously genealogized, 4. 97.

Karabhanjakas, variant of Karabhanjikas, 2. 187.

Karabhanjikas, a people, 2. 187.

Karakas, a people, 2. 178.

Kárakukshiyas, the same as Sálwas, 2. 156.

Karambha, Karambhaka, variants of Karambhi, 4. 68.

Karambhi, son of S'akuni, 4. 68.

Karandhama, variously genealogized, 3. 243, 244.

Karandhama, son of Traisámba, 4. 116.

Karanin, what, in philosophy, 5. 241.

Karanthas, variant of Kunthakas, 2. 180.

Kárapatha, Kárapatha, a country, 3. 319.

Karatas, a people, 2. 180.

Karátaba, a country, 2. 179.

Karatoyá, a river, 2. 149, 154.

Karavíra, a mountain-range to the south of Mount Meru, 2. 124.

Kardama, son of Brahmá, P. 42; 1. 101, &c.; 2. 86. Called son of Daksha, 1. 103, 108, 110, 157; 2. 99, &c., 263; 3. 164.

Kardama, a Devarshi, son of Pulaha, 1. 154, 155; 3. 68.

Kardama, a Lokapála, (?) 2. 263.

Karenumatí, wife of Nakula, 4. 159, 160.

Kardshakas, a people, 2. 175.

Karishiní, a river, 2. 145.

Karishiní (another), a river, 2. 148.

Kárishus (?), Kauśika Bráhmans, 4. 28.

Karitis, a people, 2. 164.

Karkara, variant of Jharjhara, 2. 69.

Karkataka, variant of Karkotaka, 2. 289.

Karkotaka, a serpent, son of Kaśyapa, 2. 74, 285, &c.

Karmajit, variant of Senajit, 4. 174.

Karmánga, certain ceremonies, 3. 147.

Karma - pradípa - bháshya, the, a work by Áśáditya, referred to, 3. 40, 111.

Karmaśa, variant of Kardama, son of Pulaha, 1. 154.

Karmaśreshtha, son of Pulaha, 1. 155.

Karnavatí, daughter of Ugrasena, 4. 99.

Karna, king of Anga, variously genealogized, 4. 102, 126, 142; 5. 130, 131, 133. Slain by Arjuna, 5. 157, 161, 163.

Karnaprávaranas, a people, 2. 162.

Karnata, sprung from Turvasu, 4. 117.

Karnata, a country, the Carnatic, 2. 178.

Karnatakas, a people, 2. 178 (where correct the spelling); 5. 389.

Karniká, an Apsaras, 2. 81.

Karnikas, variant of Jillikas, 2. 178.

Karniu, a sort of arrow so called, 2. 218.

Karabaka, a wind so called, 4. 303.

Kárshńi, patronym of Pradyumna, 5. 75, 116, 120.

Kárta (?), variant of Kunti, son of Dharmanetra, 4. 54.

Kártavírya, patronym of Arjuna, son of Kŕitavírya, 4. 21. He carries off Jamadagni's cow, &c., 4. 21, &c. He takes Rávańa prisoner, 4. 56. He is slain by Paraśuráma, 4. 22, 56. See also 2. 20; 4. 55, 57, 59, 241.

Kárti (?), variant of Kunti, son of Dharmanetra, 4. 54.

Kárttika, a month, Oct.–Nov., 2. 261, &c.; 3. 168, 217.

Kárttika-máhátmya, a part of the Padma-puráńa, P. 33; 2. 275.

Kárttikeya, son of the Kŕittikás, by a father variously named, P. 76, 82, 87, 89; 2. 23, 118, 119; 3. 22; 4. 283; 5. 115, 116. See also Kraunchadáraśa, Kraunchári, Shadánana, and Skanda.

Karundhaka, son of S'úra, son of Devamídhusha, 4. 101, 113.

Karúshas, Kárúshas, a people, 2. 133, 134, 158, 170; 3. 239, 240; 4. 103; 5. 122.

Karúsha, son of Vaivaswata, 2. 158; 3. 14, 232, 233, 239.

Kárúsha, variant of Karúsha, 3. 232.

Káśa, son of S'unahotra, 4. 30, 32, 40, 137.

Káśajas (?), a people, 2. 341.

Káśakas, variant of Kátakas, 4. 184.

Káśára, a promulgator of the Ŕig-veda, 3. 49.

Káśaya (?), variant of Káśi, son of Káśa, 4. 32.

Kaśera, a Bhárgava so called, 5. 218.

Kaśeru, a portion of Bháratavar-sha, 2. 112, 129.

Kaśerumat = Kaśeru, 2. 129.

Kasetu, variant of Kaśeru, 2. 129.

Káśeyas, variant of Kálakas, 4. 184.

Káśeya, variant of Káśi, son of Káśa, 4. 32, 40.

Káśeyi, variant of Káśi, wife of Bhímasena, 4. 159.

Kásheyas, variant of Kálakas, 4. 184.

Kashfaníra, variant of Kachchha-níra, 2. 289.

Káshthá, daughter of Daksha, and wife of Kaśyapa, 2. 26.

Káshthá, a measure of time, variously estimated, 1. 47, 48; 2. 253; 5. 189.

Káśis, a people, and certain kings, 2. 161; 4. 38–40, 137–139, 181, 343; 5. 46, 389, 390.

Káśi, son of Káśa, 4. 32, 39, 137.

Káśi, patronym of Káśa, 4. 344.

Káśí, wife of Bhímasena, son of Páńḍu, 4. 159.

Káśi or Káśí, doubt as to whether any city or kingdom was anciently so called, &c. &c., P. 72, 107; 2. 163; 3. 218, 221, 328, 333; 4. 33, 36, 37, 40, 345; 5. 46, 122, 124–128, 349, 389, 390.

Káśika, variant of Kauśika, son of Vasudeva, 4. 113.

Káśika, variant of Káśa, 4. 136.

Káśiká, the, a grammatical work, referred to, 2. 135.

Káśí-khańḍa, the, a part of the

Skanda-puráńa, P. 72, &c.; 1. 127, 132; 2. 228, 229, 230 .(where correct the spelling), 342; 3. 328; 4. 33.

Káśí-khańda-dípiká, the, a commentary, referred to, 2. 229.

Káśikośala, a people, 2. 157, 172.

Káśí-máhátmya, the, a part of the Kúrma-puráńa, P. 79; 3. 224.

Káśínátha Bhaṭṭa, a modern author, referred to, P. 47-49.

Káśípati, the same as Káśirája, 5. 124, 126.

Káśípurí, the city of the Káśís, 5. 125.

Káśirája, i.e., king of the Káśis, 4. 87; 5. 122, 124, 127. And so the word should be understood in 4. 32, 33, 39, 343-345. But see 4. 137 (note **).

Káśíya, variant of Káśí, son of Káśa, 4. 32 (where correct the spelling), 343.

Káśmíras, peoples so called, 2. 173, 184.

Káśmíra, a country, Cashmere, 4. 223, 224.

Kastaka (?) = Karshaka, 4. 303.

Káśya, son of Senajit, 4. 141.

Káśyá, variant of Kámyá, the Apsaras, 2. 81.

Káśya, variant of Káśa, 4. 30.

Káśyá, variant of Káśí, wife of Bhímasena, 4. 159.

Káśya, ' of the Káśí tribe,' 5. 46.

Kaśyapa, son of Maríchi, 1. 153. Self-born, 2. 338. Called son of Brahmá, 3. 343. His wives, 2. 10, 20, 26. His offspring, 2. 27, &c., 69, &c. See also 1. 102; 2. 27, 108, 285, &c., 306,

307; 3. 3, 4, 8, 11, 13, 15, 18-20, 23, 64, 68, 117, 230, 281, 297; 4. 23-25; 5. 87. See Arishṭanemi.

Kaśyapa, son of Parvasa, 1. 153.

Kaśyapa, an astronomer, referred to, 2. 276, 277.

Kaśyapa, son of Arshṭisheńa, 4. 31.

Kaśyapa, patronym of Akrita-brańa, 3. 64-66.

Kaśyapa, a star so called, in the tail of the Śiśumára or celestial porpoise, 2. 306.

Kaśyapa = Áditya, the sun, 3. 117.

Káśyapa (?), variant of Kaśyapa, son of Maríchi, 2. 288.

Kathá, technical use of, 5. 182.

Kathájava, disciple of Báshkali, and promulgator of the Rig-veda, 3. 50.

Kathaka, a section of the Black Yajur-veda, 3. 173.

Kathá-sarit-ságara, a composition, referred to, 2. 177, 211; 4. 163.

Kaṭha-upanishad, or the commentary on it, quoted, or referred to, 3. 174, 175, 224.

Kati, son of Sálávatí, 4. 28.

Kátyáyanas, sprung from Kati, 4. 28.

Kátyáyana, the grammarian, referred to, 2. 188, 189.

Kátyáyana, his Rigvedánukrama-ńiká referred to, 4. 343.

Kaukundakas, variant of Kaukuṭṭakas, 2. 178.

Kaukuńḍihi, a Rishi in the third Manwantara, 3. 7.

Kaukuntakas, variant of Kaukuṭṭakas, 2. 178.

Kaukuttakas, a people, 2. 178.

Kaulútas, variant of Kolúkas, 2. 174.

Kaumára, a Sarga, or kind of creation, 1. 76, 77.

Kaumára-bhŕitya, ' midwifery and management of children,' 4. 33.

Kaumodakí, a mace borne by Kŕishńa, 5. 51.

Kaurmuda = Kárttika, the month, 4. 268.

Kaunkańas = Konkańas, 2. 178.

Káuntalas = Kuntalas, (?) 3. 293.

Kaunteya, metronym of Arjuna, son of Páńďu. 5. 150, 155, 158.

Kauntí, a country (?), 4. 224.

Kauravas, descendants of Kuru, 3. 237; 5. 131, 133–135, 164.

Kauravyas (?), a people, 2. 175, 341.

Kauravya, a serpent, father of Ulúpí, 4. 160.

Kaurma-puráńa = Kurma-puráńa, P. 23, 77, 78; 3. 67.

Kaurma-upapuráńa, P. 87.

Kauśa = Kuśa-dwipa, 2. 110.

Kauśálí, variant of Vaiśálí, 4. 110.

Kauśálya = Hirańyanábha, 3. 58, 59, 324.

Kauśalya = Yájnavalkya, son of Brahmaráta, 3. 324.

Kauśalya = son of Hirańyanábha, an error in the Raghuvaṁśa, 3. 324.

Kauśalyá, wife of Satwata, 4. 71.

Kauśalyá = Bhadrá, wife of Vasudeva, 4. 109.

Kausalya, ' of Kosala,' 5. 82.

Kauśámbí, a city, 2. 158, 341; 4. 15, 124, 164; 5. 135.

Kauśáravi, patronym of Maitreya, 1. 6.

Kaushítaki, a Śákhá of the Rigveda, 3. 50.

Kaushítaki-bráhmańa, the, referred to, 3. 248.

Kaushítaki - bráhmańa-upanishad, the, referred to, 3. 50, 338; 4. 120, 181.

Kauśijas, a people, 2. 160.

Kauśikas, the, a family, P. 108; 4. 26, 28, 138, 139.

Kauśika, son of Vidarbha, 4. 67.

Kauśika, son of Vasudeva, 4. 110, 113.

Kauśika = Viśwámitra, 3. 293; 3. 23.

Kauśikí, rivers so called, 2. 143, 146, 151. Affluents of one of them, 2. 146. Satyavatí becomes one of them, 4. 18.

Kauśilya (?), variant of Kauśálya, or Hirańyanábha, 3. 58, 324.

Kaustubha, a jewel, produced from the ocean, and possessed by Vishńu, 1. 147; 2. 94.

Kautilya, destroyer of the Nandas, 4. 185, 186.

Káverí, a river, daughter of Yuvanáśwa, and wife of Jahnu, 2. 130, 148; 4. 14, 343.

Káverí (another), a river, 2. 148.

Kavi, son of Chakshusha, 1. 177.

Kavi, son of Práńa, 1. 200; 4. 47.

Kavi, a Ŕishi in the fourth Manwantara, 3. 8.

Kavi, son of Vaivaswata, 3. 232.

Kavi, son of Kŕishńa and Kálindí, 5. 79.

Kavi (another?), 3. 28.

Kavi (still another?), 3. 162.

Kavi, variant of Kapi, son of Urukshaya, 4. 138.

Kaviratha, variant of Suchidratha, 4. 164.

Kavyas, Kávyas, a class of Pitris, 2. 303; 3. 163, 164, 166, 339.

Kávyas, sprung from Kavi (or Kapi?), son of Urukshaya, 4. 138.

Kávya, a Rishi in the fourth Manwantara, 3. 8.

Kávya = Uśanas, 4. 47.

Kávya (?), variant of Káśya, 4. 141.

Kavya, what, 2. 58; 3. 181.

Kavyaváhana, son of Pávaka, (?) 1. 156; 5. 387.

Káya-śuddhi = Chikitsá, 'medical treatment,' 4. 33.

Káya-tírtha, what, 3. 99, 148.

Káyavadha, the same as Kálanemi, the Asura, 4. 250.

Kedáreśwara, a place of. pilgrimage in the Himálayas, P. 75.

Koknyas, a people, 2. 169; 4. 103, 121. See Knikeyas.

Kekaya, variant of Kaikeya, 4. 82, 121; 5. 103.

Kelikilá, variant of Kilikilá, 4. 211.

Kenava, disciple of Śákapúni, and teacher of the Rig-veda, 3. 49.

Kennedy, Col. Vans, his controversial correspondence with Professor Wilson, 5. 257–380.

Keralas, a people, 2. 177; 3. 293.

Kerala, sprung from Turvasu, 4. 117.

Kerala, a country, 2. 165, 179, 341; 4. 24.

Kesari, Kesarin, variants of Keśarin, 2. 199.

Keśarin, a mountain-range in Sáka-dwípa, 2. 199.

Kesava — Vishńu or Kŕishńa, 1. 63, 119, &c. &c.; 2. 7 (where correct the spelling twice), &c.; 3. 79, 85, 253; 4. 88, 277, 289, 297, 306, 322, 334, 341; 5. 2, 8–11, 23, 38, 45, 70, 77, 83, 86, 89, 97, 104, &c. &c., 388. Etymology of the word, 4. 341.

Keśidhwaja, son of Kŕitadhwaja, 3. 333; 5. 213, &c.

Keśikí, mother of Jahnu, son of Suhotra, 4. 14.

Keśin, son of Vasudeva, 4. 109.

Keśin, a Daitya, 4. 250, 272, 320, 335, 339–341; 5. 8, 34, 87, 97. Slain by Kŕishńa, 4. 340.

Keśiní, wife of Viśravas, 1. 154.

Keśiní, daughter of Vidarbha, and wife of Sagara, 3. 297, 298.

Keśiní, wife of Ajamídha, 4. 140.

Keśiní, variant of Keśikí, 4. 14.

Keśisúdana, an epithet of Kŕishńa, 5. 8, 97. See Keśin, the Daitya.

Ketua, a hundred in number, 2. 72.

Ketu, a Dánava, the descending node, son of Viprachitti and Simhiká, 1. 148; 2. 72, 258, 259, 305, 308; 5. 387. Ketu is also called son of Mŕityu, 2. 259.

Ketu, son of Támasa, Manu of the fourth Manwantara, 3. 8.

Ketumála, son of Agnídhra, and king of Gandhamádana, 2. 102.

Ketumála, a region between the

Gandhamádana mountain and the sea, 2. 112, 120, 122, 123, 125, 126, 207.

Ketumálaka = Ketumála, the region, 2. 111.

Ketumat, a Lokapála, son of Rajas, 1. 155; 2. 86, 262, 263.

Ketumat, son of Ambarísha, son of Nábhága, 3. 257.

Ketúmat, son of Dhanwantari, 4. 33.

Ketumat, son of Kshema, son of Sunítha, 4. 37.

Kevala, son of Nara, 3. 245.

Kevala (?), variant of Kerala, the country, 2. 165.

Kha = Ákáša, 5. 198, 255.

Khagaňa, variant of Sankhanábha, 3. 322, 323.

Khalá, daughter of Raudráśwa, and wife of Prabhákara, 4. 129.

Khaláya, Khálaya, variants of Khálíya, 3. 46.

Khálíya, disciple of Śákalya, and promulgator of the Rig-veda, 3. 46.

Kháliya, variant of Khálíya, 3. 46.

Khanapána, variant of Pára, 4. 123.

Khaňdas, 'portions.' Of the Padma-puráňa, P. 30. Of the Skanda-puráňa, P. 72-74. Of Bháratavarsha, &c., 2. 112.

Khaňdas, variant of Shaňdas, 2. 164.

Khaňdapáňi, son of Ahínara, 4. 165.

Khaňdaváyanas, certain Bráhmans, 4. 23.

Khaňdika, patronym of Dharmadhwaja, 5. 217.

Khaňdika, patronym of Mitadhwaja, 5. 217.

Khaňdikya, patronym of Janaka, son of Mitadhwaja, 3. 333; 5. 213, &c., 217, &c. See Janaka.

Khaňdikyajanaka = Janaka, son of Mitadhwaja, 5. 217, 220, 223.

Khaninetra, son of Viviṁśa, 3. 243.

Khanitra, son of Kalmáshapáda, 3. 314.

Khanitra, son of Prajáni, 3. 242, 243.

Khara, a Rákshasa slain by Ráma, 3. 316; 4. 297.

Kharvaťa, what, 4. 266.

Khasá, daughter of Daksha, wife of Kaśyapa, and mother of the Yakshas and Rákshasas, 2. 26, 75.

Khasas, a people, 2. 184, 186, 339; 3. 292.

Khasákas, variant of Khasíras, 2. 186.

Khasíkas, variant of Khasíras, 2. 186.

Khasíras, a people, 2. 185.

Khastima, son of Viprachitti, the Dánava, 2. 1.

Khaťwánga, a royal sage so called, 3. 303.

Khaťwánga = Dilípa, son of Aṁśumat, 3. 303.

Khaťwánga = Dilípa (another), 3. 311-313.

Khaťwángada, the same as the last, 3. 313.

Kheťa, what, 4. 266.

Kheťaka, 'hamlet,' 1. 94.

Khyáti, son of Ulmuka, 1. 178.

Khyáti, son of Támasa, Manu of the fourth Manwantara, 3. 8.

Khyáti, 'celebrity,' daughter of Daksha, and wife of Bhrigu, 1. 109, 118, 150, 152.. Called daughter of Kardama, 1. 110.

Khyáti, a river in Krauncha-dwípa, 2. 198.

Khyáti, variant of Swáti, son of Urú, 1. 178, 179.

Khyáti, variant of Swáhi, 4. 61.

Khyáti, what, in philosophy, 1. 32.

Kíkatas, peoples so called, 5. 178.

Kíkata, a country, South Behar, 5. 178, 351.

Kilagila, a certain mountain and fortress (?), 4. 211.

Kilakalas, variant of Kailakilas, 4. 211.

Kilakilas, variant of Kailakilas, 4. 209, 211, 212.

Kíla-nipátana, what, in the pancratium, 5. 37.

Kilikilá, a city, 4. 211.

Kilikilas, variant of Kailakilas, 4. 211.

Kilinakilas, variant of Kailakilas, 4. 211.

Kimnaras, horse-headed creatures, their origin, &c., 1. 82, 87; 2. 45, 124, 213; 5. 59, 247.

Kimnara, son of Sunakshatra, 4. 168.

Kimnaravarsha = Kimpurusha, a region to the north of Bháratavarsha, 2. 111.

Kimpurushas = Kimnaras, 3. 234; 4. 52.

Kimpurusha, son of Agnídhra, and king of Hemakúta, 2. 102.

Kimpurusha, a Rishi in the second Manwantara, variously genealogized, 3. 5.

Kimpurusha, a region between Himavat and Hemakúta, 2. 103, 114, 125. See Kimnaravarsha.

Kings. Of different orders of beings, 2. 85, 86. Of the Solar race, 3. 229, &c. Of Vaisáli, 3. 246, &c. Of Mithilá, 3 327, &c. Of the Lunar race, 4. 13, &c. Of the Kásis, 4. 30, &c. Of Máhishmatí, 4. 52, &c. Of Chedi, 4. 67, &c. Of Anga, 4. 123, &c. Of Magadha, 4 150, 151, 173, &c., 210, 218. Of future periods, 4. 162, &c. Of Vidisá, 4. 213. Of the Mekalas, 4. 213, &c. Of the Vindhya race, 4. 213, &c. Of the Mahishas, 4. 214. Of Kosalá, 4. 214, 215 (note *). Of the Naishadhas, 4. 215. Of Padmávatí, 4. 217. Of the seashore, 4. 219. Of Kalinga, 4. 220. Of the Naishádns, 4. 221. Of the Kali age, in general, 4. 224, &c.

Kinkiña, variant of Kríkaña, 4. 72.

Kirántís, the now current name of an Himalayan tribe, 2. 130

Kirátas, a people, 2. 129, 130, 162, 171, 176, 184, 187; 3. 295; 5. 88. Their origin, 1.182.

Kirátakas = Kirátas, 2. 186, 339.

Kirmíra, a demon, his abode, 2. 211.

Kírtti, 'fame,' daughter of Daksha, and wife of Dharma, 1. 109, 110; 2. 21.

Kírtti, variant of Kunti, son of Dharmanetra, 4. 54.

Kírttimat, son of Angiras, 1. 154.

Kírttimat, son of Uttánapáda, 1. 159.

Kírttimat, son of Vasudeva, 4. 110.

Kírttiráta, son of Mahádhṛiti, 3. 332.

Kírttiratha, son of Pratíndhaka, 3. 331.

Kisádhyas, variant of Sukuṭyas, 2. 157.

Kishkindhas, a people, 3. 293.

Kitavas, a people, 2. 185.

Kleśa, 'affliction of soul,' 1. 69.

Kodaví, variant of Koṭaví, 5. 117.

Koká, variant of Kośá, 2. 153.

Kokabakas, a people, 2. 179 (where correct the spelling), 341.

Kokanakhas, variant of Kokarakas, 2. 179.

Kokarakas, a people, 2. 179.

Kolas (?), a people, 3. 293.

Kola, sprung from Turvasu, 4. 117.

Koláhala, a certain mountain, 3. 219.

Koláhala, variant of Kálánara, 4. 120.

Kolakilas, variant of Kailakilas, 4. 211.

Kolasarpas (?), a people, 3. 293.

Kolikilas, variant of Kailakilas, 4. 211.

Kollaka, a certain mountain, 2. 141.

Kolúkas, a people, 2. 174.

Komalá (?), variant of Kosalá, 4. 216.

Konáditya, apparently an epithet of Vishṇu, P. 28.

Konárka, evidently the right reading, and synonymous with Konáditya. See Kanárka.

Konkas, a people, 2. 104, 105.

Konkaṇas, a people, 3. 293.

Konkaṇa, districts so called, 2. 179; 4. 211, 222.

Kontalas (?) = Kuntalas (?), 3. 293.

Konwa = Kollaka, a certain mountain, 2. 141.

Kora, a certain hill, 2. 142.

Kośá, a river, 2. 153.

Kosalas, Kośalas, a people, 2. 157, 172, 173, 341; 4. 215, 219, 220.

Kosala, Kośala, countries so called, 2. 145, 172, 173; 3. 264, 318, 319, 323, 324; 4. 171; 5. 82.

Kosalá, Kośalá, a city, 2. 172; 4. 215, 216.

Kosi (??), vulgarly Coosy, a river, and its affluents, 2. 146; 3. 330.

Koṭaví, a goddess so called, 5. 117.

Koṭívarsha = Soṇitapura, 5. 112.

Koṭṭaví, variant of Koṭaví, 5. 117.

Kovida, a caste in Kuśa-dwípa, 2. 197.

Krakacha, a hell, 2. 215.

Kramaṇa, variant of Kṛikaṇa, 4. 72.

Kramu, a river in Plaksha-dwípa, 2. 192.

Kramunja, a mountain-range running eastward from Mount Meru, 2. 117.

Kratha, son of Vidarbha, 4. 67.

Kratu, son of Brahmá, 1. 8, 100, &c.; 2. 285, &c.; 3. 3, 68. His wife, 1. 109, 110. His offspring, 1. 155.

Kratu, son of Uru, 1. 177. Called son of Ulmuka, 1. 178.

Kratu (who?), husband of Hayaśirá, 2. 71.

Kratu, one of the Viśwe devas, 3. 189-191.

Kratu, son of Krishńa and Jámbavatí, 5. 79.

Kratu, a certain star, 4. 233.

Kratu = Indra (?), 1. 123.

Kratudhwaja, variant of Ritadhwaja, 1. 117.

Kratujit, variant of Ritajit, a Yaksha, 2. 289, 292.

Kratujit, variant of Ritujit, son of Anjana, 3. 334.

Kratumat, son of Viśwámitra, 4. 28.

Kraturáta, variant of Kírttiráta, 3. 332.

Kratusthalá, an Apsaras, 2. 81-83, 285, 291.

Krauncha, disciple of Śákapúńi, and promulgator of the Rigveda, 3. 47.

Krauncha, an Asura, slain by Kárttikeya, 2. 119.

Krauncha, a mountain-range in Krauncha-dwípa, 2. 118, 119, 197.

Kraunchadáraña, an epithet of Kárttikeya, 2. 119.

Krauncha-dwípa, a fabulous continent so called, 2. 101, 109, 110, 197, &c.

Kraunchári, an epithet of Kárttikeya, 2. 119.

Kraunchí, daughter of Kaśyapa, wife of Garuḍa, and mother of curlews, &c., 2. 73.

Kraushťuki, named in the Márkańḍeya-puráńa, P. 56 ; 5. 381.

Kravyádas, a class of Pitris, 3. 339.

Kríḍá-khańḍa, a part of the Gańeśa-puráńa, P. 91.

Krikaňa, son of Bhajamána, son of Satwata, 4. 71.

Krikańeyu, son of Raudráśwa, 4. 128.

Krimi, son of Uśínara, 4. 121.

Krimi, wife of Uśínara, 4. 121.

Krimi (?), a river, 2. 146.

Krimi, variant of Nimi, 4. 72.

Krimi, variant of Kritaka, son of Chyavana, 4. 149.

Krimibhaksha = Krimibhojana, 2. 217.

Krimibhojana, a hell, 2. 214, 215.

Krimilá, a city founded by Krimi, son of Uśínara, 4. 121.

Krimilápurí = Krimilá, 4. 122.

Krimiláśwa, variant of Kámpilya, son of Haryáśwa, 4. 145.

Krimipúyavaha, variant of Púyavaha, 2. 218.

Krimíśa, Krimíśa, a hell, 2. 214, 217.

Kripa, a Rishi in the eighth Manwantara, son of Śaradwat, 3. 23 ; 4. 162.

Kripa, variously genealogized, 4. 146, 147 ; 5. 135.

Kripá, a river, 2. 155.

Kripaňa, variant of Krikaňa, 4. 72.

Kripí, variously genealogized, wife of Droña, 4. 146, 147.

Kripí (?), variant of Kritwí, 4. 142.

Kriśángí, an Apsaras, 2. 82.

Kriśáśwa, his wives, 2. 21, 337. His offspring, various weapons, &c., 2. 29 ; 3. 81, 82.

Kriśáśwa, variously genealogized, 3. 247.

Kriśáśwa, son of Saṁhatáśwa, 3. 265, 266.

Krishna, son of Vasudeva and

Devakí, 4. 111, 268. An epiphany of Vishńu, P. 4, 15, 28, &c.; 4. 247; 5. 1. Identified with the Rishi Náráyańa, and also with the supreme Brahma, 4. 247. An impersonation of a black hair of Vishńu, 4. 258, 259. His birth, 4. 268, &c. Is brought up by Nanda and Yaśodá, 4. 275, &c. He slays Pútaná, a female fiend, 4. 276. He overturns a waggon, 4. 279. He throws down two Arjuna-trees, 4. 281. He contends with, overcomes, and banishes, Káliya, a formidable serpent, 4. 286, &c. Is hymned by the serpent, 4. 291, &c. He dissuades Nanda from worshipping Indra, 4. 308, &c. He lifts up Mount Govardhana, and supports it for seven nights, 4. 315; 5. 34. Is made, by Indra, monarch of kine, 4. 318, &c. Is known as Upendra, &c., and why, 4. 318, &c. He sports with the Gopís, 4. 323, &c. He slays the demon Arishťa, in the form of a bull, 4. 333, 334. Is attacked by, and slays, the demon Keśin, in the form of a horse, 4. 339, 340. Is lauded by the Bráhman Nárada, 4. 340, &c. Is hymned by Akrúra, 5. 14, &c. Is conveyed, by Akrúra, towards Mathurá, 5. 17, 18. He slays Kamsa's washerman, 5. 18, 19. Blesses a polite flower-seller, 5. 19, 20. Straightens a crooked maid-servant of Kamsa, 5. 21, 22. Breaks a bow, 5. 23. Kills

Kamsa's elephant, 5. 29, 30. Slays Chámúra, a pancratiast, 5. 39. Slays Kamsa, 5. 41. Inaugurates Ugrasena king, in the place of Kamsa, his son, 5. 45. Studies the science of arms under Sándípani, 5. 46, 47. Slays the Daitya Panchajana, and possesses himself of the conch-shell Pánchajanya, 5. 48. Is besieged, in Mathurá, by Jarásandha, 5. 50, &c. He builds the city of Dwáraká, 5. 56. He destroys Kálayavana, the Yavana king, 5. 57. Repairs to Dwáraká, 5. 63. He is falsely suspected of having killed Prasena, in order to come by the Syamantaka jewel, 4. 76. He recovers the jewel from Jámbavat, king of the bears, 4. 79. He slays Śatadhanwan, the Yádava, 4. 83. He discovers the Syamantaka jewel in the possession of Akrúra, 4. 90. He is acquitted of the theft of it, 4. 91. He falls in love with, and carries off, Rukmińí, 5. 69, &c. He marries Jámbavatí, daughter of the bear Jámbavat, 4. 79. He marries Satyabhámá, daughter of Sattrájita, 4. 80. His other wives besides Rukmińí, &c., 5. 78, &c. He slays Muru, a demon, 5. 89. He slays Naraka, another demon, 5. 90. Is hymned by Aditi, 5. 90, &c. Visits the garden of Indra, and carries away the Párijáta-tree, 5. 93, &c. His 16.100 or 16.108 wives, 4. 112; 5. 82,

705. His 180,000 sons, 5. 108. Rescues Aniruddha from Bána, 5. 112, &c., &c. He overpowers Siva, 5. 115, &c. Is propitiated by him, 5. 119, 120. He slays Paundraka, the false Vasudeva, 5. 125. He burns Benares, 5. 128. Is recalled, by the gods, to heaven, 5. 143. He brings about the destruction of the Yádavas, 5. 149. Is shot by a hunter, Jaras by name, 5. 152. He is burned, and his wives with him, 5. 154. See also 1. 42, 53, 143, 151; 2. 50, 57; 3. 83, 84; 4. 75, &c., 230, 234, 235, 245, &c. &c.

Kŕishńa, son of Havirdhána, 1. 193.

Kŕishńa, a king, variously genealogized, 4. 195, 200, 201.

Kŕishńa, a hell, 2. 214, 219.

Kŕishńa, a caste in S'álmala-dwípa, 2. 194.

Kŕishńa = Vyása, 5. 162. See Kŕishńadwaipáyana.

Kŕishńa, variant of Madhu, son of Arjúna, 4. 57.

Kŕishńá (?) = Kŕishńaveńí, a river, 2. 132, 141, 144, 150, 152.

Kŕishńadwaipáyana, son of Parásara and Satyavatí, 4. 158. The last Vyása, 3. 36, 37. Author of the Mahábhárata, 3. 41. He divided the original Veda into four, &c., 3. 43. See also P. 17, 98; 5. 183.

Kŕishńa-janma-khańda, a part of the Brahma-vaivarta-puráńa, P. 65, 67; 4. 245.

Kŕishńáksha (?), variant of Vŕishńa, 4. 57.

Kŕishńángí, variant of Kŕishángí, 2. 82.

Kŕishńasútra, a hell, 2. 215.

Kŕishńaveńá = Kŕishńaveńí, 2. 130, 150, 152.

Kŕishńaveńí, two rivers so called, one of which is the Kŕishńá, popularly called Kistna, 2. 130, 132, 144, 150, 152.

Kŕita, son of Samnatimat, and disciple of Hiráńyanábha, 3. 60, 61; 5. 390. He compiled six, or else twenty four, Samhitás of the Sáma-veda, 4. 143.

Kŕita, son of Viśwámitra, 4. 27, 28.

Kŕita, son of Vasudeva, 4. 109.

Kŕita, the first age of the world, 1. 96; 3. 29, 31; 4. 157, 229, 236, 237; 5. 170, 179, 181, 184, 185. Its duration, &c., 1. 49, 50.

Kŕita, variant of Yajnakŕita, 4. 44.

Kŕita (?), variant of Kŕiti, son of Kírttiratha, 3. 331.

Kŕita (?), variant of Ŕita, 3. 335.

Kŕita (?), variant of Kŕitaka, son of Chyavana, 4. 149.

Kŕitadharma, variant of Kŕitavarman, 4. 55.

Kŕitadharman, son of Sankŕiti, 4. 44.

Kŕitadhwaja, son of Dharmadhwaja or Janaka, 3. 333; 5. 217.

Kŕitágni, son of Dhanaka, 4. 55.

Kŕitaka, son of Vasudeva, 4. 109.

Kŕitaka, son of Chyavana, son of Suhotra, 4. 149.

Kŕitaka, variant of Kŕikańa, 4. 72.

Kŕitamálá, a river, 2. 130, 132, 155.

Krítanandana, son of Dharma, son of Rámachandra, 4. 211.

Krítanjaya, Vyása of the seventeenth Dwápara age, 3. 35, 37.

Krítanjaya, son of Dharmin, 4. 169.

Krítaratha, variant of Kírttiratha, 3. 331.

Krítasarman, variant of Viswasaha, 3. 314.

Krítasmara, a certain hill, 2. 142.

Kritasthalá, variant of Kratusthalá, 2. 285, 292.

Krítasthalí, variant of Kratusthalá, 2. 285.

Krítaujas, son of Dhanaka, 4. 55.

Krítavarman, son of Dhanaka, 4. 55, 80, 82.

Krítavarman, son of Hrídika, 4. 99; 5. 148.

Krítavatí, variant of Dhrítavatí, 2. 149.

Krítavirya, son of Dhanaka, 3. 81; 4. 2, 54–56.

Krítavrata, disciple of Lomaharshaña, 3. 65.

Krítayajna, variant of Krítaka, son of Chyavana, 4. 149.

Kríteyu, son of Raudráswa, 4. 128, 129.

Kríti, son of Kírttiratha, son of Pratíndhaka, 3. 331.

Kríti, son of Bahuláswa, 3. 335.

Kríti, son of Nahusha, 4. 45.

Kríti, wife of Samhráda, 2. 69.

Kríti (?), variant of Kríta, son of Samnatimat, 3. 60, 61; 4. 143; 5. 390.

Kríti, variant of Yajnakríta, 4. 43.

Kríti, variant of Babhru, son of Romapáda, 4. 67.

Kríti, variant of Dhríti, son of Babhru, 4. 67.

Krítimat, variant of Dhrítimat, son of Yavínara, 4. 142.

Krítin, variant of Riñajya, 3. 35

Krítin (?), variant of Kríta, son of Samnatimat, 4. 143.

Krítin, variant of Krítaka, son of Chyavana, 4. 149.

Krítiráta, variant of Kírttiráta, 3. 332.

Krítiratha, variant of Kírttiratha, 3. 331.

Krítiroman, variant of Mahároman, 3. 332.

Krítma, variant of Kutsa, son of Chákshusha, the Manu, 1. 178.

Krittikás, certain stars so called, 2. 23. Their names, as early reckoned, 2. 337.

Krittiká, a certain asterism, 2.256, &c.; 3. 132; 4. 234, 235.

Krittiratha, variant of Kírttiratha, 3. 331.

Krítwí, daughter of Suka, and variously wedded, 4. 142.

Krítyá, a river, 2. 146.

Krítyá, a certain being produced by magic, 5. 126–128.

Kriyá, 'devotion,' daughter of Daksha, and wife of Dharma, 1. 109, 110. Called daughter of Kardama, and wife of Kratu, 1. 110.

Kriyá-yoga-sára, a reputed portion of the Padma-puráña, P. 30, 33, 34.

Krodha, 'wrath,' 1. 102. Called son of Daksha, 1. 103. Called son of Lobha, 1. 111. Also called son of Mrítyu, 1. 112.

Krodhá = Krodhavaśá, 2 74, 75.

Krodhana, son of Ayuta, son of Rádika, 4. 153.

Krodhavaśá, daughter of Daksha, wife of Kaśyapa, and mother of sharp-toothed monsters in general, 2. 26, 74.

Krodhodana, variant of S'uddhodana, 4. 169.

Kroshṭri, variant of Kroshṭu, 4. 53.

Kroshṭri, variant of Vṛishṇi, 4. 74, 94.

Kroshṭu, son of Yadu, 4. 53, 61.

Kshamá, 'patience,' daughter of Daksha, and wife of Pulaha, 1. 109, 154.

Kshamá, one of the Bháva-prishpas, 4. 294.

Kshamávarta, son of Devala, the Rishi, 2. 24.

Kshaṇa, a measure of time, variously estimated, 1. 47, 48.

Kshánti, variant of Khyáti, the river so called, 2. 198.

Kshapaṇaka, an author, referred to the court of King Vikramáditya, P. 8.

Kshárakardama, a hell, 2. 215.

Kshatadháman (?), variant of Ṛitadháman, 3. 27.

Kshattra (?), son of S'waphalka, 4. 95.

Kshattradharma, variant of Kshattravṛiddha, 4. 43.

Kshattradharma, variant of Kshattradharman, 4. 44.

Kshattradharman, variously genealogized, 4. 43, 44.

Kshattradharman, variant of Kshattravṛiddha, 4. 43.

Kshattraujas, variously genealogized, 4. 180, 181.

Kshattravṛiddha, son of Ayus, son of Purúravas, 4. 30, 38, 43, 44, 138, 344.

Kshattravṛiddha (?), variant of Kshattradharman, 4. 44.

Kshattriyas, 'the martial caste.' Born from the breast of Brahmá, 1. 89, 90. Their duties, 3. 86, 87. Destroyed by Paraśuráma, 4. 23. How preserved, 4. 24, &c. Races of them converted into Brahmans, 3. 258, 259; 4. 29, 130, 137, 145.

Kshattropakshattra (?), son of S'waphalka, 4. 95.

Kshattropeta(?), son of S'waphalka, 4. 95.

Kshaya, variant of Gurukshepa, 4. 167.

Kshema, 'prosperity,' son of Dharma, the Prajápati, 1. 110, 111.

Kshema, son of Idhmajihwa, king of Plaksha-dwípa, 2. 193.

Kshema, son of Sunítha, 4. 37.

Kshemá, an Apsaras, 2. 81, 83.

Kshema, a region in Plaksha-dwípa, 2. 193.

Kshema, variant of Kshemya, son of Ugráyudha, 4. 143.

Kshema, variant of Kshemaka, son of Niramitra, 4. 166.

Kshema, variant of Kshemya, son of S'uchi, 4. 174.

Kshemabhúmi, variant of Devabhúti, 4. 192.

Kshemadhanwan, son of Puṇḍaríka, 3. 320.

Kshemadharman, son of Kákavarṇa, 4. 180.

Kshemádhi, variant of Kshemári, 3. 334.

Kshemajit, variant of Kshattraujas, 4. 180.

Kshemaka, son of Medhátithi, king of Plaksha-dwípa, 2. 191.

Kshemaka, son of Niramitra, 4. 166.

Kshemaka, a Rákshasa, slain by Alarka, 4. 37.

Kshemaka, a division of Plaksha-dwípa, 2. 191.

Kshemakarí, variant of Kshemaukarí, 4. 262.

Kshemakarman, variant of Kshe-madharman, 4. 180.

Kshemankarí, the same as Yoga-nidrá, 4. 262.

Kshemárchis, variant of Kshat-traujas, 4. 18᾿.

Kshemári, son of Sanjaya, son of Supárswa, 3. 334.

Kshemavarman, variant of Kshe-madharman, 4. 180.

Kshemavat, variant of Kshemári, 3. 334.

Kshemavit, variant of Kshattrau-jas, 4. 180.

Kshemya, son of Ugráyudha, 4. 143.

Kshemya, son of Suchi, son of Vipra, 4. 174.

Kshemyá = Yoganidrá, 4. 262.

Kshepaka (?), variant of Kshe-maka, son of Niramitra, 4. 166.

Kshepana, what, in the pancra-tium, 5. 36.

Kshetra = Nakshatra, 2. 257.

Kshetradharman, variant of Kshat-tradharman, 4. 44.

Kshetrajna, variant of Kshattrau-jas, 4. 180.

Kshetrajna, 'embodied spirit,' form of Vishńu, 1. 29; 5. 241.

Kshetropeksha, son of Swaphalka, 4. 96.

Kshipraka, variant of Sipraka, 4. 194.

Kshíra, a sea of milk, encompassing Sáka-dwípa, 2. 201.

Kshudhi, son of Kríshńa and Mi-travindá, 5. 79.

Kshudra, 'elated by petty gain,' 3. 135.

Kshudrabaka, variant of Kshu-draka, 4. 170.

Kshudraka, son of Prasenajit, 4. 170.

Kshulika (?), variant of Kuńďaka, 4. 171.

Kshullaka, variant of Kuńďaku, 4. 171.

Kshupa, variously genealogized, 3. 242, 243.

Kubera, god of wealth, a Devarshi, son of Visravas, 1. 119, 122, 154; 2. 86, 112; 3. 32, 68, 116, 246, 273; 4. 281; 5. 15, 100, 137, 138, 386, 388. His city, 2. 112, 118.

Kuchchhilá, variant of Pichchhilá, 2. 151.

Kuchídi (?), variant of Kushídin, 3. 60.

Kuchírá, a river, 2. 150.

Kudmala, a hell, 2. 215.

Kuhaka, a Nága, 2. 38.

Kuhú, daughter of Angiras, 1. 153.

Kuhú, a river in India, 2. 155.

Kuhú, a river in Sálmala-dwípa, 2. 195.

Kuhú, 'the last day of the moon's wane,' 2. 261, 342.

Kujambha, a demon, slain by Indra, 4. 3, 334.

Kujámbha, a Daitya, slain by Vidúratha, 3. 242.

Kukkuras = Daśárhas, 2. 178.

Kukkurángáras (?), a people, 2. 178

Kukuheyu, variant of Kakaheyu, 4. 128.

Kukshi, disciple of Paushpinji, and promulgator of the Sáma-veda, 3. 61.

Kukshi, son of Ikshwáku, 3. 297.

Kukshí, daughter of Priyavrata, 2. 100.

Kukuras, a people, 2. 162, 178; 5. 147, 150.

Kukura, son of Andhaka, 4. 96, 97; 5. 132.

Kuláchala = Kula-parvata, 2. 113, 125.

Kuláchárya, what, 3. 260.

Kulachchhas (?), variant of Kulat-thas, 2. 182.

Kuládya (?), a country, 2. 165.

Kula-guru, what, 3. 292.

Kulaka, a caste in Kuśa-dwípa, 2. 197.

Kulaka, variant of Kuńḍaka, 4. 171.

Kúlakas, variant of Kálakhanjas, 2. 71

Kulála, variant of Kuśála, 4. 189.

Kula-parvata, 'a mountain-range,' 2. 127

Kulatthas, a people, 2. 182.

Kulika, variant of Kuńḍaka, 4. 171.

Kúlika, a king, 4. 171.

Kulindas, a people, 2. 180.

Kalindopatyakas, a people, 2. 176.

Kullúka, a commentator on the

Mánava-dharma-śástra, referred to, or cited, 1. 194; 2. 134, 143, 215, 216, 303; 3. 89, 100, 104, 107–109, 114, 131, 138, 148, 154, 168, 174, 176, 179, 187, 225; 4. 26; 5. 115.

Kulpa (?), sprung from Turvasu, 4. 117.

Kulútas, a people, 2. 174.

Kulútas (?), variant of Utúlas, 2. 174.

Kumálaka = Sauvíra, 2. 174.

Kumáras, certain saints so called, 1. 77, &c., 115.

Kumára, a Prajápati, 1. 102.

Kumára, son of Agni or Anala, 2. 23. See Kárttikeya, especially in 4. 283.

Kumára, son of Bhavya, king of S'áka-dwípa, 2. 198.

Kumára, a division of S'áka-dwípa, 2. 198.

Kumárá, a river, 2. 131.

Kumáragupta, a king, 4. 219.

Kumára-sambhava, the, a poem by Kálidása, referred to, 2. 181.

Kumárasiṁha, an astronomer, referred to the court of King Vikramáditya, P. 9.

Kumára-tantra = Kaumára-bhúti-tya, 4. 33.

Kumárí, a river in India, 2. 154. See Kumárá.

Kumárí, a river in S'áka-dwípa, 2. 199.

Kumárí, Cape Comorin, 2. 127. 132.

Kumárí (?) = Kumárá, 2. 131, 132.

G

Kumáriká, a portion of Bhárata-váraha, 2. 112, 129.

Kumáriká-khánd'a, a part of the Skanda-puráña, 4. 195.

Kamári-pújá, what, 5. 316, 332.

Kumbhaka, what, in the Yoga philosophy, 4. 308 ; 5. 231.

Kúmbhakarña, son of Viśravas, 1. 154.

Kumbhánd'a, minister of Báña, son of Bali, 5. 109.

Kumbhi, variant of Kunti, son of Kratha, 4. 67.

Kumbhípáka, a hell, 2. 215.

Kumodaka, an epithet of Kŕishña, 5. 51.

Kumuda, disciple of Pathya, and teacher of the Atharva-veda, 3. 62.

Kumuda, a mountain to the north of Mount Meru, 2. 115, 116 ; 3. 9.

Kumuda, a mountain-range in S'álmala-dwípa, 2. 194, 195.

Kumudádi, disciple of Pathya, and teacher of the Atharva-veda, 3. 62.

Kumuda-dwípa = Kuśa-dwípa, the mythological island so called, 2. 129.

Kumudáhi (?), variant of Kumu-dádi, 3. 62.

Kumudári, variant of Kumudádi, 3. 62.

Kumudwatí, a river in India, 2. 155.

Kumudwatí, a river in Krauncha-dwípa, 2. 198.

Kunakas, variant of Karaṣas, 2. 180.

Kuṇakhin, what, 3. 176.

Kunda, a mountain in S'álmala-dwípa, 2. 195.

Kuńd'aka, son of Kshudraka, 4. 171.

Kuńd'alá, a river, 2. 148.

Kuńd'alas, variant of Kuńthakas, 2. 180.

Kuńd'áśin, what, 2. 218.

Kuńd'ina = Condavir, 2. 159 (where correct the spelling) ; 5. 69–71, 389.

Kuńd'inapura, the same as Kuńd'ina, and yet identified, by Professor Wilson, with Kundapoor, 5. 69.

Kuńi, son of Satyadhwaja, 3. 334.

Kuńi, variant of Túńi, 4. 93.

Kúnika, son of S'reńika, 5. 391.

Kuntas (?), a people, 2. 169.

Kuntala, countries so called, 2. 157.

Kuntalas, peoples, two or more, 2. 157, 172, 178.

Kuntalas, variant of Kulatthas, 2. 182.

Kuntala S'átakarńi, son of Mahendra S'átakarńi, 4. 202.

Kuntalaswátí (?), variant of Kuntalaswátikarńa, 4. 200.

Kuntalaswátikarńa, son of Mŕigendra, 4. 200.

Kuntaprávarañas, a people, 2. 169.

Kuńthakas, a people, 2. 180.

Kuntis, a people, 2. 162.

Kunti, variously genealogized, 4. 54.

Kunti, son of Kratha, 4. 67.

Kunti, son of Kŕishña and Satyá, 5. 79.

Kunti, wife of Páńd'u, 4. 80, 159, 321 ; 5. 96, 150, 155.

Kunti, a country, 2. 164.

Kuntí, a river, 2. 132.

Kunti = Kuntibhoja, 4. 101.

Kunti = Kachchha, 2. 164.

Kuntibhoja, father of Pŕithá, 4. 101, 321.

Kuntijit, variant of Ŕitujit, 3. 334.

Kuntikas, variant of Kuntalas, 2. 178.

Kupathas, a people, 2. 182.

Kurara, variant of Kurarí, 2. 117.

Kurarí, a mountain-range to the east of Mount Meru, 2. 117.

Kuraŕas, variant of Karaŕas, 2. 180.

Kurávas (?), a class of Apsarases, 2. 82.

Kúrcha, what, 5. 383.

Kúrma, an epiphany of Vishńu as a tortoise, P. 78.

Kúrma-puráńa, analysis of it, &c., P. 20, 24, 26, 76, &c., 83; 5. 286, 288, 298, 301, 322, 325, 375.

Kurus, a people, 2. 132, 133, 143, 156, 182.

Kurus, a dynasty, 4. 184; 5. 132, 133, 140.

Kuru, son of Saḿvarańa, 1. 191; 3. 79; 4. 145, 148, 152, 237; 5. 231, 133, 134, 150, 164.

Kuru, son of Agnídhra, and king of a country abutting on the Śŕingavat range, 2. 102.

Kuru, a region, 2. 111, 123, 125, 126, 156, 176, 207.

Kuru, a caste in Plaksha-dwípa, 2. 193.

Kuru (?), variant of Kuruvaśa, 4. 69.

Kurujángalas, a people, 2. 156, 176.

Kurujángala, a country, 2. 176.

Kuruka, variant of Ruruka, 3. 289.

Kurukhet, where situated, P. 76; 2. 143. See Kurukshetra, of which it is a popular corruption.

Kurukshetra, a district, P. 55, 76; 2. 133, 143; 3. 343; 4. 8, 148, 164; 5. 248. See Kurukhet.

Kuruńdí, a Ŕishi in the third Manwantara, 3. 7.

Kurura, variant of Kuru, a caste so called, 2. 193.

Kurúttháma, variant of Varuttha, 4. 117.

Kuruvaḿśa, son of Madhu, son of Devakshattra, 4. 70.

Kuruvaḿśaka = Kuruvaḿśa, 4. 70.

Kuruvaŕńakas, a people, 2. 176.

Kuŕuvaśa, son of Madhu, son of Devakshattra, 4. 69.

Kuruvat, variant of Puruvat (?), 3. 191.

Kuruvatsa, son of Anavaratha, 4. 69.

Kuśa, son of Ráma, 2. 172, 173; 3. 318-320.

Kuśa, variously genealogized, 4. 15, 16, 343.

Kuśa, variant of Leśa, 4. 31, 43, 343.

Kuśa, variant of Kauśika, son of Vidarbha, 4. 67.

Kuśa, variant of Kuśámba, son of Vasu, 4. 149.

Kuśabindus, a people, 2. 176.

Kuśachírí, a river, 2. 149.

Kuśadhárá, a river, 2. 149.

Kuśadhwaja, variously genealogized, 3. 333.

Kuśádhyas, variant of Sukuŕyas, &c., 2. 157, 165.

Kuśádi (?), variant of Kushídin, 3. 60.

Kuśa-dwípa, a fabulous continent, surrounded by a sea of wine, 2. 101, 109, 195, &c. See Kauśa.

Kuśa-dwípa, an island, the same as Kumuda-dwípa, 2. 129.

Kuśágra, son of Bṛihadratha, son of Vasu, 4. 150.

Kuśágrya (?), variant of Kuśágra, 4. 150.

Kuśájas, variant of Kuśalas, 2. 172, 341.

Kuśalas, a people, 2. 172; 4. 216.

Kuśalas, a caste in Kuśa-dwípa, 2. 197.

Kuśala, son of Dyutimat, king of Krauncha-dwípa, 2. 197.

Kuśála, son of Aśokavardhana, 4. 189.

Kuśala, a region in Krauncha-dwípa, 2. 197.

Kuśála (?), variant of Kusumoda, son of Bhavya, and a region, 2. 198.

Kuśala, variant of Sumálya, 4. 185.

Kuśalyas, variant of Sukutyas, &c., 2. 157.

Kuśámba, son of Kuśa, 4. 15, 16.

Kuśámba, son of Vasu, 4. 149, 150.

Kuśanábha, son of Kuśa, 4. 15, 16.

Kuśanábha, variant of Práṁśu, 3. 232.

Kuśanára, variant of Kuśadhárá, 2. 149.

Kuśáṅḍas, variant of Sukutyas, &c., 2. 157, 165.

Kuśanku, variant of Rushadgu, 4. 61.

Kuśárava, patronym of Maitreya,

Kuśastamba, variant of Kuśámba, son of Kuśa, 4. 15.

Kuśasthalí = Dwáraká, P. 107; 2. 172; 3. 249, 253, 255, 320; 5. 56.

Kuśasthalí = Kuśávatí, 2. 172; 3. 319, 320.

Kuśáśwa (??), variant of Kuśámba, son of Kuśa, 4. 15.

Kuśávatí, a city, 2. 172; 3. 320. See Kuśasthalí.

Kuśávirá, variant of Kuśachírá, 2. 149.

Kuśeśaya, a mountain in Kuśa-dwípa, 2. 196.

Kushídin, disciple of Paushpinji, and teacher of the Sáma-veda, 3. 60.

Kushmáṇḍas, Kúshmáṇḍas, certain demigods, 1. 166; 3. 116; 4. 277; 5. 94.

Kuśída, disciple of Paushpinji, and teacher of the Sáma-veda, 3. 61.

Kuśídi (?), variant of Kushídin, 3. 60.

Kuśídin (?), variant of Kushídin, 3. 60.

Kuśika, a family named from the father of Viśwámitra, 3. 16, 23.

Kuśika (?), variant of Rushadgu, 4. 61.

Kuśika, son of Kuśa, 4. 15, 16.

Kuśin (?), variant of Kushídin, 3. 60.

Kuśíti (?), variant of Kushídin, 3. 60.

Kusumapura = Páṭaliputra, a city, 4. 182, 204.

Kuśumi (?), variant of Kuthumi, 3. 60.

Knsumi, variant of Subhúmi, son of Ugrasena, 4. 99.

Kusumoda, son of Bhavya, king of S'áka-dwípa, 2. 198.

Kusumoda, a region in S'áka-dwípa, 2. 198.

Kúta (?), a mountain-range to the north of Mount Meru, 2. 117. See S'ankhakúta.

Kúťágára, what, 5. 194.

Kúťakas, a people, 2. 104, 105.

Kúťaka, a mountain, 2. 141.

Kutapa, the term explained, 3. 187, 188.

Kúťaśaila, a certain hill, 2. 142.

Kúťaśálmali, a hell, 2. 215.

Kuthami (?), variant of Kuthumi, 3. 60.

Kuthapravarayas (?), variant of Kantaprávaraňas, 2. 169.

Kuthumi, disciple of Paushpinji, and teacher of the Sama-veda, 3. 60, 61

Kuťí, what, 5. 30.

Kuťílá, a river, 2. 155.

Kutsa, son of Chákshusha, Manu of the sixth Manwantara, 1. 178.

Kuťťáparántas, a people, 2. 169.

Kuťťapracharaňas, a people, 2. 169.

Kuťťaprávaraňas, a people, 2. 169.

Kuva, variant of Gova, 2. 164.

Knvaláśwa, variant of Kuvala-yáśwa, 3. 264.

Kuvalaya, Pratardana's horse, 4. 36.

Kuvalayápíďa, a Daitya, in the form of an elephant, slain by Kŕishňa, 4. 320, 336, 337; 5. 24, 87.

Kuvalayáśwa = Dhundhumára, son of Bŕihadaśwa, 3. 264.

Kuvalayáśwa = Pratardana, 4. 36.

Kuveňá, variant of Tungaveňá, 2. 150.

Kuvírá, variant of Kuchírá, 2. 150.

Laghiman, the term defined, 3. 311.

Laghu, a measure of time, 1. 48, 49.

Laghu-śiva-puráňa, a mythological work, P. 36.

Lagna, in astrology, 4. 66.

Lainga-puráňa = Linga-puráňa, P. 23, 67; 3. 67.

Lajjá, 'modesty,' daughter of Daksha, and wife of Dharma, 1. 109, 110.

Lajjádhára, variant of Jaládhára, 2. 198.

Lakshaňá, an Apsaras, 2. 81–83.

Lakshmaňa, son of Daśaratha, son of Aja, 3. 314, 316, 318; 4. 247.

Lakshmaňá, an Apsaras, 2. 81.

Lakshmaňá, daughter of the king of the Madras, and wife of Kŕishňa, 5. 78, 80, 81, 83, 107.

Lakshmaňá, daughter of Duryodhana, 5. 130.

Lakshmí, 'prosperity,' a goddess. Daughter of Daksha and Prasúti, 1. 109. Wife of Dharma, 1. 110; 2. 21. By another account, daughter of Bhŕigu and Khyáti, and wife of Nárá-yaňa or Vishňu, 1. 118, &c., 152. By still another account, born from the ocean, when churned, and taken by Vishňu, 1. 144, 145 A S'akti of Vish-

ńu, P. 71 ; 1. 104, 142. Hymned by S'akra or Indra, 1. 147, &c. See also P. 100; 5. 68, 289, 291, 387. Other names of Lakshmí are Bhúti, Chalá, Kamalá, Kánti, Má, Mádhaví, Padmá, Srí, &c.

Lakshmí, a Kalpa, P. 77.

Lakshmí Náráyańa, a combination of Lakshmí and Náráyańa, P. 32.

Lakshmípura, the city of Bhrigu, on the river Narmadá, 1. 150.

Lakshmívallabha, a modern author, referred to, 2. 163, 165; 4. 124, 171.

Lákulas (?), an heretical sect, 5. 380.

Lálábbakaha, a hell, 2. 215, 218.

Lalitá Deví, a form of Durgá, P. 86.

Lambá, 'an arc of the heavens,' daughter of Daksha, and wife of Dharma, 2. 21, 22.

Lambá = Kot'aví, &c., 5. 117.

Lambana, son of Jyotishmat, king of Kuśa-dwípa, 2. 195.

Lambana, a division of Kuśa-dwípa, 2. 195.

Lambodara, son of Sátakarńi, 4. 196, 200, 202.

Land, measures of, 1. 92, &c.

Lángalas, variant of Jángalas, 2. 176.

Lángala, variant of Rátula, 4. 170.

Lángali, disciple of Paushpinji, and teacher of the Sáma-veda, 3. 60, 61.

Lángalin = Haláyudha or Bala-bhadra, 5. 65, 66.

Lángulini, a river, 2. 155.

Lanká, an island, 2. 129; 3. 318; 5. 284.

Lanká, a city, 2. 111, 113, 207; 4. 56.

Lankápura = Lanká, the city, 2. 113.

Lárgas, variant of Bhargas, 2. 171.

Láśya, variant of Leśa, 4. 30.

Lát'a, a country, 2. 159.

Laugákshi, disciple of Paushpinji, and teacher of the Sáma-veda, 3. 60, 61.

Lauheyí, an Apsaras, 2. 82.

Lauhí, son of Alarka, 4. 38.

Lauhitya, a river, 2. 154.

Laukákshi (?), variant of Laugákshi, 3. 60.

Lava, son of Ráma, 3. 318, 319.

Lava, a measure of time, 1. 48.

Lavańa, a Rákshasa, son of Madhu, 1. 165; 3. 318.

Lavańa, variant of Savana, a hell, 2. 214, 217.

Laya, what, 5. 244.

Lekhas, a class of gods in the sixth Manwantara, 3. 12.

Length, measures of, 1. 92, &c.

Leśa, son of S'unahotra, 4. 30, 43, 343, 344.

Libations, how offered, 3. 115.

Liberation, when it is effected, 5. 241.

Light, or fire, the element, 1. 35.

Lightninga, the, their origin, 2. 28.

Likhita-amriti, the, a code of law, quoted, or referred to, 3. 189, 191.

Lílá, what, 4. 267, 326.

Lílávatí, the, a work on arithmetic, referred to, 5. 84, 188.

Linga, the, or 'phallus,' the type

of Síva, P. 67, &c. ; 5. 283, 338, 341, 354.

Linga-puráña, analysis of it, &c., P. 20, 24, 67, &c., 71, 79, 83, 89 ; 5. 264, 294, 298, 306, 308, 327, 341, 379.

Lobha, 'cupidity.' Sprung from Brahmá, 1. 102. Called son of Dharma, 1. 110. Called son of Dambha, 1. 111.

Lochana (?), variant of Rochana, 3. 191.

Lobscháriñí, variant of Lohatáriñí, 2. 147.

Lohadáraka, a hell, 2. 215.

Lohamukhas, a people, 2. 162.

Lohaśanku, a hell, 2. 215.

Lohitas, a class of gods in the twelfth Manwantara, 3. 27.

Lohitas, certain Kauśika Bráhmans, 4. 28.

Lohitádhipa = Lohitánga, 2. 259.

Lohitánga, or Mars, son of Sarva and Vikeśí, 1. 117 ; 2. 259.

Lohitárchis = Lohitánga, 2. 259.

Lohatáraní, variant of Lohatáriñí, 2. 147.

Lohatáriñí, a river, 2. 147.

Lohita, a river, 2. 154.

Lohitárña, son of Ghritapṛishṭha, king of Krauncha-dwípa, 2. 198.

Lohitárña, a region in Kraunchadwípa, 2. 198.

Lohitoda, a hell, 2. 215.

Lohityá, a river, 2. 154.

Lokas, 'worlds,' or 'spheres,' various, P. 31 ; 2. 225, &c.

Lokákshi (?), variant of Laugákshi, 3. 60, 61.

Lokáloka, a fabulous zoniform mountain, 2. 204, &c., 261, 263.

Lokapálas, four, or eight, in number, 1. 153–155 ; 2. 86, 112, 118 ; 3. 171, 172.

Lokáyatas, an heretical sect, 5. 380. And see 3. 211 (note †).

Lomaharshaña = Romaharshaña, P. 17–19, 28, 30, 45 ; 3. 42, 43, 64, 65.

Lomapála, variant of Romapáda, son of Vidarbha, 4. 67.

Lomapáda, variant of Romapáda, son of Chitraratha, 4. 124.

Lopámudrá, wife of Agastya, 4. 36.

Lunar days held sacred by the Vaishñavas, 2. 67.

Má = Lakshmí, 5. 387.

Mada, 'insanity,' sprung from Brahmá, 1. 102.

Madabhúta (?), son of Vasudeva, 4. 109.

Madana = Káma, 5. 72.

Madanotsava, a certain festival, I' 64.

Madayantí, wife of Saudása, son of Sudása, 3. 308, 310.

Mádhava = Vishñu or Kṛishña, 1. 60 ; 2. 313 ; 4. 327, 329 ; 5. 75.

Mádhava, commentator on the Paráśara-smṛiti, quoted, 3. 103.

Mádhava, founder of a religious sect. See Mádhwa.

Mádhava = Vaiśákha, a month, April–May, 2. 261.

Mádhaví, patronym of Pradyumna, 5. 75.

Mádhaví = Sri or Lakshmí, consort of Mádhava or Vishñu, 1. 60.

Madhu, a Ríshi in the sixth Manwantara, 3. 12, 14.

Madhu, a Rákshasa, slain by Kṛishṇa, 1. 165; 2. 52, &c.; 3. 34, 318; 4. 78, 278, 324, 330, 338; 5. 3, 40, 45, 58, 100, 101, 106, 114.

Madhu, son of Bindumat, 2. 107.

Madhu, variously genealogized, 4. 57, 58.

Madhu, son of Arjuna, son of Kṛitavírya, 4. 57.

Madhu, the family of, named from Madhu, its founder, 4. 58.

Madhu, son of Devakshattra, &c., 4. 68-70.

Madhu, son of Purudwat, 4. 69.

Madhu = Chaitra, a month, March-April, 2. 261.

Madhu Achárya, founder of a sect, his time, P. 16; 5. 258, 338, 347, 356.

Madhuchchhandas, variously genealogized, 4. 26, 28.

Madhudhwaja, variant of Madhu, son of Arjuna, 4. 57.

Madhudwish, an epithet of Vishṇu or Kṛishṇa, 5. 117. Compare Madhusúdana.

Madhuhan, what, 2. 219.

Madhuká, variant of Dhanuká, the river, 2. 199.

Madhukulyá, a river in Kuśa-dwípa, 2. 197.

Mádhumatas = Káśmíras, 2. 173, 341.

Mádhumatí, a river, 2. 341.

Madhumattas, a people, 2. 173.

Madhunandi, a king, 4. 212.

Madhunighátin, an epithet of Vishṇu or Kṛishṇa, 4. 330. Compare Madhusúdana.

Madhunishúdana = Madhusúdana, 4. 301.

Madhupadhwaja, variant of Jayadhwaja, 4. 57.

Madhupriya, an epithet of Akrúra, 4. 338.

Madhurá, variant of Mathurá, 3. 318.

Madhuraha, son of Ghṛitapṛishtha, king of Krauncha-dwípa, 2. 198.

Madhuraha, a division of Krauncha-dwípa, 2. 198.

Madhusúdana, an epithet of Kṛishṇa, 1. 112, 119; 3. 75; 4. 278, 279, 286, 291, 301, 317, 320, 324; 5. 8, 38, 41, 71, 86, 87, 100, 101, 106, 127, &c. &c.

Madhuváhiní, a river, 2. 150.

Madhuvana, a grove on the river Yamuná, 1.. 165; 3. 318; 5. 388.

Madhuvidwish, an epithet of Vishṇu or Kṛishṇa, 5. 117. Compare Madhusúdana.

Mádhwa, or Mádhava, founder of a sect, P. 49, 50.

Madhwáchárya. See Madhu Achárya.

Madhya, 'a thousand billions,' 5. 188.

Madhya-deśa, the country along the river Narmadá, 4. 64, 169.

Madhyamáshṭaká, a certain holiday, 3. 109.

Madhyamikas, Mádhyamikas, a Bauddha sect, 3. 210.

Madhyandina, son of Pushpárṇa, 1. 178.

Madhyandina, teacher of the Yajur-veda, 3. 57.

Madirá, wife of Vasudeva, son of
S'úra, 4. 109, 110.

Madirá = Váruñi, goddess of wine,
5. 65, 66.

Madras, peoples so called, 2. 133,
135, 163, 180, 339; 3. 293;
5. 80.

Madrá, daughter of Raudráśwa,
and wife of Prabhákara, 4. 129.

Madra, a country, 2. 156, 163; 4.
5, 159; 5. 80, 83.

Madrá, a river, 2. 155.

Madrabhujingaa, a people, 2. 161.

Mádrakas, Madrakas, a people, 2.
163, 339; 4. 121, 217.

Madraka, son of S'ibi, son of Uśinara, 4. 122.

Mádravas(?), variant of Amavat (?),
3. 189, 191.

Mádreyajángalas, a people, 2. 156.

Mádrí, wife of Vrishñi, son of
Bhajamána, 4. 73, 74, 94.

Mádrí, wife of Páñd'u, 4. 103, 159.

Mádrí, patronymy apparently, of
Suśílá, Lakshmaná, and Mitravindá, wives of Krishña, 5. 80-
83, 107.

Madura, variant of Mridura, 4.
94, 96.

Magas, heliolaters in S'áka-dwípa,
corresponding to terrestrial
Bráhmans, P. 64; 2. 200; 5.
381-385.

Magadhas, Mágadhas, a people,
2. 132, 165, 170; 4. 218; 5. 56.

Mágadhas, a dynasty, 4. 184.

Mágadhas, the Kshattriyas of
S'áka-dwípa, 2. 200. See Magasas.

Mágadha, a Rishi in the fourteenth
Manwantara, 3. 28.

Magadha, a country, 2. 134; 4. 15,
149, 151, 171, 173, 191, 203,
204, 208, 218, 231, 273, 345;
5. 50, 51, 56.

Magadhá, a city (?), 4. 216.

Mágadha, a 'bard,' or the name
of one, the origin of, 1. 184,
&c.

Mágadha, a measure, 5. 189, 190.

Magasas, the Kshattriyas of S'áka-
dwípa, 5. 382. See Mágadhas.

Maghá, the tenth lunar asterism,
2. 258, &c.; 3. 197; 4. 230,
233, 234, 236.

Mágha, a month, Jan.–Feb., 2.
261, &c.; 3. 109, 168–170.

Mághada, a caste in S'áka-dwípa,
2. 200.

Maghavat = Indra, 1. 173; 2. 78,
79.

Magi, the, identified with the Magas and the Mughs, 5. 384.

Mahábáhu, a Daitya, or else a
Dánava, 4. 272, 320.

Mahábáhu, variant of Mahábhoja,
4. 72.

Mahábala (?), son of Krishña and
Rukmiñí, 5. 78.

Mahábala, variant of Vipra, son of
Srutanjaya, 4. 174.

Mahábhadra, a lake in the grove
called Dhriti, 2. 117. See Maháhrada.

Mahábhága, variant of Mahábhoja,
4. 72.

Mahábhárata, the, a celebrated
heroic poem, its composition, 3.
41. See also P. 4, et passim.

Mahábháshya, the, a grammatical
commentary, referred to, 2. 152.

Mahábhauma, son of Ariha, 4. 128.

Mahábhoja, son of Satwata, 4. 71–73.

Mahá-buddhi, the same as Mahat, 5. 199.

Mahabulipoor, the popular name of a town on the Coromandel coast, 4. 316.

Maháchittá, an Apsaras, 2. 82.

Mahádeva, Rudra or Síva, P. 89; 1. 104, 116, 122, 124, 128, 129, 134, &c. &c.; 4. 262; 5. 53, 386.

Mahádevá, variant of Sahadevá, 4. 98.

Mahádhṛiti, son of Vibudha, 3. 332.

Mahádruma, son of Bhavya, king of Sáka-dwípa, 2. 198.

Mahádruma, a region in Sáka-dwípa, 2. 198.

Mahágaurí, a river, 2. 153.

Maháhaya, variant of Haya, 4. 53.

Maháhrada, a lake in the grove called Dhṛiti, 2. 112. See Mahábhadra.

Mahájwála, a hell, 2. 214, 217.

Mahákalpa, a certain vast measure of time, 1. 53.

Mahámanas, son of Mahámaṇi, 4. 120.

Mahámaṇḍala, son of Tulakuchi, 4. 186.

Mahámaṇi, son of Janamejaya, son of Puranjaya, 4. 120.

Mahámáyá, a form of Párvatí, P. 89.

Mahámáyá, the same as Yoganidrá, 4. 260.

Mahámoha, what, in philosophy, 1. 69.

Mahámuni, a Ṛishi in the fifth Manwantara, 3. 10, 11.

Mahánábha, son of Hiraṇyáksha, the Daitya, 2. 70.

Mahánada, a river, 2. 131, 142, 148, 155.

Mahánadí, a river, 2. 313.

Mahánandi, variant of Mahánandin, 4. 182.

Mahánandin, son of Nandivardhana, 4. 182, 183.

Mahánaraka, a hell, 2. 215.

Mahánasa, a mountain in Sáka-dwípa, 2. 200.

Mahánila, a serpent, son of Kaśyapa, 2. 74.

Mahániraya, a hell, 2. 215.

Mahánta, son of Dhímat, son of Viráj, 2. 107.

Mahápadma, king of Magadha, and one with Nanda, 4. 171, 184, 185.

Mahápadma, a serpent, son of Kaśyapa, 2. 74, 285, &c.

Mahápadma, what, in numeration, 4. 184; 5. 189, 392.

Mahápadmapati = Mahápadma, or Nanda, 4. 184.

Mahápagá, variant of Mahopamá, 2. 151.

Mahápatha, a hell, 2. 215.

Mahápaurava, son of Sárvabhauma, 4. 143.

Mahápralaya, what, 1. 23, 24; 5. 169.

Mahápurusha, 'great spirit,' a title of Vishṇu, 1. 2, 3; 2. 308.

Maháraṇa, one of the Viśwe devas, 3. 192.

Mahá-ranga, what, 5. 32.

Maháráshṭra, a country, 2. 165, 341; 3. 136; 5. 389.

Maháratha, variant of Brihadratha, son of Vasu, 4. 149.

Mahárátrí, a Sakti of Siva, 1. 104.

Maháraurava, a hell, 2. 215.

Mahar-loka, a region where dwell the saints who outlive the destruction of the world, 1. 52, 65, 98; 2. 113, 226, 228, 231; 4. 266; 5. 192, 193.

Mahároman, son of Kírttiráta, 3. 332.

Maharahi, 'great Rishi,' 3. 264.

Mahása, son of Kríshna and Mitravindá, 5. 79.

Mahásaila (?), a mountain-range in Kraunchá-dwípa, 2. 197.

Mahásakti, son of Kríshna and Lakshmaná, 5. 81.

Mahásála, variant of Mahámaní, 4. 120.

Mahásíla, variant of Mahámaní, 4. 120.

Mahaswat, son of Amarsha, 3. 325.

Mahat, a Rudra, 1. 117; 2. 25.

Mahat, son of Matinára, 4. 130.

Mahat, variously genealogized, 4. 143.

Mahat, 'intellect.' The first product of Pradhána, 1. 29. Synonyms and definitions of it, 1. 29, &c. The source of three-fold Ahamkára, 1. 32, &c. See also 1. 74, 139, 140, 170; 2. 58, 234, 235; 3. 38; 5. 196, 198, 199.

Mahátala, a Pátála, or underworld, 2. 209.

Mahá-tamas, what, in philosophy, 1. 69.

Mahátejas, son of Madhu, son of Devakshattra, 4. 69.

Mahátman, variant of Mahánta, 2. 107.

Máhátmya, what, P. 20, 29, 60, &c. &c., 109.

Mahatsena, variant of Sumati, son of Dfidhasena, 4. 176.

Mahat-tattwa, what, in philosophy, 1. 74.

Mahávíchi, a hell, 2. 215.

Mahávideha, a country, 2. 165.

Mahá-vidyá, what, in philosophy, 1. 148.

Mahávíra, variant of Mahávíta, 2. 201.

Mahávíra-charitra, the, a drama, referred to, 4. 171.

Mahávírya, son of Bríhaduktha, 3. 331.

Mahávírya, son of Bhavanmanyu, 4. 136, 137.

Mahávishuva, 'the great equinox,' 2. 257.

Mahávíta, son of Savana, king of Pushkara-dwípa, 2. 201.

Mahávíta, a region in Pushkara-dwípa, 2. 201.

Maháwamso, the, a Singhalese work, referred to, 4. 170 (where correct the spelling), 181, 182, 185-188, 345.

Mahá-yajnas, five certain sacrifices, named, 3. 40, 93.

Mahá-yuga, a vast period of time, 1. 50; 4. 157.

Máhendras. See 4. 220 (note §).

Mahendra = Indra, 1. 128, 137; 2. 306; 3. 226; 4. 311, 315, 318; 5. 102.

Mahendra, Máhendra, a mountain-range, 2. 113, 127, 131, 140, 154, 155.

Mahendra, a mountain (same as the last ?), 4. 24.

Mahendrá, a river, 2. 148.

Mahendra; a star in the tail of the Sisumára, or celestial porpoise, 2. 306.

Mahendra Sátakarńi, son of Chakora Sátakarńi, 4. 202.

Maheśa, an epithet of Śiva, 2. 80.

Mahesha, a certain demon, 2. 167.

Maheśwara, an epithet of Śiva, P. 67, 68, 72, 79, 89; l. 126, 128, 130, &c. &c.; 3. 316; 5. 113, 127, 341.

Maheśwara-máhátmya, part of the Váyu-puráńa, P. 37.

Máheśwara-upapuráńa, P. 87.

Maheśwarí, a Śakti of Śiva, P. 79.

Máheyas, a people, 2. 169.

Mahí, a river in India, 2. 155, 169, 170.

Mahí, a river in Kuśa-dwípa, 2. 196.

Mahídhara, a title of Vishńu, 4. 278.

Mahídhraka, variant of Mahádhŕiti, 3. 332.

Máhikas, a people, 2. 166.

Mahiká, variant of Makarí, 2. 149.

Mahimnára, son of Senajit, 4. 141.

Mahinasa, a form of Rudra, l. 117.

Mahírata, variant of Ahínara, 4. 165.

Mahisha; an Asura, son of Anuhráda, 2. 69, 119.

Mahisha, a mountain-range in Sálmala-dwípa, 2. 194

Máhishas, variant of Máhikas, 2. 166.

Máhishas, variant of Máhishakas, 4. 220.

Máhishakas, a people, 2. 166, 178; 4. 220.

Máhishaka, what, 2. 219.

Máhishikas, variant of Máhishakas, (?) 3. 292, 293.

Máhishiká, variant of Máhishikí, 2. 166.

Máhishikí, a river, 2. 166; 5. 389.

Mahishina, a people, 4. 214.

Máhishmas, variant of Máhishakas, 4. 220.

Mahishmat, son of Sáhanji, 4. 54.

Máhishmatí, a city, 2. 166, 167; 4. 36, 54, 55, 59.

Mahitá, a river, 2. 148.

Mahodarí, daughter of Maya, a Dánava, 2. 72.

Mahodaya, the same as Kanoj, a city, 4. 15.

Mahopamá, a river, 2. 151.

Mahyas, variant of Swakshas, 2. 165.

Mahyuttaras, a people, 2 170.

Maináka, son of Himavat, 1. 157. Identified with a mountain in Central India, 2. 141, 151, 154, 340.

Mainákaprabhava = Śońa, the river Sone, 2. 141.

Mainda, conquered by Kŕishńa, 5. 139.

Maithilas, a dynasty, 4. 184.

Maithila, 'of Mithilá,' P. 106; 5. 217.

Maitra = Anurádhá, an asterism, 2. 265, 277; 3. 167.

Maitra, variant of Mitra, an Áditya, 2. 289

Maitreyas, a tribe of Bráhmans (?) descended from Mitrayu (?), 4. 147.

Maitreya, a Rishi, son of Kuśárava, and disciple of Paráśara, 1. 6.

He relates the Vishṇu-puráṇa, and is one of the interlocutors of the Bhágavata-puráṇa, 1. 6. See also P. 41 ; 1. 7, &c. &c. ; 5. 130, 136, 167, &c., 251.

Maitreya, son of Mitráyu, 4. 147.

Maitrí, 'friendship,' daughter of Daksha, and wife of Dharma, 1. 110.

Májavas, variant of Málavas, 2. 180.

Mákandí, a city on the river Ganges, 2. 161 ; 4. 145.

Makara, a mountain-range to the north of Mount Meru, 2. 124.

Makaraváhiní, variant of Manjulá, 2. 153.

Makarí, a river, 3. 149.

Makheśa, a title of Vishṇu, 1. 124.

Málas, a people, 2. 156, 157.

Mála, a country, 2. 157.

Máladas, a people, 2. 157.

Maladas, a people (the same as the last ?), 2. 170.

Maladá, daughter of Raudráśwa, and wife of Prabhákara, 4. 129.

Máladhánya, variant of Maṇidhána, 4. 221.

Malajas, a people, 2. 170.

Malajas, variant of Malayas, 2. 166.

Málakas, variant of Málavas, 2. 180.

Málatí-mádhava, the, a drama, referred to, 2. 340, 341 ; 4. 219.

Málavas, peoples, 2. 133, 134, 158, 180, 341 ; 4. 224.

Málava, a country, P. 9 ; 4. 224, 225.

Málavá, a river, 2. 339.

Málavánakas, a people, 2. 178.

Malavánaras, variant of Málavánakas, 2. 178.

Málavartis, a people, 2. 157.

Málavikágnimitra, the, a drama, referred to, 4. 190.

Malayas, a people, 2. 165.

Malaya, a mountain-range in the south-west of India, 2. 113, 127, 130, 132, 140, 155.

Malina, variant of Ailina, 4. 130, 131.

Máliní, the old name of Champá, 4. 125.

Máliní, variant of Mániní, 3. 27.

Malivas (?), a people, 2. 180.

Mallas, a people, 2. 165, 166.

Malla, a sort of pancratiast, 4. 337 ; 5. 39.

Mallaga, variant of Manuga, 2. 197.

Mallaráshṭra, a country, 2. 165, 341.

Mallavas (?), a people, 2. 180.

Malla-yuddha, what, 5. 23, 39.

Mallinátha, a commentator, referred to, 2. 134 ; 3. 322.

Málukas, variant of Kárúshas, 2. 133.

Mályavat, a mountain-range to the east of Mount Meru, 2. 111, 117, 122, 123.

Mamádha (?), variant of Mágadha, 3. 28.

Mamatá, wife of Utathya, 4. 123, 134.

Mamatá, the term defined, 3. 275, 276.

Mamatwa, the same as the last, 4. 239, 241 ; 5. 223.

Mamsáshṭaká = Madhyamáshṭaká, 3. 109, 168.

Máua, what, 5. 253.

Mánadas, variant of Maladas or Máladas, a people, 2. 157, 170.

Mánaratha, variant of Mínaratha, 3. 334.

Manas, a Gandharva, 2. 83.

Manas, 'mind.' A synonym of Mahat, 1. 29. Definition of it, 1. 35.

Mánasas, the Vaiśyas of Sáka-dwípa, 2. 200; 5. 382.

Mánasas, the same as Sukálas, (?) 3. 165.

Mánasa, a form of Vishńu, 3. 17, 227.

Mánasa, son of Vapushmat, king of Sálmala-dwípa, 2. 193.

Mánasa, a division of Sálmala-dwípa, 2. 193.

Mánasa, a region inhabited by the Somapas and Sukálas, 3. 162, 165.

Mánasa = Mánasottara, a mythological mountain-range, 2. 237, 239.

Mánasa, a lake in the grove called Nandana, 2. 112, 117; 4. 6.

Mánasa, what, in philosophy, 3. 159.

Mánasa-sarovara, a lake in Úndes or Húndes, 2. 340.

Mánasottara, a fabulous mountain-range, 2. 201, 203, 205, 239, 242.

Manaswin, son of Devala, 2. 24.

Manaswiní, wife of Mrikańdu, 1. 152.

Manasyu, son of Mahánta, 2. 107.

Manasyu, son of Pravíra, 4. 127.

Mánava, a portion of Bháratavarsha, 2. 129.

Mánava, a Kalpa, P. 70.

Mánava, the name of a weapon used by Ráma, 3. 315.

Mánava-dharma-śástra, the legal institutes of the Mánava family, passim.

Mánavalakas, variant of Mánavarjakas, 2. 170.

Mánavarjakas, a people, 2. 170.

Mánavartikas, variant of Gavavartilas, 2. 157.

Manavaśas, son of Madhu, son of Devakshattra, 4. 69.

Mánava-upapuráńa, P. 87.

Mánaví, variant of Támasí, 2. 152.

Mancha, 'platform,' 5. 27, 28, 30, 32.

Manchágára, what, 5. 33.

Mancha-váta, what, 5. 30-32.

Mandagas, the Súdras of Sáka-dwípa, 2. 200; 5. 382.

Mandaga, variant of Manuga, 2. 197.

Mandagá, a river, 2. 155.

Mandakas, a people (the same as the next ?), 2. 163.

Mańdakas, a people, 2. 180.

Mandákiní, rivers so called, 2. 153, 154.

Mańdalaka, variant of Pattalaka, &c., 4. 197, 201.

Mandara, son of Meru, 1. 157. Identified with a mountain-range to the east of Mount Meru, 1. 129, 142, 143; 2. 2, 111, 115, 116; 5. 88, 137.

Mandara, a mountain in Kuśa-dwípa, 2. 196.

Mandaraharińa, an island, perhaps fabulous, 2. 129.

Mandaváhiní, a river, 2. 153.

Mandehas, a class of Rákshasas, inimical to the Sun, 2. 249, 250, 252.

Mandehas, a caste in Kuśa-dwípa, 2. 195.

Mándhátri, variously genealogized, 3. 265-271, 273-275, 280-282, 297; 4. 130, 240, 241; 5. 57.

Mánd'ukas, variant of Mánd'akas, 2. 180.

Mánd'úkáyanas, of the Ṛig-veda, 3. 51.

Mánd'úkeya, son and disciple of Indrapramati, and promulgator of the Ṛig-veda, 3. 45.

Mánd'ukeya, variant of Mánd'úkeya, 3. 45.

Mangalaprastha, a hill in India, 2. 141.

Mángali, disciple of Pauahpinji, and teacher of the Sáma-veda, 3. 61.

Mangu, son of S'wa halka, 4. 94, 96.

Mani, a serpent, son of Kaśyapa, 2. 74.

Mani, an author, referred to the court of King Vikramáditya, P. 9.

Mánidhána, a king, 4. 221.

Mánidhánya, variant of Mánidhána, 4. 221.

Mánidhányaka, variant of Mánidhána, 4. 221.

Mánidhára, variant of Mánidhána, 4. 221.

Mánidháva, variant of Mánidhána, 4. 221.

Mánigríva, son of Kubera, 4. 281.

Mánikúta, a mountain in Plaksha-dwípa, 2. 193.

Maningá (?), a river, 2. 153.

Mánini, an Apsaras, daughter of Pramlochá, 3. 27.

Manipúra, a city on the sea-coast of Kalinga, 4. 160.

Manishin, variant of Senajit, 4. 174.

Mánittha, an astronomer, referred to the court of King Vikramáditya, P. 9.

Mánivahana = Kuśámba, son of Vasu, 4. 149.

Mánívaka, son of Bhavya, king of Sáka-dwípa, 2. 198.

Mánívaka, a region in Sáka-dwípa, 2. 198.

Manjulá, a river, 2. 153.

Manjúshá, the term defined, 4. 126.

Manmatha = Káma, the God of Love, 5. 76.

Manodhṛiti (?), variant of Dhṛiti, son of Vítahavya, 3. 335.

Manohará, wife of Dhara, a Vasu, 2. 23.

Manohará, variant of Manoramá, 2. 81.

Manojavas, a class of gods in the eleventh Manwantara, 3. 26.

Manojava, son of Íśána, a form of Rudra, 1. 117.

Manojava, son of Anila, 2. 23; 5. 387.

Manojava, son of Medhátithi, king of Sáka-dwípa, 2. 200.

Manojava, an Indra in the sixth Manwantara, 3. 12.

Manojava, a region in Sáka-dwípa, 2. 200.

Manojavá, a river in Krauncha-dwípa, 2. 198.

Mano-maya, what, 5. 17.

Manoramá, an Apsaras, 2. 81, 82.

Manovatí, an Apsaras, 2. 81, 82.

Mantalaka, variant of Maṇḍalaka, 4. 201.

Manthu, son of Víravrata, 2. 107.

Mantra, what, P. 32; 1. 164; 2. 338; 5. 243.

Mantra, the twelve-syllabled, what, 1. 99; 5. 212, 383.

Mantradruma, an Indra in the sixth Manwantara, 3. 12.

Mantramálá, a river in Kuśa-dwípa, 2 197.

Mantra-snána, a ceremony, defined, 3. 114.

Manus, fourteen, sages presiding over periods called Manwantaras, 'patriarchates,' 1. 49, 82, 103; 5. 190, 193, 300. Their names, as given in 3. 1–32, are, as generally enumerated, as follows:—1. Swáyambhuva; 2. Swárochisha; 3. Auttami; 4. Támasa; 5. Raivata; 6. Chákshusha; 7. Vaivaswata; 8. Sávarṇi; 9. Dakshasávarṇa; 10. Brahmasávarṇa; 11. Dharmasávarṇika; 12. Sávarṇa; 13. Rauchya; 14. Bhautya.

Manu, son of Brahmá, 1. 101. Son of Vivaswat, the Sun, and hence called Vaivaswata, 3. 231, 297. Reputed author of the Mánava-dharma-śástra, P. 4, et passim. See also P. 62, 80, 81, 95; 1. 104, &c., 159, 164, &c., 187; 3. 34, 230, &c.; 4. 237, 239, 240; 5. 210.

Manu, a form of Rudra, 1. 117.

Manu, son of Kṛiśáśwa, 2. 29.

Manu, son of Madhu, son of Devana (?), 4. 69.

Manuga, son of Dyutimat, king of Krauncha-dwípa, 2. 197.

Manuga, a region in Krauncha-dwípa, 2. 197.

Manuja, variant of Amavat (?), 3. 190, 191.

Manushya-yajna, a certain sacrifice, 3. 40.

Mauu Swáyambhuva. See Manu, son of Brahmá.

Manuvaśa, son of Madhu, son of Devana (?), 4. 69.

Manwantara, 'patriarchate,' a long period of time, so called. The nature and duration of one, 1. 49, 51, &c. The Manwantaras named, 3. 1–32. See also P. 7, 10, 28, 30, 37, 38, 42, 43, 56, 57, 76, 79, 97; 2. 9, &c. &c.; 5. 6, 169, 244, 246, 259, 299, 311.

Manwat, son of Purushaprabhu, 4. 70.

Manyu, a form of Rudra, 1. 117.

Manyu, variant of Bhavanmanyu, 4. 136.

Maraka, what, 4. 87.

Márasiṁha Deva, a king of the Konkan, 4. 211.

Márgas, variant of Mṛigas, the caste so called, 2. 200.

Márgaśírsha, a month, Nov.–Dec., 2. 285, &c.; 3. 168.

Marícha, son of Sunda, 2. 69.

Márícha, in the guise of a golden deer, slain by Ráma, 3. 315.

Maríchi, son of Brahmá, P. 27, 28; 1. 100, 135, &c., 153; 3. 2. His wives, 1. 109, 110;

3. 160, 297, 343. His offspring, 2. 303.

Maríchi, son of Samráj, son of Chitraratha, 2. 107.

Márichi, an Apsaras, 2. 81, 82.

Márichi, wife of Parjanya, son of Agni, 1. 154; 2. 263.

Márichi, patronym of Kaśyapa, 2. 71.

Maríchigarbhas, a class of gods in the ninth Manwantara, 3. 24.

Maríchigarbha, a region tenanted by the Pitris called Havishmats, 3. 163.

Márishas (?), a people, 2. 178.

Márishá, daughter of Kańdu, and wife of the Prachetasas, 2. 2, &c.

Márishá, wife of S'úra, son of Devamídhusha, 4. 100.

Márishá, a river, 2. 154.

Márjas, variant of Bhargas, a people, 2. 171.

Márjári, variant of Somápi, son of Sahadeva, 4. 151, 173.

Márkańd'a-puráńa = Márkańd'eya-puráńa, P. 53.

Márkańd'eya, son of Mrikańd'u, P. 44, 53, 54, &c.; 1. 152, 155.

Márkańd'eya (?), variant of Máńd'úkeya, 3. 45.

Márkańd'eya-puráńa, analysis of it, &c., P. 20, 21, 23, 24, 53, &c., 59, 60; 3. 67; 5. 311, 319, 327.

Márkańd'eyí, wife of Rajas, son of Vasishtha, 1. 155; 2. 263.

Marriage, rules for, &c., 3. 101, &c.

Márshi, son of Sáraña, 4. 109.

Márshimat, son of Sáraña, 4. 109.

Márshtí, wife of Dulísaha, P. 56.

Maru, son of S'íghra or S'íghraga, 3. 314. He is still living, 3. 325. See Devápi.

Maru, son of Haryaśwa, 3. 331.

Maru (?), sprung from Ikshwáku, 4. 237.

Marubhaumas, variant of Merubhútas, 2. 169.

Marubhúmis, a people, 2. 169.

Marubhúmi, a country, 2. 169; 4. 222.

Marudeva, son of Supratíka, 4. 168.

Marudvridhá, a river, 2. 121.

Márukas, variant of Kárúshas, 2. 133.

Marul-loka, the same as Deva-loka, 1. 98.

Marunandana, variant of Pulindaka, 4. 192.

Marúńd'as, variant of Murúńd'as, 4. 206.

Marúńd'achí (?), variant of Makarí, 2. 149.

Maruta, 'winds.' Sons of Kaśyapa and Diti, 2. 78–80. Called sons of Rudra and Pris'ni, 2. 79, 80. Forty-nine in number, 3. 79, 80; 3. 15. Their chief, Vásava, 2. 85. Etymology of the word, 2. 79, 80. See also 1. 142 (where correct the spelling), 200; 2. 22; 3. 14, 244; 4. 134, 135, 249, 293; 5. 2, 43, 101, 143, 234.

Márutas = Maruta, 3. 158.

Máruta, a heaven, assigned to diligent Vaiśyas, 1. 97, 98.

Maruta, variant of Maru, son of S'íghra, &c., 3. 325.

H

Maruta, variant of Marutta, son of Uśanas, &c., 4. 63, 64.

Marutta, son of Avikshit, 3. 243–245, 336; 4. 25, 240.

Marutta, son of Uśanas, &c., 4. 63.

Marutta, son of Karandhama, 4. 116.

Marutwats, sons of Dharma and Marutwatí; the Indras, 2. 21, 22.

Marutwat = Hanumat, 1. 117.

Marutwatí, daughter of Daksha, and wife of Dharma, 2. 21, 22.

Máshí, variant of Márishá, wife of Súra, 4. 100.

Mási śráddham, a particular sacrifice, 3. 114.

Mátali, Indra's charioteer, who visited Pátála, 2. 209.

Mathurá, a holy city in India. Founded by Śatrughna, 1. 165; 3. 318. Subáhu and Śúrasena reigned there, 3. 319. See also P. 12, 70, 71, 107; 4. 218, 269, 275, 338; 5. 9, 10, 18, 23, 42, 49, 50, 54, 55, 57, 63, 64, 160, 248, 249, 382.

Mathurá, a district (?), 2. 156.

Mathurá-máhátmya, a part of the Varáha-puráṇa, P. 71.

Mati, 'understanding,' a synonym of Mahat, 1. 32.

Matinára, son of Ṛiksha, son of Ariha, 4. 128.

Matinára, variant of Rantinára, 3. 266 (where correct the spelling); 4. 129–131; 5. 390.

Matkuná, a river, 2. 155.

Mátrá, 'moment of time,' 5. 189. See Nimesha.

Mátṛis, 'mothers,' daughters of Daksha and Prasúti, &c., P. 82;

l. 131; 5. 386. For their names, Khyáti, &c., see 1. 109.

Matsyas, peoples so called, 2. 156, 158, 172.

Matsya, disciple of Śákalya, and promulgator of the Ṛig-veda, 3. 46.

Matsya, son of Vasu, son of Kritaka, 4. 150.

Matsya, 'fish,' an epiphany of Vishṇu, P. 81.

Matsya, a district in India, 2. 143, 158.

Mátsya = Matsya-puráṇa, P. 80; 3. 67.

Mátsya (?), variant of Matsya, disciple of Śákalya, 3. 46.

Matsya-dwípa, a certain island, in Pauránik mythology, 2. 129.

Matsya-puráṇa, analysis of it, &c., P. 7, 17, 19, 20, 24–28, 35, 36, 51, 52, 54, 60, 62–64, 66, 68, 75, 77, 78, 80, &c., 84, 86, 89; 5. 270.

Maudáki, son of Bhavya, king of Śáka-dwípa, 2. 198.

Maudáki, a region in Śáka-dwípa, 2. 198.

Maudákin, variant of Maudáki, as doubly denotative, 2. 198.

Maudga, disciple of Devadarśa, and teacher of the Atharva-veda, 3. 61.

Maudgaládi, variant of Modosha, 3. 62.

Maudgalyas, certain Bráhmans, 4. 145.

Maudgalya, son of Mudgala, son of Haryaśwa, 4. 146.

Mauhúrtikas, the same as Muhúrtajas, 2. 22.

Maulas (?), variant of Maunas, the dynasty, 4. 206, 210.

Maunas, a dynasty, 4. 204, 206, 207, 209, 218.

Maunas, variant of Pauras, 4. 210.

Maunda, variant of Maudga, 3. 61.

Mauneyas, certain Gandharvas, sprung from Muni, 3. 281.

Maurúnd'as, the same as Murúnd'as, 4. 209.

Mauryas, a dynasty, 4. 186, 187, 190, 203, 205, 232.

Mávella, son of Vasu, son of Kritaka, 4. 149.

Maya, an Asura, son of Viprachitti, P. 82; 1. 190; 2. 72.

Máyá, 'deceit,' daughter of Adharma, 1. 111. Called daughter of Anrita, and wife of Bhaya, 1. 112. See also 1. 188, 190; 3. 73, 83; 5. 316.

Máyá, the same as Yoganidrá, 4. 260.

Máyá, 'personified active will of the Creator,' 1. 46. See also P. 41; 1. 17, 25, 28.

Máyádeví, wife of S'ambara, 5. 74, 75. She marries Pradyumna, 5. 76. Nárada pronounces that formerly she was Rati, 5. 76, 77.

Máyámoha, Buddha so called, 3. 206–209; 5. 349, 350, 377.

Máyárati, variant of Máyávatí, 5. 74.

Máyávatí = Máyádeví, 5. 74–76.

Máyus, son of Purúravas, 4. 13.

Measures, of time, 1. 47, &c. Of land, 1. 92, &c.

Medasiras, variant of S'ivasrí S'átakarńín, 4. 198.

Medha = Medhas, 2. 101.

Medhá, 'intelligence,' daughter of Daksha, and wife of Dharma, 1. 109, 110, 148.

Medhádhriti, a Rishi in the ninth Manwantara, 3. 25.

Medhas, son of Priyavrata, 2. 100; 5. 388. See Medha.

Medhátithi, son of Priyavrata, 2. 100. King of Plaksha-dwípa, 2. 101, 191. But, by another account, king of S'áka-dwípa, 2. 200.

Medhátithi, son of Kańwa, 4. 130, 131, 140.

Medhátithi, a law-commentator, referred to, or cited, 3. 89, 104, 107, 131, 138, 168, 174, 176.

Medhatithi (?), Medhátithi (?), variants of Medhádhriti, 3. 25, 227.

Medhávin, variously genealogized, 4. 164, 165.

Medical science, eight branches of Hindu, 4. 33. Teachers of it, 4. 33.

Mediní-kos'a, a vocabulary, referred to, 2. 286 (where correct the spelling), 343.

Medíya (?), variant of Modosha, 3. 62.

Meghas, a people, 4. 216.

Megha, son of Nahusha, 4. 46.

Megha (?), variant of Ghoshavasu, 4. 192.

Megha-dúta, the, a poem, referred to, 2. 150, 157, 160; 3. 246; 4. 137.

Meghamála, a mountain in Plaksha-dwípa, 2. 193.

Meghaprishťha, son of Ghritaprish-

tha, king of Krauncha-dwípa, 2. 198.

Meghaprishtha, a region in Krauncha-dwípa, 2. 198.

Meghapushpa, a horse of Kríshńa, 4. 83.

Meghaswáti, variously genealogized, 4. 196, 200.

Meghaswáti, son of Pulomávi, 4. 200.

Meghayantí, a Kṛittiká, 2. 337.

Meghayáti, son of Nahusha, 4. 46.

Mekalaa, a people, 2. 159, 160.

Mekalas, a dynasty, 4. 215, 216.

Mekala, a Ṛishi, connected, perhaps, with the people called Mekalas, 2. 160.

Mekala, a mountain in Central India, 2. 151, 160, 340.

Mekalá, a city in Central India, 4. 64, 214–216.

Mekalá = Narmadá, 2. 160; 4. 215.

Mekaládri = Mekala, the mountain so called, 2. 160.

Mekalakas, variant of Mekalas, the dynasty, 4. 215.

Mekalakanyá = Narmadá, 2. 160.

Mekalakanyaká = Narmadá, 2. 160.

Men, proceeded from Brahmá, 1. 81.

Mená, wife of Himavat, variously genealogized, 1. 118, 157; 3. 159, 162.

Mená, an Apsaras, 2. 83.

Mená, a river, 2. 149.

Menaká, an Apsaras, daughter of Brahmá, 2. 75, 81–83, 285, 286, 291, 293.

Mendicants, duties of, 3. 95, &c.

Meru, wife of Nábhi, 2. 103.

Meru, a fabulous mountain in the centre of Jambu-dwípa, 2. 109–111. Its dimensions and form, 2. 111, &c. Its mountain-ridges, 2. 117. The cities of the gods in and around it, 2. 118. Its rivers, 2. 120. Its situation, boundaries, &c., 2. 121, &c. &c. See also P. 97; 1. 40, 120, 152, 157, 188; 2. 102, 112–116, &c., 205, 207, 208, 236, 239, 242–244, 272; 3. 14, 53, 259; 4. 249, 259; 5. 28, 165, 248, 386.

Merubhútas, a people, 3. 169.

Merumandara, a certain mountain, according to the Bhágavata-puráńa, 2. 115, 116, 122.

Merusávarńis, four Manus so called, the ninth, tenth, eleventh, and twelfth, 3. 24.

Merusávarńi, a Manu, son of Brahmá, 3. 25.

Metres, origin of certain, 1. 86.

Michitá, variant of Niśchitá, 2. 146.

Mídhwas, son of Daksha, son of Chitrasena, 3. 335.

Mihira, a family so called, 5. 382.

Mímáńsá, 'hermeneutics,' referred to, 3. 325; 4. 252.

Mínaratha, son of Anenas, son of Kshemári, 3. 334.

Mind, an organ of sense, 1. 38.

Mishṭánna, what, 2. 218, 331.

Miśrakeśí, an Apsaras, 2. 75, 81, 82; 4. 129.

Mita, a Ṛishi in the third Manwantara, 3. 7.

Mitadhwaja, son of Dharma-

dhwaja or Janaka, 3. 333; 5. 217.

Mitákshará, the, a law-commentary, referred to, or quoted, P. 60; 2. 216; 3. 38, 88, 104, 126, 151, 174, 175, 224, 338.

Mithi, the same as Janaka, or Janaka's father, according to varying accounts, 3. 330, 331.

Mithilá, a city, capital of Videha, 2. 341; 3. 330 (there miscalled a country), 331, 335; 4. 83, 344; 5. 225.

Mitra, an Áditya, 1. 188; 2. 27, 285, &c., 306; 3. 338; 5. 381. Presides over the anus, 1. 38; 3. 109. Associated with Varuña, 3. 172, 233, 234, 328; 4. 5.

Mitra, son of Vasishtha, 1. 155.

Mitra, one of the Viswe devas, 3. 179.

Mitra = Bhaga, the Áditya, (??) 1. 131.

Mitra = Vasishtha, 3. 305.

Mitra, variant of Niramitra, 4. 174.

Mitraghna, variant of Mitrayu, son of Divodása, 4. 147.

Mitrasaha = Saudása, son's son of Sarvakáma, 3. 305, 306, 309.

Mitrasena, variant of Chitrasena, the Gandharva, 2. 293.

Mitravana, a grove so called, 5. 381.

Mitravindá, wife of Krishña, 5. 78, 79, 62 (where she is called daughter of Rájádhideví, on I know not what authority). The same as S'aibyá, (?) 5. 107.

Mitravindá, a river in Kuśa-dwípa, 2. 197.

Mitrayu, descended from Vasishtha; a disciple of Romaharshaña, and a teacher of the Puráñas, P. 19; 3. 64–66.

Mitrayu, Mitráyu, son of Divodása, son of Badhryaśwa, 4. 147.

Mitráyu, variant of Mitrayu, Vasishtha's descendant, 3. 64, 65.

Mitreyu, variant of Mitrayu, son of Divodása, 4. 147.

Mlechchhas, degraded Kshattriyas, 3. 295. Peoples in various parts of India, 3. 296; 4. 117, 119. Kings of them, 4. 207, 210, 225, 226. See also P. 33, 41; 1. 182; 2. 141, &c.; 4. 229; 5. 54, 55, 159.

Moda, disciple of Vedasparśa, and teacher of the Atharva-veda, 3. 61.

Modáki, variant of Maudáki, as doubly denotative, 2. 198.

Modásha (?), variant of Modosha, 3. 62.

Modosha, disciple of Vedadarśa, and teacher of the Atharva-veda, 3. 62.

Moha, 'infatuation,' sprung from Brahmá, 1. 102.

Moha, what, in philosophy, 1. 37, 69; 5. 202.

Mohiní, a female form assumed by Vishñu, 1. 147.

Mohiní, will-born daughter of King Rukmángada, P. 52.

Moksha, what, 1. 186, 187; 2. 14; 5. 187.

Monotheism of the Puráñas, alleged, 1. 41, 42.

Months. Four kinds of, 2. 254. Named, 2. 261, 285, 291,

&c. Appropriation of Ádityas, Rishis, &c., to them, 2. 284, &c.

Moon, the. Produced from the ocean, when churned, 1. 144. Its chariot and horses, 2. 299. The source of a celestial beverage called Sudhá, 2. 300.

Mot of the Phœnicians, its analogy to Mahat, 1. 33.

Mountains. Bounding the earth, 2. 114. Of Meru, 2. 117, 121, &c. Of Bháratavarsha, 2. 126. Of the various Dwípas, 2. 191, &c. &c.

Mountaineers, tribes of, 1. 182, 183.

Mŕichchhakaṭiká, a drama, referred to, 4. 195.

Mŕida, a form of Rudra, 5. 386.

Mŕidara, variant of Mŕidura, 4. 94, 96.

Mŕidu, son of Nŕipanjaya, 4. 165.

Mŕidu, variant of Mŕidura, 4. 94.

Mŕidu, variant of Riju, 4. 110.

Mŕidura, son of S'waphalka, 4. 94, 96.

Mŕiduri, variant of Mŕiduvid, 4. 96.

Mŕiduvid, son of S'waphalka, 4. 96.

Mŕiga, a horse of the Moon, 2. 299.

Mŕigá, the same as Mŕigavíthí, 2. 277.

Mŕigas, variant of Magas, 2. 199; 5. 382, 385.

Mŕigaśiras, a constellation so called, 1. 132; 2. 265, &c.

Mŕigaśíraha, the same as Mŕigaśiras, 2. 308.

Mŕiga-tŕishná, what, 5. 60.

Mŕigavíthí, a certain triad of asterisms, 2. 265, &c., 276, 277.

Mŕigavíthiká, the same as Mŕigavíthí, 2. 276.

Mŕigavyádha, a Rudra, 2. 24, 25.

Mŕigendra (?), variant of Mŕigendraswátikarṇa, 4. 200.

Mŕigendraswátikarṇa, son of Skandhaswáti, 4. 200.

Mŕigí, daughter of Kaśyapa, and mother of wild animals, 2. 74.

Mŕikaṇḍa (?), variant of Mŕikaṇḍu, 1. 152.

Mŕikaṇḍu, son of Vidhátŕi, son of Bhŕigu, 1. 152.

Mŕishá, 'falsehood,' wife of Adharma, 1. 111.

Mŕishi (?), variant of Kŕimi, son of Uśínara, 4. 121.

Mŕittikávana (?), variant of Mŕittikávata, 4. 73.

Mŕittikávata, a city, 4. 344. See Mŕittikávatí.

Mŕittikávatí, a city on the river Narmadá, 4. 19, 64, 344.

Mŕityu, 'death.' Sprung from Brahmá, 1. 102. Called son of Kali and Durukti, 1. 111. Also called son of Bhaya and Máyá, 1. 112.

Mŕityu, a Rudra, 2. 25.

Mŕityu, father of S'ikhin or Ketu, 2. 259.

Mŕityu (another ?), father of Sunithá, 1. 179.

Mŕityu (another ?), a Vyása in the sixth Dwápara age, 3. 34, 36.

Muchakunda (?), variant of Muchukunda, 3. 268.

Muchukunda, son of Mándhátŕi and Bindumatí, 3. 268. He

destroys Kálayavana by a glance of his eye, 5. 57. Lauds Krishńa, 5. 58. Goes to Gandhamádana, to perform penance, 5. 62.

Mudas, a class of Apsarasas, 2. 82.

Muda, 'pleasure,' son of Dharma, 1. 111.

Mudgala, disciple of S'ákalya, and promulgator of the Ŕig-veda, 3. 45, 46.

Mudgala, son of Reńu, 4, 28.

Mudgala, variously genealogized, 4. 144-146.

Mudgala-puráńa, P. 90.

Mudrá-rákshasa, the, a drama, referred to, 4. 186.

Mugh, connected with Maga, P. 64 (where correct the spelling); 5. 381, 384.

Muhisha, variant of Mahisha, the mountain-range so called, 2. 194.

Muhúrtá, daughter of Daksha, and wife of Dharma, 2. 21, 22.

Muhúrta, a measure of time, variously estimated, 1. 47, 48; 3. 121, 187; 2. 253; 5. 190. The Muhúrta of Brahmá, when, 3. 108.

Muhúrtajas, sons of Dharma and Muhúrta, 2. 22.

Múka, son of Upasunda, 2. 69.

Múká, a town, in Mahávideha, 2. 165.

Mukhyas, a class of gods in the eighth Manwantara, 3. 23.

Mukhya, its technical sense, 1. 70; 5. 386.

Mukhyá = Sukhá, Varuńa's city, 2. 240.

Mukta, variant of Yukta, 3. 29.

Muktá, variant of S'uklá, a river in S'álmala-dwípa, 2. 194.

Mukti, what, 5. 229.

Muktimatí, a river, rising in the Ŕiksha mountains, 2. 153.

Mukunda, variant of Kramunja, a mountain-range running eastward from Mount Meru, 2. 117.

Mukuńťhas, a people, 2. 165.

Múla, a certain asterism, 2. 264, &c., 308; 5. 248.

Múladeva, assassin of Sumitra, son of Agnimitra, 4. 172, 191.

Múlaka, son of Aśmaka, son of Saudása, 3. 310, 311, 314.

Mummies, prepared by the Hindus, 3. 328, 329.

Munchátas, Kauśika Bráhmans, 4. 28.

Muńďas, certain kings, 4. 203.

Muńďa, son of Udayibhadra, 4. 186.

Muńďo, the Pálí name of the son of Anuruddhako, 4. 182.

Muni, son of Dyutimat, king of Krauncha-dwípa, 2. 197.

Muni, daughter of Daksha, wife of Kaśyapa, and mother of the Apsarasas, &c., 2. 26, 75, 81; 3. 281.

Muni, a region in Krauncha-dwípa, 2. 197.

Muni, 'sage,' 1. 7, et passim.

Muni, variant of Mahámuni, the Ŕishi, 3. 11.

Muni, variant of Dhwani, (?) 3. 190, 191.

Muni, variant of S'uchi, son of S'atadyumna, 3. 333.

Munika (?), variant of Sunika, 4. 178.

Munja, his capital, where, 5. 112.

Munja, what, 5. 383.

Munjá, variant of Manjulá, 2. 153.

Munjakésas, of the Atharva-veda, 3. 62.

Mura, slain by Kríshńa, 5. 90.

Murá, wife of Nanda, father of Chandragupta, 4. 187.

Mura, variant of Muru, the demon so called, 5. 90.

Murala = Kerala, the country so called, 2. 341.

Muralá, a river, 2. 341.

Murári, an epithet of Kríshńa or Vishńu, 2. 112.

Múrdhanyá, wife of Márkańdeya, 1. 152.

Múrdhávasikta, a caste, sprung from Bráhman fathers and Kshattriya mothers, 4. 213.

Múrta, what, 5. 161, 235, 238.

Múrtaya, son of Kuśa, 4. 15.

Múrti, a Prajápati of the second Manwantara, and son of Vasish-tha, 3. 5.

Múrti, 'form,' daughter of Dak-sha, and wife of Dharma, 1. 110, 111.

Múrtimat, what, in philosophy, 5. 198.

Muru, a demon, slain by Kríshńa, 5. 55, 89, 90.

Muru, a country (?), 5. 55.

Murúńdas, Murúńdas, a dynasty, 4. 206, 209.

Musala, a sort of club, borne by Balabhadra, 5. 51.

Musaláyudha, an epithet of Bala-bhadra, from his club, 5. 67, 131, 134.

Múshakas, a people, 2. 178, 180.

Múshikas, a people, 2. 178; 4. 222.

Múshika, a country, 2. 178.

Mushťika, a famous pancratiast, slain by Kríshńa, 4. 335, 337; 5. 23, 28, 35, 36, 39, 40, 87.

Mushťi-nipáta (?), what, in the pancratium, 5. 36.

Must (corrupted from the Persian mast), what, 5. 29.

Mútibas, a people, 2. 170.

Nabánazdista, of the ancient Pár-sís, 3. 231.

Nabha, son of Swárochisha, and a Rishi in the second Manwan-tara, 3. 5.

Nabha, son of Viprachitti, 2. 71.

Nabha = Nabhas, the month so called, 3. 168.

Nábha, variant of Nábhága, 3. 13.

Nabha, variant of Madhu, the Rishi, 3. 14.

Nábha, variant of Nábhága, 3. 303.

Nabha, variant of Nabhas, son of Nala, 3. 320.

Nábhágas, a class of Rájarshis sprung from Manu, 3. 70.

Nábhága, two persons, variously genealogized, 3. 13, 14, 231–233, 239, 241, 256, 257. One of them becomes a Vaiśya, 3. 240.

Nábhága, a Rishi in the tenth Manwantara, 3. 26.

Nábhága, variously genealogized, 3. 303, 314, 315.

Nabhága, variant of Nábhága, &c., 3. 13, 231, 256–258.

Nábhaga, variant of Nabhaga, 3. 13.

Nábhaga, variant of Nábhága, 3. 13.

Nábhága Arishťa, the same as Nábhágárishťa, 3. 233, 240, 256. See Nábhánedishťha.

Nabhágadishťa, · Nábhágadishťa, 3. 231, 241, 256. See Nábhánedishťha.

Nábháganedishťha, son of Vaivaswata, 3. 231, 256. See Nábhánedishťha.

Nábhágárishťa, son of Vaivaswata, 3. 231, 232, 240, 241, 256. See Nábhánedishťha.

Nabhakánanas, variant of Nala-kánanas, 2. 178.

Nábhánedishťha, named in the Ŕig-veda and· elsewhere, 3. 13, 231, 256, 257, 340, 341.

Nabhas, son of Nala, son of Nishadha, 3. 320.

Nabhas = Srávańa, a month, July-August, 2. 261 ; 4. 261.

Nabhas = Ákása, 2. 232.

Nabhaas, son of U'rja, son of Satyahita, (?) 4. 150.

Nabhas-tala, what, 5. 194.

Nabhaswatí, wife of Antardhána, son of Ṕrithu, 1. 193.

Nabhasya, son of Swárochisha, and a Ŕishi in the second Manwantara, 3. 5.

Nabhasya = Bhádrapada, a month, August-September, 2. 261.

Nábhi, son of Agnídhra, and king of Hima, 2. 102, 103.

Nábhigupta, son of Hirańyaretas, and a ruler in Kuśa-dwípa, 2. 197.

Nábhigupta, a region in Kuśa-dwípa, 2. 197.

Nabhíra, a Báhlika king, 4. 214.

Nádí = Nádiká, 2. 253.

Nádiká, a certain measure of time, 1. 48 ; 5. 189, 190.

Nadína, variant of Adína, 4. 43.

Nadwalá, daughter of Vairája, and wife of the Manu Chákshusha, 1. 177.

Nágas, 'serpent-gods,' sons of Kaśyapa and Kadrú, P. 42 ; 1. 144, 188 ; 2. 28, 284 ; 5. 236, 251, 383. Their king, 2. 86. They are harassed by the Gandharvas, 3. 281, 282. See also Sarpas.

Nágas, a people, 4. 212.

Nágas, kings reigning at Padmávatí, Kántipurí, and Mathurá, 4. 212, 217–219.

Nága, a serpent, son of Kaśyapa and Kadrú, 2. 74.

Nága, a mountain-range running northward from Mount Meru, 2. 117.

Nága, a range of hills to the east of Ramgarh, 2. 142.

Nága = Nága-dwípa, a portion of Bháratavarsha, 2. 112.

Nága, variant of Rambha, a serpent, 2. 287, 293.

Nágadásako, the Pálí name of a son of Muńďo, 4. 182, 185.

Nága-dwípa, a portion of Bháratavarsha, 2. 129.

Nága-kanyás, what, 2. 211.

Nága-panchamí, a certain festival, P. 64.

Nagara, defined, 1. 94.

Nágara-khańďa, a section of the Skanda-puráńa, 3. 339.

Nágasena, a king, 4. 217.

Nágavíthí, daughter of Dharma and Yámi, 2. 22.

Nágavíthí, a certain triad of asterisms, 2. 264, &c., 337.

Nágeśa Bhaṭṭa, quoted, or named, P. 84; 5. 379.

Nagnas, 'naked,' certain misbelievers, 3. 196, 201. See also 3. 208, 225.

Nagnajit, king of Kosala, and father of Nágnajití or Satyá, 5. 79, 82.

Nágnajití, patronym of Satyá, wife of Kṛishṇa, 5. 79, 82, 107.

Nagniká, the term defined, 3. 102.

Náhusha, a serpent, son of Kaśyapa and Kadrú, 2. 74.

Nahusha, son of Áyus and Prabhá, 2. 70; 4. 30, 44, 45, 240.

Nahusha, son of Ambarísha, 3. 314; 4. 1.

Naigama, disciple of Śákapúṇi, and promulgator of the Ṛigveda, 3. 49.

Naigameya, son of Kumára, son of Agni, 2. 23.

Naikapṛishṭhas, a people, 2. 160.

Naikavakrá, a deformed damsel made straight by Kṛishṇa, 5. 21, 165.

Naimisha = Naimisháraṇya, 3. 170.

Naimisha-gomatí, a river in India, 3. 170.

Naimisháraṇya, a forest on the river Gomatí, P. 28, 30, 32, 40, 52, 58, 65, 88.

Naimisháraṇya-máhátmya, a part of the Váyu-puráṇa, P. 39.

Naimishikas, a people, 4. 222.

Naimittika, what, 1. 123; 5. 186.

Naimittika-pralaya, the, what, 5. 196.

Naimittika-śráddha, a certain mortuary ceremony, 3. 146.

Nairṛitas, a people, 2. 171.

Nairṛita, or Rakshas, his city, where, 2. 112.

Naishádas, a people, 4. 221. See Nishádas.

Naishadhas, a dynasty, 4. 215, 216, 221. See Nishadhas.

Nákas, a dynasty, 4. 218, 219.

Nákála, what, 3. 125.

Nákapṛishṭha, the highest of the heavens, 3. 198.

Nakhavat, a king, 4. 212.

Nakshatras, 'lunar asterisms,' twenty-seven in number, daughters of Daksha, and wives of Soma, 2. 10, 21, 28.

Nakshatra-súchaka, what, 2. 218.

Nakshatra-yoginís, the stars of the twenty-seven lunar mansions, daughters of Daksha, and wives of Chandra, 2. 28.

Nakta, son of Pṛithu or Pṛithusheṇa, 2. 107.

Nakula, son of Násatya, 2. 136; 3. 74, 79; 4. 103, 159, 160, 163; 5. 134.

Nakula, variant of Rátula, 4. 169.

Nala, son of Nishadha, 2. 171; 3. 303, 304, 320; 4. 216.

Nala, son of Vírasena, 3. 304.

Nala, son of Yadu, son of Yayáti, 4. 53.

Nálá, a river in India, 2. 152.

Nala, variant of Dala, 3. 321.

Nala, variant of Sala, son of Sudhanwan, 3. 321.

Nala, variant of Bhava, son of Viloman, 4. 97.

Nalakálakas, variant of Nalaká-nanas; 2. 178.

Nalakánanas, a people, 2. 178.

Nalakúbara, son of Kubera, 4. 281.

Nalapura, a fortress in Bundel-khand, 2. 171.

Nalini, a river in India, 2. 120, 121.

Nalini, a river in Sáka-dwípa, 2. 199.

Nalini, variant of Nílini, 4. 144.

Nalopákhyana, the, a poëm, referred to, 2. 171.

Náman, 'essence' (?), &c., 4. 346; 5. 14, 15, 200.

Namasyu, variant of Manasyu, son of Pravira, 4. 127.

Names for persons of different castes, 3. 99, 100.

Namuchi, son of Viprachitti, 2. 70, 71. His abode, 2. 211.

Nandas, the nine, a dynasty, 4. 185-187, 232.

Nanda, a certain cow-herd, Krishńa's foster-father, 4. 111, 270, 274, 276, 278-281, 288-290, 296, 309, 310, 312, 314, 316, 326, 336, 337; 5. 1, 9, 10, 25, 40, 63.

Nanda, son of Vasudeva, 4. 109.

Nanda, son of Mahánandin, 4. 183-187, 229-231, 234.

Nanda, son of Prasenajit, 4. 186, 345.

Nandá, the story of, P. 87.

Nanda, a mountain in Kraunchá-dwípa, 2. 198.

Nandá, a river in Sálmala-dwípa, 2. 195.

Nandana, a Kumára, 1. 79.

Nandana (?), son of Súra, son of Devamídhusha, 4. 101.

Nandana, the grove of Indra, situated on Mount Sugandha, 2. 112, 116; 4. 293; 5. 97.

Nandana, a mountain in Kraunchá-dwípa, 2. 198.

Nandasára, variant of Bindusára, 4. 188.

Nandá-upapuráńa = Nandi-upapu-ráńa, P. 87.

Nandáyaniya, disciple of Báshkala, and promulgator of the Rig-veda, 3. 50.

Nandi, a bull, attendant of Siva, P. 89; 5. 116. According to the Váyu-puráńa, he was son of Kaśyapa and Surabhi, 2. 75. See Nandin and Nandíśwara.

Nandí, 'delight,' wife of Káma, 1. 111.

Nándimukhas, a class of Pitrís, 3. 98, 148, 149.

Nándí-mukha, a certain mortuary ceremony, 3. 149, 190.

Nandin = Nandi, 1. 122, 125; 5. 116. See Nandi and Nandí-śwara.

Nandi-puráńa, the, quoted, or referred to, 3. 163, 164, 166, 339.

Nandíśa = Nandi, 5. 116.

Nandíśwara = Nandi, 1. 122, 125.

Nandi-upapuráńa, P. 87; 3. 164, 166.

Nandivardhana, son of Udávasu, 3. 331.

Nandivardhana, son of Janaka, 4. 179.

Nandivardhana, son of Udayáśwa, 4. 182.

Nandiyasás, son of Dharma, son of Rámachandra, 4. 211, 212.

Naras, 'centaurs,' their origin from Brahmá, 1. 87.

Nara, a name of Vishńu, 1. 56, &c.

Nara, a Devarshi, son of Dharma, son of Brahmá, 1. 111; 3. 68; 4. 247. Arjuna identified with him, 5. 62.

Nara, a king, son of Támasa, Manu of the fourth Manwantara, 3. 8.

Nara, son of Gaya, son of Nakta, 2. 107.

Nara, son of Sudhŕiti, 3. 245.

Nara, son of Uttnara, son of Mahámanas, 4. 121.

Nara, son of Bhavanmanyu, 4. 136, 137.

Nárada, son of Brahmá, 1. 101, &c. Called son of Kaśyapa, by one of Daksha's daughters, 2. 18. Denominated a Devarshi, 3. 68. Dissuades the sons of Daksha from propagating their kind, 2. 13. Is cursed by Daksha, 2. 14. Is cursed by Brahmá, 2. 17. Warns Kamsa of his danger from the birth of Kŕishńa, 4. 259. He lauds Kŕishńa, 4. 340, 341. See also P. 41, 46, 51, 52, 64, 65, 75, 87; 1. 122; 3. 141, 288, 342; 4. 42, 248, 335; 5. 54, 74, 76, 103, 112, 123, 128, 141, 381, 382.

Nárada, a Gandharva, son of Varidása, 2. 20, 285, &c.

Nárada, a mountain-range in Plaksha-dwipa, 2. 191.

Nárada-puráńa, analysis of it, &c., P. 24, 51, &c. And see Náradíya-puráńa.

Náradíya = Nárada, son of Brahmá, P. 87.

Náradíya-puráńa = Nárada - puráńa, P. 20, 23, 51, 58, 87; 3. 67; 5. 327.

Náradíya-upapuráńa, P. 87.

Naraka, 'hell,' son of Anŕita, 1. 111, 112.

Naraka, son of Viprachitti, 2. 71; 5. 87.

Naraka, son of Vishńu and Bhúmi, and slain by Kŕishńa, 4. 250, 320; 5. 55, 87, 88, 90-93, 105, 113, 136.

Naraka, a country (?), 5. 55.

Naraka, a particular hell, 1. 99; 2. 215.

Narakas, or 'hells,' 1. 99; 2. 214, &c. See Niraya.

Nara-medha, a certain sacrifice, 1. 84.

Naranáráyańa = Kŕishńa, 5. 62, 146.

Nararatha, variant of Navaratha, 4. 68.

Narasimha, Vishńu as a man-lion, P. 80.

Narasimha-puráńa, P. 24, 87.

Narasimha-upapuráńa, P. 87.

Naravábana, son of Niramitra, 4. 166.

Náráyańa = Vishńu or Kŕishńa. Why so called, &c., P. 48, 53; 1. 52, 55, 56, &c.; 3. 262; 4. 90, 247, 249, 251, 277; 5. 3, 307. His wife, 1. 118, 120.

Náráyańa, the same as Brahmá, 5. 307.

Náráyaña, a Devarshi, son of Dharma, P. 65; 1. 111, 139; 2. 306, 308; 3. 68; 4. 247; 5. 250. Kŕishña identified with him, 5. 62.

Náráyaña, son of Bhúmimitra, son of Vasudeva, 4. 193, 194.

Náráyaña, a commentator on Sánkháyana, referred to, 3. 113.

Náráyaña-saras, a lake near the mouth of the Indus, 2. 15, 17.

Náráyaña-upanishad, the, referred to, 5. 345.

Náríkavacha, an epithet of Múlaka, 3. 310.

Narishyanta, two persons so called (?), P. 57; 3. 13, 14, 232, 233, 245, 335, 336.

Narishyat = Narishyanta, 3. 336.

Náríyas, variant of Saníyas, 2. 180.

Narmadá, the river Nerbudda. Daughter of Mekalá, 2. 160. Mind-born daughter of the Somapas, or of the Sukálas, 3. 162, 165. Called sister of the Nágas, 3. 282. Wife of Duhsaha, 3. 283. Prayer to her, 3. 283. See also P. 107; 1. 150; 2. 128 (where correct the spelling), 130, 131, 142, 151; 3. 207; 4. 56, 59, 64, 65, 215, 344; 5. 71, 118, 250, 350, 388.

Narmadá-máhátmya, a part of the Mataya-puráña, P. 82.

Násatyas = Aświns, sons of Vivaswat and Sanjná, 2. 343; 3. 158; 4. 258.

Násatya, son of Áditya, the Sun, 4. 103, 258.

Násik, the popular name of a town in Western India, 4. 198.

Nástika, what, 5. 178.

Nature, a habit, 1. 66.

Naurikŕishña (??), variant of Gaurakŕishña, 4. 200.

Navá, wife of Uśínara, son of Mahámanas, 4. 121.

Nava, variant of Bhava, son of Viloman, 4. 97.

Nava, variant of Nara, son of Uśínara, son of Mahámanas, 4. 121.

Navaráshtras, a people, 4. 121.

Navaráshtra, the kingdom ruled by Nava, 4. 121, 122.

Navaratha, variously genealogized, 4. 68.

Navárchis = Lohitánga, or Mars, 2. 257, 258.

Naya, 'polity,' son of Dharma, 1. 110; 4. 265; 5. 386. See Daňdanaya.

Naya, variant of Anagha, 4. 132.

Naya, what, 1. 118.

Nedishtha, son of Vaivaswata, 3. 231, 232, 240, 256, 336.

Namichakra, variant of Nichakru, 4. 163.

Namikŕishña, variant of Arishtakarman, 4. 197.

Netra, son of Dharmanetra, 4. 54.

Netra, variant of Subala, son of Sumati, 4. 176.

Nichakru, son of Adhisimakŕishña, 4. 163.

Nichitá, a river, 2. 147.

Nidágha, son of Pulastya, story of, 2. 330, &c.

Nidhis, nine, of Kubera, what, 3. 273.

Nidhŕiti, variant of Nirvŕiti, 4. 68.

Nidrá, 'sleep,' a female form of Brahmá, 1. 82. Produced from the ocean, when churned, 1. 147.

Nidrá, the same as Yoganidrá, 4. 260.

Nigada, a Saṁhitá, the same as the Yajur-veda, 3. 42.

Nighaṅṭu, the, a vocabulary, quoted, l. 5.

Nighna, son of Anaraṅya, son of Sarvakarman, 3. 305, 314.

Nighna, son of Anamitra, &c., 4. 74, 100.

Nihsattwa, what, in philosophy, l. 138.

Nijadhṛiti, a river in Sʼáka-dwípa, 2. 200.

Nikṛiti, 'immorality,' daughter of Adharma, and wife of Anṛita, 1. 111. Also called daughter of Dambha, and wife of Lobha, 1. 111.

Nikshubhá, daughter of Ṛijwáhs, and wife of Agni and Áditya, 5. 385.

Nikumbha, an attendant of Sʼiva, 4. 34.

Nikumbha, son of Haryaśwa, 3. 265.

Níla, son of Yadu, son of Yayáti, 4. 53.

Níla, son of Ajamíḍha, 4. 144.

Níla, a mountain-range to the north of Mount Meru, 2. 102, 111, 114, 121–123.

Níla, a mountain-range in Orissa, 2. 141.

Níla, a mountain (different from the first Níla just mentioned?), l. 61.

Nílakaṅṭha, author of the Srád-dha-mayúkha, referred to, 3. 148.

Nílakaṅṭha-stotra, part of the Váyu-puráṇa, P. 37.

Nílalohita, a form of Sʼiva, 1. 77, 115.

Nílini, wife of Ajamíḍha, 4. 144.

Nimesha, 'a twinkling of the eye,' the smallest measure of time, 1. 47, 48; 2. 253. And see Mátrá.

Nimi, son of Ikshwáku, 3. 259, 260. Is cursed by Vaśishṭha, 3. 327, 328. Is placed on the eyelids of men, and is the cause of their winking, 3. 329. Named in 5. 225.

Nimi, son of Bhajamána, son of Satwata, 4. 71.

Nimi, variant of Niramitra, son of Khándapáni, 4. 166.

Nimisha, 'wink,' its fancied ety-mology, 3. 329.

Nimitta, what, in philosophy, 1. 66, 67; 5. 196.

Nimlochá, variant of Anumlochá, 2. 292.

Nimlochaní, Varuṇa's city, by one account, 2. 240.

Nimlochi, variant of Nimi, son of Bhajamána, 4. 72.

Nimna, variant of Nighna, son of Anamitra, 4. 74.

Nine gems of King Vikramáditya, P. 7, &c.

Nípas, a race, 4. 142, 143.

Nípa, son of Pára, 4. 141–143.

Nípa, son of Kṛitin (?) or Kṛita, 4. 143.

Nípá, variant of Kośá, 2. 153.

Nirámaya (if a name), son of Dakshasávarṇa, 3. 25.

Niramitra, son of Nakula, son of Násatya, 4. 160.

Niramitra, Nirámitra, son of Khaṇḍapáṇi, 4. 165, 166.

Niramitra, Nirámitra, son of Ayutáyus, son of S'rutavat, 4. 174.

Niraya, 'hell,' son of Mṛityu, 1. 111.

Niraya = Naraka, the infernal regions generally, 2. 112.

Nirbíja, what, in the Yoga philosophy, 5. 230.

Nirdhṛiti, variant of Nirvṛiti, 4. 68.

Nirguṇa, what, in philosophy, 1. 153; 2. 328.

Nirmáṇaratis, a class of gods in the eleventh Manwantara, 3. 26.

Nirmogha, variant of Nirmoha, son of Sávarṇi, 3. 24.

Nirmoha, a Ṛishi in the thirteenth Manwantara, 3. 28.

Nirmoha, son of Sávarṇi, Manu of the eighth Manwantara, 3. 24.

Nirmoka, a Ṛishi in the thirteenth Manwantara, 3. 28.

Nirmoka, son of Sávarṇi, Manu of the eighth Manwantara, 3. 24.

Nirmoka, variant of Nirmoha, son of Sávarṇi, the Ṛishi, 3. 24.

Nirmukta, what, 5. 33.

Nirṇaya-sindhu, the, a law-book, referred to, or quoted, 3. 101, 103, 104, 146, 147, 149-151, 153, 163, 166, 174, 177, 187,

188, 190, 191, 198, 199, 338, 339.

Nirṛita, a Rudra, 2. 25.

Nirṛiti, a Rudra, 2. 25.

Nirṛiti, 'calamity,' offspring of Adharma, 1. 112. Adoptive mother of Dambha and Máyá, 1. 111.

Nirúḍha-paśu-bandha, a certain sacrifice, 3. 40, 113.

Nirukta, 'glossarial comment,' an Anga of the Vedas, 3. 46, 67; 4. 252.

Nirukta, the, a certain dictionary so called, referred to, 1. 58; 2. 121, 297; 3. 46; 5. 178.

Niruktakṛit, title of some unnamed disciple of S'ákapúṇi, and author of a glossary to the Ṛig-veda, 3. 48.

Nirupádhi, what, in philosophy, 1. 25.

Nirutsuka, a Ṛishi in the thirteenth Manwantara, 3. 28.

Nirvaktra (?), variant of Nichakru, 4. 163.

Nirváṇa, what, in philosophy, 3. 84, 210.

Nirváṇa-maya, what, in philosophy, 5. 225.

Nirváṇaruchis, by one account, a class of gods in the eleventh Manwantara, 3. 26.

Nirvindhyá, a river, 2. 130, 155.

Nirvírá, a river, 2. 146.

Nirvishaya, what, in philosophy, 2. 91; 5. 226.

Nirvṛiti, variously genealogized, 4. 68.

Nirvṛiti, variant of Susrama, 4. 175.

Nirvritti, variant of Nirvriti, 4. 68.

Nirvyúha, what, in architecture, 5. 31.
  itáchares, 'lemures,' 2. 289, 296.

Nisátha, son of Balabhadra, son of Vasudeva, 4. 109; 5. 68.

Nischala, variant of Nischara, the first named below, 3. 3.

Nischara, a Rishi in the second Manwantara, 3. 4.

Nischara, a Rishi in the eleventh Manwantara, 3. 26.

Nischira (?), variant of Nischara, a Rishi in the second Manwantara, 3. 5.

Nischirá, a river, 2. 146.

Nischitá, a river, 2. 146.

Nishádas, a people in the Vindhyas, 1. 181, &c.; 2. 171; 4. 113, 220; 5. 123. See Nisháda, the caste so called. Also see Naishádas.

Nisháda, progenitor of the Nishádas, his origin, 1. 181.

Nisháda, a caste, consisting of fishermen, &c., 4. 216. See Nishádas.

Nishadhas, a people, 2. 171. See Naishadhas.

Nishadha, son of Atithi, 3. 304, 320.

Nishadha, a country, 3. 304; 4. 216.

Nishadha, a country (?), 2. 102. The original, Naishadham varsham, may mean 'the region called Naishadha,' or 'the region of the Naishadha (mountains).'

Nishadha, a mountain-range, placed both south and east of

Mount Meru, 2. 111, 114, 117, 122, 123.

Nishadhá, a river, 2. 155.

Nishadha (?), variant of Nisatha, 4. 109.

Nishadháswa, son of Kuru, son of Samvarana, 4. 148.

Nishádin, epithet of Ekalavya, and whence, 4. 113.

Nishka, a certain weight of gold, 5. 84, 85.

Nishkumbha, one of the Viśwe devas, 3. 192.

Nishkumbhá, variant of Nikshubhá, 5. 382, 385.

Nishñátas, Kauśika Bráhmans, 4. 28.

Nishprakampa, a Rishi in the thirteenth Manwantara, 3. 28.

Nisi (?), variant of Nimi, son of Bhajamánas, 4. 72.

Nisitha, son of Pushpárña, 1. 178.

Nisritá, variant of Nischitá, 2. 146.

Nisumbha, a demon, slain by Yoganidrá, 4. 261.

Nisunda, son of Hráda, 2. 69.

Nitala, a particular Pátála, or underworld, 2. 209.

Nitána, son of Súra, son of Viduratha, 4. 99.

Nitatni, a Krittiká, 2. 337.

Níti, what, 1. 118; 4. 265.

Níti-manjari, the, a book, referred to, 2. 80.

Níti-mayúkha, the, a law-book, referred to, 2. 131, 132, 146, 155, 156, 339; 3. 190.

Nitya, what, in philosophy, 1. 113; 5. 186.

Nitya-karman, a certain religious duty, 4. 257.

Nitya-śráddha, a certain mortuary observance, 3. 114, 146.

Nivápa, what, 3. 93.

Nívárá, a river, 2. 148.

Nivátakavachas, a class of Dánavas, sprung from Prahráda, and dwelling in the depths of the sea, 2. 72.

Nivŕitta, what, in religious phraseology, 5. 200.

Nivŕittaśatru, son of Anádhŕishŧí, son of Súra, 4. 113.

Nivŕitti, a river in S'álmala-dwípa, 2. 194.

Nivŕitti, variant of Nirvŕiti, 4. 68.

Nivŕitti, variant of Suśrama, 4. 175.

Niyama, 'precept' son of Dharma, 1. 110.

Niyama, the term defined, 3. 77; 5. 222, 227, 230, 240.

Niyati, daughter of Meru, and wife of Vidhátŕi, 1. 152; 5. 387. (Correct, on the warrant of the Bhágavata-puráńa, the order in which Niyati and Áyati are named in 1. 157.)

Niyut, wife of S'iva, the Rudra, 1. 117.

Nŕibandhu, variant of Nichakru, 4. 163.

Nŕibandhu, variant of Ŕicha, 4. 164.

Nŕibhŕita, variant of Suśrama, 4. 175.

Nŕichakshus, son of Ŕicha, 4. 164.

Nŕichandra, son of Antinára or Rantinára, 4. 130.

Nŕiga = Nabhaga, 3. 13, 231, 232, 256. Changed to a lizard, 3. 335.

Nŕiga, son of Uśínara, son of Mahámanas, 4. 121.

Nŕigá, wife of Uśínara, son of Mahámanas, 4. 121.

Nŕihari, the same as Nŕisimha, 2. 66.

Nŕimańá, a river in Plaksha-dwípa, 2. 193.

Nŕipanjaya, son of Suvíra, son of Kshemya, 4. 144.

Nŕipanjaya, son of Medhávin, 4. 164, 165.

Nŕisimha, a form of Vishńu, half man and half lion, 2. 34, 66; 4. 106, 277; 5. 3.

Nŕiśwadhátu (?), variant of Praheti, 2. 292.

Nŕi-yajna, a certain religious observance, 3. 93.

Numeration, terms of, specified, 5. 187, &c.

Nyagrodha, son of Ugrasena, son of Áhuka, 4. 98.

Nyagrodha, 'the Indian fig-tree,' 1. 171; 2. 116, 202; 3. 285.

Nyarbuda, 'one hundred millions,' 5. 188.

Nyásin, 'religious mendicant,' 1. 98.

Nyáya, a certain system of philosophy, 3. 222.

Nyáyaka, Nyáyika, adjective of Nyáya, 4. 252.

Oblations, daily, with fire, to Brahmá, 3. 117.

Obsequies, rites of, three kinds, and by whom performed, 3. 155, &c.

Ocean, the churning of the, 1. 143, &c.

Oḍras, a people, 2. 177; 3. 295; 4. 220.

Oḍra, a country, now called Orissa, 2. 177; 3. 293; 4. 122, 221.

Oḍra, variant of Puṇḍra, son of Dírghatamas, 4. 122.

Oghavat, son of Pratíka, 3. 335.

Oghavat (?), variant of Vegavat, son of Bandhumat, 3. 245.

Oghavatí, daughter of Pratíka, and wife of Sudarśana, 3. 335.

Oghavatí, a river, 2. 148.

Oja, son of Kŕishńa and Lakshmańá, 5. 81.

Ojaswin, son of Bhautya, Manu of the fourteenth Manwantara, 3. 29.

Om, a mystical and initiatory syllable; the monosyllabic Brahma; a type of the three worlds, of Brahmá, and of the Vedas, 1. 1, &c.; 3. 37, &c. A type of Vásudeva, Kŕishńa, or Vishńu, 3. 39. See also P. 68; 1. 140, 142; 2. 250, 252; 3. 56.

Oṁkara = Om, 1. 1, 61; 2. 250, 252.

Orders, duties of the four, 3. 92, &c.

Orissa. See Oḍra.

Oshṭhakarńakas, a people, 2. 162.

Oxydracæ, the classical, perhaps one with Śúdrakas or Śúdras, 2. 184, 185.

Padmá = Lakshmí, 1. 119, 147, 151.

Padma, a Kalpa, P. 68 (where correct the spelling); 1. 53, 55, 78; 2. 21.

Padma, what, in numeration, 5. 188, 189, 392.

Padma-puráńa, Pádma-puráńa, analysis of it, &c., P. 18–20, 22–24, 26, 29, 30, &c., 34, 40, 58, 83, 85, 87; 3. 66, 67; 5. 285, 298, 310, 319, 327, 378.

Padmásana, what, in the Yoga philosophy, 5. 230.

Padmávatí, Padmavatí, a city, 4. 217–219.

Padmayoni = Abjayoni, an epithet of Brahmá, 5. 196.

Pádoddhúta, what, in the pancratium, 5. 37.

Padukas, a people, 4. 221.

Padumas, variant of Padukas, 4. 221.

Paḍumáyi (?), variant of Paṭumat, 4. 196.

Padurávi(?), variant of Paṭumat, 4. 196.

Pahlavas, a people, 2. 168, 184, 187, 339; 3. 290–292, 294, 295; 4. 15. See Pahnavas.

Pahnavas, by error for Pahlavas, (?) 2. 168, 185, 187; 3. 292, 295.

Paija, disciple of Játúkarńya, and promulgator of the Ŕig-veda, 3. 48.

Paila, disciple of Vyása, and teacher, &c., of the Ŕig-veda, P. 45; 3. 41, 42, 44, 49–51.

Páingangá, the modern name of an Indian river, 2. 144, 145.

Paippaláyani, disciple of Vedadarśa, and teacher of the Atharva-veda, 3. 62.

Paiśácha, a form of marriage, 3. 105.

Paitálaki, variant of Vaitálaki, 3. 47.

Paiṭhinasi, a lawgiver, quoted, 3. 102.

Páka, a Daitya, slain by Indra, 4. 317.

Páka-saṃsthás, certain sacrifices, 3. 112, 113.

Páka-śásana, an epithet of Indra, 4. 317.

Páka-yujnas = Páka-saṃsthás, 3. 87, 114; 5. 182.

Paksha, 'fortnight,' 2. 254.

Paksha, variant of Chákshusha, son of Anu, 4. 120.

Paksha, variant of Kshemya, son of S'achi, 4. 174.

Pakshaja, a certain kind of cloud, 2. 279.

Pálaka, son of Nahusha, 4. 46.

Pálaka, son of Pradyotana, 4. 178.

Pálaka, son of Chandapradyota (?), 5. 391.

Paláśiní, a river, 2. 132, 148.

Pálin, son of Pṛithu, son of Vena, 1. 192.

Pálita, variously genealogized, 4. 63, 64.

Palita, variant of Pálita, 4. 64.

Pallavas, variant of Pahlavas, 2. 187.

Pallipanjakas, variant of Sunayas, 2. 181.

Pampá, a river, 2. 141, 155.

Paṃśchi (?), variant of Panchi, 4. 46 (where correct the spelling).

Páṃśuráshtras, a people, 2. 164.

Pañava, variant of Kṛikaṇa, 4. 72.

Panchachúḍá, an Apsaras, slanderous of womankind, 3. 141.

Panchadaśa, a certain collection of Vaidik hymns, its origin from Brahmá, 1. 84.

Panchadhanus, son of Sṛinjaya, son of Haryaśwa, 4. 147.

Panchabasta, son of Dakshasávarṇa, Manu of the ninth Manwantara, 3. 25.

Panchajana, a Daitya, son of Saṃhráda, 2. 69. Slain by Kṛishṇa, 5. 48, 90.

Panchajana, the same as Víraṇa, 2. 15, 16.

Panchajana, an epithet of Asamanjas, 3. 298.

Pánchajanya, an island, perhaps fabulous, 2. 129.

Pánchajanya, a conch-shell captured and appropriated by Kṛishṇa, 5. 48.

Panchakas, a caste, established by Viśwasphání, 4. 217.

Panchaka, son of Nahusha, 4. 46.

Pánchálas, Panchálas, peoples, 2. 132, 134, 156, 160; 4. 145, 147.

Panchálas, a dynasty, 4. 184.

Panchála, countries so called, 2. 143, 160; 4. 141, 145.

Pancháлakas = Panchálas, a people, 4. 146.

Pancha-lakshaṇa, what, as applied to a literary composition, P. 7, 10, 29, 92; 5. 259, 261, 274, 275.

Panchamí (?), a river, 2. 150, 152.

Panchanada, a country, the Punjab, 5. 156.

Panchanada, a certain place of pilgrimage, 5. 156.

Panchapadí, a river in S'áka-dwípa, 2. 200.

Páncharátras, an heretical sect, 5. 379.

Panchárchis, synonymous with

Budha, or the planet Mercury, 2. 257 (foot of page).

Panchaśikha, son of Brahmá, 2. 200.

Panchāśwa, variant of Badhryaśwa, 4. 145.

Pancha-tantra, the, a collection of apologues, quoted, or referred to, 3. 102, 104, 197.

Panchi, son of Nahusha, 4. 46.

Pancratium, the Hindu analogue of the, 5. 39, 40.

Pánd'ara, a certain hill in India, 2. 142.

Pánd'avas, descendants of Pánd'u, P. 12; 4. 147, 159, 232, 246; 5. 82. 86. See Pánd'us.

Pánd'ava, patronym of Arjuna, son of Pánd'u, 5. 150, 166.

Pánd'avárańi, an epithet of Kunti, wife of Pánd'u, 5. 96.

Pánd'us, certain persons, and a people, P. 55; 5 '140. See Pánd'avas.

Pánd'u, son of Kŕishńadwaipáyana, 3. 229; 4. 80, 101, 102, 126, 158, 232; 5. 167.

Pánd'u, variant of Práńa, 1. 152, 155.

Pánd'ya, sprung from Turvasu, 4. 117.

Pánins, Kauśika Bráhmans, 4. 28.

Pánini, the grammarian, his age, &c., P. 60, 61; 2. 135, 136, 187, &c.; 3. 47, 48, 54, 55.

Pankti, a metre, its origin from Brahmá's marrow, 1. 86. Identified with a horse of the Sun, 2. 239.

Pannagas, synonymous with Sarpas, 5. 94.

Pannagáni, variant of Pannagári, 3. 50.

Pannagári, disciple of Báshkala, and promulgator of the Ŕigveda, 3. 50.

Pantbána, a hell, 2. 215.

Pápa, a hell, 2. 215.

Pápahará (?), a river, 2. 148, 153.

Pápamochana, a Tírtha at Benares, P. 75.

Páras, Paras, a class of gods in the ninth Manwantara, 3. 24.

Pára, son of Anga, son of Bali, 4. 123.

Pára, son of Samara, 4. 141.

Pára, variously genealogized, 4. 141.

Pára, two rivers, so called, 2. 131, 147.

Pará, a river, 2. 147.

Para, 'the duration of Brahmá's life,' 1. 46; 5. 188.

Para and Pára, what, in philosophy, &c., 2. 6; 3. 251; 4. 253; 5. 119, 232.

Para (?), variant of Púru, 3. 13.

Parabhú, variant of Paraśu, son of Auttami, 3. 6 (where correct the spelling).

Para-brahman, what, 4. 107, 252; 5. 210.

Páradas, a people, 2. 168, 181, 183–185; 3. 290–292, 294, 295.

Parájit, variant of Paráv̇rit, 4. 64.

Para-jnána-maya, what, in philosophy, 2. 328.

Paramákshara, synonymous with Om, 3. 56.

Paramáńu, a measure of time, 1.48.

Paramanyu, variant of Kálánara, 4. 120.

Paramapadátmavat, what, 3. 205.
Paramarshi, what, 3. 205.
Paramártha, what, 2. 39, 326; 3.
208; 4. 292; 5. 242.
Paramárthártha, what, 2. 62.
Paramártharúpin, what, 2. 6.
Paramátman, a name of Vishńu,
the term explained, &c., 1. 3,
41, 56, &c.; 2. 328; 3. 312;
4. 253; 5. 14, 91, 211.
Paramekshu, son of Anu, son of
Yayáti, 4. 120.
Parameśa, the term etymologized,
5. 387.
Paramesht'hin, an epithet of Brah-
má, 2. 19, 330.
Paramesht'hin, an epithet of Vish-
ńu, 4. 264.
Paramesht'hin, son of Indradyum-
na, 2. 106. Called son of Deva-
dyumna, in the Bhágavata-pu-
ráńa, 2. 107.
Parameshu, variant of Paramekshu,
4. 120.
Parameśwara, the term explained,
&c., P. 77; 1. 41, 172; 3. 251;
5. 14, 200.
Paranjaya, variant of Puranjaya,
3. 261, 263.
Parántas, a people, 2. 168.
Parapaksha, variant of Paramek-
shu, 4. 120.
Párapára, what, 2. 6.
Paraparabhúta, what, 2. 6.
Parápareśa, what, 5. 214.
Parapuranjaya, son of Śesha, king
of the Nágas, 4. 212.
Parapuranjaya, variant of Puran-
jaya, 4. 210.
Parárdha, 'the duration of half of
Brahmá's life,' 1. 47; 5. 187, 188.

Paraśakti, a certain divinity, P.
86.
Parasanchárakas, variant of Samavegavaśas, 2. 179.
Paráśara, grandson of Vasishťha,
1. 6.   Son of Śakti, 1. 6, 8;
3. 35, 36.   Disciple of Kapila,
1. 5.   He is taught the Vishńu-
puráńa by Pulastya, 1. 9, &c.
He relates it to Maitreya, 1. 11.
(Perhaps the Paráśara, disciple
of Báshkala, and also Páráśarya
(?), named below, are the same
person.) And see P. 17, 34, 41;
3. 37, 74, 79; 4. 24, &c. &c.
Paráśara, disciple of Báshkala, and
promulgator of the Ŕig-veda,
3. 45.
Paráśara, an astronomer, referred
to, or quoted, 2. 255, 277.
Paráśara (?), 3. 60.   See Páráśarya.
Páráśara, variant of Paráśara, disciple of Báshkala, 3. 44.
Paráśara-smŕiti, a code of law, referred to, 3. 103.
Páráśara-upapuráńa, P. 87.
Páráśarya (?), son of Kuthumi, and
promulgator of the Sáma-veda,
3. 61.
Párasikas, Párasíkas, 'Persians,'
2. 133, 136, 182, 183.
Paraśu, a Ŕishi in the third Manwantara, son of Auttami, 3. 6.
Paraśu, what, 4. 22.
Paraśuráma, a Ŕishi, son of Jamadagni, 4. 18.   Beheads his own
mother, Reńuká, 4. 20.   Slays
the Kshattriyas, 4. 23.   Gives
the earth to the Bráhmans, 4.
23.   Retires to Mount Mahen-

dra, 4. 24. See also P. 108;
1. 151; 2. 72, 119; 3. 23,
311, 316; 4. 21, 56, 184; 5.
283.

Parasurámakshetra, a region on
the Malabar coast, 2. 179.

Páratakas, variant of Párasikas, 2.
182.

Paratanganás, a people, 2. 181.

Paravallabhas, a people, 2. 176.

Parávasu, a Gandharva, 2. 293.

Párávatas, a class of gods in the
second Manwantara, 3. 3.

Parávṛit, son of Rukmakavacha,
4. 63.

Paráyaṇa, a promulgator of the
White Yajur-veda, 3. 57.

Páribhadra, ruler over the realm of
Páribhadra, and son of Yajnabáhu, king of Sálmala-dwípa,
2. 195.

Páribhadra, a region in Sálmala-
dwípa, 2. 195.

Paridhána, what, 3. 95.

Parigha, variant of Pálita, 4. 64.

Párijáta, a tree produced from
churning the ocean, 1. 144, 147;
5. 97. Kṛishṇa takes it away
from Indra's garden, at the in-
stigation of Sachí, 5. 98. It
returns to heaven, 5. 155. See
also 2. 200; 5. 102–105, 113,
133.

Parikara, what, 4. 287.

Parikaha, variant of Parikshit, 4.
162.

Parikaha (?), variant of Parikshit,
4. 152.

Parikshi, variant of Parikshit, 4.
162.

Parikshit, variously genealogized,

P. 40, 41, 44; 4. 148, 152,
160–163, 229–234, 236; 5.
155, 167. The Bhágavata-puráṇa narrated to him, P. 53.

Parikshita, variant of Parikshit, 4.
162.

Párimardana (?), variant of Arimardana, son of Swaphalka, 4.
95.

Pariṇáma, 'digestion,' 3. 128.

Pariṇáma, 'decay,' &c., 5. 254.

Pariṇámin, an epithet of Pradhána,
1. 27.

Páripátra, the northern portion of
the Vindhya chain of mountains, 2. 127, 128, 130, 133,
141, 144, 152, 155, 340; 3.
240, 321. See Páriyátra.

Páripátra, variant of Páriyátra, 3.
320, 321.

Páriplavas, a class of gods in the
fifth Manwantara, 3. 10.

Pariplava, son of Sukhábala, 4.
165.

Pariśraya, variant of Pariplava, 4.
165.

Parítas, variant of Parántas, 2.
168.

Parivatsara, a certain cyclic year,
2. 255.

Parivettṛi, the term defined, 4.
155.

Parivitti, the term defined, 4. 154.

Parivráj, what, 3. 96, 123, 215.
See Bhikshu.

Páriyátra, variously genealogized,
3. 321, 323.

Páriyátra, a mountain-range to the
west of Mount Meru, 2. 123,
124.

Páriyátra = Páripátra, part of the

Vindhya mountains, 2. 113, 128; 3. 321.

Parjanya = Indra, 2. 44; 4. 309. King of clouds, &c., 2. 86; 4. 156, 157.

Parjanya, a Prajápati, son of Agni, 1. 154; 2. 86, 263.

Parjanya, a Ŕishi in the fifth Manwantara, 3. 10.

Parjanya, an Áditya, 2. 285, &c.

Parjanya (who?), 2. 83. See Arvágwasu.

Parńa, a promulgator of the White Yajur-veda, 3. 57.

Parńas, variant of Shańďas, 2. 164.

Parńása, a river, 2. 152; 4. 73.

Parńiká, variant of Parńiní, 2. 81.

Parńiní, an Apsaras, 2. 81–83.

Parokaha, variant of Paramekshu, 4. 120.

Parokshá, variant of Yavakshá, 2. 151.

Pártha, metronym of Arjuna, son of Páńďu and Pŕithá, 4. 28; 5. 156, 159, 161–164.

Párthivas, Kaušika Bráhmans, 4. 28.

Parushńí, the same as Irávatí, a river, 2. 121.

Parvakárin, what, 2. 219.

Parvans, certain ceremonial days, 3. 143, 147.

Párvańa, a particular sacrifice, 3. 113.

Párvańa-śráddha, a certain mortuary observance, 3. 147, 173, 189, 190.

Parvasa, son of Paurńamása, 1. 153.

Parvasí, wife of Parvasa, 1. 153.

Parvata, a Devarshi, son of Kaś-yapa, 1. 122; 2. 20; 3. 68.

Párvatí = Umá, or Satí, daughter of Himavat, P. 32, 71, 89; 1. 157; 2. 80, 234; 4. 33; 5. 108, 109, 321.

Párvatí = Párá, a river so called, 2. 147, 340.

Párvatíyas, a people of mountaineers, 2. 177.

Paryávartana, a hell, 2. 215.

Paryushita, what, 3. 126, 196.

Páśivářas, a people, 2. 180.

Paśu, 'sacrificial animal,' 1. 84; 3. 158; 5. 59, 94, 234, 236, 247.

Paśu = Paśu-bandha, 3. 40.

Pnáus, variant of Pattis, 2. 186.

Paśu-bandha, a certain ceremony, 3. 40 (where correct the spelling), 337.

Paśu-bhartŕi, what, 1. 124.

Páśupatas, an heretical sect, 5. 380.

Paśupati, a form of Rudra, 1. 116, 122; 5. 59, 386. Kŕishńa identified with him, 5. 15.

Paśu-yajna, a certain ceremony, 3. 40.

Pátálas, 'underworlds,' 2. 110, 207–209, &c., 231; 5. 191, 192, 196.

Pátála, one of the Pátálas, P. 31; 1. 145; 2. 209; 3. 19, 24, 299; 5. 6, 191, 251. Its king, Bali, according to one authority, 2. 211.

Patala, variant of Patara, 5. 191.

Pátála-khańďa, a section of the Padma-puráńa, P. 30, 31, 34.

Párálávatí, a river, 2. 148, 340.

Pátaliputra, capital of Magadha, 4. 182, 186, 204.

Patanga, a caste in Plaksha-dwípa, 2. 193.

Patanga, a mountain-range extending southward from Mount Meru, 2. 117.

Patanga, a sun, 5. 191.

Patangí, daughter of Dakaha, wife of Kaśyapa, and mother of grasshoppers, 2. 28.

Pátanjala, the Yoga philosophy so called, 3. 325.

Patanjali, a teacher of the Yoga philosophy, 5. 226, 240.

Pat'arn, a sun, 5. 191.

Path, heavenly, of the Pitris, 2. 264. Of the gods, 2. 269. Of Vishńu, 2. 270.

Pat'bitanga, what, 5. 383.

Pathya, disciple of Kabandha, &c., and teacher of the Atharva-veda, 8. 61, 62.

Pattalaka, son of Hála, 4. 197.

Pattanas, a people, 2. 180.

Pattan Somnáth, the popular name of the site of a once celebrated temple, 5. 47.

Pattis, a people, 2. 184.

Pat'us, a caste, established by Viśwaspháńi, 4. 217.

Pat'umat, son of Meghaswáti, 4. 196.

Pat'umávi (?), variant of Pat'umat, 4. 196.

Pat'umitras, a dynasty, 4. 212, 214, 215.

Pat'umitra, a king, 4. 215.

Paulomas, certain Dánavas, sons of Kaśyapa and Pulomá, 2. 71. Identified with the Nivátaka-vachas, and slain by Arjuna, 2. 72.

Paulomí, patronym of S'achí, wife of Indra, 5. 99.

Paulomí, wife of Bhrigu, 1. 152; 5. 99.

Pauńd'ras, a people, 2. 177; 3. 295; 4. 220, 221; 5. 121.

Pauńd'ra, the same as Pauńd'raka, epithet of the false Vásudeva, 5. 129.

Pauńd'ra, variant of Puńd'ra, son of Dírghatamas, 4. 122.

Pauńd'rakas, a people, 2. 177, 184; 3. 295; 4. 220, 221.

Pauńd'raka, epithet of Vásudeva the impostor, slain by Krishńa, 5. 70, 121–125, 128, 129.

Pauńd'raka, variant of Puńd'ra, son of Dírghatamas, 4. 122.

Pauńd'rikas, a people, 2. 177; 3. 295.

Pauras, a dynasty, 4. 207, 209, 210.

Pauravas, a dynasty, 4. 144, 184.

Pauraví, daughter of Báhlika, and wife of Vasudeva, 4. 108–110.

Pauraví, variant of Yaudheyí, 4. 159.

Pauŕńamása, son of Maríchi and Sambhúti, 1. 153; 3. 17.

Pauŕńamása, a Sádhya, 2. 22.

Pauŕńamása, variant of Púŕńotsanga, 4. 195.

Pauŕńamásí, day of full moon,' 2. 260.

Paurusha, variant of Paurusheya, 2. 289.

Paurusheya, a Rákshasa, 2. 285, &c.

Pausha, a month, Dec.–Jan., 2. 261, &c.; 3. 162.

Paushña = Revatí, an asterism, 2. 277.

Paushpanji, son of Pushpanja, disciple of Sukarman, and teacher of the Sáma-veda, 3. 58–61. See Paushpinji.

Paushpinji, disciple of Hiranyanábha, and teacher of the Sáma-veda, 3. 58, 59. (Almost without doubt, Paushpinji and Paushpanji are one, and Paushpinji is the right name.)

Pava, son of Nahusha, 4. 46.

Pávaka, son of Vahni or Agni, 1. 141, 156, 193 ; 4. 283; 5. 387. Called son of Antardhána, 1. 193. Chief of the Vasus, 2. 85.

Pávakis, the, who, 4. 283.

Pávaki, patronym of Kárttikeya, 4. 283.

Pavamána, son of Vahni or Agni, 1? 156, 193. Called son of Antardhána, 1. 193.

Pavamána, ruler over the realm of Pavamána, and son of Medhátithi, king of S'áka-dwipa, 2. 200.

Pavamána, a region in S'áka-dwipa, 2. 200.

Pavana, son of Auttami, Manu of the third Manwantara, 3. 7.

Pávana, son of Krishña and Mitravindá, 5. 79.

Pavana = Váyu, 5. 46.

Pavana, a mountain-range to the west of Mount Meru, 2. 124.

Pavanásin, what, 5. 12.

Pavana-tanaya, 'son of Pavana,' the same as Hanumat, 1. 117.

Pávaní, a river, 2. 120, 121.

Pavitras, a class of gods in the fourteenth Manwantara, 3. 28.

Pavitrá, a river in India, 2. 148.

Pavitrá, a river in Kuśa-dwípa, 2. 196.

Pavitra, what, in the religion of the Magas, 5. 384.

Pavitravatí, a river in Krauncha-dwípa, 2. 198.

Payas, 'fluid,' 2. 203.

Payoda, son of Yadu, 4. 53, 57.

Payoshñí, a river, or rivers, so called, 2. 130, 144–147, 171.

Payoshñiká, the same as Payoshñí, 2. 144.

Perfection, its eight varieties, 1. 91.

Phálguna, the same as Arjuna, son of Pándu, 3. 84; 5. 140, 160.

Phálguna, a month, Feb.–March, 2. 261, &c. ; 3. 168.

Pheña, variant of Hema, son of Ushadratha, 4. 122.

Phenapas, a class of Pitris, 3. 339.

Pichchhilá, a river, 2. 151.

Píd'a, in astronomy, 'occultation,' 3. 164.

Pináka, the name of S'iva's bow, 1. 141.

Pinákadhrik, an epithet of Virabhadra, 4. 339.

Pind'as, 'balls of food offered to the manes of relatives,' 3. 148.

Pind'a-múlaka, what, as a vegetable production, 3. 195.

Pind'áraka, son of Vasudeva and Rohiñí, 4. 109 ; 5. 141.

Pind'áraka, a place of pilgrimage in Gujerat, 5. 141.

Pind'ini, an Apsaras, 2. 82.

Pingáksha, a sort of bird, P. 55.

Pingala, a Rudra, 2. 25.

Pingala, a writer on prosody, P. 60.

Pinjalá, a river, 2. 150.

Pippala, a region in Sudaréana or Jambu-dwípa, 2. 110.

Pippalá, a river, 2. 148.

Pippala, a certain great tree, where specially growing, according to various accounts, 2. 111, 116.

Pippaláda, disciple of Davadaráa, and teacher of the Atharva-veda, 3. 61.

Pippalávatí, variant of Pátalávatí, 2. 148.

Piśáchas, certain goblins. Created by Brahmá, 1. 87. Offspring of Kaśyapa and Krodhavaśá or else Piśáchá, 2. 74, 75. See also 1. 82; 3. 116, 119; 4. 250; 5. 94, 203.

Piśáchá, daughter of Dakaha, wife of Kaśyapa, and mother of the Piśáchas, 2. 26, 75.

Piśáchiká, a river, 2. 155.

Pishpaláda (?), variant of Pippaláda, 3. 62.

Piśitásin, what, 2. 87.

Pítas, a caste in Śálmala-dwípa, 2. 194.

Pitámaha = Brahmá, 1. 141; 4. 4, 251; 5. 114.

Pitámaha, an ancient lawgiver, cited, 3. 108.

Pítha-sthána, 'a spot where the goddess Deví is worshipped,' P. 90; 4. 261, 262.

Pitris, certain demigods. Their origin from Brahmá's side or armpits, 1. 80, 81, 156; 3. 340. Sons of Angiras and Swadhá, by another account, 2. 29. Their wife, Swadhá, 1. 109, 156. Their offspring, 1. 157. Their king,

Yama, 2. 85; but Agni, 2. 86. Classes and kinds of, 1. 123; 3. 157, &c., 339, 340. Their songs, 3. 170, 197; 5. 249: and see Pitri-gítá. Food grateful to them, 3. 193. See also P. 37, 38, 81, 83; 1. 82, 97, 156, 188; 3. 56, 98, 119, 146, 148, 149; 5. 193.

Pitri-gaña, what, 1. 119.

Pitri-gítá, &c., a certain kind of hymn, 3. 66 (note §), 170, 197, 340; 5. 249.

Pitri-loka, 'the heaven of the Pitris and of Bráhmans,' 1. 97, 98. See Prájápatya.

Pitri-yajna, a particular sacrifice, 3. 40, 93.

Pitri-yána, 'path of the Pitris,' 2. 264, 269.

Pitryá = Maghá, a certain asterism, 2. 258.

Pívara, a Rishi in the fourth Manwantara, 3. 8.

Pívara, ruler over the realm of Pívara, and son of Dyutimat, king of Krauncha-dwípa, 2. 197.

Pívara, a region in Krauncha-dwípa, 2. 197.

Pívarí, wife of Vedaśiras, variously genealogized, 1. 152, 155; 3. 160, 161. Etymology of the word, 2. 342.

Piyadasi, Páli of Priyadarśin, 4. 189.

Piyadassano, Páli, the same as Piyadasi, 4. 189.

Plakaha-dwípa, a continent, particulars regarding, 2. 101, 109, 191, &c.

Plakahagá, a river, 2. 121.

Plakshavatí, a river, 2. 339.

Poison. Produced from the ocean, 1. 144. Swallowed by Síva, 1. 147.

Prabala, son of Kríshńa and Lakshmańá, 5. 81.

Prabhá, wife of Pushpárńa, 1. 178.

Prabhá, daughter of Swarbhánu, and wife of Namuchi, 2. 70; 4. 30.

Prabhá, wife of Vivaswat, son of Kaśyapa, 3. 20.

Prabhákara, ruler over the realm of Prabhákara, and son of Jyotishmat, king of Kuśa-dwípa, 2. 195.

Prabhákara, a Ríshi, sprung from Atri, 4. 129.

Prabhákara, a region in Kuśadwípa, 2. 195.

Prabhánu, son of Kríshńa and Satyabhámá, 5. 81.

Prabhása, a Vasu, 2. 23. His wife, 2. 24. His sons, Devarshis, 3. 70.

Prabhása, a place of pilgrimage on the coast of Gujerat, 5. 47, 146, 147.

Prabháta, son of Vivaswat, son of Kaśyapa, 3. 20.

Prabhava, a Sádhya, 2. 22.

Prabhavápyaya, what, in philosophy, 1. 21, 56.

Prabhávatí, an Apsaras, 2. 82.

Prabhu, variant of Vipra, son of Srutanjaya, 4. 174.

Prabbútas, variant of Prasútas, 3. 12.

Prachetases, ten sons of Práchínabarhis, 1. 102, 127, 157, 195, &c.; 2. 1, &c., 337; 3. 230.

Prachetas, son of Angiras, 3. 297.

He presides over the tongue, 1. 38.

Prachetas, variously genealogized, 4. 119.

Prachetas, the same as Varuńa, 5. 88.

Práchetasa, the same as Daksha, 1. 102.

Práchínabarhis, son of Havirdhána, 1. 157, 192, &c. Of the family of Atri, 1. 193.

Prachinwat, son of Janamejaya, son of Púru, 4. 127.

Práchinwat, the same as Prachinwat, on the authority of the Mahábhárata, 4. 128.

Práchyas, a people, 2. 178.

Pradarśanas, a class of gods in the third Manwantara, 3. 6.

Prádhá, wife of Kaśyapa, son of Maríchi, 2. 81.

Pradhána, 'primary matter,' 1. 4. A form of Vishńu, 1. 18, 19. Properties of it, 1. 20, &c. The same as Prakríti, 1. 20. 'Equipoise of the three qualities,' 1. 26; 5. 199. One with Brahma, 1. 23, &c. Agitated, influenced, or entered into, by Purusha or Vishńu, 1. 27, &c. Merges into spirit, 5. 199. See also P. 94; 1. 67, 75, 164, 169, 172; 2. 37, 58, 94, 232-235; 3. 129, 202; 4. 258; 5. 260.

Pradhánátman, a name of Vishńu, 1. 3.

Prádhánika, what, in philosophy, 1. 24.

Pradosha, son of Pushpárńa, 1. 178.

Pradyotas = Pradyotanas, 4. 178, 179.

Pradyota, variant of Pradyotana, 4. 178, 231.

Pradyotanas, certain kings, 4. 179.

Pradyotana, son of Sunika, 4. 178.

Pradyumna, son of Chákshusha, 1. 178, 179.

Pradyumna, son of Kṛishṇa and Rukmiṇí, 5. 71. Is carried off, when six days old, by S'ambara, a demon, 5. 73. Is reared by Máyádeví, 5. 74. Slays S'ambara, 5. 75. See also 3. 166; 4. 112; 5. 16, 72, 75, 76, 83, 107, 108, 110, 113, 115, 116, 118, 120, 141, 148.

Pradyumna, variant of S'atadyumna, 3. 333.

Prádyumni, patronym of Aniruddha, 5. 84, 120.

Praghosha, son of Kṛishṇa and Lakshmaṇá, 5. 81.

Prágjyotisha, the same as Assam, 5. 55, 88–90, 113.

Praharaṇa, son of Kṛishṇa and Bhadrá, 5. 82.

Praheti, a Rákshasa, 2. 285, &c.

Prahládas, a people, 2. 166.

Prahláda, son of Hiraṇyakaśipu, 2. 30. His descendants, 2. 69. His devotion to Vishṇu, 2. 36. Is persecuted by his own father, 2. 38. Vishṇu appears to him, 2. 62, &c. He becomes king of the Daityas and Dánavas, 2. 64, 85. His abode, in a division of Pátála, 2. 211. See also P. 43, 52, 96; 1. 188; 3. 1, 19; 4. 41. And see Prahrádu.

Prahráda = Prahláda, 1. 190; 2. 30.

Prahwa-swágatokti, what, 3. 130.

Prajáni, son of Prámśu, 3. 242.

Prajápatis, 'mind-born sons of Brahmá.' Variously enumerated, and originating from various parts of Brahmá's body, &c., 1. 100, &c. Married to the daughters of Daksha, 1. 109. Their chief, Daksha, 2. 85. See also P. 42, 95, 96; 1. 78, 79, 89, &c., 110, 131; 2. 9; 5. 144.

Prajápati = Brahmá, 1. 55, 97, 100, 130; 2. 249; 3. 93, 99, 115, 117, 340; 5. 183, 234, 236.

Prajápati, the same as Kaśyapa, 2. 21.

Prajápati, the same as Daksha, 2. 29; 3. 82.

Prajápati, the Vyása of the second Dwápara age, 3. 34, 36. (On what authority is he identified with Manu, in 3. 34?)

Prajápati (which of the Prajápatis named above is intended?), 2. 123, 148, 307.

Prajápati (which of the Prajápatis?), presiding over the genitals, 1. 38.

Prajápatipati = Brahmá, 1. 55; 2. 86.

Prajápati-yajna, a certain sacrifice, 3. 93.

Prájápatya (who?), 3. 166.

Prájápatya, a heaven, 1. 98; 5. 183.

Prájápatya, a certain wind, 5. 204.

Prájápatya, a form of marriage, 3. 105.

Prájápatya-tírtha, what, as applied to the hand, 3. 99.

Prajas, variant of Aja, son of Auttami, 3. 6.

Prajáti, variant of Prajáni, 3. 242.

Prajuá, a synonym of Mahat, 1. 32.

Prákára, what, in architecture, 5. 57, 128, 134.

Prákkośalas, a people, 2. 172.

Prakoshńá, variant of Pramlochá, 2. 293.

Prákrits, what, in philosophy, 1. 24, 26, 74, 76, 78, 114.

Prákrita-pralaya, what, 5. 169, 201.

Prakritis, the seven, what, in the Sánkhya philosophy, and in the Puráńas, 5. 199.

Prakriti, what, P. 93; 1. 18, &c., 109, 139, 140, 172, 197; 2. 232, 233, 235, 316, 320, 325, 328; 4. 254, 264; 5. 186, 198–200, 214, 225, 260. See Pradhána.

Prákritika, what, in philosophy, 1. 113; 5. 186.

Prakriti-khańd'a, a part of the Brahma-vaivarta-puráńa, P. 65, 67.

Prakriyá-páda, a part of the Váyu-puráńa, P. 37.

Pralamba, a Daitya, subject to Kańsa, 4. 250, 272, 300, 301, 322, 335. Slain by Balabhadra, 4. 304, 305.

Pralaya, 'dissolution.' Fourfold, 1. 113, &c. Account of, 5. 169, &c. Three kinds of, 5. 186. Incidental, 5. 186. Elemental, 5. 195, &c. Final, 5. 202. See also P. 81; 1. 4. See also Dissolution.

Pramada, a Rishi in the third Manwantara, 3. 7.

Pramatha, an attendant of S'iva, 5. 113, 115, 116, 128.

Pramáthiní, an Apsaras, 2. 81.

Pramati, son of Rantinára, 4. 129.

Pramati (who?), 5. 251.

Pramati, variant of Prajáni, 3. 242.

Pramati, variant of Sumati, 3. 247.

Pramátri, 'mother's mother,' 3. 115.

Pramita, variant of Pramati, 5. 251.

Pramlá, variant of Pramlochá, 2. 81.

Pramlochá, an Apsaras who beguiles the sage Kańd'u, 2. 2, &c., 75, 81–83, 285, 287, 291, 293; 3. 27,

Pramlochantí, an Apsaras, 2. 81, 83.

Pramlová (?), variant of Pramlochá, 2. 287.

Pramoda, 'hilarity,' sprung from Brahmá, 1. 102,

Pramoda, son of Drid'háśwa, son of Kuvalayáśwa, 3. 265.

Prámsu, son of Vaivaswata or S'raddhádeva, the Manu presiding over the current Manwantara, 3. 14, 232, 233.

Prámsu, son of Vatsaprí, 3. 242.

Pramucha, a Muni, fosterer of the nymph Revatí, 3. 9.

Práńa, son of Dhátri and Áyati, 1. 152.

Práńa, son of Dhara, a Vasu, 2. 23.

Práńa, a Rishi in the second Manwantara, variously genealogized, 3. 3, 4.

Práńa, a certain measure of time, 1. 48.

Pránakrishna-sabdámbudhi, 3. 131.
(The more correct name of the
work intended here follows.)

Pránakrishníya-sabdábdhi, a modern Sanskrit dictionary, referred to, 5. 390. See the last
article.

Pránarodha, a hell, 2. 215.

Pranava, the same as Om, 3. 38.

Pránáyáma, what, in the Yoga
philosophy, 2. 89, 272; 3. 55;
4. 308; 5. 230-232, 240.

Pranetri, 'promulgator,' 3. 30, 39.

Pranidhána, what, in the Yoga
philosophy, 5. 229, 239(note§§).

Prápti, daughter of Jarásandha,
and wife of Kamsa, 5. 50.

Prasáda, 'favour,' son of Dharma,
1. 111.

Prasáma, son of Vasudeva, son of
Súra, 4. 111.

Prasandhi, son of Manu in the
Krita-yuga, 3. 243.

Prasannateyu, son of Raudrásva,
4. 128.

Prasanneyu, son of Raudrásva, 4.
128.

Prasena, son of Nighna, son of
Anamitra, 4. 74, &c. Is killed
by a lion, 4. 77.

Prasena, variant of Devavat, son
of Akrúra, 4. 96.

Prasenajit, son of Viswasáhwan,
3. 325.

Prasenajit, variously genealogized,
3. 265, 266, 297.

Prasenajit, son of Rátula, 4. 170.

Prasenajit, king of Kosala, son of
Mahápadma, 4. 171.

Prasenajit, king of Magadha, 4.
171.

Prasenajit, son of Mahámandala,
4. 186.

Prasenajit, the same as Renu, 4. 19.

Prasiddhaka, variant of Pratíndhaka, 3. 331.

Praskanwa, descended from Medhátithi, son of Kanwa, 4. 130.

Prasna-upanishad, commentary on
the, referred to, 3. 340.

Prasraya, 'affection,' son of Dharma, 1. 111 (where correct the
spelling); 4. 265.

Prastiahta, Prastishta, what, 5. 37.

Prasrita, son of Vasudeva, son of
Súra, 4. 111.

Prasritas, variant of Prasútas, 3.
12.

Prasriti, son of the Manu Swárochisha, and a Rishi in the second
Manwantara, 3. 5.

Prastára, variant of Prastáva, 2.
106.

Prastáva, son of Udgítha, 2. 106.

Prástávi, variant of Prastáva, 2.
107.

Prastútas (??), variant of Prasútas,
3. 12.

Prasuhmas, a people, 2. 165.

Prasusruka, son of Maru, son of
Síghra or Síghraga, 3. 314.
See Prasusruta.

Prasusruta, variant of, or later substitute for, Prasusruka, 3. 325.

Prasútas, a class of gods in the
sixth Manwantara, 3. 12.

Prasúti, daughter of Swáyambhuva, and wife of Daksha, 1.
108; 3. 162; 5. 386.

Prásyas, variant of Práchyas, 2.
178.

Pratah. 'dawn,' son of Pushpárna,

1. 178 (where correct the spelling) ; 2. 253.

Prátak, a Yaksha, 2. 285, 287, 292, 293.

Pratápa-mártaǹd'a, a work on law, referred to, 2. 153.

Pratardana, son of Divodása, son of Bhímaratha, 4. 24, 33-36, 39, 40, 343.

Pratardana, son of Manwat, 4. 70.

Pratardanas, variant of Pradarśanas, 3. 6.

Prátastana, variant of Prátak, son of Pushpárńa, 2. 253.

Prati, variant of Pratikshattra, 4. 44.

Pratibáhu, son of S'waphalka, 4. 96.

Pratibáhu, son of Vajra, son of Aniruddha, 4. 113.

Pratibandhaka, variant of Pratíndhaka, 3. 331.

Pratibhánu, son of Kŕishńa and Satyabhámá, 5. 81.

Pratíha, son of Parameshťhin, son of Devadyumna, 2. 107. See Pratihára and Pratihartŕi.

Pratihára, son of Parameshťhin, son of Indradyumna, 2. 106. See Pratíha and Pratihartŕi.

Pratihartŕi, son of Pratihára, 2. 106. He is called son of Pratíha, 2. 107.

Pratíka, son of Vasu, son of Bhútajyotis, 3. 335.

Pratíka, variant of Pratíndhaka, 3. 331.

Pratíkáśwa, variant of Supratíka, 4. 168.

Pratikshattra, variously genealogized, 4. 43, 44.

Pratikshattra, son of S'amin, 4. 99.

Pratimásyas, a people, 2. 172.

Pratimatsyas, variant of Pratimásyas, 2. 172.

Pratíndhaka, son of Maru, son of Haryaśwa, 3. 331.

Pratípa, son of Dilípa, son of Bhímasena, 4. 153.

Pratípaka, variant of Pratíndhaka, 3. 331.

Pratipaksha, son of Kshattradharma or Kshattradharman, &c., 4. 43, 44.

Pratipáśwa, variant of Supratíka, 4. 168.

Pratiratha, son of Chyavana, son of Mitrayu, (?) 4. 147.

Pratiratha (?), variant of Apratiratha, 4. 130.

Pratisanchara, what, 1. 52 ; 5. 186, 196.

Pratisarga, 'secondary creation,' P. 63, 93 ; 1. 55.

Pratishťhána, a town, or towns, P. 107 ; 2. 165 ; 3. 237, 238.

Pratíta, son of Bhánuratha, son of Bŕihadaśwa, 4. 168.

Pratítáśwa, son of Bhánuratha, son of Bŕihadaśwa, 4. 168.

Prativáha, son of S'waphalka, 4. 95, 96.

Prativindhya, son of Yudhishťhira, 4. 159.

Prativyoma, son of Vatsavyúha, 4. 167.

Prativyúha, variant of Prativyoma, 4. 167.

Pratyagra, variant of Pratyagraha, 4. 149, 150.

Pratyagraha, son of Vasu, son of Kŕitaka, 4. 149.

Pratyagratha, variant of Pratya-graha, 4. 149.

Pratyáhára, what, in the Yoga philosophy, 4. 307; 5. 199, 232, 240.

Pratyangirasas, certain Riches or verses, sons of Angiras, 2. 28, 29.

Pratyatmya, 'reflexion,' a form of Brahmá, 1. 82.

Pratyaya, a Sarga, 1. 76.

Pratyúsha, a Vasu, 2. 23; 3. 68.

Pravá, instead of Arishta, daughter of Daksha, and wife of Kaśyapa, according to the Váyu-puráńa, 2. 26.

Pravaha, a certain wind, 2. 305, 306.

Praváhas, variant of Ápaváhas, 2. 165.

Praváhita, a Rishi in the third Manwantara, 3. 7.

Pravará, a river, 2. 149; 5. 389.

Právaranas (?), a people, 2. 169.

Pravarasena (??), variant of Pravíra, son of Dharma, 4. 212.

Pravasu, son of Ailina or Ilina, 4. 132.

Pravijayas, a people, 2. 166.

Pravilasena, son of Pattalaka, 4. 197.

Pravillasena (?), variant of Pravila-sena, 4. 197, 202.

Pravíra, variously genealogized, 4. 127.

Pravíra (another), variously genealogized, 4. 132.

Pravíra, son of Haryaśwa, son of Chakshus, 4. 144.

Pravíra, son of Dharma, son of Rámachandra, 4. 211, 212, 214.

Pravíraka, a certain Yavana king, 4. 211.

Právrisheyas, a people, 2. 170.

Pravritta, what, as an epithet of 'works,' 5. 200.

Prayága, a sacred city, now Allahabad, 3. 246; 4. 218, 219; 5. 248.

Práyaśchitta, 'expiation,' proceeding from Brahmá, 1. 85.

Prekshágára, 'theatre,' 5. 29, 33.

Prema-ságara, a Hindí translation from the Bhágavata-puráńa, referred to, 4. 246.

Pretas, 'ghosts,' 3. 119.

Preta-kalpa, a part of the Garuḍa-puráńa, P. 84.

Preta-kárya, 'funeral ceremonies,' 5. 155.

Preta-rája, an epithet of the god Yama, 5. 61.

Pŕishadarbha, variant of Vŕisha-darbha, 4. 121.

Pŕishadaśwa, son of Virúpa, 3. 257.

Pŕishadaśwa, son of Anarańya, 3. 284.

Pŕishadhra, son of Vaivaswata, Manu of the current Manwantara, 3. 14, 232, 233, 238, 239.

Pŕishata, grandson of some Nípa, 4. 143, 144.

Pŕishata, son of Somaka, son of Sahadeva, 4. 148.

Pŕishokta, variant of Vŕishańa, son of Arjuna, 4. 57.

Pŕishťhaja, son of Kumára, son of Agni, 2. 23.

Pŕiśni, variously genealogized. 4. 94.

Pŕiśni, 'earth,' mother of the Maruts, 2. 79.

Pṛithá, daughter of S'úra, son of Devamíḍhusha, and wife of Páńḍu, 4. 101, 102, 126, 320, 321; 5. 156, 164, 167.

Pṛithagas, variant of Pṛithugas, 3. 12.

Pṛithiví, 'earth.' The element, produced from the rudiment of smell, 1. 35, 36. Turns into a cow, and is milked, 1. 187, &c. Whence the name, 1. 183. Mother of the Maruts, 2. 80. See also Diti and Maruts. Lauds Vishńu incarnate as a boar, 1. 59, &c.

Pṛithu, one of the Viswe devas, 3. 192.

Pṛithu, according to the Bhágavata-puráńa, son of Támasa, Manu of the fourth Manwantara, 3. 8.

Pṛithu, a Ṛishi in the fourth Man-wantara, 3. 8. A descendant of Kaśyapa, according to the Váyu-puráńa, 3. 8.

Pṛithu, son of Vena, son of Anga, P. 42; 1. 178, &c.; 2. 85; 4. 240; 5. 388.

Pṛithu, son of Prastáva, 2. 107. See Pṛithusheńa.

Pṛithu, variously genealogized, 3. 263, 297.

Pṛithu, son of Ruchaka, 4. 64.

Pṛithu, son of Chitraka, 4. 96; 5. 148.

Pṛithu, son of Pára, son of Sa-mara, 4. 141.

Pṛithu, variant of Chakshus, son of Purujánu, 4. 144.

Pṛithudána, son of Saśabindu, 4.63.

Pṛithudharma, variant of Pṛithu-karman, 4. 62, 63.

Pṛithudhátṛi, variant of Pṛithu-dána, 4. 63.

Pṛithugas, a class of gods in the sixth Manwantara, 3. 12.

Pṛithujaya, son of Saśabindu, &c., 4. 62, 63.

Pṛithukas, variant of Pṛithugas, 3. 12.

Pṛithukarman, son of Saśabindu, &c., 4. 62, 63.

Pṛithukírtti, son of Saśabindu, 4. 62, 3.

Pṛithukírtti, daughter of S'úra, son of Devamíḍhusha, and mo-ther of Dantavaktra, by one account, 4. 104.

Pṛithula, variant of Pṛithuláksha, 4. 125.

Pṛithuláksha, son of Chaturanga, 4. 125.

Pṛithumat, son of Saśabindu, 4. 63.

Pṛithunjaya, variant of Pṛithujaya, 4. 62.

Pṛithu-rai-charitra, a poem in old Hindí, referred to, 3. 207.

Pṛithurukma, variously genealo-gized, 4. 63, 64.

Pṛithusas (?), variant of Pṛithugas, 3. 12.

Pṛithusattama, son of Pṛithu-śravas, son of Saśabindu, 4. 63.

Pṛithusena, son of Ruchiráswa, 4. 141.

Pṛithusheńa, son of Vibhu, son of Prastáva, 2. 107.

Pṛithushańs, variant of Pṛithusena, 4. 141.

Pṛithuśrava (?), son of Dakshasá-varńa, Manu of the ninth Man-wantara, 3. 25.

Pṛithuśravas, instead of Pṛithu-śrava (?), according to the Váyu-puráńa, 3. 25.

Pṛithuśravas, son of S'aśabindu, &c., 4. 63.

Pṛithuśravas, son of Raghu, son of Dírghabáhu, according to the Bhágavata-puráńa, 3. 313.

Pṛithuyaśas, son of S'aśabindu, 4. 62.

Prīti, 'affection,' daughter of Daksha, and wife of Pulastya, 1. 109, 154.

Priyá, daughter of Daksha, and mother, by one account, of four Manus, known as the Merusá-varńis, 3. 24.

Priyadarśaná, one of Kṛishńa's wives (?), 5. 81.

Priyadarśin, the same as Aśoka, 4. 189 (where correct the spelling), 345.

Priyamedha, son of Ajamíd'ha, 4. 140.

Priyamukhyá, variant of Guńa-mukhyá, 2. 81.

Priyaśiahyá, an Apsaras, 2. 82.

Priyavrata, son of Swáyambhuva Manu, 1. 104, &c., 155, 159; 3. 2, 5, 7, 11; 5. 250. His offspring, 2. 100, 108, 193, 195, 197, 198, 200, 203.

Properties of sensible objects, 1. 37.

Proshakas, a people, 2. 187.

Proshṭhas, a people, 2. 179.

Ptolemy Euergetes, name of, in an ancient Indian inscription, 4. 189.

Pudakas, variant of Padukas, 4. 221.

Pulaha, a Prajápati, son of Brahmá, 1. 8–10, &c., 100, &c., 2. 103, 285, &c.; 3. 3, 8, 11, 68, 160, 164. His wife, Kshamá, 1. 109, 110. His offspring, 1. 154.

Pulaha, a certain star, 4. 233.

Pulaka, variant of Pattalaka, 4. 197.

Pulastya, a Prajápati, son of Brahmá, P. 30, 31, 41, 75; 1. 8, 9, 100, &c.; 2. 103; 284, &c., 330, 3. 3–5, 8, 11, 68, 160, 161, 164, 246. His wife, Prīti, 1. 109, 110. His offspring, 1. 154. Progenitor of the Rák-shasas, 1. 10.

Pulastya, variant of Vasishṭha, 5. 251.

Pulika, variant of Sunika, &c., 4. 178.

Pulimat, son of Gotamíputra, 4. 198.

Pulindas, certain barbarous people, 2. 159, 160, 170, 179, 341; 4. 217. Their origin, 1. 182.

Pulinda, variant of Pulindaka, 4. 192.

Pulindaka, the same as Pulindas, 2. 159.

Pulindaka, son of Árdraka, son of Vasumitra, 4. 192.

Pulindasena, variant of Pravila-sena, 4. 297.

Pulomá, daughter of Vaiśwánara, wife of Kaśyapa, and mother of the Paulomas, certain Dánavas, 2. 71, 72.

Puloman, a Dánava, son of Kaś-yapa, 2. 70; 5. 99. His abode, 2. 211 (where correct Pulomat); 5. 389.

Puloman, son of Viprachitti, son of Kaśyapa, 2. 72.

Puloman, variant of Pulomárchis, 4. 199, 202.

Pulomárchis, son of Chandrasri, and the last of the Andhrabhṛitya kings, 4. 199. See Pulomat.

Pulomat, variant of Pulimat, 4. 198, 201.

Pulomat, variant of Pulomárchis, 4. 199, 201, 203, 204, 231, 236.

Pulomávi, son of Swátikarṇa, 4. 200.

Pulomávit (?), variant of Pulomávi; 4. 200.

Pulovápi (?), variant of Pulomárchis, 4. 199.

Puṁs, 'spirit,' &c., 1. 3, 23, &c.; 2. 233, 323, 332; 3. 202; 4. 258; 5. 59, 199. And see Purusha.

Punarvasu, son of Puru, son of Madhu, 4. 69.

Punarvasu, variously genealogized, 4. 98, 99.

Punarvasu, Punarvasú, a certain asterism, 2. 265, &c., 308; 3. 132, 167.

Puṇḍaríka, a serpent, son of Kaśyapa, son of Maríchi, 2. 74.

Puṇḍaríka, son of Nabhas, son of Nala, 3. 320.

Puṇḍaríká, daughter of Vasishṭha, and wife of Páṇḍu (or of Prásu?), 1. 152, 155.

Puṇḍaríká, an Apsaras, 2. 81–83.

Puṇḍaríkí, a river in Krauncha-dwípa, 2. 198.

Puṇḍaríkáksha, 'lotos-eyed,' a title of Vishṇu or Krishṇa, 1. 1–3;

2. 57, 94; 3. 204; 4. 104, 289, 340.

Puṇḍaríkanayana = Puṇḍaríkáksha, 4. 104, 112.

Puṇḍaríkavat, a mountain-range in Krauncha-dwípa, 2. 197.

Puṇḍras, a people, 2. 132, 170, 185. See Puṇḍrakas.

Puṇḍra, son of Vasudeva, son of Súra, 4. 110.

Puṇḍra, son of Bali, the Daitya, · 4. 122.

Puṇḍra; countries so called, 2. 134, 170, 171, 177; 4. 221.

Puṇḍra, a fabulous city, between the Himavat and Hemakúṭa mountains, 2. 282.

Puṇḍrakas; a people, 4. 220. See Puṇḍras.

Punjal, a festival; observed in the south of India, 4. 313.

Panjikasthalá, an Apsaras, 2. 81–83, 285, 286, 291; 292.

Punjikasthali, variant of Punjikasthalá, 2. 286.

Punnámnyṛiksha; an epithet of ten particular asterisms, 3. 132.

Puṇyá; daughter of Kratu, and wife of Yajnaváma, 1. 155 (where correct the spelling), 260.

Puṇyá, a river; 2. 154.

Puṇyajanas; certain Rákshasas, destroyers of the city of Kuśasthalí, 3. 255.

Pur, synonymous with Mahat, 1. 32.

Pura, 'city,' its extent, form, &c., 1. 94.

Purajánu, variant of Purujánu, 4. 144.

Purajit, son of Aja, son of Úr-
dhwaketu, 3. 334.

Púraka, 'inspiration,' in the Yoga
philosophy, 4. 308; 5. 231.

Puramálini, a river, 2. 148.

Púraña, son of Viswámitra, 4.
28.

Puráñas, 'mythological digests,'
P. 7; 5. 300. Their scope, &c.,
P. 5, &c.; 3. 72, 73. Subjects
of them; P. 7. Their probable
age, P. 16. Their extent, P. 24.
Their names, P. 20, 23; 3. 66,
67. Classes of them, P. 19, &c.
Notices and analyses of them,
severally, P. 27–86. Taught by
Vyása, 3. 42. Taught by Súta,
3. 64. Original Samhitás of
them, 3. 64, &c.

Puráñárñava, the title of a work
connected with the Puráñas, P.
49.

Purañḍas, variant of Puruñḍas, 4.
206.

Purandara, the Indra of the current
Manwantara, 3. 13, 18; 5. 46.

Puranjaya, son of Vikukshi, 3.
261–263.

Puranjaya, son of Bhajamána, son
of Satwata, 4. 72.

Puranjaya, son of Srinjaya, son of
Kálánara, 4. 120.

Puranjaya, son of Vindhyaśakti,
4. 210.

Puranjaya, variant of Nṛipanjaya,
son of Suvíra, 4. 144.

Puranjaya, variant of Nṛipanjaya,
son of Medhávin, 4. 165.

Puranjaya, variant of Ripunjaya,
son of Viśwajit, 4. 176.

Purári, an epithet of S'iva, signi-

fying 'enemy of Pura,' a demon
so called, 2. 112.

Purávatí, a river, 2. 149.

Purikasheña, variant of Pravila-
sena, 4. 197.

Purikáya, Puríkáya, a certain king,
4. 213.

Purikáyá, a city (?), 4. 213.

Purimat, variant of Pullmat, 4.
198.

Puríndrasena, variant of Pravila-
sena, 4. 197, 201.

Puríshabhíru, variant of Pravila-
sena 4. 197.

Puríshasena (?), variant of Pravilasena, 4. 197.

Puríshataru (?), variant of Pravila-
sena, 4. 197.

Puríshí, a particular holy fire, 1.
85 (where correct Puríshin).

Púrñá, a river, 2. 145.

Púrñá, a river (another), 2. 154.

Púrñaka, what, in the worship of
the Magas, 5. 384.

Púrñamása, son of Kṛishña and
Kálindí, 5. 79.

Púrñáśá, a river, 2. 152 (where
correct the spelling); 5. 389.

Púrñotsanga, son of Sríśatakarñí,
4. 195, 200, 202.

Purodaśa, 'a sacrificial cake of
ground rice,' 1. 119.

Purohita, 'priest,' 4. 62.

Purojava, ruler over the realm of
Purojava, and son of Medhátithi, king of S'áka-dwípa, 2. 200.

Purojava, a region in S'áka-dwípa,
2. 200.

Púrta-kamalákara, the, a work on
law, referred to, 2. 131, 132,
339; 3. 190.

Púru, Puru, son of Chákshusha, 1. 177, 178; 3. 13.

Púru, an incarnation of Dharma, and son of Vasudeva, 4. 111.

Púru, son of Yayáti, 3. 266; 4. 46, 48, &c., 116, 117, 120, 126-128, 130, 133, 139, 152, 237.

Púru, son of Jahnu, son of Suhotra, 4. 14, 15, 24.

Puru, son of Madhu, son of Devakshattra, 4. 69.

Purudwat, variously genealogized, 4. 69, 70.

Puruhotra, variously genealogized, 4. 69.

Puruhuta, son of Dravavasu, 4. 70.

Puruja, variant of Purujánu, 4. 144.

Purujánu, son of Susánti, 4. 144.

Purujáti, variant of Purujánu, 4. 144.

Purujit, son of Ruchaka, son of Uśanas, 4. 64.

Purujit, son of Krishna and Jámbavatí, 5. 79.

Purukutsa, son of Mándhátrí, 1. 17; 3. 268, 281-283; 5. 250.

Purukutsa, son of Durgaha, 3. 268.

Purukutsa, son of Anu, son of Purudwat (?), 4. 69.

Puromídha, son of Hastin, 4. 140.

Puruńdas, Puruńdas (?), a dynasty, 4. 206.

Purunjas, variant of Puruńdas, 4. 206.

Púrúravas, son of Budhá and Ilá, 3. 236; 4. 5. His progeny, 4. 53. The city of Pratishthána is bestowed on him, 3. 237. Becomes enamoured of Urvasí, 4. 6, &c. Strikes fire, and makes it threefold, 4. 10. Traditions of him, 4. 11. See also P. 107; 3. 168; 4. 30, 31, 343.

Purúravas, king of the Madras, 4. 5.

Purúravas, variant of Puruvat (?), 3. 189-191.

Purushas, a caste in Kraunchádwípa, 2. 193.

Purusha, 'the male portion of Brahmá,' 1. 106. See Viráj.

Purusha, 'spirit.' A form of Vishńu, 1. 16; 2. 295; 3. 72, 83, 252. For 'disciple,' 4. 73. See also P. 94; 1. 3, 4, 27, 58; 2. 37, 58; 5. 200, 201. And see Puńs.

Purusha, son of Chákshusha, Manu of the sixth Manwantara, 3. 13.

Purushakutsa (?), variant of Purukutsa, son of Mándhátrí, 3. 268.

Purushaprabhu, son of Madhu, son of Devakshattra, 4. 70.

Purusha-swarúpin, what, 3. 252.

Purushavara, variant of Purúravas, son of Budhá, 3. 237.

Purushottama, 'supreme spirit,' a title of Vishńu, P. 73; 1. 16, 27, 63, 167; 170, 196, &c.; 2. 57, &c. &c.; 3. 282, 299; 4. 75, 247, 248, 256; 5. 2, 7, 119, 161, 166, 184, 200, 216, 254, 344.

Purushottama, a disquisitionist on the Bhágavata-puráńa, referred to, P. 48.

Purushottama, a region (?), 'Áyatana,' of Vishńu, 2. 5.

Purushottama-kshetra, a holy place in Orissa, sacred to Purushottama, P. 28, 73.

Puruvaśa, son of Mahátejas (?), 4. 69.

Puruvat (?), one of the Viśwe devas, 3. 191.

Puruvatsa (?), variant of Puruvaśa, 4. 69.

Púrva, son of Mídhwas, 3. 335.

Púrva-bhádrapadá, a certain asterism, 2. 268, &c.; 3. 132, 167, 179.

Púrvábhirámá, a river, 2. 148.

Púrvachitti, an Apsaras, 2. 75, 81–83, 285, 288, 293.

Púrvábña, 'forenoon,' 2. 295.

Púrvaja, an epithet of Vishńu, 1. 2, 3.

Púrvajá = Aświní (?), an asterism, 2. 264.

Púrva-phálguní, an asterism, 2. 259, &c.

Púrva-proshťhapadá = Púrva-bhádrapadá, 2. 265.

Púrváshádhá, an asterism, 2. 259, &c., 308; 4. 230, 234.

Púshan, an Áditya, 1. 131, 141, 180; 2. 27, 285; 4. 339.

Pushkalas, a caste in Krauncha-dwípa, 2. 197.

Pushkalas, variant of Múshakas, 2. 178.

Pushkala, variant of Pushkara, son of Bharatá, 3. 319.

Pushkala, variant of Rátula, 4. 169.

Pushkalávartaka = Pushkarávartaka, 2. 280.

Pushkaras, the Bráhmans of Krauncha-dwípa, 2. 197.

Pushkara, son of Bharata, son of Daśaratha, and king of Pushkarávatí, 3. 319.

Pushkara, a famous lake, near Ajmere, P. 30; 2. 96; 4. 26; 5. 243.

Pushkara, variant of Kiṁnara, son of Sunakshatra, 4. 168.

Pushkara-dwípa, a certain continent, 2. 101, 109, 110, 201, &c., 245.

Pushkara-máhátmya, a Pauráńik composition, 2. 12.

Pushkaráruńí, variant of Pushkarin, 4. 138.

Pushkarávartaka, a kind of cloud, 2. 280.

Pushkarávatí, a city, identified with Arrian's Peukolaotis, 3. 319.

Pushkarin, son of Urukshaya, 4. 138.

Pushkariní, daughter of Avaraúya, and wife of Chakshusha, 1. 177, 179. Called daughter of Víraña, and also wife of Vyushťa, 1. 178.

Pushkariní, wife of Bhumanyu, 4. 138.

Pushkasas, a dynasty, 4. 206.

Pushpadaṁshťra, a serpent, son of Kaśyapa, 2. 74.

Pushpajáti, a river, 2. 155.

Pushpamitras, a dynasty, 4. 212, 214, 215.

Pushpamitra, the first S'unga king, 4. 189–191.

Pushpamitra, king of Mekalá, 4. 213, 215; 5. 392.

Pushpanja, father of Paushpanji, 3. 58.

Pushpárña, son of Vatsara, son of Dhruva, 1. 178.

Pushpavarsha, a mountain in Sálmala-dwípa, 2. 195.

Pushpavat, variously genealogized, 4. 150.

Pushpavat, a mountain in Kuśa-dwípa, 2. 196.

Pushpaveńí, a river, 2. 154.

Pushtí, 'thriving,' daughter of Daksha, and wife of Dharma, 1. 109, 110.

Pushtí, daughter of Paurńamása, 1. 153.

Pushtí, daughter of Dhruva, 1. 178.

Pushtímat, variant of Tushtimat, 4. 99.

Pushtí-śráddba, a particular mortuary ordinance, 3. 147.

Pushya, son of Reńu, 3. 297.

Pushya, variously genealogized, 3. 324.

Pushya, a certain asterism, 2. 259, &c., 308; 3. 132, 167; 4. 229.

Pushya = Pausha, the month so called, 3. 168.

Pushya, variant of Satyadhríta, 4. 150.

Put, a hell, that of the sonless dead, 1. 183.

Pútaná, a she-demon, daughter of Bali, 2. 69. Is slain by Kŕishńa, 4. 272, 276, 278, 281, 335; 5. 33, 87. And see 4. 272.

Pútauá, variant of Jharjhara, 2. 69.

Pútimŕittika, a hell, 2. 215.

Pútisŕinjayas, variant of Ghatasŕinjayas, 2. 180.

Putra, son of Vasishtha, son of Brahmá, 1. 155.

Putra, son of Priyavrata, 2. 100, 101.

Putra, son of Brahmishtha, 3. 324.

Putravat, variant of Pushpavat, 4. 150.

Púyavaha, a hell, 2. 215, 218.

Púyoda, a hell, 2. 215.

Qualities, three, Satya, Rajas, Tamas, 1. 3, 13, 26. See Guńas.

Rabhasa, sprung from Rambha, son of Áyus, 4. 43.

Rádhá, wife of Kŕishńa, P. 21, 22, 66, &c.; 4. 245, 329, 330; 5. 264, 269, 283, 285, 321, 342, 345.

Rádhá, wife of Adhiratha, 4. 126, 143; 5. 391.

Rádheya = Karńa, and why so called, 4. 126, 142.

Rádhika, son of Jayasena, son of Sárvabhauma, 4. 153.

Rága, 'attachment,' its place in philosophy, 1. 69.

Rághava, patronym of Ráma, 1. 151; 3. 81; 4. 104, 241.

Raghus, the, descendants of Raghu, 4. 240.

Raghu, variously genealogized, 3. 305, 313-316; 4. 241.

Raghu, son of Yadu, son of Yayáti, 4. 53.

Raghunandana, a modern law compiler, 3. 328.

Raghuvamśa, the, a poem, referred to, P. 9, 30, et passim.

Rahasyá, a river, 2. 147.

Rahasya, the term explained, 5. 47.

Ráhu, son of Viprachitti and Simhiká, 2. 55, 72 : but see 5. 387. King of meteors, 2. 86.

His car and horses, 2. 304.
Eclipse personified, 2. 308.
Áyus, eldest son of Purúravas,
marries his daughter Prabhá,
4. 30. At the churning of the
ocean, he obtains a portion of the
Amrita, is beheaded by Vishńu,
is transferred to the skies, &c.,
1. 147, 148. See also 2. 258,
259. Another name of Ráhu is
Swarbhánu.

Ráhula, variant of Rátula, 4. 169,
170.

Ráhulasú, the same as S'ákya, 4. 170.

Raibhyas, a class of gods in the
fifth Manwantara, 3. 10.

Raibhya, son of Sumati, son of
Rautinára (?), 4. 130.

Rain. How formed, 2. 279. Kinds
of it, 2. 280.

Raiva, variant of Revata, 3. 249.

Raivata, a Rudra, 2. 24, 25.

Raivata, a Manu in the fifth Manwantara, variously genealogized,
2. 100; 3. 1, 9, 11, 17, 18, 20,
227, 337.

Raivata, son of Revata, king of
the Ánartas, 3. 249. He founds
and dwells in the city of Kuśasthalí, 3. 249; 5. 56. He visits
Brahmá, 3. 249, &c. Bala-
bhadra marries his daughter,
Revatí, 3. 254; 5. 68. And
see 5. 137. Another name of
Raivata is Kakudmin.

Raivata (?), variant of Viloman, 4.
97.

Raivataka = Raivata, son of Revata, 3. 249.

Raivataka, a mountain-range,
branching off from the Vindhyas, 2. 141.

Raivataka, a mountain-range in
S'áka-dwípa, 2. 198.

Raivataka, a lake on Mount Kumuda, 3. 9.

Raja, son of Viraja or Virajas, 2.
107. See Rajas.

Rájá (rájan), 'king,' its etymology,
1. 184.

Rája-bhata, what, in legal terminology, 2. 217.

Rájádaswátí (?), variant of Chakoraswátikarńa, 4. 201.

Rájádhideví, variously genealogized, wife of Jayasena, the
Ávantya, 4. 101, 103; 5. 82
(where she should have been
called paternal aunt of Krishńa).

Rájagriha, a city in Magadha, 4.
171 (where correct the spelling),
180, 181, 345.

Rajaka, 'dyer' (?), 5. 18.

Rájaka, variant of Janaka, son of
Viśákharúpa, 4. 179.

Rájaní, a river, 2. 148.

Rajauí, a river in S'álmala-dwípa,
2. 195.

Rája-nighańtu, the, a metrical
work, referred to, 2. 147.

Rájanyas, the same as Kshattriyas,
3. 90, 153.

Rájarshis, 'royal sages,' their abode,
&c., 3. 69, 262; 4. 104.

Rajas, son of Vasishtha, son of
Brahmá, 1. 155; 2. 86, 263;
3. 7.

Rajas = Raja, son of Viraja or
Virajas, 2. 107.

Rajas, 'quality of foulness, pas-
sion, activity,' P. 20; 1. 4, 35,
44.

Rajasas, a class of gods in the fifth
Manwantara, 3. 17.

Rájasa, adjective of Rajas, P. 20–22 ; 5. 267, 285, 310, 317, &c.

Rájasravas, Rájasravas, Vyása in the twenty-second Manwantara, 3. 35. He is assigned to the twenty-first Manwantara, 3. 37.

Rájasúya, a particular sacrifice, 3. 288 ; 4. 2.

Rája-tarangiń, the, a metrical history, referred to, 2. 178, 179, 186 ; 4. 223.

Rájavat, son of Dyutimat, son of Páńd'u (or of Práńa ?), 1. 153.

Rájeyu, variant of Riteyu, 4. 128.

Raji, son of Áyus, son of Purúravas, 4. 30, 40, 41, &c.

Rájin, a horse of the Moon, 2. 299.

Rájívalochaná, daughter of Jarásandha, and consort of Kamsa, 4. 273.

Rájní, daughter of Raivata, the fifth Manu, and wife of Vivaswat, 3. 20.

Rájyábhishekapaddhati, a modern work, on the consecration of kings, referred to, 2. 339 ; 3. 190.

Rájyádhideva, variant of Ráshťrádhideva, 4. 99.

Rájyavardhana, a medieval king, 2. 341.

Rájyavardhana, son of Dama, son of Narishyanta, 3. 245.

Ráká, 'day of full moon,' daughter of Angiras, 1. 153 ; 2. 261.

Ráká, a river in Sálmala-dwípa, 2. 195.

Rákhí-púrńímá, the Hindí name of a certain festival, 4. 276.

Rakshá, 'amulet,' 4. 276.

Rakshasas, the same as Rákshasas, 5. 247.

Rakshas, son of Kaśyapa and Khasá, and progenitor of the Rákshasas, 2. 75.

Rakshas, the same as Nairrita, 2. 112.

Rákshasas, certain demons. Descendants of Pulastya, 1. 10. They proceed from Brahmá, 1. 82. Originate from Kaśyapa and Surasá, 2. 74. Offspring of Kaśyapa and Khasá, 2. 75. Sprung from Rákshas, son of Kaśyapa and Khasá, 2. 75. Twelve of them named, 2. 285, &c. Etymology of the word, 1. 82, 83. And see 1. 87, 188 ; 4. 250, 266, 277 ; 5. 94, 203, 246, 247, 383.

Rákshasa, a form of marriage, 3. 105 ; 5. 71, 72.

Rakshogańabhojana, a hell, 2. 215.

Rakshoghna-mantra, the term explained, 3. 182.

Rakshoha (?), variant of Heti, 2. 292.

Raktapúya, a hell, 2. 215.

Rámas, a people, 2. 133, 135.

Ráma, son of Daśaratha, P. 4, 15, 31, 32, 59, 62 ; 1. 165 ; 3. 81, 248, 314–318, 320, 332 ; 4. 220, 259.

Ráma, the same as Paraśuráma, 1. 151 ; 3. 23, 311 ; 4. 19, 20, &c.

Ráma = Balaráma, 4. 280, 283, 285, 286, 288, 291, 297, 298, 305, 306, 323, 335, 336 ; 5. 8–11, 17, 18, 20, 23, 35, 48, 50, 51, 54, 64, 66–68, 70, 84,

110, 116, 120, 130, 134, 135, 138, &c. &c.

Rámá, an Apsaras, 2. 83.

Rámachandra, 1. 157; 5. 283, 284. See Ráma, son of Daśaratha.

Rámachandra, son of Puranjaya, son of Vindhyaśakti, 4. 210.

Rámachandra, a certain king, 4. 212.

Rámagangá, another name of the river Suváma, 2. 151.

Rámagiri, variant of Kámagiri, 2. 141.

Rámakrishńa, a writer on exequial ceremonies, 3. 190.

Ramánas, a people, 2. 182.

Ramaña, son of Dhara, a Vasu, 2. 23.

Ramańaka, ruler over the kingdom of Ramańaka, and son of Yajnabáhu, king of Sálmala-dwípa, 2. 195.

Ramańaka, son of Vítihotra. 2. 203.

Ramańaka, a region in Sálmaladwípa, 2. 195.

Ramańaka, an island, perhaps fabulous, 2. 129; 4. 287.

Rámanátha, a commentator on the Káśí-khańd'a, referred to, 2. 229.

Rámáunja, a religious reformer, his time, &c., P. 16, 71; 5. 257, 338, 347, 356.

Rámáśrama, a commentator on the Amara-kośa, referred to, P. 7.

Rámáśrama, a dissertator on the Bhágavata-puráńa, referred to, P. 47.

Rámaťhas, a people, 2. 183.

Rámáyańa, a famous poem, the genuine and the spurious, referred to, P. 4, &c. &c.; 2. 120, 145–147, 150, 151, 153–164, 166–178, 180–183, 185–287, 189, 190, 337, 339; 3. 317; 5. 280, 281, 284.

Rambha, a serpent, 2. 285, 287, 291, 293; 5. 12.

Rambha, son of Vivińśati, 3. 243.

Rambha, son of Áyus, son of Purúravas, 4. 30, 43.

Rambhá, an Apsaras, 2. 75, 81–83, 285, 287, 289, 291, 293; 5.165.

Rámeśwara, the same as Setubandha, 3. 328.

Ramya, son of Agnídhra, and king of Ramyaka, the country between Mount Meru and Mount Níla, 2. 102.

Ramyaka, a fabulous region, to the north of Mount Meru, 3. 111, 114.

Ramyaka, the same as Ramya, 2. 102.

Rańachhor, the Hindí name of a modern form of Krishńa, 5. 156.

Rańadhrishťa, son of Dhrishťa, son of the Manu Vaivaswata, 3. 255, 256.

Rańadhrishťa, son of Ntíga or Nabhaga, 3. 335.

Rańadhrishťa, by one account, son of Vrishńi, son of Kunti, 4. 68.

Rańaka, variant of Kuńďaka, 4. 171.

Rańanjaya, son of Kŕitanjaya, son of Dharmin, 4. 169.

Rańastambabbramara, a district in India, 2. 158.

Rańostambha (?), a district in India, 2. 158.

Ranáśwa, son of Samhatáśwa, 3. 265.

Ráńáyaníya, disciple of Laugákshi, and promulgator of the Sáma-veda, 3. 60, 61.

Ráńáyaníyi, son of Ráńáyaníya, 3. 61.

Randhra, variant of Bradhna, 3. 29.

Rangavalí, wife of Rantideva, 4. 137.

Rangopajívin, what, 2. 218.

Rantibhára, variant of Rantinára, 4. 129.

Rantideva, son of Sankriti, son of Nara, 4. 137.

Rantinára, son of Riteyu, 3. 266 (where correct the spelling); 4. 129; 5. 390.

Raptee, the popular name of a river of which the Rohiní is an affluent, 4. 170.

Rása, a sort of dance, practised by Krishna and the Gopís, 4. 324, 328, 329.

Rasádu (?), variant of Rushadgu, 4. 61.

Rasakulyá, a river in Kuśa-dwípa, 2. 197.

Rása-mańdala, a sort of dance, 4. 329, 330.

Rasátala, a Pátála, or underworld, 1. 62; 2. 209; 3. 281, 282; 4. 251; 5. 118.

Rasawáhiní, the, a Pálí work, referred to, 4. 189.

Rasáyana, 'alchemical therapeutics,' 4. 33.

Rása-yátrá, a certain annual festival, 4. 330.

Ráshtra (?), son of Káśi (?), 4. 32, 343.

Ráshtrabhrit, an Apsaras, 2. 81.

Ráshtrádhideva, son of Vidúratha, son of Bhajamána, 4. 99.

Ráshtrapála, son of Ugrasena, son of Áhuka, 4. 99.

Ráshtrapálá, variant of Ráshtrapálí, 4. 99.

Ráshtrapálí, daughter of Ugrasena, son of Áhuka, 4. 99.

Ráshtravardhana, variant of Rájyavardhana, 3. 245.

Raśmipas, a class of Pitris, 3. 339.

Rasollásá, what, according to the Yoga philosophy, 1. 91.

Rathabhrit, variant of Rathakrit, 2. 293.

Rathachitra, a Yaksha, 2. 285, &c.

Rathachitrá, a river, 2. 150.

Rathajit, in the Linga-purána, instead of Ritajit, the Yaksha, 2. 293.

Rathakrichchhra, in the Váyu-purána, instead of Rathakrit, 2. 291.

Rathakrit, a Yaksha, 2. 285, &c.

Rathamitra, variant of Rathachitra, the Yaksha, 2. 293.

Rathantara, a Sádhya, 2. 22.

Rathántara, corrupted from Rathitara, the same as Śákapúni, 3. 45-47, 50.

Rathantara, a Kalpa, P. 65, 66.

Rathantara, a portion of the Sáma-veda, 1. 128; 2. 295, 343; 3. 48. Its origin from Brahmá, 1. 84.

Rathasthá, a river, 2. 121.

Rathaswana, a Yaksha, 2. 285, &c.

Rathasyana, variant of Rathaswana, 2. 289.

Rathaujas, a Yaksha, 2. 285, &c

Rathavara, son of Bhímaratha, son of Vikriti, 4. 68.

Ratha-yátrá, a festival so called, P. 64, 71.

Rathítaras, a race descended from Rathítara, 3. 259.

Rathítara, son of Prishadaśwa, son of Virúpa, 3. 258, 259.

Rathítara = Śákapúni, 3. 45, 47, 48.

Rati, daughter of Daksha, and wife of Káma, 5. 76. 77. See Nandí.

Ratnagarbha Bhattáchárya, a commentator on the Vishńu-puráńa, P. 115, 116.

Ratnakútí (?), daughter of Raudráśwa, and wife of Prabhákara, 4. 129.

Ratnapála, a certain king, 4. 223.

Ratnávalí, a drama, referred to, 2. 341.

Rathoragas (?), a people, 2. 175.

Rátri, 'night,' a body of Brahmá, 1. 81.

Rátri, a river in Krauncha-dwípa, 2. 198.

Rátula, variously genealogized, 4. 169, 170.

Rauchya, Manu, according to various accounts, of the ninth, and of the thirteenth, Manwantara, son of Ruchi and Mánini, 3. 25, 27.

Raudra = Árdrá, an asterism, 3. 167.

Raudráśwa, variously genealogized, 4. 127, 128.

Raudrí-saṁhitá. See Rudra-saṁhitá.

Rauhińeya, metronym of Balabhadra, 4. 189, 300–302.

Raumas, a class of demigods, originating from the pores of Vírabhadra's skin, 1. 130.

Raupyanábha, a Rákshaka, 1. 188.

Raurava, a hell, 1. 112; 2. 214–216; 3. 198; 5. 386.

Rávaṇa, son of Viśravas, 1. 10, 154. He slays Anarańya, 3. 284. Carries off Sítá, 3. 317. Is taken captive by Kártavírya, 4. 56. His former existence as Śiśupála, 4. 104, 106.

Ravaṇa (?), variant of Ramańa, 2. 23.

Ravi, the same as Súrya, 1. 180. And see Sun.

Rays of the sun, 2. 297, 298; 5. 191.

Raya, son of Purúravas, son of Budha, 4. 13.

Ráyáńayíya (?), variant of Báńáyaniya, 3. 60.

Rechaka, what, in the Yoga philosophy, 4. 308; 5. 231.

Rechaka, a certain disposition of the feet in dancing, 4. 291.

Religion, periods of the Hindu, P. 1, &c.

Reńus, certain Kauśika Bráhmans, 4. 28.

Reńu, son of Vikukshi, 3. 297; 4. 18, 28.

Reńuka, son of Reńu, 4. 28.

Reńuká, daughter of Reńu, and wife of Jamadagni, 4. 18, 19.

Reńuká, a river in Śáka-dwípa, 2. 199.

Reva, variant of Revata, 3. 249.

Revá-khańďa, a part of the Skanda-puráńa, P. 73, 87.

Revá-máhátmya, a composition, P. 24, 35, 80, 87.

Revá-máhátmya, a composition (another), 2. 132, 144, 148, 151, 341; 5. 118.

Revanta, son of Vivaswat, son of Kaśyapa, 3. 20, 21.

Revata, variously genealogized, 3. 249.

Revata, variant of Viloman, 4. 97.

Revatí, an Apsaras, 3. 9.

Revatí, daughter of Raivata, and wife of Balabhadra, 3. 249, 254; 4. 109; 5. 68, 137, 154.

Revatí, an asterism, 2. 258, &c.; 3. 9.

Ribhus, a class of gods in the current Manwantara, 3. 15.

Ribhus, variant of Bhavyas, the gods so called, 3. 12.

Ribhu, mind-born son of Brahmá, 1. 77. Legend of him, 2. 330, &c. He receives the Vishńu-puráńa from Brahmá, 5. 250 (where correct the spelling), 392.

Riches, 'hymns of the Rig-veda,' 3. 43. Thirty-five particular ones, accounted children of Angiras, 2. 28, 29.

Rich, the same as Rig-veda, 5. 211.

Richa, son of Sunítha, son of Sushena, 4. 164.

Richeyu, variant of Riteyu, 4. 127, 128.

Richíka, son of Úrva, 3. 80; 4. 16, 17, &c., 25, 26.

Rig-veda, the, its origin, P. 2; 1. 84, 171. Its Samhitás, &c., 3. 40—51; 5. 200.

Rig-vidhána, a work connected with the Rig-veda, referred to, P. 60.

Rijísha, a hell, 2. 215.

Riju, son of Vasudeva, son of S'úra, 4. 110.

Rijudása, son of Vasudeva, son of S'úra, 4. 110.

Rijwáhwa, a sage of the Mihira family, 5. 382, 385.

Riksha, sprung from Bhrigu, and Vyása in the twenty-fourth Dwápara age, 3. 35.

Riksha, son of Ariha, son of Devá-tithi, 4. 128.

Riksha, son of Ajamídha, 4. 148, 153.

Riksha, son of Devátithi, 4. 152, 153.

Rikshá, wife of Ajamídha, 4. 148.

Riksha, a chain of mountains in Central India, 2. 127, 128, 130, 141, 144, 145, 151, 153, 155, 171; 4. 24.

Riksha (correct the spelling), variant of Chakshus, son of Puru-jánu, 4. 144; 5. 391.

Rikshaka, the same as Riksha, the chain of mountains so called, 2. 113.

Rikshavat, the same as Riksha, the chain of mountains so called, 2. 145, 160, 340; 4. 64, 77.

Rikshya (??), variant of Riksha the Vyása, 3. 35.

Rińadya, variant of Rińajya, 3. 35.

Rińajya, Vyása of the eighteenth Dwápara age, 3. 35.

Rińavya (??), variant of Rińajya, 3. 35.

Rińin (??), variant of Rińajya, 3. 35.

Ripu, son of S'lishti, l. 177. Also called son of Udáradhí, l. 178.

Ripu, son of Yadu, son of Yayáti, 4. 53.

Ripu, son of Babhru, son of Druhyu, 4. 118.

Ripukáyán (?), a king, 4. 213.

Ripunjaya, son of S'lishti, l. 177.

Ripunjaya, son of Viswajit, son of Satyajit, 4. 170, 171, 176, 178.

Ripunjaya, variant of Nripanjaya, son of Suvíra, 4. 144.

Ripunjaya, variant of Vipra, son of S'rutanjaya, 4. 174.

Rishabhas, a caste in Krauncha-dwípa, 2. 198.

Rishabha, son of Nábhi, 2. 103. Has a hundred sons, 2. 103. Adopts a religious life, &c., 2. 103. Is the first teacher of Jaina doctrines, 2. 104, &c.

Rishabha, a Rishi in the second Manwantara, variously genealogized, 3. 3, 4.

Rishabha, father of S'waphalka, 4. 93, 94.

Rishabha, son of Kuságra, 4. 150.

Rishabha, a mountain-range running north from Mount Meru, 2. 117.

Rishabha (?), a mountain in India, 2. 141, 340. See Vrishabha.

Rishabhá = Árshabhí, certain asterisms so called, 2. 277.

Rishabha (??), variant of Rushadgu, 4. 61.

Rishis, seven in number, the same as Prajápatis, 1. 101, &c. Twelve in number, and attendants on the Sun, 2. 284, &c. Classes

of them, 3. 68. Appearing in various Manwantaras, 3. 2, &c. &c. As an asterism, 4. 230–236. One with Ursa Major, 2. 226, 269, 307. Their year, 1. 49. Mocked by the Yádavas, 5. 142. Whence their name, 3. 68. See also P. 38; 1. 174, 175; 5. 193, 195, 247.

Rishi-anukramañs, a work connected with the Vedas, by S'aunaka, referred to, 4. 31.

Rishikas, peoples so called, 2. 167, 181. See Rishtikas.

Rishiká, a river, 2. 132 (where correct the spelling), 154, 167, 339.

Rishikulyá, a river, 2. 130–132, 154.

Rishikulyá = Gangá, the river Ganges, 2. 154.

Rishtikas, in the genuine Rámáyaña, perhaps the same as Rishikas, 2. 167.

Rishtisheña, father of Devápi, according to the Rig-veda, 4. 153.

Rishya, variant of Rikaha, son of Devátithi, 4. 153.

Rishyamuka, a mountain in the Deccan, 2. 141.

Rishyanta, variant of Sushyanta, 4. 132.

Rishyasringa, a Rishi in the eighth Manwantara, sprung from Kasyapa, 3. 23.

Rishyasringa, a hermit, named in the Rámáyaña, 4. 124.

Rita, son of Chákshusha, Manu of the sixth Manwantara, 1. 178.

Rita, son of Vijaya, son of Jaya, 3. 335.

Rita (??), son of Dharma, the Prajápati, 1. 111.

Ritadhámán, Manu, by one account, of the thirteenth Manwantara, 3. 25.

Ritadhámán, Indra of the twelfth Manwantara, 3. 27.

Ritadhwaja, a form of Rudra, 1. 117.

Ritadhwaja, son of S'atrujit, 4. 36 (where correct the spelling).

Ritadhwaja, another name of Pratardana, son of Divodása, 4. 36.

Ritadhwaja, variant of Kritadhwaja, 5. 217.

Ritajit, a Yaksha, 2. 285, &c.

Ritambhará, a river in Plakshadwípa, 2. 193.

Rituparná, variant of Rituparná, 3. 303.

Ritavách (?), a Manu, who brought down Revatí from heaven, 3. 9.

Ritavírya, variant of Kritágni, 4. 55.

Ritavratas, a caste in S'áka-dwípa, 2. 200.

Ritáyus, son of Purúravas, son of Budha, 4. 13.

Riteyu, son of Raudrás'wa, 4. 128, 129.

Ritu, Manu, by one account, of the twelfth Manwantara, 3. 25.

Ritujit, son of Anjana, son of Kuní, 3. 334 (where correct the spelling; 5. 391.

Ritumálá, variant of Kritamálá, 2. 132.

Rituparná, son of Ayutás'wa, 3. 303, 304, 315.

Rituparná, king of Ayodhyá, 3. 304.

Kitusthalá, an Apsaras, 2. 81, 83.

Ritwig, 'superintending priest,' 3. 327.

Rochaka (?), variant of Rochana 3. 190, 191.

Rochamána, son of Ánarta, son of S'aryáti, 3. 249.

Rochamána (?) variant of Rochana, 3. 190, 191.

Rochana, one of the Vis'we devas, 3. 189-191.

Rochaná, wife of Vasudeva, son of S'úra, 4. 110.

Rodha, a hell, 2. 214, 216.

Rohi, a river, 2. 151.

Rohiní, wife of Mahádeva, the Rudra, 1. 117.

Rohiní, daughter of Kas'yapa and Surabhi, and mother of horned cattle, 2. 75.

Rohiní, wife of Vasudeva, son of S'úra, 4. 110, 111, 259, 260, 264, 275, 280, 289, 300-302 ; 5. 141, 154.

Rohiní, or Pauraví, wife of Vasudeva, son of S'úra, 4. 108, 109 ; 5. 79 (where, in note **, it should have been specified that Krishńa had two stepmothers named Rohiní).

Rohiní, wife of Krishńa, 5. 78, 79, 81, 83, 107.

Rohiní, a river, 4. 170.

Rohiní, an asterism, 2. 265, &c. ; 3. 132.

Rohiní, denoting a young woman, the term defined, &c., 3. 102, 197, 198.

Rohitas (??) a caste in S'álmaladwípa, 2. 194.

Rohitas, instead of Lohitas, a class

of gods in the twelfth Manwantara, 3. 27.

Rohita, ruler over the realm of Rohita, and son of Vapushmat, king of Sálmala-dwipa. 2. 193.

Rohita, son of Hariśchandra, 4. 27.

Rohita, the same as Dakshasávarni, Manu of the ninth Manwantara, 3. 24.

Rohita, a division of Sálmala-dwípa, 2. 193.

Rohita, variant of Rohitáswa, 3. 288, 289.

Rohitapura, a city, founded by Rohita or Rohitáswa, 3. 288.

Rohitás, the same as Rotás, 3. 288.

Rohitáswa, son of Hariśchandra, 3. 288.

Romas, variant of Rámas, 2. 133.

Romaharshana, disciple of Vyása, &c., P. 17, 19, 46; 3. 42, 64, 65, 227. See Lomaharshana and Súta.

Romaharahaṇiká, a Pauráṇik Saṁhitá, 3. 66, 227.

Romaka, a city, 2. 111, 113. It is situated in Ketumála, 2. 207.

Romans, a people, 2. 176.

Romapáda, son of Vidarbha, 4. 67 (where correct the spelling in note 4); 5. 391.

Romapáda, another name of Chitraratha, son of Dharmaratha, 4. 124, 125.

Ropans, variant of Romans, 2. 176.

Rotás, the popular name of a fort in Behar, 3. 288.

Ruchas, a class of Apsarases, 2. 82.

Ruchaka, son of Uśanas, 4. 63 (correct the spelling); 5. 391.

Ruchaka, a mountain-range running south from Mount Meru, 2. 117.

Ruchaka, variant of Ruruka, 3. 289.

Ruchi, a Prajápati, 1. 101, 108; 3. 16, 27.

Ruchi (?), variant of Richa, 4. 164.

Ruchirá, a river, 2. 155.

Ruchira, variant of Ruchiráswa, 4. 141.

Ruchiradhí, son of Sankriti, son of Nara, 4. 137.

Ruchiráswa, son of Sénajit, son of Viswajit, 4. 140, 141.

Rudhirámbhas (??), variant of Rudhirándha, 2. 214.

Rudhirándha, a hell, 2. 214, 219.

Rudiment, or element of an element, 1. 37. See Tanmátrá.

Rudrás, born from Brahmá, 1. 115. Eight in number, 1. 116. Eleven in number, and sons of Kaśyapa and Surabhi, &c. &c., 1. 116, 117, 124; 2. 24, 25, 29. Sons of Kaśyapa and Ilá, 2. 75. The Maruts identified with them, 2. 79. A class of gods in the current Manwantara, 3. 13, 15. See also 1. 141; 4. 249, 258; 5. 100, 143, 234, 388.

Rudra, one with Siva, P. 35, 36, &c. Born from the forehead of Brahmá, 1. 103. Becomes androgynous, and parts into eleven male forms and as many female, 1. 104. Has a thousand and eight names, 2. 25.

Etymology of the word, 1. 115; 2. 80. See also 1. 13, 41, 60, 77, 78, &c., 103, &c., 115, &c.; 3. 22, 24, 27, 83, 252; 4. 2, 3, 293; 5. 2, 43, 113, 120, 191–193, 247, 386.

Rudrá, wife of Vasudeva, son of Súra, 4. 110.

Rudrá, daughter of Raudráśwa, and wife of Prabhákara, the Ŕishi, 4. 129.

Rudras, variant of Puńḍras, 2. 132.

Rudradáman, a king of Suráshṭra, 4. 205.

Rudrakálí, a form of Umá, the sanguinary goddess, 1. 130.

Rudra-loka, a supernal region, 2. 230.

Rudráńís, certain goddesses, wives of the Rudras, eleven, their names, &c., 1. 117.

Rudráńí, (11), goddess of the Daityas, 5. 117. See Koťaví.

Rudra-saṁhitá, an appendage to the Váyu-puráńa, 2. 151.

Rukma, son of Ruchaka, son of Uśanas, 4. 64.

Rukmadhara, son of Mahápaurava, 4. 143.

Rukmakavacha, son of Síteshu, &c., 4. 63, 64.

Rukmángada, a king, father of Mohiní, P. 52.

Rukmángada-charita, said to be a part of the Śrí-nárada-puráńa, P. 51.

Rukmaratha, son of Mahat, 4. 143.

Rukmavatí, the same as Kakudmatí, 5. 83.

Rukmeshu, variously genealogized, 4. 63, 64.

Rukmin, son of Bhíshmaka or Bhíshma, king of the Vidarbhas, 4. 112; 5. 69, 70, 83, 85. Founds and dwells in the city of Bhojakaťa, 2. 159; 5. 71, 84. Slain by Balabhadra, 5. 86.

Rukminí, daughter of Bhishmaka, king of the Vidarbhas, 5. 69. Is affianced to Śiśupála, 5. 69. Kŕishńa abducts her, 5. 70; but with her own consent, 5. 72. Is married to Kŕishńa, 5. 71. One of Kŕishńa's principal wives, 4. 112; 5. 79. Gives birth to Pradyumna, 5. 71, 108. Her other children by Kŕishńa, 5. 78. Burns herself with him, after his death, 5. 154. Is identified with Śrí, 1. 151. See also 5. 75–77, 86, 97, 103, 107.

Rumańwat, son of Jamadagni, 4. 20.

Rúpá, variant of Kŕipá (?), the river, 2. 155, 164.

Rúpa, its import, 3. 205, 252; 5. 15.

Rúpapas (?), variant of Rúpasas, 2. 164.

Rúpasas (?), a people, 2. 164.

Rúpaváhikas, a people, 2. 164.

Rúpavásikas, variant of Rúpaváhikas, 2. 164.

Rupavatí, a river in Krauncha-dwípa, 2. 198.

Ruru, one of the Viśwe devas, 3. 192.

Ruru, son of Ahínagu, 3. 320.

Ruru, variously rendered, as the name of an animal, 1. 72; 3. 193.

L

Ruruka, son of Vijaya, son of Chunchu, 3. 289.

Rusadratha (??), in the Bhágavata-puráña, instead of Rushadratha, 4. 122.

Ruśaná, wife of Mahinasa, the Rudra, 1. 117.

Ruseku (??), in the Bhágavata-puráña, instead of Rushadgu, 4. 61.

Rushadgu, son of Swáhi, son of Vṛijinívat, 4. 61.

Rushadratha, in several Puráñas, instead of Uahadratha, 4. 122.

Ŝabala (?), variant of Savana, 2. 214.

Ŝabaláśwas, a thousand, sons of Daksha, 2. 14, 16.

Ŝabaras, a people, 2. 170.

Sabda-brahma, what, 4. 252, 253; 5. 210.

Ŝabda-kalpa-druma, the, a diction-ary, referred to, 2. 147; 3. 71, 108, 131, 187, 293; 4. 309; 5. 3.

Sabhánara, son of Anu, son of Yayáti, 4. 120.

Sabhoga, a country, 3. 221.

Sabhya, a certain holy fire, 3. 175; 5. 114, 115.

Sabíja, what, in the Yoga philo-sophy, 5. 230.

Sacæ. See Ŝakas.

Sachaitanya, what, 5. 204.

Ŝachí, daughter of Puloman, and wife of Indra, 1. 136 (where correct the spelling), 200; 2. 72; 4. 45, 320; 5. 46, 97, 99, 102, 133. See Ŝakráñí.

Ŝáchí (?), variant of Somá, an Ap-saras, 2. 81, 82.

Ŝachípati, 'lord of Ŝachí,' an epi-thet of Indra, 4. 320; 5. 46, 133.

Sadáchandra, a king, 4. 212.

Sadáchárás, certain observances so called, enumerated, 3. 107, &c.

Sadaikarúpa, what, in philosophy, 1. 15.

Sadákántá, a river, 2. 149.

Sadánírá, two rivers so called, 2. 149.

Sadasadátmaka, what, in philo-sophy, 1. 20.

Sadáśiva, the same as Ŝiva, P. 32.

Sadáśwa, Sadaśwa (?), son of Samara, 4. 141.

Sádhus, 'pious men,' 3. 107.

Sádhyas, certain gods. Sons of Dharma and Sádhyá, 2. 22. Personified rites and prayers of the Veda, born of the metres, 2. 22. A reproduction of the Jayas, 2. 26, 27. See also 1. 82, 123, 141, 142; 3. 7, 14; 4. 249 (where "the Saints" re-presents Sádhyas); 5. 101, 143, 247.

Sádhyá, daughter of Daksha, wife of Dharma, and mother of the Sádhyas, 2. 21, 22.

Ŝádhya (??), variant of Ŝákya, 4. 169.

Sad-veśa-dhárin, what, 4. 228.

Sadwatí, daughter of Pulastya, and wife of Agni, 1. 154, 155.

Sagara, a sage, son of Báhu, 3. 289-291. Subdues sundry bar-barous tribes, 3. 291. Imposes marks upon them, 3. 294. His

sixty thousand sons destroyed, 3. 298. See also P. 53; 2. 272; 3. 80, 81, 85, 98, &c., 297, &c.; 4. 60, 240, 241; 5. 388.

Ságara, the 'ocean,' why so called; 3. 302.

Ságara, an island at the mouth of the Ganges, 3. 302.

Saha, son of Kŕishńa and Lakshmańá, 5. 81.

Saha = Sahas, a month, Nov.-Dec., 2. 291, 293.

Sahadeva, son of Śŕinjaya, 3. 247.

Sahadeva, son of Dasra, 4. 103, 159; 5. 134.

Sahadeva, variously genealogized. 4. 147, 148.

Sahadeva, son of Jarásandha, 4. 150, 173, 177, 231.

Sahadeva, son of Bhánuratha, 4. 168.

Sahadeva, son of Divákara, son of Prativyoma, 4. 168.

Sahadeva, son of Sudása, 4. 148.

Sahadevá, daughter of Devaka, son of Áhuka, and wife of Vasudeva, son of Śúra, 4. 98, 110, 111.

Sahadeví (?), variant of Sahadevá, 4. 98.

Sahajanyá, an Apsaras, 2. 75, 81-83, 285-287, 291, 293.

Sáhajit, variant of Sáhanji, 4. 54.

Sahálin, son of Kákavarńin, 4. 186.

Sahalya (?), variant of Sumálya, 4. 185.

Sáhanja, variant of Sáhanji, 4. 54.

Sáhanjanípurí, a city, the capital of King Sáhanja, 4. 54.

Sáhanji, son of Kunti, 4. 54.

Saharaksha, son of Pavamána, 1. 156.

Sahas = Márgaśírsha, a month, Nov.-Dec., 2. 261.

Sahasrabala, variant of Sahasráśwa, 3. 321.

Sahasrada, variant of Sahasrajit, son of Yádu, 4. 53, 54.

Sahasrajit, son of Yadu, 4. 53.

Sahasrajit, son of Kŕishńa and Jámbavatí, 5. 79.

Sahasrájit, son of Bhajamána, son of Satwata, 4. 72.

Sahasráksha, an epithet of Indra, 4. 261, 321, 334. (Compare Bhaganetŕa, another epithet of the same god.)

Sahasráníka, son of Śatáníka, 4. 163.

Sahasrári (??), variant of Vatsaprí, 3. 242.

Sahasrasrotas, a mountain in Śáka-dwípa, 2. 200.

Sahasraśruti, a mountain in Śálmala-dwípa, 2. 195.

Sahasrástuti, a river in Śáka-dwípa, 2. 200.

Sahasráśwa, son of Ahínagu, 3. 321.

Sahásráya, variant of Sahasráśwa, 3. 321.

Sahaswat, variant of Mahaswat, 3. 325.

Sahasya = Pausha, a month, Dec.-Jan., 2. 261.

Sáhi (?), variant of Swáhi, 4. 61.

Sahishńu, son of Pulaha, 1. 155. Also called son of Vanakapívat, 1. 155.

Sahishńu, a Rishi in the sixth Manwantara, 3. 12.

Sahitá, variant of Mahitá, 2. 148.

Sahya, a mountain-range in Western India, 2. 113, 127, 128, 130, 140, 155; 5. 66.

Sahya, variant of Satya, a Rishi in the tenth Manwantara, 3. 26.

Sahya (?), variant of Bhavya, the Rishi, 3. 25.

S'aibas, a people, 4. 121.

S'aibya, a tribe, 4. 159.

S'aibya, a horse of Krishńa, 4. 83.

S'aibyá, wife of Satadhanu, 3. 217, &c.

S'aibyá, wife of Jyámagha, 4. 65, &c.

S'aibyá, wife of Krishńa, 5. 107.

S'aibyá = Sudattá, wife of Krishńa, (?) 5. 82.

S'aibyá, a river, 2. 149.

S'aibyá, variant of Sumati, daughter of Arishťanemi or Kaśyapa, 3. 297.

Saililávatí, a district somewhere in India, 2. 165.

Saimhikeyas, a class of demons, sons of Simhiká, 2. 72.

Saindhavas, a people, 2. 133, 134; 5. 389. And see Sindhus.

Saindhavas, of the Atharva-veda, 3. 62.

Saindhava, a teacher of the Atharva-veda, 3. 62.

Saindhaváyanas, Kauśika Bráhmans, 4. 28.

Saindhaváyana, descendant of Saindhava, disciple of S'aunaka, &c., and teacher of the Atharva-veda, 3. 62.

S'aineyas, a branch of the Yádavas, descended from S'ini, 4. 93, 137 (where correct the spelling).

S'aineya, the same as Satyaka (?), 5. 148.

S'ainyas, a dynasty, sprung from S'ini, 4. 137. And see S'aineyas.

S'aishiri (?!), variant of S'aiśiri, 3. 57.

S'aiśikas, S'aiśikas (?), a people, 4. 221.

Saiśikatas (?), a people, 2. 177.

Saiśinas, variant of S'aiśikas, 4. 221.

S'aiśireya, disciple of S'ákalya, and promulgator of the Rig-veda, 3. 46.

S'aiśiri, teacher of the Yajur-veda, 3. 57.

S'aiśítas, variant of S'aiśikas, 4. 221.

S'aiśunágas, a dynasty, sprung from S'iśunága or Siśunáka, 4. 171, 182, 183, 186, 231.

S'aiválas, S'aivalas, a people, 2. 175.

S'aiva-puráńa, = S'iva-puráńa, P. 23, 35, 36; 3. 66.

S'ájya (?!), variant of S'ákya, 4. 169.

S'akas, a people, P. 9; 2. 165, 171, 179, 181, 182, 184, 186, 339; 3. 290, 292, 294, 295, 336; 4. 60. Vanquished by King Sagara, 3. 291. Kings of their race, 4. 184, 202, 206. Identified with the classical Sacæ, 4. 208.

S'aka-dwípa, a continent, P. 64; 2. 101, 109, 110, 198, &c.; 5. 382, 385.

Sakákola, a certain hall, 2. 215.

S'ákalas, of the Rig-veda, 3. 51.

S'ákala, the capital of the Báhíkas,

a city in the Punjab, identified with the Sagala of Ptolemy, 2. 133, 135, 340.

S'ákalya, son and disciple of Mán-d'úkeya, &c., and promulgator of the Rig-veda, 3. 45, 48, 50.

S'ákapúńa, father of S'ákapúńi, 3. 47.

S'ákapúńi, an author, son of S'ákapúńa, disciple of Satyaśrí, and promulgator of the Rig-veda, 3. 18, 46–48. And see S'ákapúrńi and Rathántara.

S'ákapúrńi, corrupted from S'ákapúńi, 3. 46–50.

S'akavarńa, S'ákavarńa, variants of Kákavarńa, 4. 180.

S'áketa (?), a city, 4. 218.

S'áketu, variant of S'áketa, 4. 218.

S'ákha, son of Kumára, son of Agni, 2. 23 ; 4. 283.

S'ákhá, 'a subdivision of the Vedas,' 3. 49, 51, &c.

S'akra = Indra, P. 77 ; 1. 50, 125, 136, &c.; 2. 78, 79, 240, 293 ; 3. 1, 3, 30, 123, 202, 252 ; 4. 3, 102, 159, 261, 284, 308–310, 314, 317, 320, 322, 341 ; 5. 13, 87, 89, 93, 99, 100, &c., &c.

S'akra, an Áditya, 2. 27.

S'akradhwajotthána = S'akrotthána, 4. 308, 309.

S'akra-gopa, a certain insect, 2. 284.

S'akrajit, son of S'úra, son of Vidúratha, 4. 99.

S'akrajit (?), variant of Sattrájita, 4. 74.

S'akráńí = S'achí, wife of Indra, 5. 96.

S'aktidgrahas, a people, 2. 182.

S'aktidguhas, variant of S'aktidgrahas, 2. 182.

S'aktidwahas, variant of S'aktidgrahas, 2. 182.

S'akrotthána, a festival so called, in honour of Indra, 4. 308.

S'akrotthánadhwajotsava = S'akrotthána, 4. 308.

S'akru, son of S'úra, son of Vidúratha, 4. 99.

S'áksha (?), a certain king, 4. 214 (note ||).

S'áktas, worshippers of S'akti, P. 21, 79, 80, 86, 88–90 ; 5. 267, 280, 286, 299, 309, 310, 316–319, 326, 348, 380.

S'akta, son of Manasyu, 4. 127.

S'akti, 'the female double of a god.' The S'aktis of Rudra or S'iva, white and black, 1. 104 ; 4. 260. Vaishńaví, a S'akti of Vishńu, 4. 260. Rádhá, a S'akti of Kŕishńa, 5. 264. See, further, in explanation of the term, &c., P. 21, 22, &c.; 5. 235, 245, 267, 285, 310, 316–318, &c.

S'akti, Vyása in the twenty-fifth Dwápara age, son of Vasishtha, and father of Parás'ara, 1. 8 ; 3. 35–37, 306. Slain by King Kalmáshapáda changed to a Rákshasa, 1. 8.

S'aktimat (?), variant of S'uktimat, a mountain-range, 2. 140.

S'aktiputra, patronym of Parás'ara, 3. 36.

S'aktu, what, 3. 127.

S'akuni, son of Hirańyáksha, 2. 69.

S'akuni, son of Ikshwáku, 3. 259, 260.

S'akuni, son of Daśaratha, son of Navaratha; 4. 68.

S'akuni, daughter of Bali, the Daitya, 2. 69.

S'akuni, variant of Kuni, 3. 334.

S'akuni, 'bird-seller' and 'ornithomancer,' 2. 219.

S'akuntalá, an Apsaras, wife of Dushyanta, 3. 81; 4. 133.

S'akuntala, the, a drama, referred to, 4. 133.

S'ákyas, a tribe, 4. 187.

S'ákya, S'akya (??), a Buddha, variously genealogized, 3. 246; 4. 5, 169, 170, 171, 181, 182, 186, 187; 5. 178.

S'akyamánábhava (?), a king, 4. 214.

S'ala, son of Somadatta, 4. 157; 5. 134.

S'ala, variant of Chhala, 3. 321.

S'ala, variant of Leśa, 4. 30.

S'ala (??), variant of S'atha, 4. 109.

S'aladá, daughter of Raudráśwa, and wife of Prabhákara, the Rishi, 4. 129.

S'álagráma, a certain place of pilgrimage, 2. 103, 106, 312, 313, &c.

S'álagráma, 'ammonite,' a stone held sacred by the Hindus, P. 34; 2. 313.

S'álákya, 'treatment of external organic affections,' a branch of surgery, 4. 33.

S'álankáyanas, Káuśika Bráhmans, 4. 28.

S'álankrityas, Kauśika Bráhmans, 4. 29.

S'álaváñakas, variant of Málaváñakas, 2. 178.

S'álávatí, mother of Devaśravas, &c., 4. 28.

S'áligotra (??), variant of S'álihotra, 3. 60, 61.

S'álihotra, teacher of the Sámaveda, 3. 61.

S'álin, teacher of the Yajur-veda, 3. 57.

S'áliśúka, variously genealogized, 4. 190.

S'áliváhana, King, P. 61.

S'álíya, disciple of S'ákalya, and promulgator of the Rig-veda, 3. 46.

S'álmala-dwípa, a continent, 2. 101, 109, 110, 193, &c.

S'álmali, S'álmalí, a certain hell, 2. 215.

S'álmali, S'álmalí, a certain tree, 4. 240; 5. 101.

S'álmali-dwípa = S'álmala-dwípa, 2. 101, 109.

S'álokya, a kind of emancipation, 5. 242.

Salomadhi (??), variant of Pulomárchis, 4. 199, 204.

S'álwas, S'álwas (?), a people, 2. 133-135, 156; 3. 293.

S'álwa, king of the Saubhas, 5. 70.

S'álwa, a country, 4. 158.

S'álwasenis, a people, 2. 179.

S'ályas, variant of S'álwas, 2. 135.

S'alya, son of Viprachitti, 2. 71.

S'alya, 'extraction of extraneous bodies,' a branch of surgery (??), 4. 33.

S'álya (??), variant of S'álwa, 5. 70.

Sama, son of Dharma, the Prajápati, 1. 111.

S'ama, what, in ethics, 4. 294.

S'ama (?), variant of S'uchi, son of Andhaka, 4. 97.

S'ama (?), variant of Nara, son of Us'inara, 4. 121.

S'ama (??), variant of Suśrama, 4. 175.

Samádhi, what, in the Yoga philosophy, 2. 91, 315; 3. 21, 298, 307; 5. 228, 230, 240, 241.

Sámun, the same as Sáma-veda, 1. 171.

Sáman, what, in the science of polity, 5. 52.

Samánasalilas = Samánodakas, 3. 151.

Samangas, a people, 2. 178.

Samánodakas, 'relatives by offerings of water,' 3. 151.

Samantapanchaka, a holy spot in Kurukshetra, 4. 23.

Samantaras (??), variant of Bhargas, 2. 171.

Samara, variously genealogized, 4. 141.

Samaratha (??), variant of Mínaratha, 3. 334.

Sámarshañas, Kauśika Bráhmans, 4. 28.

Samása-samhitá, the, an astronomical work, quoted, 2. 277.

Samashtí, mystical explanation of, viz., to denote Vasudeva, 5. 215.

Samaujas, son of Asamaujas, 4. 100.

Sáma-veda, the. Its origin, 1. 85. Its divisions, &c., 3. 58-60; 4. 143; 5. 200, 321.

Samavegavaśas, a people, 2. 179.

Samaya, 'precept,' son of Dharma, 1. 111.

Sámba, son of Kŕishńa and Rukmińí, 4. 112. Called son of Kŕishńa and Jámbavatí, 5. 79, 107, 130, 142: Is taken captive by the Kurus, 5. 130. Is recovered by Balabhadra, 5. 134, 135. Is cursed by the Ŕishis, 5. 142. He introduces heliolatry into the north-west of India, 5. 381-385. See also P. 64 (where correct the spelling); 5. 131, 132, 148.

Sambandhin, what, in legal language, 3. 175.

Sámbapura, a city so called, founded by Sámba, son of Kŕishńa, 5. 382.

S'ambara, an Asura, son of Kaśyapa, 2. 31, &c., 52, &c., 70; 5. 73-76. Carries off Pradyumna, and is slain by him, 5. 72, 75.

Sámba-upapuráńa, P. 87 (where correct the spelling).

Sambhala, Sambhala (??), a village, where Kalki is to be born, 4. 229.

S'ámbhavas, an heretical sect, 5. 380.

Sámbhava, variously genealogized, 4. 150.

Sambhávya, variant of Susambhávya, 3. 11.

S'ambhu, a Rudra, or form of S'iva, 1. 180; 2. 24, 234; 5. 108, 111.

S'ambhu, Indra of the tenth Manwantara, according to the Bhágavata-puráńa, 3. 25.

S'ambhu, son of Ambarísha, son of Nábhága, 3. 257.

S'ambhu, wife of. Dhruva, son of Uttánapáda, 1. 177.

S'ambhu (?), variant of Sudyumna, son of Abhayada, 4. 128.

Sambhúta, son of Trasadasyu, 3. 283, 284.

Sambhúti, son of Dukaaha, 3. 283.

Sambhúti, 'fitness,' daughter of Daksha, and wife of Maríchi, 1. 109, 153; 3. 17, 227.

Sambhúti, wife of Jayadratha, 4. 125.

Samhana (?), variant of Sáhanji, 4. 54.

Samhanana, son of Manasyu, 4. 127.

Sambára, what, in cosmology, 5. 196.

Samháta, a certain hell, 2. 215.

Samhata (?), variant of Sáhanji, 4. 54.

Samhatáswa, son of Nikumbha, 3. 265, 266.

Samhitá, 'collection.' Applied to the Veda, 3. 42, 44, &c. How it differs, in later literature, from Puraná, P. 19, 78.

Samhitáswa (??), variant of Samhatáswa, 3. 265.

Samhláda, the same as Samhráda, 3. 30, 69.

Samhráda, son of Hiranyakasipu, 2. 30, 69.

S'ami (?), variant of S'uchi, son of Andhaka, 4. 97.

S'ami (??), variant of Nara, son of Us'ínara, 4. 121.

S'amíka, a Muni to appear at the end of the Kali age, P. 55; 5. 251.

S'amíka, son of S'úra, son of Deva-mídhusha, 4. 101, 113.

S'amin, variant of S'uchi, son of Andhaka, 4. 97.

Sámin, son of S'úra, son of Vidúratha, 4. 99.

Sámípya, a kind of emancipation, 5. 242.

Samíras, a people, 2. 173.

Sammada, the sovereign of the fish, 3. 268, 276.

Sammardana, son of Vasudeva, son of S'úra, 4. 110.

Sammati, son of Harsha, 4. 190.

Sammati, a river in Kuśa-dwípa, 2. 196.

Sammita, a Rishi in the third Manwántara, son of Vasishtha, 3. 7.

Samnaddha, a certain ray of the sun, 2. 297 (where correct the spelling).

Samnateyu, son of Raudráswa, 4. 127, 128 (in both which places correct the spelling). See Santatateyu.

Samnati (correct Sannati), son of Alarka, 4. 37.

Samnati, 'humility,' daughter of Daksha, and wife of Kratu, 1. 109, 155; 4. 265.

Samnati (?), variant of Samnatimat, 4. 143.

Samnatimat, son of Sumati, son of Supárswa, 4. 143.

Samnipáta, what, in wrestling, 5. 36.

Sampadwasu, a certain ray of the sun, 2. 298; 5. 191 (where correct the spelling, and expunge the mark of interrogation).

Sampára, son of Samara, 4. 141.

Sampáti, son of Aruña and S'yení, 2. 73.

Sampáti, variant of Samyáti, 4. 128.

Sampratápana, a certain hell, 2. 215.

Samráj, son of Chitraratha, son of Gaya, 2. 107.

Samráj, daughter of Priyavrata, 2. 100.

Samráj, the term, as used in theology, explained, 1. 170, 172.

S'ámśapáyana, disciple of Romaharshaña, and a promulgator of the Puráñas, P. 19; 3. 64, 65, 332.

S'ámśapáyani, variant of S'ámśapáyana, 3. 64, 66.

Samskáras, certain ceremonies at birth, &c., P. 63; 3. 100, 147.

Samskfiti, variant of Sankfiti, 4. 137.

Samudra, 'ocean,' king of rivers, 1. 157; 2. 86; 5. 388.

Samudragupta, a certain king, 4. 219.

Sámudrí, daughter of Samudra, and wife of Práchínabarhis, 1. 157. See Savarñá.

Samuttaras (?), variant of Bhargas, 2. 171.

Samvaraña, variously genealogized, 4. 145, 148.

Sámvarañi, a Muni named in the Rig-veda, 3. 337.

Samvarta, a lawgiver, referred to, or cited, 3. 96, 198.

Samvarta, son of Angiras, 3. 244, 245.

Samvarta, a Kalpa so called, 1. 53.

Samvarta, a wind so called, 1. 54.

Samvartakas, certain clouds so called, 4. 314; 5. 193 (where erase note †).

Samvatsara, a certain cyclic year, 2. 254, 255, 306. As personified, king of times and seasons, 2. 86.

Samvid, what, in philosophy, 1. 32, 172.

Sámya, what, as one of the Siddhis, 1. 91.

Samyadwasu, or Sacrifice (?), 2. 83.

Samyama, what, in the Yoga philosophy, 1. 11, 26, 114, 171; 5. 216, 231, 245.

Samyama, variant of Samnaddha, 2. 297.

Samyama (??), variant of Srinjaya, 3. 247.

Samyamani, Yama's city, where situated, 2. 240. And see 2. 112.

Samyáti, son of Nahusha, son of Áyus, 4. 45, 46.

Samyáti, variously genealogized, 4. 128.

Samyoga, what, in the Yoga philosophy, 5. 227.

Sana, a mind-born son of Brahmá, 1. 78.

Sanadhwaja, according to the Bhágavata-puráña, son of S'uchi, son of S'atadyumna, 3. 334.

S'anaíschara, or Saturn, son of Rudra, &c., 1. 117; 2. 257, 258, 304. Called son of the Sun and Sanjná, 2. 259. Called son of the Sun and Chháyá, 3. 21. See S'ani, Saptárchis, and Saura.

Sanaka, a mind-born son of Brahmá, 1. 59, 77; 2. 200; 5. 195.

Sananda, a mind-born son of Brahmá, 1. 77, 79; 2. 200.

Sanandana, a famous sage, son of Brahmá, 1. 61. He dwells in Jano-loka, 1. 63; 2. 226, 228. See also 5. 13, 233.

Sanátana, a mind-born son of Brahmá, 1. 77; 2. 200.

Sanátana, a Loka, the abode of the Vairájas, Pitris so called, 3. 159.

Sanatkumára, son of Brahmá, P. 72, 88; 1. 77, 78, 122; 2. 200; 3. 168; 4. 12.

Sanatkumára-saṃhitá, a part of the Skanda-puráña, P. 73.

Sanatkumára-upapuráña, P. 87.

Sandaṃśa, a certain hell, 2. 215, 220.

Sandhi (?), variant of Susandhi, 3. 325.

Sandhyá, 'twilight,' &c. A form of Brahmá, 1. 81. Daughter of Brahmá, P. 89. Prayer to be used at it, 2. 250-252. Duration of it, 2. 253. The period preceding a Yuga, 1. 49, 50. See also P. 63; 2. 249; 3. 129, 135; 5. 12, 384.

Sandhyá, a river in Krauncha-dwípa, 2. 198.

Sandhyáṃśa, the period succeeding a Yuga, 1. 49, 50.

S'áńd'ilya, an heresiarch so called, 5. 379.

Sándípani, a teacher of the science of arms, 5. 46-48.

Sandoha, what, 4. 312.

Sandrocottus, Sandrocoptus, Chandragupta identified with, 4. 186.

Sanga (?), variant of Asanga, son of Yuyudhána, 4. 93.

Sangata, son of Dasáratha, son of Suyasas, 4. 189.

Sangati (?), variant of Sammati, the river so called, 2. 196.

Sangava, 'forenoon,' 2. 253.

Sangba (?), variant of Megha-swáti, 4. 200.

Sanghára (?), variant of Saṃpára, 4. 141.

Sanghátá, a certain hell, 2. 215.

Sanghátántargata, what, in legal phraseology, 3. 155, 156.

Sangraha, the technicality, as used of literature, explained, 5. 47.

Sangrámajit, son of Kṛishṇa and Bhadrá, 5. 82. Son of Kṛishṇa and S'aibyá, 5. 107.

S'ani, son of Atri, 1. 154.

S'ani, the same as Saura, 2. 259.

Sanika (?), S'anika (?), variants of Samíka, the Muni, 5. 251.

Sanika (?), variant of S'amíka, son of S'úra, 4. 101.

Saviyas, a people, 2. 180.

Sanjátas (?), variant of Sujátas, 4. 59.

Sanjaya, son of Supárs:wa, 3. 334.

Sanjaya, son of Dhṛitahavya, 3. 335.

Sanjaya, son of Bratikshattra, 4. 44.

Sanjaya, son of Rananjaya, 4. 169.

Sanjaya (?), variant of Sáhanji, 4. 54.

Sanjaya (?), variant of Asanga, son of Yuyudhána, 4. 93.

Sanjaya (?), variant of Sṛinjaya, 4. 144.

Sanjívana, a certain hell, 2. 215.

Sanjívini, 'the herb of immortality,' 1. 146.

Sanjná, variously genealogized, wife of Vivaswat, 2. 259; 3. 20, &c.

Sanjneya, variant of Sábanji, 4. 54.

Sanjnita (?), variant of Sáhanji, 4. 54.

Sanka (?), variant of Sanku, son of Ugrasena, 4. 98.

Sankalpa, a Prajápati, son of Brahmá, 1. 101.

Sankalpa, son of Dharma and Sankalpá, 2. 23.

Sankalpá, daughter of Daksha, and wife of Dharma, 2. 21, 23.

Sankalpa, what, in philosophy, 4. 241.

S'ankara, a form of Rudra or Siva, 1. 13, 119, 124, &c.; 2. 118; 4. 3; 5. 108, 111, 115, 116, 119, 126, 386.

S'ankara, son of Kaśyapa, son of Maríchi, 2. 70.

S'ankara Áchárya, a writer and religious reformer, his time, &c., P. 16, 48, 49; 1. 125; 3. 113, 174, 191, 223, 340; 5. 177, 257, 337, 347, 356.

Sankarshaña = Balabhadra, son of Vasudeva, 2. 211, 212; 3. 166; 4. 110, 111, 260, 297, 301; 5. 16, 40, 44, 144, 215. See Sesha.

Sánkáśyá, a kingdom, its situation, 3. 333.

S'ankha, son of Kaśyapa and Kadrú, 3. 74.

S'ankha, son of Vasishṭha, and a Rishi in the third Manwantara, 3. 7.

S'ankha, a mountain-range, 2. 117 (note §). See S'ankhakúṭa.

S'ankha, a forest so called, 2. 118.

S'ankha, variant of Vátsya, disciple of S'ákalya, 3. 46.

S'ankha, variant of S'ankhanábha, 3. 322.

S'ankha-dwípa, an island, perhaps fabulous, 2. 129.

S'ankhakúṭa, a mountain-range running north from Mount Meru, 2. 117.

S'ankhaña, variously genealogized, 3. 314, 322, 323.

S'ankhaña (?), variant of Sáhanji, 4. 54.

S'ankhanábha, son of Vajranábha, 3. 322.

S'ankhapá, variant of S'ankhapád, 2. 261, 262.

S'ankhapád, the Lokapála of the south, son of Kardama and Sruti, 1. 155; 2. 86, 261–263, 338; 5. 387. (Correct S'ankhapáda, wherever found.)

S'ankhapád, one of the Viśwedevas, 3. 192.

S'ankhapála, a serpent, presiding over the month of Bhádrapada, &c., 2. 285, &c.

S'ankha-smriti, the, a code of law, referred to, 3. 190.

S'ánkháyana, of the Ṛig-veda, 3. 51.

S'ánkháyana, compiler of a S'ákhá of the Ṛig-veda, 3. 49, 50.

S'ánkháyana, author of a Gṛihyasútra, 3. 113, 168.

Sánkhya, a system of philosophy, referred to, P. 12, 41, 42, 94; 2. 14, 43; 3. 39; 4. 253.

Sánkhya-káriká, the, quoted, or referred to, 1. 20, 33, 34, 37, 69, 71, 76; 2. 43; 5. 60, 199, 202.

Sankhyá-parimáná, the, referred to, 1. 48.

Sánkhya-pravachana, the, referred to, 1. 33, 37; 3. 202.

Sánkhya-pravachana-bháshya, the, referred to, 1. 31; 5. 378.

Sánkhya-sára, the, referred to, 1. 33–35; 3. 301.

Sankírṇa (?), variant of Sankírṇára, 2. 291.

Sankírṇára, a serpent, presiding over the months of Madhu and Mádhava, 2. 291.

Sankocha, what, in philosophy, 1. 29.

Sankṛitis, a branch of the Kávyas, 4. 138.

Sánkṛiti, son of Reṇu, 4. 28.

Sankṛiti, son of Jayatsena, son of Adína, 4. 43, 44.

Sankṛiti, son of Nara, son of Bhavanmaṇyu, 4. 137.

Sánkṛityas, Kauśika Bráhmans, 4. 29.

Sankus, Kauśika Bráhmans, 4. 28.

Sanku, an author, referred to the court of King Vikramáditya, P. 8.

Sanku, son of Ugrasena, son of Ahuka, 4. 98.

Sanku, son of Kṛishṇa and Satyá, 5. 79.

Sanku (?), variant of Sanku, son of Ugrasena, son of Ahuka, 4. 98.

Sankura (?), variant of Sankara, son of Kaśyapa, 2. 70.

Sankuśiras, son of Kaśyapa, son of Maríchi, 2. 70.

Sánta, son of Idhmajihwa, king of Plaksha-dwípa, 2. 193. See Sántabhaya.

Sántá, daughter of Daśaratha, son of Aja, and wife of Rishyaśṛinga, 4. 124.

Sánta, a region in Plaksha-dwípa, 2. 193. See Sántabhaya.

Sántabhaya, son of Medhátithi, king of Plaksha-dwípa, 2. 191. See Sánta.

Sántabhaya, a region in Plaksha-dwípa, 2. 191. See Sánta.

Sántahaya, son of Támasa, Manu of the fourth Manwantara, 3. 8.

Sántakarṇa (?), variant of Sríśátakarṇi, 4. 195.

Santána, son of Ugra, 1. 117.

Sántánika a Loka, tenanted by the Vairájas, Pitṛis so called, 3. 159.

Sántanu, Santanu, son of Pratípa, 4. 144, 146, 152, 154–158.

Santanu (?), variant of Sutanu, 4. 110.

Sántaraya, sprung from Anenas, son of Áyus, 4. 43.

Santardana, son of Dhṛishṭaketu, the Kaikeya, 4. 103.

Santardana (?), variant of Sammardana, 4. 110.

Santateyu, son of Raudráśwa, 4. 128, 129. See Samnateyu.

Sánti, Indra of the tenth Manwantara, 3. 25.

Sánti, disciple of Angiras, son of Daksha, 3. 28, 29.

S'ánti, son of Níla, son of Ajamíd'ha, 4. 144.

S'ánti, son of Kŕishńa and Kálindí, 5. 79.

S'ánti, 'placidity,' daughter of Daksha, and wife of Dharma, 1. 109, 110. Called daughter of Kardama, and wife of Atharvan, (?) 1. 110, 200.

S'ánti, a certain ceremony, 3. 44 (where correct the spelling); 5. 390.

S'ánti, what, in philosophy, 1. 37.

S'ánti (?), variant of Swáhí, 4. 61.

S'ántidevá, daughter of Devaka, son of Áhuka, and wife of Vasudeva, 4. 98, 110, 111.

S'ántideví, variant of S'ántidevá, 4. 98.

S'ántihavya (?), variant of S'ántahaya, 3. 8.

S'ántihaya (?), variant of S'ántahaya, 3. 8.

Santimat (?), variant of Sumati, 4. 143.

Santosha, 'content,' son of Dharma and Tushti, 1. 110.

Santosha, what, in ethics, 3. 77.

S'ápemin (??), variant of S'ápeyin, 3. 57.

S'ápeyin, teacher of the Yajurveda, 3. 57.

Sapińd'as, certain relatives, in legal phraseology, 3. 151.

Sapińd'ana, a certain S'ráddha, 3. 147. See the next.

Sapińd'í-karańa = Sapińd'ana, 3. 154, 156, 157.

Saptabhangins, the Jainas so called, 3. 209.

Saptadaśa, a certain collection of hymns, its origin from Brahmá's western mouth, 1. 85.

Saptajit (?), variant of Satyajit, 2. 289.

Saptaketu (?), variant of Satyaketu, 3. 26.

Saptárchis = S'anaiśchara, or Saturn, 2. 257, 258.

Sáptatantavas, a sect so called, 3. 340.

Saptavádins, the Jainas so called, 3. 209.

Sáras (?), a people, 2. 179.

S'arabha, a fabulous animal so called, 1. 63, 72, 83, 84.

S'aradwat, a Rishi in the current Manwantara, son of Gotama, 3. 15, 16, 23; 4. 146.

S'áradwatí, an Apsaras, 2. 81–83.

Saramá, daughter of Daksha, and wife of Kaśyapa, son of Maríchi, 2. 26, 73.

Sára-mara, the same as Avyanga, 5. 383.

Sárameya (?), variant of Arimejaya, son of S'waphalka, 4. 96.

Sárameyádana, a certain hell, 2. 215.

S'arańa, S'árańa, son of Vasudeva, son of S'úra, 4. 109.

Sárani-vyúha (??), what, in architecture, 5. 30, 31.

Sára-pradhána, the same as Avyanga, 5. 383.

Sára-sangraha, the, referred to, 3. 191.

Sáraswatas, a people, P. 104; 3. 70, 71.

Sáraswata, an epithet of Kapila, the Rishi, 1. 5, 17; 5. 250.

Sáraswata, Vyása of the ninth Dwápara age, 3. 34, 37.

Sáraswata, a Ṛishi, son of Saraswati, the goddess so called, P. 104; 3. 70.

Sáraswata, a modification of Sanskrit, P. 104.

Sáraswata, a Kalpa so called, P. 40, 49.

Saraswati, a S'akti of S'iva, P. 71; 1. 104.

Saraswatí, goddess of learning, daughter of Daksha, and wife of Dharma, P. 105; 1. 131, 148; 2. 21; 3. 70. As one with various rivers, P. 46, 104–106; 2. 121, 142–144, 154, 155; 3. 71, 170.

Saraswati, wife of Matinára, 4. 131.

Saraswatí, a river in S'álmaladwípa, 2. 195.

S'arávatí, a river, 2. 147.

S'arayú, a river, the Sarjoo, 2. 121 (where correct the spelling), 147, 149, 172, 340; 5. 388.

Sarga, what, P. 93; 3. 72; 5. 259, 299.

Sarga, variant of Swarga, son of Bhíma and Disá, 1. 117.

Saríśipa, what, 1. 84; 2. 55, 92; 3. 158; 5. 59, 94, 162, 203, 236, 247.

S'arman, a name appropriate for a Bráhman, 3. 99.

S'armishṭhá, daughter of Vṛishaparvan, and wife of Yayáti, 2. 70; 4. 46–48.

S'árnga, a bow borne by Kṛishńa, 5. 113, 116, 125.

S'árngadhanwan, an epithet of Kṛishńa, derived from the name of his bow, S'árnga, 5. 113, 116.

S'árngin, an epithet of Kṛishńa, derived from the name of his bow, S'árnga, 5. 114.

Saro-máhátmya, a part of the Vámana-puráńa, P. 75.

Sarpas (?), a people. 3. 293.

Sarpa, a Rudra, 2. 25.

Sarpa, a Rákshasa, presiding over the month of Nabhas, &c., 2. 285, 288, 292, 293.

Sarpa, 'serpent,' whence the term, 1. 83.

Sarpa-bali, a certain sacrifice, 3. 114.

Sarpapungava, in place of Rambha, a serpent presiding over the months of S'ukra and S'uchi, 2. 293.

Sarpis, wife of Ṛitadhwaja, a form of Rudra, 1. 117.

Sarpis, 'clarified butter,' 2. 109.

Sárshṭi, a kind of emancipation, 5. 242. (It is very inadequately translated in 2. 270.)

Sarúpá, wife of Bhúta, the patriarch, and mother of the Rudras, 2. 25.

Sárúpya, a kind of emancipation, 5. 242.

S'arútha (?), variant of Varuttha, 4. 117.

S'urva, a Rudra, 1. 116; 2. 24, 272; 5. 121, 386.

S'arva, son of Dhanusha, 4. 150.

Sárvabhauma, son of Ahaṁyáti, 4. 128.

Sárvabhauma, variously genealogized, 4. 143.

Sárvabhauma, son of Vidúratha, 4. 153.

Sárvabhauma (?), variant of Sarvakáma, 3. 304.

Sarvabhúta = Sarvátman, 5. 34, 164, 246.

Sarva-bhúta-dayá, what, 4. 294.

Sarvadamana, epithet of Bharata, son of Dushyanta, 4. 134.

Sarva-darśana-sangraha, the, quoted, 3. 213.

Sarvadharman,. a king, son of Dharmasávarńika, the Manu, 3. 27.

Sarvaga, son of Páurńamása, son of Maríchi, 1. 153.

Sarvaga, a king, son of Dharmasávarńika, the Manu, 3. 27.

Sarvaga, son of Bhímasena or Bhíma, by one account, 4. 159.

Sarvaga, what, in philosophy, 1. 27.

Sarvagata, instead of Sarvatraga, in the Bhágavata-puráńa, 4. 159.

Sarvagata, what, in theology, 3. 251.

Sarvajit (??), variant of Satyajit, son of Suníta, 4. 176.

Sarvakáma, variously genealogized, 3. 304, 305, 315.

Sarvakarman, variant of Sarvakáma, 3. 305, 314; 4. 24.

Sarva-múrti, what, 5. 200.

Sarvasangá, a river, 2. 154.

Sárvaseni, daughter of a king of the Káśis, 4. 136.

Sarvátman, what, in theology, 1. 142.

Sarvatobhadra, a mountain in Krauncha-dwípa, 2. 198.

Sarvatobhadra, a fabulous grove, so called, 2. 117, 122.

Sarvatraga, son of Bhímasena or Bhíma, 4. 159.

Sarvatraga (?), variant of Sarvaga, son of Dharmasávarńika, the Mánu, 3. 27.

Sarvávasu, a certain ray of the sun, 2. 297.

Sarvavega, son of Dharmasávarńika, the Manu, 3. 27.

S'aryáta, a race descended from S'aryáti, son of Vaivaswata, 3. 255.

S'aryáta, son of Manu, 3. 248, 342.

S'aryáti, son of Nabusha, son of Áyus, 4. 46.

S'aryáti, Saryáti (?), son of Vaivaswata, the Manu, 2. 172; 3. 13, 14, 232, 233, 248, 255; 4. 40.

S'aśa, a portion of Sudarśana, the continent, 2. 110.

S'aśabindus, a tribe, 4. 61.

S'aśabindu, son of Chitraratha, son of Rushadgu, 4. 61, 63.

S'aśáda, an epithet of Vikukshi, 3. 261, 262.

S'aśáda (??), variant of Vimśati, 3. 260.

S'aśi (?), variant of S'uchi, son of Andhaka, 4. 97.

S'aśigupta, a certain king, 4. 219.

S'aśikas, a people, 2. 167.

S'aśikántá, variant of Sadákántá, 3. 149.

S'aśin, the same as Kubera, 2. 112.

S'astra, technical use of, in theology, 1. 85, 200; otherwise, 5. 38, 147.

S'astra-devatás, 'deified weapons,' sons of Kríśáśwa, 2. 29 (where correct the spelling), 5. 388.

S'áśwata, son of S'ruta, 3. 334.

S'atabalá (?), a river, 2. 148, 153.

S'atabaláka, disciple of S'ákapúni, and promulgator of the Rigveda, 3. 49.

S'atabhishá, the same as S'atabhishaj, 2. 308.

S'atabhishaj, an asterism, 2. 265, &c.; 3. 167, 169.

S'atadhanu, a certain king, 3. 217, &c.

S'atadhanus, son of Hrídika, 4. 82, 90, ·99. He slays Sattrájita, 4. 81. Is slain by Krishńa, 4. 83. See S'atadhanwan.

S'atadhanus, for S'atadhanwan, son of Somaśarman, 4. 190.

S'atadhanwan = S'atadhanus, son Hrídika, 4. 80, &c., 99.

S'atadhanwan, son of Somaśarman, 4. 190.

S'atadhanwan (?), variant of Bindusára, 4. 188.

S'atadhara, son of Devavarman, 4. 189.

S'atadhwaja (?), variant of Satyadhwaja, 3. 333.

S'atadrú, S'atadru, the river Satlej, 2. 130, 131, 142, 144; 3. 170; 4. 118.

S'atadyumna, a king, son of Chákshusha, the Manu, 1. 177; 3. 13.

S'atadyumna, son of Bhánumat, 3. 333.

S'atajit, son of Raja, 2. 107. Also called son of Viraja, 2. 107.

S'atajit, variously genealogized, 4. 53.

S'atájit, son of Bhajamána, son of Satwata, 4. 72.

S'atajit, son of Krishńa and Jámbavatí, 5. 79.

Sátakarńi, S'átakarńi, variously genealogized, 4. 195, 200, 202, 205.

S'átakarńi, son of Yantramáti (?), 4. 202.

S'átakarńi, &c., variants of Sundara-śátakarńin, 4. 197.

S'átakarńí (?), variant of Vijaya, son of Yajnaśrí, 4. 199.

S'átakarńí (?), variant of Swáti, 4. 200.

S'atakesara, a mountain in S'ákadwípa, 2. 200.

S'atakratu, an epithet of Indra, 1. 150; 4. 42, 309; 5. 43.

S'atakumbhá, a river, 2. 147.

S'atamakha, an epithet of Indra, 2. 112.

S'atánanda (as the name doubtless should be written), a Rishi in the eighth Manwantara, according to one account, 3. 23.

S'atánanda, son of S'aradwat or Gautama, 4. 146.

S'atáníka, a king of the Pánd'u family, P. 63.

S'atáníka, king of Kauśámbí, 4. 124, 165.

S'atáníka, son of Nakula, 4. 159, 163.

S'atáníka, son of Janamejaya, 4. 162, 163, 166.

S'atáníka, son of Vasudána, son of Bríbadratha, 4. 165.

S'atáníka, son of Sattrájit, 4. 165.

S'atánkrú (?), daughter of Ugrasena, son of Ahuka, 4. 99.

S'atapas, a class of gods in the eighth Manwantara, 3. 23.

S'atapatha-bráhmaña, the, referred to, or cited, 1. 45; 3. 35, 244, 342; 4. 11, 247. Its length, 3. 63.

S'átaprasúti, son of Kambalabarhis, 4. 63.

S'ataratha, variant of Daśaratha, son of Múlaka, 3. 314.

S'atarúpá, the first woman, the female portion of Brahmá, wife of Swáyambhuva Manu, &c., P. 95 (where twice correct the spelling); 1. 104, &c.

S'atasankhyas, a class of gods in the tenth Manwantara, 3. 25.

S'ataśŕínga, a mountain in S'álmala-dwípa, 2. 195.

S'atatejas, Vyása of the twelfth Dwápara age, according to one account, 3. 37.

S'atavapus (??), variant of S'iteshu, 4. 63.

S'atávari (??), variant of S'arávatí, 2. 147.

S'atayajna (?), variant of S'rutanjaya, 4. 174.

S'atáyus, son of Purúravas, son of Budha, 4. 13.

S'atáyus, son of Bhajamána, son of Satwata, 4. 72.

S'atáyus (??), variant of S'rutáyus, son of Arishťanemi, 3. 334.

S'atáyus (??), variant of S'iteshu, 4. 63.

S'atha, son of Vasudeva, son of S'úra, 4. 109.

Satí, a S'akti of S'iva, P. 79; 5. 321.

Satí, 'truth,' daughter of Daksha, and wife of Bhava, &c., P. 89; 1. 109, 110, 117, &c., 157; 4. 261, 262. Also called daughter of Kardama, 1. 110. She burns herself, 1. 127.

Sati, wife of some Angiras, 2. 29.

Satírthas, variant of Saníyas, 2. 180.

Satíyas, variant of Saníyas, 2. 180.

Satkarman, variant of Satyakarman, 4. 126.

Sátpudá, a mountain-range, popularly so called, in India, 2. 128, 144, 150, 339.

S'atrughna, son of Daśaratha, son of Aja, 1. 165; 3. 315, 318, 319.

S'atrughna (who ?), 4. 85.

S'atrughna, son of Swaphalka, 4. 95, 96.

S'atrughna, son of Devaśravas, son of S'úra, 4. 113.

S'atruhan, variant of S'atrughna, son of S'waphalka, 4. 95, 96.

S'atrujit, epithet of Pratardana, son of Divodása, 4. 34, 35.

S'atrujit, son of Vatsa, son of Pratardana, 4. 36.

Sattá, what, in philosophy, 5. 200.

Sattámátrátman, what, in philosophy, 3. 312.

Sattrájit, father of some S'atáníka, 4. 165.

Sattrájit, variant of Sattrájita, 4. 74, 100.

Sattrájita, son of Nighna, and friend of Áditya, 4. 74. Receives the Syamantaka jewel, 4. 75. Gives his daughter Satyabhámá to Kŕishña, in marriage, 4. 80. Is slain by Satadhanwan, 4. 81. See also 4. 112; 5. 81, 148.

Sáttrájití, the same as Satyabhámá, 5. 81.

M

Sattwa, what, in philosophy, P. 20; l. 3, 35, 74, 138.

Sáttwika, adjective of Sattwa, what, P. 20, 21; l. 34, 74; 2. 296; 5. 285, 310.

Satwa, variously genealogised, 4. 69, 70.

Sátwatas, a dynasty descended from Satwata, 4. 70.

Satwata, Sátwata, a Yádava king, variously genealogised, 4. 69–71, 74, 86.

Satyas, certain gods, appearing in the third and fourth Manwantaras, 3. 6, 7, 17. Their origin, 2. 26; 3. 17.

Satya, a form of Vishṇu, 3. 17.

Satya, one of the Viśwe devas, 3. 189–191.

Satya, two Ṛishis, appearing in the ninth Manwantara, and in the tenth, respectively, 3. 25, 26.

Satya, son of Havirdhána, 1. 193.

Satya, an astronomer, referred to the court of King Vikramáditya, P. 9.

Satya (?), son of Sáraṇa, 4. 109.

Satya, the same as Satya-loka, 2. 231.

Satyá, mother of Tushita, 3. 17.

Satyá, or Nágnajití, a wife of Kṛishṇa, 4. 91, 92; 5. 78, 79, 82. Confounded with Satyabhámá, 5. 97, 99, 104.

Satyá, wife of Bṛihanmanas, 4. 125.

Satya, what, in philosophy, 3. 77; 4. 294.

Satyabhámá, daughter of Sattrá-
jita, and wife of Kṛishṇa, 4. 80, 81, 91, 92 (where the Sanskrit has Satyá, another person, wherefore note * should be altered), 112; 5. 78, 79, 81, 89, 92, 96–99, 102, 103, 105, 107, 148, 154.

Satyábhidháyin, what, in theology, l. 73, 89.

Satyadharman, a king, son of Dharmasávarṇika, the Manu, 3. 27.

Satyadhṛita, son of Pushpavat, 4. 150.

Satyadhṛiti, son of Sáraṇa, 4. 109.

Satyadhṛiti, son of Dhṛitimat, son of Yavínara, 4. 142.

Satyadhṛiti, son of S'atánanda, son of S'aradwat, 4. 146.

Satyadhṛiti, variant of Sudhṛiti, son of Maháviírya, 3. 331.

Satyadhwaja, son of Úrjaváha, 3. 333.

Satyahita, son and disciple of Satyasravas, and promulgator of the Ṛig-veda, 3. 45.

Satyahita, variant of Satyadhṛita, 4. 150.

Satyajit, a Yaksha, 2. 285, &c.

Satyajit, Indra of the third Manwantara, by one account, 3. 6.

Satyajit, son of Suníta, 4. 176.

Satyajit (?), variant of Jayadratha, son of Bṛihatkarman, 4. 140.

Satyajita (?), variant of Satyadhṛita, 4. 150.

Satyakas, a class of gods in the fourth Manwantara, according to one account, 3. 7.

Satyaka, a king, son of Raivata,

Manu of the fifth Manwantara, 3. 11.

Satyaka, son of S'ini, 4. 93.

Satyaka, son of Krishna and Rohini, 5. 79, 148.

Satyaka (?), variant of Andhaka, 4. 96.

Satyakarman, son of Dhritavrata, son of Dhriti, 4. 126.

Satyakarna, son of Janamejaya, son of Chandrapida, 4. 163.

Satyaketu, a Rishi in the tenth Manwantara, 3. 26.

Satyaketu, variously genealogized, 4. 37, 38.

Satyaki = Yuyudhana, 4. 93; 5. 123, 148.

Satya-loka, 'the world of infinite wisdom and truth,' 1. 98; 2. 113, 227, 228; 4. 319.

Satyambhara, a river in Plaksha-dwipa, 2. 193.

Satyanetra, son of Atri, 1. 154.

Satyangas, a caste in Plaksha-dwipa, 2. 193.

Satyaratha, son of Minaratha, 3. 334.

Satyaratha, son of Romapada, son of Dharmaratha, 4. 124.

Satyarathá, wife of Harischandra, 3. 287.

Satyarathi, son of Satyaratha, son of Minaratha, 3. 334.

Satyasena, a form of Bhagavat or Vishnu, in the third Manwantara, 3. 17.

Satyasravas, son and disciple of Mandukeya, and promulgator of the Rig-veda, 3. 45.

Satyasravas, son of Vitihotra, 3. 335.

Satyasri, son and disciple of Satyahita, and promulgator of the Rig-veda, 3. 45-47, 50.

Satyavach, son of Chakshusha, the Manu, 1. 177.

Satyavat, son of Chakshusha, the Manu, P. 83; 1. 178.

Satyavati, wife of Harischandra, 3. 288.

Satyavati, daughter of Vasu, and wife of S'antanu and of Parasara, 4. 150, 157, 158; 5. 181.

Satyavati, daughter of Gadhi, 4. 16, &c. Becomes the river Kausiki, 4. 18.

Satyavratas, a caste in S'aka-dwipa, 2. 200.

Satyavratas, a class of gods, appearing in the third Manwantara, according to one account, 3. 17.

Satyavrata, a Manu (?), 3. 236.

Satyavrata, or Trisanku, variously genealogized, 3. 284, 286.

Satya-yajna, a particular sacrifice, 3. 93.

Satyayu, son of Pururavas, son of Budha, 4. 13.

Satyeyu, son of Raudrasva, 4. 127-129.

Saubalyas, a people, 2. 157.

Saubhas, a people, 5. 70.

Saubhari, a Rishi, legend of, 3. 268, &c.

Saucha, what, 3. 77.

Saudamini, daughter of Kasyapa and Vinata, 2. 73.

Saudamini, an Apsaras, 2. 81.

Saudasa, son of Sudasa, son of Sarvakama, 3. 304-307, 310; 4. 24.

Saudása, son of Sudása, son of Chyavana, 4. 147, 148.

Saudása, son of Apílaka or Ivilaka, 4. 202.

S'auddhodani, patronym of S'ákya, 4. 170.

Saudhas (?), variant of Sodhas, 2. 163.

Sauhfidas, a people, 2. 178.

Sankara (?), variant of S'úkara, 2. 214.

S'aulkáyani, disciple of Devadarsa, &c., and teacher of the Atharvaveda, 3. 61, 62.

S'aulkyáyani (?), variant of S'aulkáyani, 3. 61.

Saumas, an heretical sect, 5. 380.

Saumadatti, patronym of Sávarni, disciple of Romaharshana, 3. 66.

Saumaka (?), variant of Somaka, 2. 191.

Saumanasya, son of Yajnabáhu, king of S'álmala-dwípa, 2. 195.

Saumanasya, a region in S'álmala-dwípa, 2. 195.

Saumasushmáyaña, Vyása in the twenty-third Dwápara age, 3. 35.

Saumitri, teacher of the Sámaveda, 3. 60, 61.

Saumyas, a class of Pitris, 2. 303; 3. 166.

Saumya, a portion of Bháratavarsha, 2. 112, 129.

S'aunaka, disciple of Pathya, and teacher of the Atharva-veda, 3. 62, 72; 4. 163.

S'aunaka, variously genealogized, 4. 31, 32, 40.

S'aunakáyani (?), variant of S'aulkáyani, 3. 62.

Saunanda, a famous club which came down from heaven, 5. 51.

Sauparña-puráña = Garuda-puráña, P. 24.

Saura (correctly), the same as S'ani, or Saturn, 2. 259.

Saurapatas (in correct spelling), a sect worshipping the sun, 5. 280.

Saura-puráña = Brahma-puráña, P. 27.

Saura-samhitá, a part of the Skanda-puráña, P. 73.

Sauráshtras, a people, 2. 133, 134; 4. 222, 224.

Saura-upapuráña, P. 87.

S'auri, a name of Vishñu or Kfishña, 1. 119; 4. 323; 5. 22, 84, 87, 115, 121, 125.

Sauri = S'ani, or Saturn, 2. 226, 259.

Saurí-samhitá, a part of the Kúrma-puráña, P. 77.

Sausalyas, variant of Saubalyas, 2. 157.

S'ausíta, variant of S'aisíkas, 4. 221.

Sausratas, Kausíka Bráhmans, 4. 28.

Sausruta, a medical work, by Susruta, referred to, P. 60, &c.

Sausúlyas (?), variant of Saubalyas, 2. 157.

Sauti, son of Súta or Lomaharshaña, 3. 43.

Sautrámañí, a particular sacrifice, 3. 109, 113.

Sauvíras, peoples so called, 2. 133, 134, 174; 5. 389.

Sauvíra, a country, 2. 174, 318; 5. 389.

Savana, son of Vasishtha, 1. 155.

Savana, son of Priyavrata, and king of Pushkara-dwípa, 2. 100, &c., 201.

Savana, a Ŕishi in the ninth Manwantara, 3. 25.

Savana, a hell, 2. 214.

Sávarńa, Manu of the twelfth Manwantara, son of Rudra, 3. 27.

Sávarńá, daughter of Samudra, and wife of Práchínabarhis, 1. 194 (where 'ocean' represents Samudra). See Sámudrí.

Sávarńa, variant of Sávarńi, the Manu, 3. 22.

Sávarńaka, variant of Sávarńika, 3. 23.

Sávarńi, Manu of the eighth Manwantara, son of the Sun and Chháyá, 3. 21-24.

Sávarńi, descended from Somadatta (?), disciple of Romaharshaŕa, and a teacher of the Puránas, 3. 64-66.

Sávarńi (who?), P. 65.

Sávarńi (who?), 2. 113.

Sávarńi (?), variant of Sávarńa, 3. 27.

Sávarńika, the eighth Manwantara, 3. 23.

Sávarńyas, of the Atharva-veda, 3. 62.

S'ávasta (?), variant of S'rávasta, 3. 263.

S'ávasti (?), variant of S'rávasta, 3. 263.

S'ávastí (?), variant of S'rávastí, 3. 263.

Savibhása (?), variant of Vibhása, a sun, 5. 191.

Savisha, a hell, 2. 215.

Sávitra, a Rudra, 2. 25.

Sávitra, a peak of Mount Meru, 1. 120.

Savitŕi = Parjanya, &c., an Áditya, 1. 142 (where correct the spelling), 200 ; 2. 27, 250, 251 ; 3. 56, 117.

Savitŕi, Vyása of the fifth Dwápara age, 3. 34, 36.

Sávitrí, wife of Satyavat, P. 83.

Sávitrí, daughter of Daksha, and wife of Dharma, 2. 21.

Sávitrí, a river in Plaksha-dwípa, 2. 193.

Sávitrí, a form of the Gáyatrí, 1. 108.

Sáya, son of Pushpárńa and Doshá, 1. 178.

Sáyańa Áchárya, a commentator, referred to, 3. 338 ; 5. 178.

S'ayanottama, what, in architecture, 5. 33.

Seas, seven, surrounding the seven Dwípas, 2. 109, 110. That of salt water, 2. 191. That of cane-juice, 2. 193. That of wine, 2. 195. That of clarified butter, 2. 197. That of whey, 2. 198. That of milk, 2. 200, 201. That of fresh water, 2. 202.

Sana (?), variant of Hema, son of Ushadratha, 4. 122.

S'ená (?), variant of Mená, the river so called, 2. 149.

Senajit, a Yaksha, 2. 285, 288, &c.

Senajit, son of Viśwajit, son of Jayadratha, 4. 140.

Senajit, son of Bŕihatkarman, son of Sukshatŕra, 4. 174.

Senajit, the same as Prasenajit, 3. 265.

Senáni, a Rudra, 2. 25.

Sarpas, 'serpents.' Transformed hairs of Brahmá's head, 1. 83. Offspring of Kaśyapa and Kadrú, 2. 74. Their king, S'esha, 2. 85; but Takshaka, 2. 86. Twelve of them named, and their function mentioned, 2. 285, &c.

Sense, organs of, how produced, and by whom presided over, and the number of them, 1. 38.

S'esha, son of Kaśyapa and Kadrú, 2. 74. King of serpents, 2. 85. See also P. 42; 4. 269; 5. 12, 65, 130, 139, 149, 192, 195, 393. A form of Vishńu, dwelling below the seven Pátálas, supporter of the world on his head, and a teacher of astronomy, and also the couch of Vishńu, P. 31; 2. 211–213; 3. 30, 31; 4. 260. See also Balabhadra (bis).

S'esha, a Prajápati, 1. 102.

S'esha, a king, 4. 212.

S'eshanága (?), a king, 4. 212, 218.

Setu, variously genealogized, 4. 118.

Setubandha, a place in the south of India, 3. 328.

Shad'ánana, an epithet of Kárttikeya, 2. 118.

Shad'ja, a note of the musical scale, 2. 329.

Shańd'as, a people, 2. 163.

Shod'aśárchis, an epithet of S'ukra,

or Venus, the planet so called, 2. 257, 258.

Shod'aśín, a particular sacrifice, 1. 85; 3. 113 (where correct the spelling).

S'ibapura (?), a city, ruled over by S'ibi, son of Uśínara, 4. 121.

S'ibi, Indra in the fourth Manwantara, 3. 7. See S'ikhi.

S'ibi, son of Chákshusha, the Manu, 1. 178.

S'ibi, son of Samhráda, or else of Anuhráda, 2. 69.

S'ibi, son of Uśínara, 4. 121, 122.

S'ibi (who?), 4. 24.

S'ibi (who?), 5. 82, 83.

S'ibi (?), variant of S'ini, son of Garga, 4. 137.

S'ibiká, the weapon of Kubera, 3. 22.

Siddhas, a people in India, 2. 176.

Siddhas, a sort of sages, 1. 122, 144; 5. 14, 59, 88, 94, 105, 150, 195, 246, 247.

Siddha, son of Dharma, the Prajápati, 1. 111.

Siddhakshetra, a region in India, 5. 118.

Siddhapura, a fabulous city, 2. 111, 113.

Siddhártha, an epithet of S'ákya, 4. 170.

Siddhártha, variant of Rátula, 4. 169.

Siddhásana, in the Yoga philosophy, 5. 230.

Siddhi, 'perfection,' daughter of Daksha, and wife of Dharma, 1. 109, 110.

Siddhis, 'attributes of perfection,' eight, specified, 1. 91. See also,

for other senses of Siddhi, 2. 7 ; 5. 146.

Siddhimanwantara, a place of pilgrimage on the river Narmadá, 2. 151.

S'íghra, the same as S'íghraga, 3. 325.

S'íghrá, a river in India, 2. 151.

S'íghraga, son of Agnivarńa, 3. 314. See S'íghra.

S'ikhańd'ini, wife of Antardháua, 1. 192.

S'ikhańd'ini, two Apsarases so called, 2. 80, 81.

S'íkhi, variant of S'ibi, Indra in the fourth Manwantara, according to one account, 3. 7.

S'íkhí, a river in Plaksha-dwípa, 2. 192.

S'ikhin, the same as Ketu, 'the descending node,' 2. 259.

S'ikhivásas, a mountain-range extending westward from Mount Meru, 2. 117.

S'íkshá, an Anga of the Veda, defined, 3. 67 ; 4. 252.

S'íkya (?), a certain king, 4. 214 (note ||).

S'íla, son of Páriyátra, 3. 321.

S'ilpa-s'ástra, ' mechanics, sculpture, and architecture,' 1. 148.

Simha, the same as Nrisimha, 5. 3.

Simha, son of Krishńa and Lakshmańá, 5. 81.

Simhala, an island, 2. 129.

Simhiká, daughter of Kas'yapa, and wife of Viprachitti, her halfbrother, 1. 148 ; 2. 30, 55, 71, 259.

Simhiká, daughter of Daksha, and wife of Kas'yapa, 2. 26.

Simhapáyana (?), variant of S'áms'apáyana, 3. 64, 65.

S'ims'apáyana, variant of Vais'ampáyana, 3. 66.

Sindhus, a people, 2. 159 ; 5. 389. See Saindhavas.

Sindhu, the river Indus, 2. 120, 121, 142 ; 3. 170 ; 4. 118, 223 ; 5. 381.

Sindhu, a river (another), 2. 148, 341.

Sindhudwípa, variously genealogized, 3. 303, 315.

Sindhuka, a king, 4. 195. See S'ipraka.

Sindhupulindakas (?), a people, 2. 158, 159.

Sindhusauvíras, a people, 2. 134, 173 ; 5. 389.

S'íneyus (?), variant of S'íteshu, 4. 63.

S'ini, son of Vrishńi, son of Bhajamána, 4. 73, 74, 93.

S'ini, son of Anamitra, 4. 93, 94.

S'ini, son of Garga, son of Bhavanmanyu, 4. 137.

S'ini (??), variant of S'uchi, son of Andhaka, 4. 97.

S'ini (?), variant of Pratikshattra, son of S'amin, 4. 99.

S'inibáhu, a river rising in the Vindhya mountains, 2. 155.

S'iníka (??), variant of S'amíka, a future Muni, 5. 251.

S'iníválí, daughter of Angiras, 1. 153.

S'iníválí, a river in S'álmala-dwípa, 2. 195.

S'iníválí, 'the day when the new moon is first seen,' 2. 260.

S'iphá, a river in India, 2. 155.

Síprá, a river, 2. 131 (where correct the spelling), 155, 339.

Sípraka, founder of the Andhrabhŕitya dynasty, 4. 194.

Síra, 'ploughshare,' 3. 332; 5. 51. Compare Hala.

Síradhwaja, an epithet of Balabhadra, 3. 253.

Síradhwaja, an epithet of Janaka, son of Hraswaroman, 3. 332, 333.

Sirálas (??), variant of Páśivátas, 2. 180.

Siráyudha, an epithet of Balabhadra, 3. 254.

Sírin, an epithet of Balabhadra, 4. 82 ; 5. 137.

S'ishŕi (??), variant of S'lishŕi, son of Dhruva, 1. 179.

S'ishyanandi (??), variant of Sushinandi, 4. 211.

Siśira, son of Dhara, a Vasu, 2. 23.

Siśira, son of Medhátithi, king of Plaksha-dwípa, 2. 191.

Siśira, disciple of Sákalya, and a promulgator of the Ŕig-veda, 3. 46.

Siśira, a region in Plaksha-dwípa, 2. 191.

Siśira, a mountain-range extending southward from Mount Meru, 2. 117.

Siśiráyana (rightly, Saiśiráyana), son of Siśira, 5. 53.

Síśu, son of Sárana, 4. 109.

Siśuka, son of Dharma, &c., 4. 211, 213.

Siśuka (??), variant of Sindhuka, 4. 195, 200.

Siśumára, what, in astronomy, 2. 306, 307.

Siśunága, the same as Siśunáka, 4. 180, 185, 231.

Siśunáka, a king, 4. 180. See also Saiśunágas.

Siśunandi, a Yavana king, 4. 211, 212.

Siśupála, son of Damaghosha, 4. 67, 104–106, 246, 316; 5. 69, 70.

Sítá, daughter of Janaka, and wife of Ráma, 1. 151 ; 3. 316, 317, 331, 332 ; 4. 146.

Sítá, Síté, a river, the Sihoun (?), 2. 112, 120–122, 272 ; 5. 388.

Sítá-kund', the popular name of a hot well near Monghir, on the Ganges, 4. 286.

Sítánta, a mountain-range extending eastward from Mount Meru, 2. 117, 124.

Síteshu, son of Uśanas, 4. 63, 64.

Síteyus (?), variant of Síteshu, 4. 63.

Sítíkahu (??), variant of Síteshu, 4. 63.

Sívas, a class of gods in the third Manwantara, 3. 6.

Siva, a god of the first order. The same as Vishnu in the character of destroyer, 1. 41. Born, as a Kumára, from Brahmá, in every Kalpa, and differing, in each, in colour, 1. 77–79. King of the Bhútas, 2. 86. His city, &c., 2. 112, 230. Spoils Daksha's sacrifice, 1. 120, &c. Bears the river Alakanandá on his head, 2. 272. Intercedes for Bána, 5. 118, &c. See also P. 4. &c. &c. ; 1. 1, &c.; 5. 14, 76, 92, 94, 108, 114, &c. &c. And see Hara, Ísa, Íśwara, Mahádeva, Maheśa, Maheśwara, Náráyana, Sankara,

S'úlapáṇi, Trilochana, Umápati, &c.

S'iva, a Rudra, 1. 117; 5. 386.

S'iva, son of Úru, son of Chákshusha, the Manu, 1. 177.

S'iva, son of Medhátithi, or else of Idhmajihwa, king of Plaksha-dwípa, 2. 191, 193.

S'ivá, a S'akti, sprung from S'iva, and wife of Íśána, P. 79; 1. 117.

S'ivá, wife of Anilá, the Vasu, 2. 23; 5. 387.

S'iva, a region in Plaksha-dwípa, 2. 191, 193.

S'ivá, a river in India, 2. 149.

S'ivá, a river in Kuśa-dwípa, 2. 196.

S'iva, the name of a Kalpa, P. 74.

S'ivadatta, a king of the Ábhíras, 4. 208.

S'iva-dharma, a part of the Skanda-puráṇa (?), 2. 216, 221.

S'iva-dharma-upapuráṇa, P. 87.

S'iva-gítá, a poem encomiastic of S'iva, 3. 65.

S'ivapura, the city of S'iva, P. 38. For S'iva's city, see 2. 112.

S'iva-puráṇa, P. 20, 24, 35, 88, 89. And see S'aiva-puráṇa.

S'iva-rahasya-khaṇḍa, a part of the Skanda-puráṇa, P. 73.

S'iva-rátri, a certain festival, P. 89.

S'iva-saṁhitá. See Rudra-saṁhitá.

S'ivaskanda (??), variant of S'iva-skandha, 4. 198.

S'ivaskandaśátakarṇi, &c. (??), variants of S'ivaskandha, 4. 201, 202.

S'ivaskandha, variously genealo-gized, 4. 198, 202.

S'ivaśri, variant of S'ivaśriśátakar-ṇin, 4. 201:

S'ivaśriśátakarṇin, son of Pulimat, 4. 198.

S'ivaswámin, variant of S'ivaswáti, 4. 198.

S'ivaswáti, son of Chakoraśátakar-ṇin, &c., 4. 197, 201.

Sivatas (??), variant of Páśivátas, 2. 180.

S'iva-tantra, a composition, quoted, 2. 206.

S'iva-tattwa-viveka, the, by Ap-payya Díkshita, quoted, 5. 391.

S'iva-upapuráṇa, P. 36, 87, 88.

Skanda = Kárttikeya, P. 72; 4. 283.

Skanda, a Prajápati, 1. 78.

Skanda, son of Paśupati, a form of Rudra, 1. 117.

Skanda-puráṇa, Skánda-puráṇa, analysis of the, &c., P. 20, 23, 24, 27, 72, &c., 78, 85; 3. 67; 5. 264, 316.

Skandaswáti, son of Ávi (??), son of Saudása, 4. 202.

Skandhastambbi, son of Púrṇot-sanga, 4. 200.

Skandhaswáti, son of Swáti, 4. 200.

Skandhaswáti (??), variant of S'iva-skandha, 4. 201.

Sleeping, rules of, 3. 131, &c.

S'lishṭi, son of Dhruva, 1. 177; 5. 388.

Smártas, a religious sect, 5. 340, 342.

Smaya, 'wonder,' son of Dharma, 1. 111.

Smṛita, a Prajápati, son of Va-sishṭha, 3. 5.

Smṛiti, 'memory,' daughter of Daksha, and wife of Angiras,

1. 109, 153. Called daughter of Dharma, 1. 111.

Smṛiti, what, in philosophy, 1. 32.

Snehas, a caste in Kuśa-dwípa, 2. 195.

S'obhayantyas, a class of Apsarases, 2. 75, 82.

Society, origin and progress of, 1. 92, &c.

Sodhas, a people, 2. 161.

Sohanji (?), variant of Sáhanji, 4. 54.

S'oka, 'sorrow,' son of Mṛityu, 2. 112.

Soma, son of Atri, 1. 154; 2. 11; 4. 2, 129. Called son of Dharma, 2. 259. Called son of the Ṛishi Prabhákara, 4. 129. Churned from the ocean, 2. 11. By origin, a Bráhman, 5. 388. His wives, 2. 20, 21. His offspring, 2. 28. Carries off Tárá, wife of Bṛihaspati, 4. 2. Has Budha, or Mercury, by her, 1. 174; 2. 259; 4. 4. His city, Vibhávari or Vibhá, 2. 118, 240, 241. Soverrign of the vegetable world, 2. 1. Monarch of the stars and planets, of Bráhmans and of plants, of sacrifices and of penance, 2. 85; 4. 2. Lord of progenitors, 3. 181. One with the Moon, P. 3; 2. 337; 5. 47, &c. One with the moon-plant. 2. 337, 342. See also 1. 188, 190; 4. 3, 4, 103, 104, &c. &c.

Soma, a Vasu, 2. 23.

Soma, one of the Viśwe devas, 3. 179.

Soma (?), variant of Devakshattra, 4. 68.

Somá, an Apsaras, 2. 81.

Somadatta, son of Kṛiśáśwa, 3. 247.

Somadatta, son of Panchadhanus, 4. 147; 5. 134.

Somadatta, son of Váhlika, 4. 157.

Somádbi (?), variant of Somápi, son of Sahadeva, 4. 151, 173.

Somáśushmáyaṅa, &c., variants of Saumaśushmáyaṅa, 3. 35.

Somakas, a family sprung from Somaka or Ajamídha, 4. 147.

Somaka, a second birth of Ajamídha, 4. 147.

Somaka, son of Sahadeva or Saudása, 4. 148.

Somaka, son of Kṛishṇa and Kálindí, 5. 79.

Somaka, a mountain-range in Plaksha-dwípa, 2. 191.

Soma-loka, a region tenanted by various classes of Pitṛis, 3. 159, 160.

Somanátha, the temple of, 5. 47.

Somapas, a class of Pitṛis, sons of Kavi and Swadhá, 1. 123, 157; 3. 159, 160, 162, 165, 174, 339.

Somápi, son of Divodása, son of Badhryaśwa, 4. 147.

Somápi, son of Sahadeva, son of Jarásandha, 4. 151, 173.

Somasada, a class of Pitṛis, sons of Viráj, 3. 159.

Soma-saṁsthás, certain sacrifices, 3. 112, 113.

Somaśarman, son of S'áliśúka, 4. 190.

Somaśushma, named in the S'atapatha-bráhmaṇa, &c., 3. 35.

Soma-tírtha, a place of pilgrimage on the coast of Gujerat, 5. 47.

Somávarta, the region between the river Payoshní and Váráha, 2. 144.

Somavit (??), variant of Somápi, son of Sahadeva, 4. 151.

Soma-yajna, a particular ceremony, 3. 40.

Soña, an Indian river, the Sone, 2. 141, 151, 340.

Sonáksha (??), variant of Pratikshattra, son of Samin, 4. 99.

Sonáśwa (??), variant of Pratikshattra, son of Samin, 4. 99.

Soñi, son of Súra, son of Vidúratha, 4. 99.

Soñitapura, Bána's city, 5. 112, 118.

Soshayantyas, a class of Apsarases, 2. 82.

Sparta, the pancratium of, 5. 39, 40.

Spheres of the sun and planets, 2. 224, &c.

Sphúrja, a Rakshasa, 2. 285, &c.

Sraddhá, 'faith,' daughter of Daksha, and wife of Dharma, 1. 109, 110. Called daughter of Kardama, and wife of Angiras, 1. 110. See also 1. 148; 3. 121.

Sraddhá, wife of Vaivaswata, 3. 233-235, 337.

Sráddha, 'devotion to the manes of one's progenitors,' 3. 113, &c. For prosperity, 3. 98, 99, 146, &c. Kinds of Sráddhas, 3. 146, 147. The perpetual Sráddha, 3. 122. Sráddha for kindred newly deceased, 3. 149,

&c. Monthly Sráddha for deceased relations, 3. 153, &c. Annual Sráddha, 3. 154. Occasional Sráddhas, 3. 157, &c. Bráhmans to be entertained at Sráddhas, 3. 173, &c. Prayers to be used at Sráddhas, 3. 181, &c. Things sacred at Sráddhas, 3. 186, &c. Sráddhas how vitiated, 3. 194, &c.

Sraddhádeva (correctly), an epithet of Vaivaswata, 3. 13, 337.

Sráddhadeva, an epithet of Yama, 3. 337.

Sráddha-gñña-pati, the, a work on exequial law, referred to, 3. 190.

Sráddha-kalpa, a part of the Váyupuráña, P. 38.

Sráddha-kalpa, the, a work on exequial law, referred to, or quoted, 3. 148, 189, 199, 339.

Sráddha-mayúkha, the, a work of like character, referred to, 3. 148, 198.

Sráddha-tattwa, the, another similar treatise, referred to, 3. 190.

Srama, son of Ápa, 2. 23.

Sránta, son of Ápa, 2. 23.

Srastara, the term defined, &c., 3. 131, 150; 5. 204.

Srava (?), one of the Viśwa devas, 3. 191.

Srávaka, what, among the Buddists, &c., 3. 41.

Sravaña, Sravaná, a certain asterism, 2. 265, &c., 308; 3. 132.

Srávaña, a month, July–Aug., 2. 261, &c.; 3. 114; 4. 261, 276.

Srávaní, a certain sacrifice, 3. 113.

Srávantí, error for Srávastí, noted as such, 3. 264.

Srávasta, son of Yuvanáśwa, 3. 263, 264.

Srávastí, Sravastí (?), a city, its position, 3. 263, 264, 319.

Sravishťhá, the same as Dhanishťhá, an asterism so called, 2. 259.

Sreníka, the same as Bimbisára, 4. 171.

Sreníka (another?), 5. 391.

Sreyas, what, in theology, 2. 326.

Srí, daughter of Bhṛígu, and wife of Vishńu, 1. 2, 118, 135, 142, 144, &c. &c. ; 5. 99. Hymned by Indra, 1. 148, &c. See Lakshmí (at the end of the article) and Rukminí.

Srí Bhágavata, Srí Bhágavata-puráńa. See Bhágavata-puráńa.

Sríbhánu, son of Kṛishńa and Satyabhámá, 5. 81.

Srídáman, a friend of Kṛishńa, 4. 300.

Srídevá, daughter of Devaka, son of Áhuka, and wife of Vasudeva, son of Súra, 4. 98, 110, 111.

Srídeví (?), variant of Srídevá, 4. 98.

Srídhara, the same as Vishńu, 1. 119.

Srídhara Swámin, the same as Srídhara Yati, P. 46, 47, &c., 114, &c.

Srídhara Yati, commentator on the Vishńu-puráńa, P. 114-116, et passim. See Srídhara Swámin.

Sríjavána, son of Dyutimat, son of Páńďu (?), 1. 152.

Srímallakarńí, variant of Srísátakarńí, 4. 200.

Srí-nárada-puráńa, a mythological work, P. 51.

Srínáthdwár, a temple so called in the living languages of India, P. 22 ; 5. 318.

Sṛíngavat, the same as Sṛíngin, 2. 102, 111, 256.

Sṛíngin (rightly), a mountain-range to the north of Mount Meru, 2. 114, 115. See Sṛíngavat.

Sṛíní (?), variant of Túńi, 4. 93.

Sṛínjayas, a people, 2. 180; 4. 144.

Sṛínjaya, son of Auttami, the Manu, 3. 7.

Sṛínjaya, son of Dhúmráśwa, 3. 247.

Sṛínjaya, son of Súra, son of Devamíďhusha, 4. 101, 113.

Sṛínjaya, son of Kálánara, 4. 120.

Sṛínjaya, son of Haryaśwa, son of Chakshus, 4. 144, 147.

Sṛínjayá, the name of two wives of Bhajamána, son of Satwata, 4. 72.

Sṛínjaya, variant of Sanjaya, son of Pratikshattra, 4. 43 (where correct Sṛínjaya), 44, 344.

Sríparvata, a mountain in Telingana, 2. 141 ; 4. 208. See Srísaila.

Sríparvatíyas, a branch of the Andhras, 4. 208.

Sríranga, the temple of, in the Deccan, P. 34.

Srísaila, a mountain near the river Kṛishńá, 2. 141; 5. 118. See Sríparvata.

Srísántakarńa (?), Srísántakarńi

(11), variants of S'riśátakarńi, 4. 195.

S'riśátakarńi, S'riśátakarńi (1), son of Kŕishńa, brother of S'ipraka, 4. 195, 196, 198, 201, 202, 345.

S'tishti (11), variant of Yuddha-mushti, 4. 99.

S'rishti (11), variant of S'lishti, son of Dhruva, 5. 388.

S'rishti-khańda, a part of the Padma-puráńa, P. 30, 83.

S'rishti-lílá, 'sport of creation,' P. 41.

S'rí-súkta, a supposititious Vaidik hymn, 1. 144.

S'ritala, a Pátála, or underworld, 2. 209.

S'titanjaya (11), variant of S'rutanjaya, son of Senajit, 4. 174.

S'rivatsa, a mystical mark borne by Kŕishńa, 2. 94; 4. 268; 5. 5, 13, 35, 124, 238.

S'rivatsa, the Jaina mystical mark so called, 5. 124.

S'rońi, a river in India, 2. 155.

S'rońi, variant of Yoni, the river so called, 2. 194.

S'rotas, S'rotas (1), substituted, perhaps wrongly, for Prátáh, the Yaksha, 2. 287, 292.

S'rotriya, the term defined, 3. 174–176.

S'ruta, 'sacred tradition,' son of Dharma, the Prajápati, 1. 110.

S'ruta, son of Bhagiratha, 3. 303, 315.

S'ruta, son of Upagu, 3. 334.

S'ruta, son of Kŕishńa and Kálindí, 5. 79, 107.

S'ruta (11), variant of Suśruta, son of Subhása, 3. 334.

S'rutadevá, daughter of S'úra, son of Devamíd'husha, variously married, 4. 101, 103, 104.

S'rutadharas, a caste in Sálmala-dwípa, 2. 195.

S'rutakarman, son of Sahadeva, son of Dasra, 4. 159.

S'rutakarman (11), variant of S'ruta-śravas, son of Somápi, 4. 151.

S'rutakírtti, son of Arjuna, son of Páńd'u, 4. 159.

S'rutakírtti, daughter of S'úra, son of Devamíd'husha, and wife of Dhŕishtaketu, king of the Kai-keyas, 4. 101, 103; 5. 82.'

S'rutanjaya, son of Senajit, son of Bŕihatkarman, 4. 174.

S'rutaśarman (11), variant of S'ruta-śravas, son of Somápi, 4. 151.

S'rutasena, an astronomer, referred to the court of King Vikramá-ditya, P. 9.

S'rutasena, variously genealogized, 4. 152, 162.

S'rutasena (11), variant of S'úrasena, son of S'atrughna, 3. 319.

S'rutasena (1), variant of S'ruta-soma, 4. 159.

S'rutasoma, son of Bhímasena or Bhima, son of Páńd'u, 4. 159.

S'rutaśravas, son of Somápi, son of Sahadeva, 4. 151, 173.

S'rutaśravas, daughter of S'úra, son of Devamíd'husha, and wife of Damaghosha, 4. 101, 103.

S'rutavat, the same as S'rutaśravas, son of Somápi, 4. 173.

S'rutavindá, a river in Kuśa-dwípa, 2. 197.

S'rutáyu (1), variant of S'rutáyus, son of Purúravas, 4. 13.

Srutáyus, son of Bhánuratha, son of Chandragiri, 3. 321.

Srutáyus, son of Arishṭanemi, 3. 334.

Srutáyus, son of Purúravas, son of Budha, 4. 13.

Srutáyus (??), variant of Ayutáśwa, 3. 303.

Srutáyus (??), variant of Ayutáyus, son of Srutavat, 4. 173.

Sruti, daughter of Atri, and wife of Kardama, 1. 154, 155; 2. 263.

Srutiratha (??), variant of Kírttiratha, 3. 331.

Stamba, variant of Stambha, a Rishi, 3. +

Stambamitra (?), variant of Tambamitra, 5. 250.

Stambha, a Rishi in the second Manwantara, variously genealogized, 3. 3–5.

Stanabálas, variant of Tanabálas, 2. 180.

Stanapas (??), variant of Tanayas, 2. 181.

Stanapáyikas, variant of Stanayoshikas, 2. 187.

Stanaposhikas, variant of Stanayoshikas, 2. 187.

Stanayodhikas, variant of Stanayoshikas, 2. 187.

Stanayoshikas, a people, 2. 187.

Stávás (??), a class of Apsarases, 2. 82.

Sthala (??), variant of Chhala, 3. 321, 323.

Sthaleyu, son of Raudráśwa, 4. 128, 129.

Sthandileyu, son of Raudráśwa, 4. 127, 128.

Stháṇu, a name of Rudra or Siva, 1. 103; 5. 389.

Stháṇu, a Tírtha sacred to Siva, P. 75.

Stháṇwíśwara, a district in India, 2. 143; 5. 388.

Sthávara, what, in philosophy, 5. 236.

Sthirátman, what, in philosophy, 1. 59.

Sthiti, what, in philosophy, 3. 31, 315; 5. 169.

Sthúla-maya, what, in philosophy, 1. 60 (where correct the spelling); 5. 386.

Stoma, 'hymn,' sprung from Brahmá, 1. 85, 200.

Strírájya, 'a polyandrous kingdom,' 4. 222.

Student, duties of a religious, 3. 92, 93.

Stuti, 'prayer,' sprung from Brahmá, 1. 85.

Stutyavrata, ruler over the realm of Stutyavrata, and son of Hiraṇyaretas, sovereign of Kuśadwípa, 2. 197.

Stutyavrata, a realm in Kuśadwípa, 2. 197.

Subáhu, a Yaksha, 2. 293.

Subáhu, son of Satrughna, son of Daśaratha, 3. 319. Slain by Ráma, 3. 316.

Subáhu, son of Chitraka, 4. 96.

Subáhu, son of Krishṇa and Káliudí, 5. 79.

Subáhú, an Apsaras, 2. 81–83.

Subáhu (??), variant of Bahugava, 4. 128.

Subáhu (??), variant of Dhruva, son of Rantinára, 4. 130.

Subáhuka = Subáhu, the Yaksha, 2. 293.

Subala, son of Bhautya, the Manu, 3. 29.

Subala, Subála (?), son of Sumati, son of Dṛiḍhasena, 4. 176.

Subaláśwa (?), variant of Baláśwa, 3. 243.

S'ubhás (?), a class of Apsarases, 2. 82.

S'ubha, son of Dharma, the Prajápati, 1. 111.

S'ubha, son of Sahasráśwa, (?) 3. 321.

Subhadra, ruler over the realm of Subhadra, and son of Idhmajihwa, 2. 193.

Subhadra, son of Kṛishńa and Bhadrá, 5. 82.

Subhadra, a division of Plakshadwípa, 2. 193.

Subhadrá, daughter of Vasudeva, son of Súra, 4. 110; 5. 344.

Subhadrá, granddaughter of Rukmin, and wife of Aniruddha, 4. 112; 5. 84.

Subhadrá, wife of Arjuna, son of Páńḍu, 4. 159, 160.

Subhagá, an Apsaras, 2. 81, 82.

Subhágá, daughter of Raudráśwa, and wife of Prabhákara, the Ṛishi, 4. 129.

S'ubhancharás, a class of Apsarases, 2. 82.

Subhánu, son of Kṛishńa and Satyabhámá, 5. 81.

Subhása, son of Sudhanwan, son of S'áśwata, 3. 334.

Subháshańa (??), variant of Subbhása, 3. 334.

Subháswaras, a class of Pitṛis, 3. 339.

Subhávya (??), variant of Subhása, 3. 334.

Subhímá, wife of Kṛishńa, son of Vasudeva, 5. 83.

S'ubhra, husband of Vikuńṭhá, 3. 17.

Subhujá, an Apsaras, 2. 82.

Subhúmi, son of Ugrasena, son of Áhuka, 4. 99.

Subhúmi, variously genealogized, 4. 96.

Subháshańa (??), variant of S'anku, son of Ugrasena, 4. 98.

Substance, imperceptible, how perceptible, 1. 66.

Suchakshu, variant of Chakshu, the river Oxus, 2. 120 (note ||), 126.

Suchandra, son of Hemachandra son of Viśála, first king of Vaiśálí, 3. 247.

Suchandrá, (??), variant of Subhadrá, granddaughter of Rukmin, 4. 112.

Suchará, an Apsaras, 2. 82.

Sucháru, son of Pratibáhu, son of Vajra, 4. 113.

Sucháru, son of Kṛishńa and Rukmińí, 4. 113; 5. 78, 148.

Suchchháyá, wife of S'lishṭi, 1. 177.

Suchetas, son of Prachetas, son of Durgama or the like, 4. 119.

Suchi, son of Vahni or Agni, 1. 156, 193. Also called son of Antardhána, son of Pṛithu, 1. 193.

S'uchi, Indra of the fourteenth Manwantara, 3. 28.

S'uchi, a Rishi in the fourteenth Manwantara, 3. 28.

S'uchi, son of S'atadyumna, son of Bhánumat, 3. 333.

S'uchi, sprung from Anenas, son of Áyus, 4. 43.

S'uchi, son of Andhaka, 4. 97.

S'uchi, son of Vipra, son of S'rutanjaya, 4. 174.

S'uchi, daughter of Kas'yapa, son of Marichi, mother of waterfowls, 2. 73.

S'uchi = Áshádha, a month, June—July, 2. 261, 286.

S'uchi, variant of Kavi, son of Chákshusha, 1. 179.

S'uchidratha, S'uchidratna (??), S'uchidrava, variants of S'uchiratha, 4. 164.

S'uchiká, an Apsaras, 2. 81, 82.

Súchímukha, a certain hell, 2. 215.

S'uchiratha, son of Chitraratha, son of Ushna or the like, 4. 164.

S'uchis'ravas, a Prajápati, 1. 102.

Sudakshina, son of a king of the Kás'is, 5. 126, 128.

Sudámana, a people, 2. 175.

Sudamshtra, son of Samaujas, 4. 100.

Sudantá, an Apsaras, 2. 82.

Sudars'ana, variously genealogized, 3. 314, 325.

Sudars'ana (who?), 3. 335.

Sudars'ana, son of Ajamídha, 4. 148.

Sudars'ana, a name of Jambúdwípa, 2. 110.

Sudars'ana, Krishna's discus, 2. 52; 5. 89, 101, 117, 127, 128.

Sudás, ancestor of certain Bhojas, 2. 159.

Sudása, variously genealogized, 3. 303, 304, 306, 315.

Sudása, son of Chyavana, son of Mitrayu, 4. 147.

Sudása (??), variant of Vasudána, son of Brihadratha, 4. 165.

Sudattá, one with Mitravindá, wife of Krishna, (??) 5. 82. (The Harivams'a clearly distinguishes Sudattá and Mitravindá.)

S'uddha, a Rishi in the fourteenth Munwantara, 3. 28.

S'uddha, sprung from Anenas, son of Áyus, 4. 43.

S'uddhi-s'ráddha, a certain mortuary ceremony, 3. 147.

S'uddhi-tattwa, the, a law-book, referred to, 3. 131.

S'uddhoda (??), variant of S'uddhodana, 4. 169.

S'uddhodana, variously genealogized, 4. 5, 169, 170, 181.

S'uddhodanasuta, patronym of S'ákya, 4. 170.

Suddhodano, Páli of S'uddhodana, 4. 170.

Sudellas, a people, 2. 166.

Sudeshñas (Sudeshtas?), variant of Sudellas, 2. 166.

Sudeshña, son of Krishna and Rukminí, 5. 78.

Sudeshtas, a people, 2. 171. See Sudeshñas.

Sudeva, son of Chunchu, 3. 289.

Sudeva, son of Haryas'wa, king of the Kás'is, 4. 40.

Sudeva, son of Devaka, son of Áhuka, 4. 98.

Sudhá, wife of Vámadeva, the Rudra, 1. 117.

Sudhá, 'certain divine food,' 2. 148. Compared with Amŕita, 2. 300. See also Sudhámŕita.

Sudhámans, certain gods in the third and tenth Manwantaras, 3. 6, 25.

Sudháman, a Lokapála, son of Virajas or Viraja, &c., 1. 153; 2. 261, 262. See Sudhanwan, the Lokapála.

Sudháman, ruler over the realm of Sudháman, and son of Ghŕitapŕishtha, king of Krauncha-dwípa, 2. 198.

Sudháman, two Ŕishis so called, in the fifth and sixth Manwantaras, 3. 10-12.

Sudháman, a division of Krauncha-dwípa, 2. 198.

Sudháman, a mountain in India, 2. 142.

Sudhámŕita, what, 2. 300—302; 3. 56.

Sudhanu (?), variant of Sujantu, 4. 14.

Sudhanus, son of Kuru, son of Samvaraṇa, 4. 148.

Sudhanwan, a Lokapála, son of Vairája, 2. 86, 262, 263. See Sudháman, the Lokapála.

Sudhanwan, son of Sambhúta, 3. 284.

Sudhanwan, son of Abínagu, 3. 321.

Sudhanwan, lord of Sánkáśyá, 3. 333.

Sudhanwan, son of S'áśwata, 3. 334.

Sudhanwan, the same as Sata-dhanwan, son of Hŕidika, 4. 83.

Sudhanwan, son of Supárśwa, 4. 143.

Sudhanwan, son of Satyadhŕita, 4. 150.

Sudhanwan (?), variant of Sambhúti, son of Duŝsaha, 3. 283.

Sudhanwan (??), variant of Sudyumna, son of Abhayada, 4. 128.

Sudhanwan, variant of Sudhanus, 4. 148.

Sudhanwan (??), variant of Subala, son of Sumati, 4. 176.

Sudhárá (??), variant of Sutárá, 4. 95.

Sudharmá, the same as Sudharman, Ugrasena's palace or hall, 5. 46.

Sudharmans, certain gods in the ninth and thirteenth Manwantaras, 3. 24, 28.

Sudharman, a king, son of Dharmasávarṇika, the eleventh Manu, 3. 27.

Sudharman, one of the Viśwe devas, 3. 192.

Sudharman, son of Supárśwa, 4. 143.

Sudharman, Ugrasena's palace or hall, 5. 46, 155.

Sudharman (??), variant of Suśarman, 4. 193.

Sudharmátman (??), variant of Saryadharman, 3. 27.

Sudhásúka, son of Chitraka, 4. 96.

Sudhávats, a class of Pitŕis, 3. 339.

Sudhís, a class of gods in the fourth Manwantara, 3. 7.

Sudhŕit, in the Bhágavata-puráṇa, alternative of Sudhŕiti, son of Mahávírya, 3. 331.

N

Sudhŕiti, son of Rájyavardhana, 3.
245.

Sudhŕiti, son of Mahávírya, son of
Bŕihaduktha, 3. 331.

Sudhŕiti (?), variant of Dhŕiti, son
of Babhru, 4. 67.

Súdras, a people, 2. 133, 183–
185; 4. 222. See Sudraci and
Súdrakas.

Súdras, 'the servile caste.' Sprung
from the feet of Brahmá, 1. 89,
90. Their duties, 3. 87. Names
fitting for them, 3. 99, 100.
And see the article last preceding.

Súdrá, daughter of Raudráśwa,
and wife of Prabhákara, the
Ŕishi, 4. 129.

Sudraci, the, of Pliny, Súdras, 2.
185.

Súdra-dharma-tattwa, the, a law-
book, on the duties of Súdras,
referred to, or cited, 3. 89.

Súdrakas = Súdras, the people so
called, 2. 184.

Súdraka, a king named in the
Harshacharita, 3. 318.

Súdraka, a king (another?), named
in the Skanda-puráña, 4. 195.

Súdrakamalákara = Súdra-dharma-tattwa, 3. 89.

Sudyota (?), variant of Pradyotana, son of Sunika, minister of
Ripunjaya, 4. 178.

Sudyu (?), variant of Sudyumna,
son of Abhayada, 4. 128.

Sudyumna, or Ilá, offspring of
Vaivaswata, the Manu, P. 101,
107; 3. 234–237, 239.

Sudyumna, son of Chákshusha,
the Manu, 1. 177; 3. 13.

Sudyumna, son of Abhayada, 4. 127.

Sudyumna (?), variant of Satadyumna, son of Bhánumat, 3. 333.

Sugandha, in place of Gandhamádana, the mountain so called, 2.
111.

Sugandhá, an Apsaras, 2. 81–83.

Sugandhí, mistress of Vasudeva,
son of Súra, 4. 110.

Sugavi, variant of Susandhí, son
of Praśruta, 3. 325.

Sughora, husband of Upadánaví,
by one account, 4. 132.

Sugríva, a horse of Ќŕishña, 4. 83.

Sugríví, daughter of Kaśyapa and
Támrá, and mother of horses,
camels, and asses, 2. 73.

Suhmas, a people, 2. 165; 4. 122.

Suhma, son of Bali, son of Sutapas, 4. 122.

Suhma, a country said to lie to
the east of Bengal, 2. 165, 177;
4. 123.

Suhotra, variously genealogized,
4. 138–140.

Suhotra, son of Kánchana, 4. 14,
138, 139.

Suhotra, son of Sudhanus, 4. 148.

Suhotra, son of Sahadeva, son of
Dasra, 4. 159.

Suhotra (?), variant of Sruta, son
of Bhagíratha, 3. 303.

Suhotra (?), variant of Sujantu, 4.
14.

Suhotra, variant of Sunahotra, 4.
30, 31, 138, 139. Peculiarly
genealogized, 4. 136.

Suhotŕi, son of Vitatha or Bharadwája, 4. 136.

Suhú (?), variant of Subhúmi, son
of Ugrasena, 4. 99.

Sujahnu (??), variant of Sujantu, 4. 14.

Sujantu, son of Jahnu, son of Suhotra, 4. 14.

Sujátas, a tribe, 4. 59.

Sujáta, son of Bharata, son of Tálajangha, 4. 57.

Snjyeshťha, variously genealogized, 4. 191.

S'uka, son of Vyása, P. 40, 41, 46, 49, 53, &c.; 4. 142, 230.

S'uka (??), variant of As'okavardhana, &c., 4. 188.

Sukálas, sons of Vasishťha, Pitris of the Bráhmans, dwelling in the region called Mánasa, 3. 159, 163, 165.

Sukálins, the same as Sukálas, 3. 163, 165, 339.

Sukandakas, a people, 2. 173.

Sukanyá, daughter of S'aryáti, son of the Manu Vaivaswata, and wife of Chyavana, the Ŕishi, 3. 248, 342, 343.

S'úkara, Súkara (??), a hell, 2. 214, 216. See the next.

Súkaramukha (??), a hell, 2. 215. See the last.

Sukarmans, certain gods in the twelfth and thirteenth Manwantaras, 3. 27, 28.

Sukarman, son of Sumantu, &c., disciple of Jaimini, and teacher of the Sáma-veda, 3. 58, 60, 61.

Sukarman, son of S'waphalka, 4. 96.

Sukes'í, an Apsaras, 2. 82.

Suketana (??), variant of Suketu, 4. 37.

Suketu, son of Nandivardhana, son of Udávasu, 3. 331.

Suketu, variously genealogized, 4. 37.

Suketu (??), variant of Bhavanmanyu, 4. 136.

Sukha, 'enjoyment,' son of Dharma, the Prajápati, 1. 110, 111.

Sukhá, Varuńa's city, 2. 240. See Mukhyá, &c., named in the same page.

Sukhábala, son of Nŕichakshus, 4. 164, 165.

Sukhada, a division of Plaksha-dwípa, and ruled over by Sukhodaya, 2. 191.

Sukhínala (??), variant of Sukhábala, 4. 165.

Sukhinandi (??), variant of Susbinandi, 4. 211.

Sukhodaya, ruler over the realm of Sukhada, and son of Medhátithi, sovereign of Plaksha-dwípa, 2. 191.

S'uki, daughter of Kas'yapa, wife of Garuďa, and mother of parrots, owls, and crows, 2. 73.

S'ukla, son of Havirdhána, 1. 193.

S'ukla, a mountain in Krauncha-dwípa, 2. 198.

S'ukla, the same as S'weta, a mountain in India, 2. 111.

S'uklá, a river in S'álmala-dwípa, 2. 194.

S'uklá, a river in Krauncha-dwípa, 2. 198.

S'ukra, son of Bhava, 1. 117. Said to have sprung from Bhŕigu, 2. 259. Preceptor of the Daityas, 3. 19. Identified with the planet Venus, &c., 1. 117, &c.; 4. 2, 47. His car and horses, 2. 304. And see Us'anas.

S'ukra, son of Vasisht'ha, the Prajápati, 1. 155.

S'ukra, son of Havirdhána, 1. 192.

S'ukra, a R'ishi in the fourteenth
Manwantara, 3. 28.

S'ukra, the same as Jyaisht'ha, or
else Ashád'ha, a month, 2. 261,
286.

S'ukrá (??), variant of S'uklá, a river
in S'álmala-dwípa, 2. 194.

Sukr'íta, a Prajápati in the second
Manwantara, son of Vasisht'ha,
3. 5.

Sukr'íta, a river in Plaksha-dwípa,
2. 191.

Sukr'íti, a R'ishi in the tenth Manwantara, 3. 26.

Sukr'íti, son of Pr'ithu, son of Pára,
4. 141.

Sukr'íti (??), variant of Kr'ítwí, 4.
142.

Sukshattra, son of Niramitra, son
of Ayutáyus, 4. 174.

Sukshetra, son of Brahmasávarn'a,
3. 26.

Sukshetra (??), variant of Sukshattra, 4. 174.

S'uktá (??), variant of S'uklá, a
river in S'álmala-dwípa, 2. 194.

S'ukti, the same as S'uktimat, 2. 113.

S'uktimat, a mountain-chain in
India, the east and north portions of the Vindhya range, 2.
127, 128, 131, 132, 140, 141,
153-155, 340 ; 4. 64.

S'uktimatí, a river in India, 2.
132, 153.

S'uktimatí, a city near the R'ik-
shavat mountain, 4. 64.

Sukulya (??), variant of Sumálya,
4. 185.

Sukumára, ruler over the realm of
Sukumára, and son of Bhavya,
king of S'áka-dwípa, 2. 198.

Sukumára, variously genealogized,
4. 37, 38.

Sukumára, son of S'wetakarn'a, 4.
163.

Sukumára, a division of S'áka-
dwípa, 2. 198.

Sukumáraka, son of Jámbavat, 4.
76, &c.

Sukumárí, a river in S'áka-dwípa,
2. 199.

Sukut'yas, a people, 2. 156.

S'úlapán'i, an epithet of S'iva, 5.
119. King of the Bhútas, 2.
86.

S'úlapán'i, an author, cited, or referred to, 3. 89, 90, 102.

S'úlaprota, a hell, 2. 215.

Sulochaná, an Apsaras, 2. 82.

Sumálin, a Rákshasa, 1. 188
(where correct the spelling).

Sumallikas, a people, 2. 175.

Sumálya, son of Nanda, son of
Mahánandin, 4. 185.

Sumályaka, the same as Mályavat,
2. 111.

Sumaná, wife of Dama, son of
Narishyanta, 3. 245.

Sumanases (plural of Sumanas), a
class of gods in the twelfth Manwantara, 3. 27.

Sumanas, son of Úru, 1. 177. Also
called son of Ulmuka, 1. 178.

Sumanas, son of Haryaswa, 3. 284.

Sumanas, a mountain-range in
Plaksha-dwípa, 2. 191.

Sumanas (??), variant of Sudhanwan, son of Satyadhr'íta, 4. 150.

Sumangá, a river in India, 2. 154.

Sumahta (??), variant of Sushyanta, 4. 132.

Sumautra (??), variant of Suvarńa,
son of Antariksha, 4. 169.

Sumantu (who?), rehearser of the
Bhavishya-puráńa, P. 63.

Sumantu, disciple of Vyása, and
teacher of the Atharva-veda, 3.
42, 61, 62.

Sumantu, son and disciple of Jaimini, and teacher of the Sáma-
veda, 3. 58.

Sumantu (??), variant of Sujantu,
4. 14.

Sumati, the fifth Tírthakara; or
Jaina saint, son of Bharata, son
of Rishabha, 2. 105-107.

Sumati, descended from Atri; disciple of Romaharshańa, and
teacher of the Puráńas, 3. 64,
65.

Sumati, variously genealogized, 3.
247, 248.

Sumati, son of Nŕiga or Nábhága,
3. 335.

Sumati, in the Bhágavata-puráńa,
instead of Tamsu, 4. 129, 130.

Sumati, variously genealogized, 4.
143.

Sumati, son of Dŕiďhasena, 4. 176.

Sumati, daughter of Kratu, and
wife of Yajnaváma, 1. 155.

Sumati, daughter of Kaśyapa, son
of Maríchi, and wife of Sagara,
3. 297, 298.

Sumátya (??), variant of Sumálya,
4. 185.

Sumbha, a demon slain by Yoganidrá, 4. 261.

Sumbha (??), variant of Suhma,
son of Bali, 4. 122.

Sumedhas, a class of Pitris, sons
of some Kardama, 3. 164.

Sumedhases (plural of Sumedhas),
a class of gods in the fifth Manwantara, 3. 9.

Sumedhas, a Rishi in the sixth
Manwantara, 3. 12.

Sumeru, the same as Meru, the
fabulous mountain, 1. 129; 5.
387.

Sumitra, son of Vŕishńi, son of
Satwata, 4. 73, 74.

Sumitra, father of a Chitraka, according to the Linga-puráńa, 4.
94.

Sumitra, instead of Chitraka, in
the Bhágavata-puráńa, 4. 96.

Sumitra, son of Suvarńa, son of
Antariksha, 4. 169.

Sumitra, son of Suratha, son of
Kuńďaka, 4. 172. He is the
last of the race of Ikshwáku.

Sumitra, son of Agnimitra, son of
Pushpamitra, 4. 172, 191.

Sumitra, son of Krishńa and Jámbavatí, 5. 79.

Sumitra (??), variant of Sukshattra,
4. 174.

Sumukhí, an Apsaras, 2. 81-83.

Sumúrtyas (??), variant of Mauryas, 4. 190.

Sun, the. Offspring of Kaśyapa
and Aditi, 2. 27, 259; 3. 117,
230, 231, 296, 343. Called
son of Brahmá, 3. 343. His
wife and progeny, 3. 20; 4.
102, 103, 126. An object of
worship in the Veda, P. 3. An
object of worship in the Puráńas, P. 27; 3. 56, 116, 117;
5. 261, 263, &c. Especially

worshipped by the Magas, 5.
381–385. Originator of the
Solarian dynasty, 3. 230, &c.
His car and seven horses, the latter being the metres of the Veda,
or Gáyatrí, Bṛihatí, Ushṇih,
Jagatí, Trishṭubh, Anushṭubh,
Pankti, 2. 239. His city, on
Mount Meru, 2. 118, 124.
Called lord of cattle, 4. 249.
He presides over the eyes, 1.
38. His diurnal course, 2. 242.
His northern declination, and
his southern, 2. 245, 246. The
cause of rain, 2. 279; 4. 249.
His attendants in the several
months of the year, 2. 284, &c.
Mystical account of him, 2. 295,
&c. His functions, 2. 297. His
seven principal rays, 2. 297,
298. At the end of the world,
his rays dilate into seven suns,
called Ároga, Bhrája, Paṭara,
Patanga, Swarṇara, Jyotishímat,
and Vibhása, according to the
Taittiríya - áraṇyaka, but elsewhere named somewhat differently, 5. 191. He has his teeth
knocked down his throat by
Vírabhadra, 1. 131; 4. 339.
He is harassed by the Mandehas, certain Rákshasas, 2. 249,
250, 252. He is placed on a
lathe, by Viśwakarman, and an
eighth part of his effulgence
is ground off, 3. 21, 22. In the
form of a horse, he communicates the White Yajur-veda to
Yájnavalkya, 3. 57. He be-
friends Sattrájita, and bestows
the Syamantaka jewel on him,

4. 74, 75. See also Áditya,
Ádityas, Aświns, Bháskara, Kaś-
yapa, Násatyas, Savitṛí, Ravi,
Súrya, Vivaswat.
Sunábha (?), variant of Sunáman,
4. 98.
Sunaha (?), variant of Sujantu, 4.
14.
Sunahotra, son of Kshattravṛid-
dha, 4. 30, 31. See Suhotra.
Sunahśepha, variously genealo-
gized, 3. 289; 4. 25, &c.
Sunaka, disciple of Pathya, and
teacher of the Atharva-veda, 3.
62.
Sunaka, son of Gṛitsamada, 4. 31,
32, 40.
Sunaka (another?), 5. 218.
Sunaka (?), variant of Sunaya, son
of Ṛita, 3. 335.
Sunaka (?), variant of Sunika, 4.
176, 178.
Sunakshatra, son of Marudeva, 4.
168.
Sunakshatra (?), variant of Su-
kshattra, 4. 174.
Sunáman, son of Ugrasena, son of
Áhuka, 4. 98; 5. 41.
Sunámní, wife of Vasudeva, son
of Súra, 4. 110.
Sunandá, daughter of Vidúratha,
and wife of Vatsaprí, 3. 242.
Sunandá, characterized as Sárva-
seni, wife of Bharata, son of
Dushyanta, 4. 136.
Sunandana (?), variant of Sun-
daraśátakarṇin, 4. 197.
Sunasá, a river, 2. 151.
Sunayas, a people, 2. 181.
Sunaya, son of Ṛita, son of Vijaya,
3. 335.

Suraya, son of Pariplava, 4. 165.

Sunda, son of Nisunda, 2. 69; 4. 250.

Sundara (??), variant of Kukura, 4. 97.

Sundarasâtakarñin, Sundaraswâtikarña, son of Pravilasena, &c., 4. 197, 201, 202.

Sundarí, daughter of Vaiswânara, 2. 71.

Sundarí (??), variant of Sutârá, 4. 95.

Sunetra (?), variant of Dharma, son of Suvrata, 4. 175.

Sonetra (??), variant of Drídhasena, 4. 175.

Sanetra (??), variant of Susrama, 4. 175.

Sunetra, variant of Suníta, 4. 176.

Sungas, a dynasty, 4. 190, 192, 203, 212, 232.

Sunika, minister of Ripunjaya, 4. 178.

Suníta, son of Subala, son of Sumati, 4. 176.

Sunítha, son of Samnati, son of Alarka, 4. 37.

Sunítha, son of Susheña, 4. 164.

Sunítha, daughter of Mrítyu, and wife of Anga, a descendant of Atri, 1. 177, 179.

Sunítha (??), variant of Suníta, 4. 176.

Suníti, wife of Uttánapáda, 1. 159, &c.

Súnrítá, wife of Uttánapáda, 1. 159, 175, 176.

Súnrítá, an Apsaras, 2. 82, 83.

Sunuta (??), variant of Sujantu, 4. 14.

Sunwat, son of Sumantu, and

teacher of the Sáma-veda, 3. 58, 60.

Súnyabandhu, son of Trinabindu, 3. 246.

Sunyáti (??), variant of Saryáti, son of Panchi (?), 4. 46.

Supáras (??), variant of Táras, a class of gods so called, 3. 27.

Suparña, the same as Garuda, son of Kasyapa, 1. 191; 2. 73, 74.

Suparñá, the same as Vinatá, 2. 28, 73.

Suparña, a mountain in Plakshadwípa, 2. 193.

Suparña, variant of Suvarña, son of Antariksha, 4. 169.

Suparñá, variant of Puñyá, the river, 2. 154.

Supáréwa, son of Suvarchas, 3. 334.

Supáréwa, son of Srutáyus, son of Arishtanemi, 3. 334.

Supáréwa, variously genealogized, 4. 143.

Supáréwa, a mountain serving as buttress to Meru, on the north, 2. 111, 115, 116.

Supáréwa (??), variant of Suyasas, 4. 188.

Supáréwaka, the same as Supáréwa, son of Srutáyus, 3. 334.

Supáréwaka, son of Chitraka, 4. 96.

Suparvas, a class of gods in the twelfth Manwantara, according to the Váyu-puráña (??), 3. 27. (Táras may be the correct name.)

Suparvan, one of the Viswe devas, 3. 192.

Suparvan (??), variant of Suvarña, son of Antariksha, 4. 169.

Suprabha, ruler over the realm of Suprabha, and son of Vapushmat, king of S'álmala-dwípa, 2. 194.

Suprabhá, wife of Kṛiśáśwa, 2. 337.

Suprabha, a division of S'álmala-dwípa, 2. 194.

Suprabhá, variant of Prabhá, daughter of Swarbhánu, 2. 70. (Probably Suprabhá is the preferable reading.)

Suprabhátá, a river in Plaksha-dwípa, 2. 193.

Supraníta (?), variant of Supratíka, 4. 168.

Supratíka, variously genealogized, 4. 168.

Supratíka, a Báhlika king, 4. 214.

Supratípa, son of Pratíkáśwa (?), 4. 168.

Supratishṭhitá, an Apsaras, 2. 82.

Suprayogá, a river in India, 2. 148.

Supreme condition of Vishṇu, 2. 90.

Supriyá, an Apsaras, 2. 81.

Suras, a general term for the gods, 4. 147, 190; 5. 109, 247.

S'úras, a people, 2. 133, 134, 185; 4. 222, 224.

S'úras, a tribe, 4. 61.

S'úra, son of Arjuna, son of Kṛitavírya, 4. 57.

S'úra, son of Bhajamána, son of Satwata, 4. 72.

S'úra, son of Vidúratha, son of Bhajamána, 4. 99, 100.

S'úrá, son of Devamídhusha, son of Hṛidika, 4. 100 (where once correct the spelling); 5. 391.

S'úra, son of Vasudeva, son of S'úra, 4. 109.

S'úra, a king (who?), 4. 126.

S'úra, son of Ailina or Ílina, 4. 132.

S'úra, son of Kṛishṇa and Bhadrá, 5. 82.

Surá, the goddess of wine, 1. 147. See Madirá and Váruṇí.

Surá, a zoniform sea of wine, surrounding S'álmala-dwípa, and surrounded by Kuśa-dwípa, 2. 195.

Surabhi, daughter of Daksha, wife of Kaśyapa, and parent of cows and buffaloes, 2. 25, 26, 75.

Surabhi, a fabulous cow, yielding every desire, produced when the ocean was churned, 1. 144, 147. Kártavírya carries her off, 4. 21. Comes from Goloka, in company with Indra, and visits Kṛishṇa, 4. 319.

S'úrabhú (?), variant of Sutanu, daughter of Ugrásena, son of Áhuka, 4. 99.

Suradhí (?), variant of Ruchiradhí, 4. 137.

S'úraka (?), variant of S'údraka, 4. 195.

Suraksha, perhaps the name, in the Váyu-puráṇa, of the Vyása in the fourteenth Dwápara age, 3. 37.

Surakshaya (?), variant of Gurukshepa, 4. 167.

Suramá (?), variant of Surasá, the Apsaras, 2. 81.

Suramídha (?), variant of Purumídha, 4. 140.

Suraṇá, a river in India, 2. 151.

Surangá (?), variant of Maningá (?), 2. 154.

Surápas (११), variant of Táras, a class of gods so called, 3. 27.

Suráraṇi, an epithet of Aditi, daughter of Daksha, 5. 96.

Surasá, daughter of Daksha, wife of Kaśyapa, and mother of a thousand many-headed serpents or dragons, 2. 26, 73, 74.

Surasá, an Apsaras, 2. 81-83.

Surasá, daughter of Raudráśwa, and wife of Prabhákara, the Rishi, 4. 129.

Surasá, a river in India, 2. 130, 132.

S'úrasenas, a people, inhabiting Mathurá, 2. 156, 173, 341. See Suraseni.

S'úrasenas, a dynasty, 4. 184.

S'úrasenas, a tribe, 4. 58.

S'úrasena, S'úrasena (११), son of Satrughna, 3. 319.

S'úrasena, son of Arjuna, son of Kártavírya, 4. 57.

S'úrasena, the upper part of the Doab, 2. 143.

Suraseni, the, of Arrian, identified with the people called S'úrasenas, 2. 156.

Surásht́ras, a people, 2. 169.

Surásht́ra, a country, now popularly called Surat, 4. 205.

Suratha, a king, subsequently born as the Manu Sávarṇi, 3. 22.

Suratha, variously genealogized, 4. 152, 153.

Suratha, son of Nŕibandhu, 4. 164.

Suratha, son of Kuńd́aka, 4. 171.

Suratha (११), variant of Dhruva, son of Rantinára, 4. 130.

Suratha (११), variant of Sunaya, son of Pariplava, 4. 165.

Surathá (११), variant of Surasá, an Apsaras, 2. 81.

Surendra, an epithet of Indra, 4. 314.

Sureśwara, a Rudra, 2. 25.

Surgery, branches of, specified and defined, 4. 33.

Súrmyá, wife of Anubráda, 2. 69.

Súrṇitá (११), an Apsaras, 2. 82.

Surochana, ruler over the realm of Surochana, and son of Yajnabáhu, king of S'álmala-dwípa, 2. 195.

Surochana, a division of S'álmala-dwípa, 2. 195.

Surochis, son of Vasisht́ha, the Prajápati, 1. 155.

Surottamá, an Apsaras, 2. 82.

S'úrpáraka, a certain maritime district, of uncertain locality, 4. 24.

Suruchi, a Gandharva, 2. 285, &c.

Suruchi, wife of Uttánapáda, 1. 159, &c.; 3. 5.

Suruńd́as (११), variant of Guruńd́as, 4. 206.

Surúpas, a class of gods in the fourth Manwantara, 3. 7.

Surúpas (११), variant of Táras, a class of gods so called, 3. 27.

Surúpá, an Apsaras, 2. 81, 82.

Súrya, the Sun, P. 27; 2. 124; 3. 56; 4. 75, 126, 249, 339; 5. 261, 263, &c. &c., 381, 382. See Sun.

Súryaka (११), variant of Janaka, son of Viśákharúpa, 4. 179.

Súryakánta, a certain precious stone, 4. 85.

Súryápíd́a, son of Parikshit, 4. 163.

Súrya-siddhánta, the, an astronomical work, referred to, 1. 51; 2. 207; 3. 163.

Súryavarchas, a Gandharva, 2. 285, &c.

Susambhávya, son of Raivatá, Manu of the fifth Manwantara, 3. 11.

Susamedhases (?), variant of Sumadhases, 3. 9.

Susanágo, Páli name of a king, 4. 185. (He is confounded with the Síšunága or Síšunáka of the Puráńas.)

Susandhi, son of Mándhátri, 3. 297.

Susandhi, son of Prasuśruta, 3. 325.

Sušánti, Indra of the third Manwantara, 3. 5.

Sušánti, son of Šánti, son of Níla, 4. 144.

Sušarmans (??), variant of Sutrámans, 3. 28.

Sušarman, son of Náráyaṇa, son of Bhúmimitra, 4. 193, 194.

Sushena, a Yaksha, 2. 285, &c.

Sushena, son of Jamadagni, 4. 20.

Sushena, son of Vasudeva, son of Súra, 4. 110.

Sushena, variously genealogized, 4. 163, 164.

Sushena, son of Krishńa and Rukmiṇí, 5. 78.

Sushinandi, son of Dharma, son of Rámachandra, 4. 211.

Sushirnandi (??), variant of Sushinandi, 4. 211.

Sushmins, a caste in Kuśa-dwípa, 2. 195.

Sushomá, the same as Sindhu, the river Indus, 2. 121.

Sushumńá, a certain ray of the sun, 2. 297, 298; 3. 55; 5. 191.

Sushyanta, variously genealogized, 4. 132.

Sušílá, daughter of a Madra king, and wife of Krishńa, 5. 78, 81. (If the Puráńas harmonize, of the various Mádrís it is not Sušílá, but Mitravindá, that is referred to in 5. 107.)

Susíma, son of Bindusára, 4. 186.

Susráma, son of Dharma, son of Suvrata, 4. 175.

Susravas, a Prajápati, according to the Váyu-puráńa, 1. 102.

Susruta, a writer on medicine, his probable age, &c., P. 61; 4. 33.

Susruta, variously genealogized, 3. 334.

Susruta (??), variant of Susráma, 4. 175.

Sustuta, son of Supáréwa, son of Suvarchas, 3. 334.

Suswadhas (??), a class of Pitris, sons of Kardama, 3. 159, 164.

Suswadhá, the same as Swadhá, 'a benediction,' 3. 185.

Sútas, a caste, comprising genealogists, bards, and charioteers, 4. 126.

Súta, the original herald, or bard, his origin, 1. 184, &c. See also P. 18, 30, and Sútas.

Súta, the same as Romnharshaṇa, P. 18, 33, 37, 38, 40, 52, 58, 65, 77, 78, 81; 3. 42, 64, 65, 72, 332. Called son of Lomaharshaṇa, P. 45.

Suta (??), one of the Viśwe devas, 3. 192.

Sútaka, what, in legal phraseology, 3. 130.

Sutala, a particular Pátála, or underworld, 2. 209.

Sntánu, son of Ugrasena, son of Áhuka, 4. 99.

Sutanu, daughter of Ugrasena, son of Áhuka, 4. 99.

Sutanu, mistress of Vasudeva, son of Súra, 4. 110.

Sutapas, a class of gods in the eighth Manwantara, according to the Bhágavata-puráńa, 3. 24.

Sutapas (identifiable with Sutapas, a Rishi, named below?), son of Vasishťha, 1. 155.

Sutapas, a king, son of Támasa, Manu of the fourth Manwantara, 3. 8.

Sutapas, a Rishi, or Rishis, so called, in the twelfth and thirteenth Manwantaras, 3. 27, 28.

Sutapas, son of Hema, son of Usbadratha, 4. 122.

Sutapas (?), variant of Tanayas, 2. 181.

Sutapas (?), variant of Sunaya, son of Pariplava, 4. 165.

Sutapas (?), variant of Suvarńa, son of Antariksha, 4. 169.

Sutárá, daughter of Swaphalka, 4. 95.

Súta-saṁhitá, a part of the Skanda-puráńa, P. 73.

Sutejas (?), variant of Sudeva, son of Chunchu, 3. 289.

Sútiká, what, in legal phraseology, 3. 196.

Sutírtha (?), variant of Sunítha, son of Sushena, 4. 164.

Sutoya, son of Suvarchas, 3. 334.

Sutrámana, a class of gods in the thirteenth Manwantara, 3. 28.

Sutudrí, the same as Satadrú, 2. 121.

Suvámá, a river, identified, by Colonel Wilford, with what is now known as the Rámgangá, 2. 151.

Suvarńá, son of Vasudeva, son of Súra, 4. 111 (where correct the spelling), 344.

Suvapus, variant of Vapus, an Apsaras, 2. 81.

Suvarchalá, wife of Rudra, one of the Rudras, 1. 117.

Suvarchas, son of Swágata, 3. 334.

Suvarman, son of Chitraka, 4. 96.

Suvarman, son of Dṛiḍhanemi, 4. 143.

Suvarńa, son of Antariksha, son of Kimnara, 4. 169.

Suvarńa, a weight of gold, equivalent to 80 Raktis, or about 175 grains Troy, 2. 216; 5. 84.

Suvarńaroman, son of Mahároman, 3. 332.

Suvárthácbí (?), a river in India, 2. 149.

Suvaśa, son of Sudaṁshťra, 4. 100.

Suvásiní, the term defined, 3. 124.

Suvastrí, variant of Suvástu, 2. 149.

Suvástu, a river in India, 2. 149, 340.

Suvasu, an Apsaras, 2. 83.

Suvátá, an Apsaras, 2. 83.

Suvela, the same as Trikúťa, the mountain, 2. 141.

Suvibhu, son of Vibhu, son of Satyaketu, 4. 37, 38.

Suvidarbhas, a people, their origin, 4. 121.

Suvíra, son of Síbi, son of Uśínara, 4. 121.

Suvíra, son of Kshemya, son of Ugráyudha, 4. 144.

Suvíra (?), variant of Pravíra, 4. 127.

Suvrata, son of Kritanjaya, son of Dharmin, 4. 169.

Suvrata, son of Kshemya, son of Suchí, 4. 175.

Suvrata, son of Nribhrita, 4. 175.

Suvratá, an Apsaras, 2. 83.

Suvratá, daughter of Daksha, the Prajápati, 3. 24.

Suvrata, variant of Darva, son of Uśínara, 4. 121.

Suvrata, variant of Suśrama, 4. 175.

Suvrittá, an Apsaras, 2. 81 (where correct the spelling), 82, 337.

Suyajna, variant of Tamas, son of Prithuśravas, 4. 63.

Suyaśá, an Apsaras, 2. 81.

Suyaśas, son of Aśokavardhana, 4. 188.

Suyodhana, variant of Anenas, son of Kakutstha or Puranjaya, 3. 263.

Swabháva, what, in philosophy, 1. 68.

S'wabhojana, a certain hell, 2. 215, 220.

Swabhúmi (?), variant of Subhúmi, son of Ugrasena, 4. 99.

Swadhá, 'oblation.' Daughter of Daksha and Prasúti, 1. 109, 119. Daughter of Agni, wife of Kavi, and mother of the Somapas, 3. 162. Wife of the

Pitris, particularly of the Agnishwáttas and Barhishads, 1. 109, 119, 156, 157. A name of Vishnu, 5. 253. Identified with a mystical ejaculation, 1. 148; 3. 123, 186; 4. 267; 5. 179. See also 1. 110, 188, and Suswadhá.

Swadhá, wife of Angiras, according to the Bhágavata-puráṇa, 2. 29.

Swadhámans, variant of Sudhámans, 3. 6.

Swadháman (?), variant of Sudháman, the Rishi so called, 3. 10.

Swadhís (?), variant of Sudhís, 3. 7.

Swádhyáya, what, 3. 77; 5. 137, 216, 229.

Swágata, variously genealogized, 3. 334.

Swáhá, 'offering.' Daughter of Daksha and Prasúti, and wife of Vahni, 1. 109. Wife of Abhimánin, one of the Agnis, 1. 155, 156. A name of Vishnu, 5. 253. Identified with a mystical ejaculation, 1. 148; 3. 123, 181, 338. See also 1. 110, 119; 4. 267; 5. 179.

Swáhá, wife of Paśupati, the Rudra, 1. 117.

Swáha (?), variant of Swáhi, 4. 61.

Swáhi, son of Vrijinívat, 4. 61.

Swairatha, ruler over the realm of Swairatha, and son of Jyotishmat, king of Kuśa-dwípa, 2. 195.

Swairatha, a division of Kuśa-dwípa, 2. 195.

Swaketu, variant of Suketu, son of Nandivardhana, 3. 331.

Swakshas (??), variant of Suhmas, 2. 165.

Swáloya (??), variant of Kháliya, 3. 46.

Swamati (?), variant of Sumati, 3. 247.

S'waphalka, variously genealogized, 4. 87, &c., 93, 94, 335 (where the accent is broken off).

S'wáphalki, patronym of Akrúra, 4. 88.

Swa-prakáśa, a commentary on the Vishńu-puráńa, P. 115.

Swaráj, the same as Brahmá, 1. 170, 172.

Swaráj, a certain ray of the sun, 2. 297, 298.

Swaráńdas (??), variant of Muruńdas, 4. 206.

Swarapuranjaya, variant of Parapuranjaya, son of S'esha, 4. 212.

Swarasa, a mountain in S'álmala-dwípa, 2. 195.

Swaráshtras (??), a people, 2. 169. See Suráshtras.

Swarbhánu, son of Kaśyapa, son of Marichi, 2. 70.

Swarbhánu, the same as Ráhu, son of Viprachitti, 2. 71, 259, 304; 4. 30, 343.

Swarbhánu, son of Kŕishńa and Satyabhámá, 5. 81.

Swarga, son of Bhíma, the Rudra, 1. 117.

Swarga, the same as Indra-loka, 1. 98; 3. 143, 302; 5. 93, 144. On Mount Meru, 2. 125. And see Swar-loka.

Swarga-khańda, a part of the Padma-puráńa, P. 30, 31.

Swar-loka, a supernal region, some-times identified with Meru, 2. 113, 225, 231; 5. 192. See Swarga.

Swarńabháj, variant of Swarńara, 5. 191.

Swarńuprastha, an island, perhaps fabulous, 2. 129.

Swarńara, a certain sun, 5. 191.

Swarńarekhá, a river in India, 2. 154.

Swarńaroman, the same as Suvarńaroman, 3. 332.

Swarńaroman (??), variant of Swarńara, 5, 191.

Swarochis, son of Kála, the Gandharva, 3. 2.

Swárochisha, Manu of the second Manwantara, variously genealogized, 3, 1, 2, 11, 16, 17.

Swárochisha, a Manwantara, P. 76; 1. 153; 2. 26, 108; 3. 22.

Swarúpas (??), variant of Surúpas, 3. 7.

Swarúpa, what, in philosophy, 1. 68.

Swarvíthi, wife of Vatsara, son of Dhruva, 1. 178; 5. 388.

S'wása, 'asthma,' 5. 202.

Swasaṁbhávya (??), variant of Susaṁbhávya, 3. 11.

Swastika, a particular diagram used in mystical ceremonies, 2. 211.

Swastikásana, what, in the Yoga philosophy, 5. 230.

Swastyátreyas, certain Bráhman families, 4. 129.

Swastyayana, defined as a prayer to avert all evil, 4. 278.

Swaswadhas (??), variant of Sumedhas, certain Pitŕis, 3. 164.

Swáti, son of Úru, 1. 177, 179.

Swáti, son of Meghaswáti, 4. 200.

Swáti, Swáti (??), a certain asterism, 2. 264, 265, &c. ; 3. 167.

Swátikarña, son of Kuntalaswáti, 4. 200.

Swátin (??), variant of Swáhi, 4. 61.

Swátishe̥ña, son of Kuntalaśátakarñi, 4. 202.

Swavarchalá (??), variant of Suvarchalá, 1. 117.

Swayaṁbhoja, a Yadava chieftain, son of Pratikshattra, son of Samin, 4. 99.

Swayaṁbhú, an epithet of Brahmá, P. 63 (where correct the spelling); 1. 55 (where correct the spelling); 5. 386. The Vyása of the first Dwápara age, 3. 34. But see Swáyaṁbhuva, 3. 36.

Swayaṁbhú, an epithet of the first Manu, (?) 3. 96.

Swayaṁbhú, a synonym of Mahat, 1. 32 (where correct the spelling).

Swáyaṁbhuva, an epithet of the first Manu, P. 42, 95; 1. 104, 107, 109, &c., 159, 174; 3. 1, 2, 7 (in which three pages correct the spelling), 97, 107.

Swáyaṁbhuva, for Swayaṁbhú, Brahmá, as the first Vyása, in a passage from the Kúrma-puráña, 3. 36.

Swáyaṁbhuva, the name of the first Manwantara, P. 42, 56, 96; 1. 154; 2. 9, 11, 108; 3. 2, &c. &c.

Sweta, a serpent, son of Kaśyapa, son of Maríchi, 2. 74.

Sweta, ruler over the realm of Sweta, and son of Vapushmat, king of Sálmala-dwípa, 2. 193.

Sweta, a country in Jambu-dwípa, 2. 102.

Sweta, a division of Sálmala-dwípa, 2. 193.

Sweta, a mountain-range in India, 2. 102, 114, 115, 256. See Swetádri.

Sweta, the last of thirty-three Kalpas, that in which Siva was born with a white complexion, P. 35, 37.

Swetádri, a mountain-range, 4. 260. See Sweta, the mountain-range.

Sweta-dwípa, 'white island,' a certain continent, according to the Kúrma-puráña, 2. 200.

Swetajala, a lake in the grove called Vaibhrája, 2. 112.

Swetakarña, son of Satyakarña, 4. 163.

Swetaketu, son of Senajit, son of Viśwajit, 4. 141.

Swetalohita, a Kumára, in the twenty-ninth Kalpa, 1. 79.

Swetáśwatara - upanishad, the, quoted, 4. 253.

Swetaváhana, according to the Váyu-puráña, son of Súra, son of Viduratha, 4. 99.

Syádvádins, the Jainas so called, epithetically, 3. 209.

Syalantas (??), Kauśika Bráhmans, 4. 28.

Syáma, son of Súra, son of Devamídhusha, 4. 101, 113.

Syáma, a mountain-range in Śáka-dwípa, 2. 199.

Syámaka, the same as Syáma, son of Súra, 4. 101.

Syamantaka, a certain very valuable jewel. Áditya, the Sun, presents it to Sattrájita, 4. 75. It has power to yield gold, and to prevent the incursion of portents, wild beasts, fire, robbers, pestilence, famine, and dearth, 4. 76, 85. Jámbavat, king of the bears, purloins it, and takes it to his cave, 4. 76. It is presented, by Jámbavat, to Kŕishńa, after a conflict between them which lasts for twenty-one days; and Kŕishńa then restores it to Sattrájita, 4. 78, 79. Śatadhanwan slays Sattrájita in his sleep, and possesses himself of it, 4. 81. Sattrájita surrenders it to Akrúra, 4. 82. It remains in Akrúra's keeping, 4. 92. See also 4. 336; 5. 148.

Syámáyani, disciple of Vaiśampáyana, and promulgator of the Yajur-veda, 3. 52.

Syená (?), variant of Srońí, the river, 2. 155.

Syenajit (??), variant of Senajit, the Yaksha, 2. 289.

Syení, daughter of Kaśyapa, wife of Aruńa, and mother of hawks, 2. 73.

Syuvakas (??), variant of Páśivát'as, 2. 180.

Tachari. See Tochari.

Tadaikya, 'identification or unity,' 5. 227.

Tád'aká, a she-demon, slain by Ráma, 3. 315. (She was mother of Márícha, whom, also, Ráma slew.)

Taijasa, adjective of Tejas, 'fire,' &c., 1. 33.

Tairyagyonya, the name of a creation, that of animals, 1. 75.

Taitiri (??), variant of Taittiri, 4. 97.

Taittiri, son of Viloman, according to one MS. of the Vishńu-puráńa, 4. 97.

Taittiri (?), variant of Viloman, &c., 4. 97, 98.

Taittiríyas, of the Yajur-veda, 3. 54.

Taittiríya, a Śákhá, the same as Taittiríya-samhitá, 3. 54.

Taittiríya-árańyaka, the, referred to, 5. 191.

Taittiríya-bráhmańa, the, referred to, 3. 171.

Taittiríya-samhitá, the, referred to, or cited, 3. 113, 257, 341; 5. 386.

Taksha, king of Takshaśílá, son of Bharata, son of Daśaratha, 3. 319.

Takshaka, a serpent, son of Kaśyapa, son of Maríchi, P. 44; 1. 188, 191; 2. 38, 74, 285, &c. King of serpents, 2. 86. His abode, 2. 211.

Takshaka, son of Prasenajit, son of Viswaséhwan, 3. 325.

Takshaka, the same as Taksha, son of Bharata, 3. 319.

Takshaśílá, a city, capital of King Taksha, 3. 319.

Takwa, the same as Bábíka, 2. 167.

Talá, daughter of Randráśwa,

208 INDEX.

wife of Prabhákara, the Ríshi, 4. 129.

Tála, a certain hell, 2. 214, 216.

Tálajanghas, a tribe in Central India, 4. 58, 59, 61. They vanquish Báhuka, son of Vríka, 3. 289. They are all but exterminated by Sagara, 3. 291. See also 3. 292.

Tálajanghas (misprinted Tálanjanghas), one hundred sons of Tálajangha, son of Jayadhwaja, 4. 57; 5. 391.

Tálajangha, son of Vatsa, 4. 40; 5. 391. (The same as the next?)

Tálajangha, son of Jayadhwaja, 4. 57. (The same as the last?)

Talaka (??), variant of Pattalaka, 4. 197.

Tálaketu, an epithetical name of Balaráma, 3. 254.

Talátala, a Pátála, or underworld, 2. 209.

Talottama, ' a couch or bench with cushions,' 5. 33.

Táluki (??), variant of Vaitálaki, 3. 47.

Támaliptas (??), variant of Támraliptakas, 2. 177.

Tamas, son of Daksha, the Prajápati, 1. 103.

Tamas, son of Prithuśravas, son of Sasabindu, 4. 63.

Tamas, a certain hell, 2. 215.

Tamas, 'quality of darkness, ignorance, inertia,' &c., P. 20; 1. 4, 35, 69.

Tamas (??), variant of Bhava, son of Viloman, 4. 97.

Támasas (?), variant of Tomaras, 2. 187.

Támasa, Manu of the fourth Manwantara, son of Priyavrata, 2. 100; 3. 1, 7, 8, 10, 11, 337 (note on p. 11).

Tamasá, a river in India, now popularly called the Tonse, 2. 151.

Támasa, adjective of Tamas, the philosophical term, P. 20, 21, 59; 1. 34; 2. 232; 5. 198, 285, 310, &c.

Támasí, a river in India, 2. 152, 340.

Tambamitra, recipient of the Vishnu-puráña from Bháguri, 5. 250.

Tambhamitra (??), variant of Tambamitra, 5. 250.

Támisra, a certain hell, 2. 215; 3. 130.

Támisra, 'gloom, a kind of ignorance,' 1. 69.

Támrá, daughter of Daksha, and wife of Kaśyapa, son of Maríchi, 2. 26, 72.

Támrá, a river in India, 2. 151.

Támraliptas, a people, 4. 220. See Támraliptakas.

Támralipta, a country in Eastern India, 4. 220.

Támraliptakas, a people, 2. 177. See Támraliptas.

Támraliptí, a sea-port at the western mouth of the Ganges, 2. 177.

Támrapaksha, son of Krishña and Rohiní, 5. 107.

Támraparña, a division of Bháratavarsha, 2. 112, 129.

Támraparñí, a river in Tinnivelly, 2. 130, 132, 155.

Támrarasá, daughter of Raudrás-wa, and wife of Prabhákara, the Rishi, 4. 129.

Támratapta, son of Krishńa and Rohińí, 5. 79.

Támravarńa (?), variant of Támra-parńa, 2. 129.

Támravarńa (??), variant of Tám-rapakaha, 5. 107.

Támráyańa (?), promulgator of the White Yajur-veda, 3. 57.

Tamsu, variously genealogized, 4. 129-132.

Tamsurodha, variant of Tamsu, 4. 130-132.

Tamsurodya (??), variant of Tamsu, 4. 130.

Tamsurogha (??), variant of Tamsu, 4. 130.

Tanabálas, a people, 2. 180.

Tanapas (??), variant of Tanayas, 2. 181.

Tanayas, a people, 2. 180.

Tandri, 'sloth,' a form of Brahmá, 1. 82.

Tandrija, son of Kanavaka or Karundhaka, 4. 113.

Tandripála, son of Kanavaka or Karundhaka, 4. 113.

Tangańas, a people, 2. 181.

Tankańas, a people, 2. 181.

Tanmátra, 'rudiment or type of an element, devoid of qualities, and the same as the properties of an element,' 1. 37, 74; 5. 199.

Tantija (??), variant of Tandrija, 4. 113.

Tantipála (??), variant of Tandri-pála, 4. 113.

Tantras, certain mystical works so

called, P. 6, 21, 32, 59; 4. 261, 262; 5. 263, 316, 317, 326, 338.

Tantrija (??), variant of Tandrija, 4. 113.

Tantripála (??), variant of Tan-dripála, 4. 113.

Tántrika, adjective of Tantra, P. 21, 79, &c.; 5. 285, &c.

Tanwí, the same as Sudattá, (?) 5. 82.

Tapana, Tápana, a certain hell, 2. 215.

Tápaní, the same as Vetrávatí, a river, 2. 147.

Tápaníyas, of the White Yajur-veda, 3. 57.

Tapas, the same as Tapo-loka, 2. 227, 231.

Tapas, the same as Mágha, a month, Jan.—Feb., 2. 261.

Tapas, what, in philosophy, 2. 338; 3. 11, 20, 77, 95; 4. 294.

Tápasa, 'an ascetic,' 5. 183.

Tapaswin, a Rishi in the twelfth Manwantara, 3. 27. (See the next name.)

Tapaswin, son of Chákshusha, the Manu, 1. 177. (The same as the last ?)

Tapaswin, 'an ascetic,' 3. 307.

Tapasya, the same as Phálguna, a month, Feb.—March, 2. 261.

Tapatí, wife of Samvarańa, 4. 148.

Tapatí, the same as Tápí, the Taptee, 2. 144; 3. 21.

Tápí, the river popularly called Taptee, daughter of the Sun and Chháyá, 2. 130, 132, 144, 148; 3. 21; 4. 59.

Tápí, the same as Yamuná, 2. 148.

Tápiní, the same as Tápí, the Taptee, 2. 147.

Tapodhana, a Rishi in the twelfth Manwantara, 3. 27.

Tapodhṛiti, a Rishi in the twelfth Manwantara, 3. 27.

Tapodyuti, a Rishi in the twelfth Manwantara, 3. 27.

Tapo-loka, 'the world of the seven sages,' 'the sphere of penance,' inhabited by the incombustible gods called Vairájas, 1. 98; 2. 113, 227–229; 3. 159; 4. 266.

Tapomúla, son of Támasa, according to divers Puráñas, 3. 8.

Tapomúrti, a Rishi in the twelfth Manwantara, 3. 27.

Taporati, a Rishi in the twelfth Manwantara, 3. 27.

Taptabáluka, a certain hell, 2. 215.

Taptakumbha, a certain hell, 2. 214, 217.

Taptaloha, a certain hell, 2. 217.

Tapta-mudrá, ' stamping with a hot iron the name of Vishṇu on the skin,' P. 34 (where correct the spelling).

Taptasúrmi, a certain hell, 2. 215.

Táras, a class of gods in the twelfth Manwantara, 3. 27, 227.

Tárá, wife of Bṛihaspati, son of Angiras, 4. 2. She is carried off by Soma, whence a war, 4. 2, 3. Is mother of Budha, 4. 4.

Tárádhísa, variant of Tárápíḍa, 3. 321.

Táraka, son of Kaśyapa, son of Maríchi, 2. 70. (For mention of a Táraka, see also P. 82; 2. 119.)

Táraká, daughter of Sunda, 2. 69.

Táraká, an elongated form of Tárá, 4. 3.

Táraka, variant of Kálanábha, son of Hiraṇyáksha, 2. 70.

Tárakámaya, the term explained, 4. 3.

Tárakáyanas, Kauśíka Bráhmans, 4. 28.

Taraksha (?), Vyása of the fourteenth Dwápara age, by one account, 3. 37.

Tárápíḍa, son of Chandrávaloka, 3. 321 (where correct the spelling); 5. 391.

Tarka, 'logical reasoning,' 4. 310.

Tárksha, a name of Kaśyapa, son of Maríchi, 2. 21, 28, 66, 73.

Tárksha, (?), variant of Tárkshya, 2. 288, 292.

Tárkshya, a certain Yaksha, 2. 285, &c.

Taru, son of Chákshusha, the Manu, according to the Matsya-puráña, 1. 178.

Tatpurusha, a particular Kalpa, P. 72.

Tattwadaréa, a Rishi in the thirteenth Manwantara, according to the Bhágavata-puráña, 3. 28. See the next name.

Tattwadarśin, a Rishi in the thirteenth Manwantara, 3. 28. See the last name.

Tauṇḍ́ikeras (?), variant of Tuṇ́ḍikeras, 4. 59.

Tejas, 'fire,' 'heat,' 'light,' 'energy.' It is produced from the rudiment of form or colour, and produces the rudiment of taste, 1. 34, 36.

Tejeyu, son of Raudráśwa, 4. 127.

Tewar, the modern corruption of Tripurí, 5. 118.

Thanesar, the modern corruption of Sthánwíśwara, P. 76.

Thogari. See Tochari.

Tigma, son of Mrídu, son of Nrí-panjaya, 4. 165.

Tigmaketu, son of Vatsara, son of Dhruva, 1. 178.

Tigmátman, variant of Tigma, 4. 165.

Tilabháras, a people, 2. 173.

Tilaka (??), variant of Pálaka, son of Pradyotana, 4. 178.

Tilakanijas (??), variant of Nalaká-nanas, 2. 178.

Tilottamá, an Apsaras, 2. 75, 81-83, 285, 289, 291, 293; 5. 165.

Time. Measures of, 1. 46, &c.; 2. 253, &c.; 5. 170, 187, &c. Astrological divisions of, 4. 66. A form of Vishṇu, 1. 18: see Kála. Hymn on, 2. 338.

Timi, daughter of Daksha, and wife of Kaśyapa, son of Maríchi, 2. 26.

Timi, instead of Tigma, in the Bhágavata-puráṇa, 4. 165.

Tíragrahas, a people, 2. 172.

Tírtha, 'a place of pilgrimage,' P. 31, 38, 71; 2. 150; 4. 227.

Tírthakara, the same as Tírthan-kara, 2. 105.

Tírthankara, a synonym of Jina, 5. 364. See Tírthakara.

Tírthavatí, a river in Krauncha-dwípa, 2. 198.

Tiryaksrotas, what, in cosmology, 1. 71. 74.

Tishmas (?), variant of Tishyas, 2. 197.

Tishyas, a caste in Krauncha-dwípa, 2. 197.

Tishya, the same as Pushya, the asterism so called, 2. 258, 259; 4. 229.

Tithi-tattwa, the, a law-book, referred to, or cited, 3. 89, 90, 4. 309.

Titikshá, 'long-suffering,' 'patience,' daughter of Daksha, and wife of Dharma, 1. 110.

Titikshu, son of Mahámanas, 4. 120, 122.

Tittiri, disciple of Yáska, and promulgator of the Yajur-veda, 3. 54.

Tittiri (?), variant of Víloman, son of Kapotaroman, 4. 97.

Tochari, a tribe of the Sacæ or Sakas, identified with the Tu-kháras, 2. 186.

Tokháras (?), variant of Tukháras, 3. 293.

Tomaras, a people, 2. 187.

Tośala, the same as Tośalaka, 5. 39.

Tośalaka, Tosalaka, a famous pancratiast, slain by Krishṇa, 5. 39, 40.

Toshala (?), the same as Tośalaka, 5. 39.

Toshalaka (?), the same as Tośalaka, 5. 39.

Toyá, a river in India, 2. 155.

Toyá, a river in Sálmala-dwípa, 2. 194.

Toyámbudhi, a sea of fresh water in Sweta-dwípa, 2. 200.

Toyeśa, an epithet of Varuṇa, 5. 15.

Traigartas, the same as Trigartas, 2. 180.

Trairájya (??), variant of Strirájya, 4. 222.

Traisáli (??), variant of Traisámba, 4. 116.

Traisámba, son of Gobhánu, 4. 116.

Traishťubha metre, the same as Trishťubh, 1. 84.

Traiyáruña (?), the Vyása of the fifteenth Dwápara age, 3. 34. See Tryaruña.

Transmigration, stages of, 2. 221.

Trasadasyu, son of Purukutsa and Narmadá, 3. 283, 284.

Trasaddasyu, the same as Mándhátṛi, 3. 266.

Trasaddasyu, variant of Trasadasyu, 3. 283.

Trasarenu, a measure of time, equivalent to three Anus, 1. 48.

Trasu (??), variant of Tamsu, 4. 129, 130.

Trayí, 'the three Vedas collectively, or the doctrines they teach,' 4. 310.

Trayyáruña, son of Tridhanwan, 3. 284.

Trayyáruña, son of Urukshaya, 4. 138.

Trayyáruña (??), variant of Traiyáruña, (?), 3. 34.

Trayyáruñi, disciple of Lomaharshaña, 3. 65.

Trayyáruñi (?), variant of Traiyáruña (?), 3. 34.

Trayyáruñi (??), variant of Trayyáruña, son of Tridhanwan, 3. 284.

Trayyáruñi (?), variant of Trayyáruña, son of Urukshaya, 4. 138.

Tretá, the second age of the world, 1. 84, 91; 3. 31, 254, 261;

4. 11, 237; 5. 170, 181, 185. Its duration, 1. 50.

Tretágni, 'a triad of holy fires, 4. 11.

Tribandhana, son of Aruña, son of 'Haryaáwa, 3. 284.

Tribhánu, instead of Traisámba, in the Bhágavata-puráña, 4. 116.

Tridasapati, an epithet of Indra, 5. 15.

Trideva (?), variant of Rantideva, 4. 137.

Tridháman, Vyása in the tenth Dwápara age, 3. 34, 37.

Tridháman, 'triple-gloried,' &c., 2. 252.

Tridhanwan, variously genealogized, 3. 283, 284.

Tridivá, a river in India, 2. 145, 146.

Tridivá, a river in Plaksha-dwípa, 2. 192.

Tridivályá, a river in India, 2. 146.

Trigartas, a people, 2. 179.

Trigarta, a country, the same as Jálandhara, 2. 179.

Trikakud, sprung from Anenas, son of Áyus, 4. 43.

Trikáṇḍa-sesha, the, a vocabulary, referred to, 2. 148, 172, 178; 3. 264.

Trikúťa, a mountain-range running southwards from Mount Meru, 2. 117.

Trikúťa, a mountain, the same as Suvela, 2. 141.

Trilochana, an epithetical name of S'iva, 1. 141; 5. 111.

Trilochana, an author, referred to the court of King Vikramáditya, P. 9.

Trimadhus, certain Bráhmans so called, 3. 173.

Trimadhu, a certain passage of the Ríg-veda, 3. 173, 174.

Trimadhu, a certain rite, 3. 173 (note †).

Tríñabindu, son of Búdha, son of Vogavat, 3. 245 (where correct the spelling), 246, 248; 5. 390.

Tríñabindu, Vyása in the twenty-third Dwápara age, 3. 35, 37.

Triñáchiketas, certain Bráhmans so called, 3. 173, 174.

Triñáchiketas, a portion of the Káthaka branch of the Yajur-veda, 3. 173, 174.

Trinetra, variant of Dfid'hasena, 4. 175.

Tripati, the hill of, in the Deccan, 2. 141.

Trípti, ' mental satisfaction, or freedom from sensual desire,' one of the eight Siddhis, or attributes of perfection, 1. 91.

Tripura, an Asura, conquered by S'iva, P. 82, 89; 5. 118.

Tripura (?) Asuras, the, 5. 349.

Tripurí, the capital of the Chedis, where situated, 5. 118.

Tripuríkshatra, a sacred spot, where situated, 5. 118.

Trisakti-máhátmya, a part of the Varáha-puráña, P. 71.

Trisámá, a river in India, 2, 130, 132,

Trisanku, the same as Satyavrata, 3, 284; &c., 297. Viswámitra elevated him to heaven, 3. 285–287,

Trisanku, a certain Buddhist, 3. 340.

Trisanku (?), variant of Swáhi, 4. 61.

Trisánu (?), variant of Traisámba, 4. 116.

Trisári (?), variant of Traisámba, 4. 116.

Trisarví (?), a certain usage, 4. 162. See Triswachí (?).

Tríshñá, ' thirst,' daughter of Mfityu, sprung from Brahmá, 1. 112.

Trishtubb, a metre, originating from Brahmá's southern mouth, or, by another account, from his flesh, 1. 84, 86. It is identified with a horse of the Sun, 2. 239.

Trisíkha, according to the Bhágavata-puráña, Indra of the fourth Manwantara, 3. 7.

Trisrínga, a mountain-range, its position with reference to Mount Meru, 2. 123, 124.

Trisuparñas, certain Bráhmans so called, 3. 173, 174.

Trisuparña, a certain portion of the Veda, 3. 173, 174.

Triswachí (?), a certain usage, 4. 162. See Trisarví (?).

Trita, son of Chákshusha, the Manu, 1. 178.

Trivakrá, the same as Naikavakrá, 5. 21, 165.

Trivakshya (?), variant of Ríchs, 4. 164.

Trivikrama, an epithetical designation of Vishñu, P. 74; 3. 18.

Trivfisha, according to some accounts, Vyása in the eleventh Dwápara age, 3. 34, 37.

Trivṛíshan, Vyása in the eleventh Dwápara age, 3. 34.

Trivṛít, a certain collection of Vaidik hymns, its origin from Brahmá's eastern mouth, 1. 84.

Triyáruñi (?), for Traiyáruñi (?), 3. 37, 221 (where correct Triyáruña), 340.

Truthfulness, obligation of, 3. 144.

Truṭi, a measure of time, equivalent to three Trasareñua, 1. 48.

Tryambaka, a Rudra, 2. 24, 25.

Tryambaka, an epithet of Aparájita, the Rudra, on one interpretation, 2. 24 (note 2).

Tryaruña, old form of 'Traiyáruña (?), found in the Ṛig-veda, 3. 36, 65, 284.

Tukháras, a people, 2. 176, 186; 4. 203. See Tusháras, Tushkaras, &c.

Tulá (?), an Apsaras, 2. 81.

Tulakuchi, son of Sahálin, 4. 186.

Tulasí, a certain shrub, sacred to Kṛishṇa, P. 34. Produced from the ocean, when churned, 1. 147.

Tulunga, a country, 2. 179.

Tuluva, the same as Tulunga, 2. 179.

Tulyatá, 'similarity of life, form, and feature,' one of the eight Siddhis, or attributes of perfection, 1. 91.

Tumbaru, variant of Tumburu, 2. 284, 292, 293; 4. 98.

Tumburu, a Gandharva, 2. 284, &c.; 4. 98.

Tuñḍíkeras, a tribe, 4. 58, 59.

Tungabhadrá, a river, popularly called Toombudra, P. 34; 2. 150.

Tunganas (??), variant of Tangañas, 2. 181.

Tungaprastha, a mountain, 2. 142.

Tungaveñá, a river (one with the Tungabhadrá ?), 2. 150, 152.

Túñi, son of Asanga, son of Yuyudhána, 4. 93.

Turañya, a horse of the Moon, 2. 299.

Turvaśa, the old form of Turvasu, 4. 46, 48, 116.

Turvasu, son of Yayáti, 4. 46, 48, &c., 116, 117. See Turvaśa.

Turvaśu (??), variant of Turvaśu, 4. 116.

Turya (??), variant of U'rja, the Ṛishi so called, 3. 3.

Tushadratha (??), variant of Ushadratha, 4. 122.

Tusháras, a dynasty, 4. 203, 206, 208. See Tukháras, Tushkaras, &c.

Tusháras, variant of Tukháras, 2. 186; 3. 293.

Tushitas, a class of gods, variously genealogized, appearing in various Manwantaras, 1. 109; 2. 26, 27; 3. 3, 17, 18.

Tushita, a form of Vishṇu, in the third Manwantara, 3. 17.

Tushitá, wife of Vedaśiras, &c., 3. 3, 17.

Tushkaras, Tushkáras (??), variants of Tukháras, 4. 203, 206, 208. See Tusháras.

Tushṭa, son of Ugrasena, son of Khuka, 4. 99.

Tushṭavu (??), variant of Tumburu, 2. 293.

Tushṭí, 'satisfaction,' daughter of

Daksha, and wife of Dharma, 1. 109, 110.

Tushti, daughter of Pauruamása, son of Maríchi, 1. 153.

Tushtimat, son of Ugrasena, son of A'huka, 4. 99.

Twáshtra, a section of the Bhavishya-puráña, P. 63.

Twashtti, the same as Viswakarman, 1. 24; 3. 20. In 3. 273, "the divine artist" is substituted for Twashtti.

Twashtti, a Rudra, 2. 24.

Twashtti, an Áditya, 2. 27, 285, &c.

Twashtti, son of Manasyu, son of Mahánta, z. 107. According to the Bhágavata-puráña, he is son of Bhauvana, 2. 107.

Twishá, daughter of Pauruamása, son of Maríchi, 1. 153.

Ubhayaspttishti, a river in Sáka-dwípa, according to the Bhágavata-puráña, 2. 200.

Uchathya, the old form of Utathya, 3. 16.

Uchchaihsravas, a horse created at the churning of the ocean, and appropriated by Indra, 1. 147. King of horses, 2. 85.

Uchchhra (??), variant of Ushna, son of Dyutimat, king of Krauncha-dwípa, 2. 197.

Udadhi (??), variant of Udáyin, son of Vasudeva, 4. 110.

Udaksena, son of Viswaksena (see it), son of Brahmadatta, 4. 142.

Udámbhin (?), variant of Udáyáswa, 4. 182.

Udápi (??), variant of Somápi, son of Sahadeva, 4. 151.

Udáradhí, father of Ripu, by one account, 1. 178.

Udáravasu, son of Udávasu, 3. 331.

Udásin (??), variant of Udayáswa, 4. 182.

Udávasu, son of Janaka, son of Nimi, 3. 330.

Udaya (?), variant of Udayáswa, 4. 182.

Udayagiri, a mountain-range in Sáka-dwípa, 2. 198, 199.

Udayana, king of Kausámbi, son of Sahasránika, 2. 158; 4. 163.

Udayana, son of Satánika, son of Vasudána, 4. 165.

Udayana, a common variant of Udayáswa, 4. 182.

Udayáswa, son of Darbhaka, 4. 182.

Udayibhaddako, Páli for Udayibhadraka, 4. 182.

Udayibhadra, the same as Udayibhadraka, 4. 186.

Udayibhadraka, son of Ajátasatru, 4. 182. See the last.

Udáyin, son of Vasudeva, son of Súra, 4. 110.

Udáyin, son of Kúnika, 5. 391.

Udayin, variant of Udayáswa, 4. 182.

Udáyus (??), variant of Somápi, son of Sahadeva, 4. 151.

Udbhava, son of Nahusha, son of Áyus, 4. 46.

Udbhida, ruler over the realm of Udbhida, and son of Jyotishmat, king of Kusa-dwípa, 2. 195.

Udbhida, a division of Kusa-dwípa, 2. 195.

Uddala, teacher of the White Yajur-veda, 3. 57.

Uddálaka, son of Aruńa, according to the Vedas, 3. 49.

Uddálaki (?), variant of Dálaki, 3. 49.

Uddálin (??), variant of Uddála, 3. 57.

Uddhava, son of Devabhága, P. 43; 4. 113; 5. 146, 147.

Udgátrí, 'a priest who chants Sámans,' 3. 43.

Udgítha, son of Bhuva, 2. 106. Also called son of Bhúman, 2. 107.

Udibhi (??), variant of Udayáśwa, 4. 182.

Uḍras, the same as Keralas, 2. 177.

Uḍras, variant of Puńḍras, 2. 132.

Uḍras (??), variant of Oḍras or Auḍras, 4. 220.

Uḍra, a country, 2. 177.

Uḍravataara, a certain cyclic year, 2. 255.

Uḍumbaras, Kauśika Bráhmans, 4. 28.

Uḍupati, an epithet of Soma, son of Atri, 4. 4.

Ugra, a Rudra, 1. 116; 2. 25; 5. 386.

Ugrajit, an Apsaras, 2. 81.

Ugrampaśyá, an Apsaras, 2. 81.

Ugraretas, a form of Rudra, 1. 117.

Ugrasena, a Gandharva, 2. 285, &c.

Ugrasena, son of Áhuka, 4. 76, 84, 87, 88, 98, 114, 250, 337, 341; 5. 8, 41, 45, 46, 49, 63, 131-134, 142, 143, 150, 382. He burns himself at the exequies of Kŕishńa, 5. 154.

Ugrasena, son of Parikshit, 4. 152, 162.

Ugraseni, wife of Akrúra, 4. 96.

Ugraśravas, son of Lomaharshańa, P. 30.

Ugráyudha, variously genealogized, 4. 142-144.

Ujjayiní, a city in Central India, now popularly called Onjein, 2. 159; 3. 246; 4. 59; 5. 392.

Ukta (??), variant of Ushńa, 4. 164.

Uktha, son of Chhala, 3. 321.

Ukthya, a particular sacrifice, its origin from Brahmá's southern mouth, 1. 84, 85; 3. 113.

Ulbańa, son of Vasishtha, son of Brahmá, 1. 155.

Ulmuka, son of Chákshusha, the Manu, 1. 178.

Ulmuka, son of Balabhadra, 4. 109; 5. 68.

Ulúki (?), daughter of Kaśyapa and Támrá, (?) 2. 73.

Ulúpí, daughter of Kauravya, and wife of Arjuna, son of Páńḍu, 4. 160.

Ulútas, variant of Utúlas, 2. 174.

Umá, daughter of Himavat and Mená, 1. 157; 3. 159. Consort of Śiva or Náráyańa, P. 76, 82; 1. 118, 125, 133; 2. 118; 4. 247; 5. 76, 83, 118, 119. See Párvatí, Satí, and Ushas.

Umá, a Śakti of Śiva, 1. 104. (The same as the last ?)

Umá (??), variant of Ushas, wife of Bhava, 1. 117.

Umápati, an epithet of Śiva, from the name of his consort, 1. 130; 5. 118, 119.

Umávana, a synonym of Sonita-
pura, 5. 112.

Umbrella produced from the ocean,
when churned, appropriated by
Varuńa, 1. 147.

Umlochá, an Apsaras, 2. 81.

Umlochá, variant of Anumlochá,
2. 288.

Úndea, the same as Húndea, 2.340.

Unmáda, 'Insanity,' a form of
Brahmá, 1. 82.

Unnábha, son of Sila, according
to the Raghuvaṁśa, 3. 321.

Unnata, variant of Uttama, the
Ŕishi, 3. 12.

Unnata, a mountain-range in Sálmala-dwípa, 2. 194.

Unnati, 'loftiness,' daughter of
Daksha, and wife of Dharma,
1. 110.

Upabarhańa, the same as Nárada,
the Gandharva, 2. 20.

Upabarhańa, a mountain in Krauncha-dwípa, 2. 198.

Upádána, 'material cause,' 1. 66.

Upadánaví, daughter of Vŕisha-
parvan, the Daitya, 2. 70; 4.
132 (where correct the statement as to this Upadánaví's
being wife of Hirańyáksha).

Upadánaví, daughter of Vaiśwánara, and wife of Hirańyáksha,
2. 71.

Upadánaví, wife of Taṁsu, and of
Sughora (?), by various accounts,
4. 132.

Upadeva, son of Sávarńa, the
Manu, 3. 27.

Upadeva, son of Akrúra, 4. 96.

Upadeva, son of Devaka, son of
Áhuka, 4. 98.

Upadevá, daughter of Devaka, son
of Áhuka, and wife of Vasudeva,
son of Súra, 4. 98, 110, 111.

Upadeví (??), variant of Upadevá,
4. 98, 110.

Upadwípas, 'minor Dwípas,' 2.
129.

Upagu, son of Sátyarathi, 3. 334.

Upagupta, son of Upagu, 3. 334.

Upagupta (??), variant of Upagu,
3. 334.

Upagupta (??), variant of Sruta,
son of Upagu, 3. 334.

Upaguru (??), variant of Upagu,
3. 334.

Upahálakas, the same as Kuntalas,
2. 157.

Upahútas, a synonym of Havishmats, 3. 163, 339.

Upákhyána, ' a minor story or
tale,' 3. 63, 66.

Upaksha, son of Swaphalka, 4.
96.

Upakshattra (?), son of Swaphalka,
4. 95.

Upamadgu, son of Swaphalka, 4.
94.

Upamangu (??), variant of Upamadgu, 4. 94, 96.

Upauanda, son of Vasudeva, son
of Súra, 4. 109.

Upanandana, a Kumára, or transformation of Siva, 1. 79.

Upanidhi, son of Vasudeva, son of
Súra, 4. 110.

Upanishads, the, P. 2; 5. 261,
&c., 288, 291, 308, 315, 345,
354.

Upapradána, 'the giving of presents,' one of the four devices
of policy, 5. 52.

Upapuránas, their character, names, &c., P. 22, 27, 36, 83, 86, &c.

Uparichara, the same as Vasu, son of Kritaka, 4. 149, 150.

Upasamhára-páda, a part of the Váyu-puráña, P. 37, 38.

Upasamhriti, 'the end of all things,' 5. 169, 184.

Upasloka, father of Brahmasávarña, according to the Bhágavata-puráña, 3. 25.

Upasunda, son of Nisunda, 2. 69.

Upaváhas (?), variant of Apaváhas, 2. 165.

Upaveñá, a river in India, 2. 150.

Upávrittas, a people, 2. 169.

Upáyas, the, four schemes of policy, 2. 54. And see 5. 52 (text and note ‖).

Upayuta, son of Upagupta, 3. 334.

Upendra, the same as Krishña (?), presiding over the feet, 1. 38; 4. 318, 319. (Perhaps the president of the feet differs from Krishña.)

Upendrá, a river in India, 2. 150.

Upodgháta-páda, a part of the Váyu-puráña, P. 37.

Uragas, synonym of Sarpas, 2. 213; 5. 110, 246.

Uragári, 'enemy of snakes,' an epithetical designation of Garuda, 4. 87.

Úrdhwabáhu, son of Vasishtha, son of Brahmá, 1. 155.

Úrdhwabáhu, a Rishi in the fifth Manwantara, 3. 10.

Úrdhwaga, son of Krishña and Lakshmaná, 5. 81.

Úrdhweketu, son of Sanadhwaja.

Úrdhwaroman, a mountain in Kusa-dwipa, 2. 197.

Úrdhwasrotas, the third of the creations, that of the divinities, 1. 72, 74, 75.

Úrdhwavaktras, a class of Viswe devas, 3. 149.

Úrdhwáyanas, a caste in Plaksha-dwipa, 2. 193.

Úrjas (?), a class of Apsarases, 2. 82.

Úrja, son of Vatsara, son of Dhruva, 1. 178.

Úrja, a Grámañí or Yaksha, 2. 291 (where correct the spelling), 292, 343.

Úrja, a Rishi in the second Manwantara, variously genealogized, 3. 3, 4 (where correct the spelling), 5, 337.

Úrja, son of Satyahita or Satyadhrita, 4. 150.

Úrjá, 'energy,' daughter of Daksha, and wife of Vasishtha, 1. 109, 110, 155; 3. 7. Called daughter of Kardama, 1. 110.

Úrja, synonym of Kárttika, a month, Oct.—Nov., 2. 261.

Úrja (?), variant of Úrjaváha, 3. 333.

Úrjas (?), variant of Úrja, the Grámañí, 2. 292.

Úrjaswati, daughter of Daksha, and wife of Dharma, 2. 21.

Úrjaswati, daughter of Priyavrata, 2. 100.

Úrjaváha, Úrjavaha, son of Suchi, son of Satadyumna, 3. 333.

Úrjba (?), variant of Jantu, son of Sudhanwan, 4. 150.]

Urihara (?), variant of Jharjhara,

Úrjita (??), variant of Súra, son of Arjuna, son of Kŕitavírya, 4. 57.

Úrmis, six in number, namely, hunger, thirst, sorrow, stupefaction, decay, death, 2. 4. Enumeration of them in Sanskrit, 2. 337.

Úrńáyu, a Gandharva, 2. 285, &c.

Úru, son of Chákshusha, the Manu, 1. 177; 3. 13 (where correct the spelling), 337.

Uru, Úru (??), son of Bhautya, the Manu, 3. 29.

Urubuddhi, son of Indrasávarńi, the Manu, 3. 29.

Urukriya (??), variant of Gurukshepa, 4. 167.

Urukshat (??), variant of Urukshaya, son of Mahávírya, 4. 137.

Urukshaya, son of Mahávírya, son of Bhavanmanyu, 4. 137.

Urukshaya (?), variant of Gurukshepa, 4. 167.

Urukshepa (??), variant of Gurukshepa, 4. 167.

Urunjaya (??), variant of Urukshaya, 4. 137.

Urunjaya (??), variant of Gurukshepa, 4. 167.

Uruśanku(??),variant of Rushadgu, 4. 61.

Uruśravas, son of Satyaśravas, son of Vítihotra, 3. 335.

Uruśŕinga, a mountain in Śákadwípa, 2. 200.

Uruvas, son of Madhu, son of Devakshattra, 4. 69.

Úrva, grandfather (where correct father) of Jamadagni, 3. 80; 5. 399.

Úrva (??), variant of Úrja, the Rishi, 3. 3.

Úrva (?), variant of Mŕidu, son of Ntipanjaya, 4. 165.

Urvarávat (??), variant of Arvarívat, son of Sávarńi, 3. 24.

Urvarívat, probably the true reading for Arvarívat, the Rishi, 3. 5.

Urvarívat, variant of Arvarívat, son of Sávarńi, 3. 24.

Urvaśí, an Apsaras, daughter of Náráyaṇa, and mistress of Purúravas, 2. 75, 80–83, 285, 288, 291, 293; 3. 328; 4. 5, &c., 343. Mistress of Satyadhŕiti, son of Satánanda, 4. 146.

Úryás (?), a class of Apsarases, 2. 82.

Usáná, wife of Mahisása, a form of Rudra, 1. 117.

Usanas, an ancient author, referred to, 1. 174. (Possibly he is the same as the next, if not the lawgiver so named).

Usanas, son of Bhŕigu, 1. 122, 152, 175; 2. 53; 4. 2, 3, 46. Called son of Kavi (not of Vedaśiras), 1. 200. Identified with the planet Venus, 2. 225, 259, 308.

Usanas, the Vyasa of the third Dwápara age, 3. 34, 36. (Perhaps this is Usanas, son of Bhŕigu.)

Usanas, variously genealogized, 4. 63.

Ushá, daughter of Bána, and enamoured of Aniruddha, 5. 108, 109, 110, 112.

Ushá. See Ushas, wife of Bhava;

and see 2. 249 (note *), and 342 (on that note).

Ushá, part of the night. See Ushas.

Ushadgu (??), variant of Rushadgu, 4. 61.

Ushadratha, son of Titikshu, 4. 122.

Ushas, wife of Bhava, 1. 117, (where correct Ushá); 5. 387.

Ushas (later, Ushá), part of the night, 2. 249, 342.

Ushat (??), variant of Úsanas, 4. 63.

Ushávana (?), variant of Umávana, 5. 112.

Ushij (??), variant of Síva, son of Úru, 1. 179.

Ushmánaya (??), variant of Úshmápaña (?), 3. 37.

Úshmapas, Ushmapas (??), a class of Pitris, 1. 123; 3. 162, 339.

Úshmápaña (?), 3. 37. See Saumasushmáyaña.

Ushña, ruler over the realm of Ushña, and son of Dyutimat, king of Kuśa-dwípa, 2. 197.

Ushña, variously genealogized, 4. 163, 164.

Ushña, a division of Kuśa-dwípa, 2. 197.

Ushñih, a metre, its origin from the hairs of Brahmá's body, 1. 86. Considered as a horse of the Sun, 2. 239.

Ushtrakarñikas, a people, 2. 162.

Uśíka, son of Kriti or Dhriti, 4. 67.

Uśínaras, a people, 4. 120.

Uśínara, son of Vasudeva, son of Súra, 4. 109.

Uśínara, son of Mahámanas, 4. 120, 121.

Uśrayus, son of Purúravas, son of Budha, 4. 13.

Utanka (??), variant of Uttanka, 3. 264.

Utathya, son of Angiras, 1. 154; 3. 16; 4. 123, 134.

Utkalas, a people inhabiting part of Orissa, 2. 159.

Utkala, son of Sudyumna, who at first was a woman, 3. 237.

Utkala, a country included in what is now called Orissa, 2. 153, 160; 3. 237.

Utkala-khañḍa, a part of the Skanda-puráña, P. 73.

Utpalávatí, a river, 2. 154. (See the next.)

Utpalavatí, a river, rising in the Malaya mountains, 2. 155. (The same as the last ?)

Utsarpiñí, a certain period of time, a term used by the Jainas, 2. 197.

Utsavasanketas, a people, 2. 179.

Uttálaka (??), variant of Pattálaka, 4. 197.

Uttamas, a people, 2. 159.

Uttama, a Rishi in the sixth Manwantara, 3. 12, 14.

Uttama, Vyása of the twenty-first Dwápara age, 3. 35.

Uttama, son of Uttánapáda, 1. 159, &c.

Uttama, variant of Auttami, son of Priyavrata, 2. 109; 3. 1, 5, 8, 11, 337.

Uttamarñas, a people, 2. 160.

Uttamaujas, son of Brahmasávarña or Brahmasávarñi, 3. 26.

Uttánabarhis, son of Saryáti, son of Vaivaswata, the Manu, 3. 249.

Uttánahaya (?), variant of Vońu, 4. 53.

Uttánapáda, son of Swáyambhuva, 1. 108, 159, &c.; 2. 99, 306, 307; 3. 2, 5, 11; 5. 386. His offspring, 2. 108.

Uttanka, a certain Maharshi, 3. 264.

Uttará, wife of Abhimanyu, son of Arjuna, 4. 160.

Uttarabhádrapadá, an asterism, 2. 268, &c.; 3. 132.

Uttara-khańd'a, part of the Padma-puráńa, P. 20, 30, 32, 34; 4. 245.

Uttara-khańd'a, part of the Brahma-puráńa, P. 29.

Uttarakośalas, a people, 2. 172.

Uttarakośala, a country, 3. 319. See Kosala.

Uttarakośalá, a city in the region just named, 2. 172.

Uttarakuru, a people, 2. 339.

Uttarakuru, a region, 2. 112, 115, 120, 123; 3. 21.

Uttarápatha, 'the regions to the north of the Vindhya mountains,' 3. 240.

Uttaraphálguní, an asterism, 2. 265, &c.

Uttaraproshťhapadá, the same as Uttarabhádrapadá, 2. 265.

Uttara-ráma-charita, a drama, referred to, 3. 81, 317.

Uttarásháďhá, an asterism, 2. 265, &c., 308.

Uttaríyaka, 'a man's upper garment,' 3. 95.

Utúlas, a people, 2. 174.

Vách, daughter of Daksha, and wife of Kaśyapa, son of Marichi, 2. 26. Mother of the Apsarases and Gandharvas, according to the Padma-puráńa, 2. 75, 81.

Váchaspati, substituted, by the Translator, for Brihaspati, 2. 24.

Váchávriddhas, a class of gods in the fourteenth Manwantara, 3. 28.

Váchávrittas (??), variant of Váchávriddhas, 3. 28.

Vada, a Veda of the Magas, or heliolaters in S'áka-dwípa, 5. 383.

Vad'abhi, the same as Valabhi, 5. 27.

Vadaśrí (?), variant of Chandraśrí, 4. 201.

Vad'avá, mistress of Vasudeva, son of S'úra, 4. 110.

Vád'ava, a fire so called, which devours the water of the ocean, 4. 303. See the next article.

Vad'avánala, the fire called Anala, where, 2. 110.

Vadha, a Rákshasa, 2. 285, 287, 291, 293.

Vággmin, son of Manasyu, son of Pravíra, 4. 127.

Vahínara (??), variant of Ahínara, son of Udayana, 4. 165.

Váhiní, a river in India, 2. 153.

Váhlikas, Váhíkas, probably wrong for Báhlíkas, supposed to be the people of Balkh, 2. 175; 4. 157, 345.

Váhlíka, Váhlíka (?), son of Pratípa, 4. 154, 157. (Báhlíka is the more correct form.)

Váhlíśwara kings, the, seven in

number, sons of Váhlíka or Báhlíka, according to the Matsya-puráṇa, 4. 157. (Probably Báhlíśwara is the better reading of the name.)

Váhna-puráṇa, the same as Agni-puráṇa, P. 24.

Vahnayas (?), a class of Apsarases, 2. 82.

Vahnis, the same as Agnis, 4. 249.

Vahni, 'fire.' His wife, Swáhá, 1. 109. His offspring, 1, 156; for he seems to be identified with Abhimánin, eldest son of Brahmá, 1. 155. He has his hands cut off by Vírabhadra, 1. 131. He gives deadly arrows to Arjuna, 5. 158. See Agni.

Vahni, son of Turvasu, 4. 116.

Vahni, son of Kṛishṇa and Mitra-vindá, 5. 79.

Vahni (??), variant of Vṛishṭa, son of Kukura, 4. 97.

Vahnijwála, a certain hell, 2. 215, 220.

Vahni-puráṇa, the, referred to, 3. 340, 342; 5. 381.

Vaibhojas, a kingless people, who travel on rafts, sprung from Druhya or Druhyu, son of Yayáti, 4. 119.

Vaibhrája, a mountain-range in Plaksha-dwípa, 2. 191.

Vaibhrája, a grove on Mount Su-páréwa, 2. 112, 116.

Vaidehas, a people, 2. 177.

Vaideha, an epithet of Janaka, son of Nimi, 3. 330.

Vaidbeya, promulgator of the White Yajur-veda, 3. 57.

Vaidbṛita, Indra of the eleventh Manwantara, according to the Bhágavata-puráṇa, 3. 96.

Vaidhṛitis, a class of gods in the fourth Manwantara, according to the Bhágavata-puráṇa, 3. 7.

Vaidiśá, perhaps intended for Vidiśá (?), 3. 218, 221, 243.

Vaidúra, a country, 4. 216.

Vaidúrya, a mountain-range lying to the west of Mount Meru, 2. 117.

Vaidúrya, a mountain, part of the southern Vindhya range, 2. 144, 150.

Vaidyuta, ruler over the realm of Vaidyuta, and son of Vapushmat, king of Sálmala-dwípa, 2. 193.

Vaidyuta, a division of Sálmala-dwípa, 2. 193.

Vaidyuta, 'electric fire,' 1. 156. See Pávaka.

Vaijayantí, the name of Vishṇu's necklace, 2. 94.

Vaikanka, a mountain-range running eastward from Mount Meru, 2. 117. Garuḍa has his city there, 2. 118.

Vaikárika, 'pure,' 'productive, or susceptible of production,' an epithet of Ahaṁkara, 1. 33, 34, 74. See Sáttwika.

Vaikhánasa, synonymous with Vánaprastha, 3. 101, 279.

Vaikṛita, 'secondary,' adjective of Vikṛiti, 1. 76, 78. One of the creations has this epithet.

Vaikuṇṭhas, a class of gods in the fifth and sixth Manwantaras, 3. 9, 10, 18. They were trans-

formed from the Jayas, created by Brahmá, according to the Váyu-puráña, 2. 26.

Vaikuñtha, a metronym of Vishñu, as specially manifested, 3. 17, 18 (where correct the spelling); 4. 278; 5. 390.

Vaikuñtha, the name of Vishñu's city. It stands highest of all the Lokas, P. 31; 1. 98. It is surmounted by Nákapŕishťha, 3. 198. It stands on Mount Meru, 2. 112. See also 1. 62; 2. 230.

Vaimánika-devas, certain gods so characterized, and why, 1. 175.

Vainadí (??), variant of Vinadí, 2. 150.

Vainahotra, son of Dhŕishťaketu, 4. 38.

Vainateya, apparently an Asura, his abode, 2. 211. (The name signifies 'son of Vinatá;' but I find no mention of Vinatá as mother of an Asura.)

Vainya, patronym of Pŕithu, 1. 186; 5. 388.

Vairájas, a class of Pitŕis, 3. 158, 159, 339. They inhabit Tapo-loka, 2. 227, 229; but Satya-loka, 2. 228. The term etymologized, 2. 229.

Vairájas, sundry verses of the Sáma-veda, produced from Brahmá's northern mouth, 1. 85.

Vairája, son of Viráj or Brahmá, and one with Manu, 1. 106; 2. 262; 3. 159.

Vairája, a patriarch, 1. 177; 2. 86. See Virajas.

Vairája, the same as Sudháman,

the Lokapála, according to the Váyu-puráña, 2. 262.

Vairája, father of Ajita, 3. 17.

Vairámatí, variant of Vairávatí, 2. 200.

Vairatha, variant of Swairatha, son of Jyotishmat, and the name of that son's kingdom, 2. 195.

Vairávatí, a city in Sweta-dwípa, 2. 200.

Vairivíra (??), variant of Ilavila or Iḍaviḍa, 3. 314.

Vairúpas, certain verses of the Sáma-veda, their origin from Brahmá's western mouth, 1. 85.

Vaiśákha, a month, April—May, 2. 261, &c.; 3. 168.

Vaiśákhí, wife of Vasudeva, son of Śúra, 4. 110.

Vaiśálaka, adjective of Vaiśálí (??), 3. 248.

Vaiśálí, Vaiśalí (??), wife of Vasudeva, son of Śúra, 4. 110.

Vaiśálí, a city, founded by Viśála, son of Trińabindu, P. 106; 3. 221, 246, 247, 248.

Vaiśampáyana, disciple of Vyása, and teacher of the Yajur-veda, 3. 41, 43, 52, 53, 54, 55, 57; 4. 153, 162.

Vaiśampáyana, disciple of Loma-harshaña, 3. 66. (Is he the same as the last?)

Vaishñavákútachandriká, a commentary on the Vishñu-puráña, P. 116.

Vaishñava-puráña, the same as Vishñu-puráña, P. 23, 34; 3. 66, 67.

Vaishńaví, a S'akti of Vishńu, 4.
260.

Vaishńaví-saṁhitá, a part of the
Kúrma-puráńa, P. 77.

Vaiśravańa, patronym of Kubera,
1. 122. King over kings, 2.
85. How employed, when the
earth was milked, 1. 188.

Vaiśwadeva, a particular sacrifice,
in worship of the Viśwe devas,
2. 330; 3. 114, 130, 178, 186.
See Vaiśwadevika.

Vaiśwadevahoma, a particular
sacrifice, 3. 114.

Vaiśwadevika, the same as Vaiśwadeva, 3. 185, 190.

Vaiśwánara, a Dánava, 2. 71.

Vaiśwánara, three certain triads
of asterisms, 2. 265, 267.

Vaiśwánarí, a certain triad of
asterisms, 2. 265, &c.

Vaiśyas, 'members of the third
caste,' 1. 89. Sprung from the
thighs of Brahmá, 1. 90. Their
duties, 3. 87.

Vaitála, disciple of Játúkarńya,
disciple of S'ákalya, 3. 48.

Vaitálaki, disciple of S'ákapúńi,
and promulgator of the Ŕig-
veda, 3. 47.

Vaitána, 'rules for oblations according to the Vedas,' 3. 63,
338.

Vaitańd́ya, son of Ápa, a Vasu,
2. 23.

Vaitarańí, a river in India, 2. 153.

Vaitarańí, a certain hall, 2. 215,
219.

Vaivaswata, a Rudra, 2. 25.

Vaivaswata, the Manu of the
seventh Manwantara, variously

genealogized, P. 57, 106, 107;
2. 27; 3. 2, 3, 13, 14, 20, 22,
34, 79, 181, 231, 237, 248,
256; 5. 390. His wife, S'raddhá,
3. 233. Hence he is called
S'raddhádeva, 3. 337.

Vaivaswata, a Manwantara, P. 43,
56, 69; 2. 108, 259.

Vaivataka (??), variant of Raivataka, a mountain-range in S'áka-
dwípa, 2. 199.

Vájapeya, a certain sacrifice, its
origin, &c., 1. 85; 3. 113.

Vájasaneyi, the same as the White
Yajur-veda, 3. 57, 63, 325; 4.
162.

Vájaśrava, Vájasrava (??), Vájaśra-
vas (??), variants of Rájaśravas, a Vyása, 3. 35.

Vájíkarańa, 'the use of aphro-
disiacs,' 4. 33.

Vájimedha, a synonym of Aśwamedha, 5. 252.

Vájins, students of the White
Yajur-veda, 3. 57.

Vájiní (?), variant of Rájaní, a river
in India, 2. 148.

Vajra, a Yadava prince, son of
Aniruddha and Subhadrá, 4.
113. Son of Aniruddha and
Úshá, 5. 108, 150, 151, 155,
160.

Vajrá, daughter of Vaiśwánara,
according to the Padma-puráńa,
2. 71.

Vajrakámá, daughter of Maya, 2.
72.

Vajrakańt́akaśálmalí, a certain
hell, 2. 215.

Vajrakút́a, a mountain in Plaksha-
dwípa, 2. 193.

Vajramitra, son of Ghoshavasu, 4. 192.

Vajranábha, variously genealogized, 3. 321, 323.

Vajra-nipátana, 'what, in the Hindu pancratium, 5. 37.

Vajrásana, what, in the Yoga philosophy, 5. 230..

Vajravat (??), variant of Vrijinívat, 4. 61.

Vajrin, an epithet of Indra, 5. 138.

Vajrívan (??), variant of Vaprívan, 3. 34.

Vakras, variant of Chakras, 2. 165.

Vakrátapas, a people, 2. 165.

Vakrayodhin, variant of Vaktrayo-dhin, 2. 72.

Vakshu, the Oxus, 5. 388. See Vankshu, 2. 122; Suchakshu, 2. 126; &c. &c. (Chakshu looks very like a graphical corruption of Vakshu.)

Vaktrayodhin, son of Viprachitti, 2. 72.

Valabhi, what, in architecture, 5. 27, 30, 31.

Valaka (??), variant of Baláka (?), otherwise Balákáswa, 4. 15.

Valaka (??), variant of Vanaka, a Rishi, 3. 8.

Vali, what, in architecture, 5. 32.

Válikhilyas, Devarshis, sons of Kratu, 1. 98, 155; 2. 253, 289, 296; 3. 68.

Válakhilya, a Samhitá of the Rig-veda, 3. 49 (where correct the spelling), 68.

Valkajas, variant of Kalkalas, 2. 180.

Vallabhas, a people, 2. 180.

Vallabha, a religious reformer, his time, &c., 1. 16, 22; 5. 258, 318, 338, 343–345, 347, 356.

Vallabhagañi, a lexicographer, re-ferred to, 3. 102, 197.

Vallabhí, a city in Central India, 2. 180.

Valliráshtra (??), variant of Malla-ráshtra, 2. 165.

Válmíka (??), variant of Báblika, 4. 169.

Válmíki, Vyása of the twenty-fourth Dwápara age, 3. 35, 37.

Válmíki, author of the Rámáyaña, 3. 317.

Vámas, an heretical sect, P. 79; 5. 286, 287, 325, 326, 375, 380.

Vámas (??), variant of Rámas, 2. 133.

Váma, a Rudra, 2. 25.

Váma, son of Krishña and Rohiñí, 5. 79.

Váma, a horse of the Moon, 2. 299.

Vámá, the same as Suvámá, a river, 2. 151.

Vámáchárina, a sect, 1. 125 (where correct the spelling); 5. 290 (where correct the spelling), 392.

Vámadeva, a Rudra, 1. 79, 103, 117.

Vámadeva, a mountain in S'álmala-dwípa, 2. 195.

Vámaka, son of Bhajamána, son of Satwata, 4. 72.

Vámana, 'dwarf,' son of Kaśyapa and Aditi, and a form of Vishñu, 3. 18, 19; 4. 123; 5. 3.

Vámana, a mountain-range in Krauncha-dwípa, 2. 197.

Vámana (?), variant of Dálaki, 3. 49.

Vámana-purána, analysis of it, &c., P. 20, 23, 24, 74, &c.; 3. 67; 5. 270, 319, 327.

Vamra, son of Vikhanas, 3. 337.

Vamrívan (?), variant of Vaprívan, 3. 34.

Vaṁśadhárá, a river in India, 2. 155.

Vaṁśaka, variant of Darbhaka, 4. 182.

Vaṁśavánaka (?), variant of Vatsabálaka, 4. 101.

Vaṁśavartins (the spelling to be corrected), variant of Vaśavartins, 3. 6; 5. 390.

Vana (?), variant of Nríga, son of Uśínara, 4. 121.

Vanaka, a Ŕishi in the fourth Manwantara, 3. 8. (But, very likely, Varada is the preferable reading.)

Vanakapívat, son of Pulaha, 1. 155; 3. 8.

Vanapítha (?), variant of Akapívat, 3. 8.

Vánaprastha, 'hermit,' his duties, &c., 3. 95, 279; 5. 174. And see Vanaukas and Vanavása.

Vanarájí, mistress of Vasudeva, son of Śúra, 4. 110.

Vánaráśyas, variant of Várapáśis, 2. 165.

Vanaspati, ruler over the realm of Vanaspati, and son of Ghŕitapŕishṭha, king of Krauncha-dwípa, 2. 198.

Vanaspati, a region in Krauncha-dwípa, 2. 198.

Vansukas, the same as Vánaprastha, 1. 98.

Vánavas, a people, 2. 175.

Vánavadarvas (?), a people, 2. 175.

Vanavása, the same as Vánaprastha, 5. 174.

Vanavásakas, a people, 2. 178.

Vánavásikas (?), variant of Vanavásakas, 2. 178.

Vánavásins (?), variant of Vanavásakas, 2. 178.

Vánáyavas (?), variant of Vátáyanas, 2. 176.

Vánáyusas (correctly), variant of Vátáyanas, 2. 176.

Vanáyus, son of Purúravas, son of Budha, 4. 13.

Vanchu (?), variant of Chakshu, the Oxus, 2. 120.

Vansyu, son of Raudráśwa, 4. 127–129.

Vangas, a people, 2. 166; 3. 293. And see Bangas.

Vangara, variant of Varánga, 4. 211.

Vangava (?), a king, son of Varadharmin, 4. 212.

Vangiri (?), a king, 4. 211.

Váñí, variant of Pará, a river, 2. 147.

Vanju (?), variant of Chakshu, the Oxus, 2. 120. See Vakshu.

Vankŕiti (?), variant of Vikŕiti, son of Jímúta, 4. 68.

Vankshu, variant of Chakshu, the Oxus, 2. 120, 122, 339. See Vakshu.

Vankshu (?), variant of Nríchakshus, 4. 164.

Vanyá (?), a river in Kuśa-dwípa, 2. 196.

Vanya (??), variant of Prámśu, son of Vaivaswata, 3. 232.

Vapovan (??), variant of Vaprivan, 3. 34.

Vaprivan, Vyása in the fourteenth Dwápara age, 3. 34.

Vapus, 'body,' daughter of Daksha, and wife of Dharma, 1. 109, 110.

Vapus, an Apsaras, 2. 81.

Vapushmat, son of Priyavrata, and king of Sálmala-dwípa, 2. 100, &c., 193.

Vapushmat, a Rishi in the eleventh Manwantara, 3. 26.

Vapushmat, one of the Viśwe devas, 3. 192.

Vapushmat, slain by Dama, son of Narishyanta, 3. 245.

Vara, son of Swaphalka, 4. 96.

Vará, a river in India, 2. 149.

Varadas, a people, 2. 185.

Varadá, a river in India, popularly called Wurda, 2. 145, 155.

Varada, a common variant of Van-áka, a Rishi, 3. 8.

Varada Bhatta, the same as the next, 3. 223.

Varadarája, an author, 3. 136, 222, 224. And see the last article.

Varadharmin, a king, son of Nakhavat (?), 4. 212.

Varáha, an epiphany of Vishńu, in the form of a boar, for the recovery of the earth, 1. 59. Is lauded by the earth, 1. 59-61. Raises the earth from the waters, 1. 61, &c. His form, 1. 61-63. He typifies the ritual of the Vedas, 1. 63. He re-

news the world, 1. 65. See also P. 42, 66, 70; 5. 88.

Varáha, a district in India, 2. 144.

Varáha, the name of a Kalpa, that now current, P. 34; 1. 53, 54, 69; 2. 108; 3. 66.

Varáha-dwípa, an island, perhaps fabulous, 2. 129.

Varáhamihira, an astronomer, referred to the court of King Vikramáditya, P. 8; 2. 190, 275, 277; 4. 153.

Varáha-puráńa, Varáha-puráńa, analysis of it, &c., P. 20, 23, 24, 70, &c.; 3. 67; 5. 327.

Varaka (??), variant of Dhanaka, 4. 54.

Varalatta (??), a country in the south of India, 2. 179.

Váramatha, son of Kshemavat, 3. 334.

Vára-mukhyá, 'a courtesan,' 5. 25.

Varańa (??), variant of Ramańa, 2. 23.

Varańá, a river in India, 2. 152.

Váránaná, an Apsaras, 2. 82.

Váráńasí, Varáńasí, Varáńasí, Benares, 2. 152, 163; 4. 180; 5. 121, 127, 129. Burning of, 5. 128.

Várańávata, an ancient city, 4. 80, 81.

Varánga, son of Dharma, son of Rámachandra, 4. 211.

Várapásis, a people, 2. 165.

Vararuchi, an author, referred to the court of King Vikramáditya, P. 8.

Váravásis (??), variant of Várapásis, 2. 165.

Váráyásiz (??), variant of Várapásiz, 2. 165.

Varcha (??), a name of the Sun (?), 5. 383. See Varchas.

Varchárchas, an epithet of the Magas, 5. 383.

Varchas, 'light,' son of Soma, the Vasu, 2. 23.

Varchas, a particular ray of the sun, 5. 191. And see 2. 297, 298.

Varchaswin, son of Varchas, 2. 23.

Varchávasu, a Gandharva, 2. 293.

Várddrínasa, the name of some bird, 3. 194.

Vardhamána, a mountain in Krauncha-dwípa, according to the Bhágavata-puráńa, 2. 198.

Vardhana, son of Kŕishńa and Mitravindá, 5. 79.

Vareńya-rúpa, what, in theology, as characterizing Vishńu, 4. 254.

Varga (??), variant of Vahni, son of Turvasu, 4. 116.

Varidása, a Gandharva, 2. 20.

Váridhára, a hill in India, 2. 141.

Várisára (??), variant of Bindusára, 4. 188.

Variyas, son of Pulaha, a Prajápati, 1. 155.

Varman, a name appropriate for a Kshattriya, 3. 99.

Varńásá, two rivers so called, 2. 152.

Varpeyu, son of Raudrásśwa, 4. 128.

Varsama (??), the same as Varáman, 5. 384.

Varahas, divisions of Jambu-dwípa, 2. 102, 114.

Vársháyańi, an ancient author, re-ferred to, 2. 113 (where correct the spelling).

Varahayantí, a Kŕittiká, 2. 337.

Várshńeyas, the same as Vŕishńis, 4. 58.

Varáman, what, among the Magas, 5. 384 (where correct the spelling).

Vartivardhana (?), variant of Nandivardhana, son of Janaka, 4. 179.

Várttá, 'the Silpa-sástra, mechanics, sculpture, and architecture,' 1. 148. Inconsistently rendered by "the Puráńas," 2. 202. The word has another sense in 4. 310.

Varuńa, 'god of the ocean,' P. 3; 1. 119, 141, 147, 177, 178, 180; 2. 44, 76, 77, 85; 3. 118, 166, 288; 4. 5, 27, 56, 258; 5. 15, 51, 55, 65, 68, 88, 92, 93, 100. His city, Vibhávarí, Sukhá, or Nimlochaní, according to various authorities, where situated, 2. 112, 118, 239, 240. He gives a thousand horses to Richíka, 4. 16. Other names of him are Ambupa, Prachetas, and Toyeśa.

Varuńa, an Áditya, 2. 27, 285, &c., 306.

Varuńa, one of the Viśwe devas, 3. 179.

Varuńa, a Yaksha, 2. 288, 293.

Varuńa (who ?), father of the ninth Manu, according to the Bhágavata-puráńa, 3. 24.

Váruńa, a portion of Bháratavarsha, 2. 112, 129.

Váruńa, the same as Satabhishaj,

an asterism, 2. 265; 3. 167 (where correct the spelling), 169; 5. 390.

Varuńa (??), variant of Vanaka, the Ŕishi, 3. 8.

Varuńá (??), variant of Varańá, a river, 2., 152.

Váruńa-upapuráńa, P. 87.

Váruńí, 'the goddess of wine, produced from the ocean, when churned, 1. 144, 147; 2. 212; 5. 65, 66. Other names of her are Madirá and Surá.

Váruńí, variant of Áruńí, the Ŕishi, 3. 26.

Varúthiní, an Apsaras, 3. 2.

Varuttha (?), sprung from Turvasu, 4. 117.

Vasá, a river in India, 2. 152.

Vásaná, 'imagination,' 5. 224.

Vasana (??), variant of Savana, son of Vasishťha, 1. 155.

Vaśáti (??), Vaśáti (??), variants of Vimśati, son of Ikshwáku, 3. 260.

Vásava, a name of Indra, 1. 136; 2. 239; 5. 45, 89, 99, 101, 234. King of the Maruts, 2. 85.

Vásava, the same as Dhanishťhá, an asterism, 3. 167.

Vásavadattá, the, a tale, its Preface referred to, 2. 158, 159, 164, 341; 3. 268, 318, 340; 4. 137, 172, 178, 180, 191, 217; 5. 81.

Vaśavartins, a class of gods in the third Manwantara, 3. 6.

Vashať, the same as Vashaťkára, 1. 60; 2. 29; 3. 123, 234.

Vashaťkára, a mystical exclama-tion, deified, &c., 1. 60, 142; 2. 29; 3. 295; 5. 137, 179. (In several of the passages re-ferred to, it is variously and very erroneously translated.) And see Vashať.

Vaśin, according to the Bhágavata-puráńa, son of Kŕiti, son of Bahuláśwa, 3. 335.

Vásishťhas, seven sons of Vasish-ťha, the Prajápati, 1. 155; 3. 5, 6, 7.

Vasishťha, a Prajápati, Brah-marshi, or son of Brahmá, 1. 100. His wife, Úrjá, 1. 109, 155; but Arundhati, by a dis-crepant account, 1. 110, 200. His seven sons, according to conflicting accounts, 1. 155; 3. 5, 6, 7. He has another son, Śakti, father of Paráśara, 3. 35, 36, 306. The Barhishads, certain Pitŕis, are regarded as his sons, 3. 161; and so are the Sukálins, other Pitŕis, 3. 165. He figures as a Ŕishi in the current Manwantará, 3. 13. His hermitage, where, 2. 132. He allays the wrath of Paráśara, 1. 7. He curses Pávaka and others, 1.193. Is family-priest to the house of Ikshwáku, 3. 260, 261. Priest of Manu, 3. 234. Ghostly adviser of Pŕish-adhra, 3. 239. Is family-priest of Sagara, 3. 291, 292. Dis-putes with Viśwámitra, P. 39, 56, 108; 1. 7; 3. 261, 306; 4. 22. His cow is killed by Satya-vrata or Triśanku, and the con-sequences, 3. 286. Viśwámitra

curses him, and he is changed into a starling, 3. 288. He curses Saudása, 3. 307, 310. He curses Nimi, 3. 327. Is cursed by Nimi, 3. 328. See also P. 32, 33, 58, 64; 1. 6, &c., 137, &c.; 2. 285, &c.; 3. 3, 4, 8, 11, 23, 68, 201, 233, 237, 285, 287, 292, 305; 5. 251. Etymology of the word Vasishťha, as against Vasishťha, a common corruption of it, 2. 339. Another name of Vasishťha, is said to be Mitra, 3. 305.

Vasishťha, the Vyása of the eighth Dwápara age, 3. 34, 37. (The same as the last?)

Vasishťha, or Ápava, son of Varuńa, god of the ocean, 4. 56.

Vásishťha, patronym of Sakti, father of Parásara, 1. 7.

Vásishťha, patronym of Mitrayu, 3. 66.

Vásishťha, variant of Mahámuni, 3. 11.

Vasishťha-samhitá, the, referred to, 3. 190.

Vasishťha-smriti, the, a code of law, quoted, or referred to, 3. 102, 110.

Vásishťha-upapurána, P. 87.

Vastrá, variant of Vástu, a river, 2. 149.

Vástu, a river in India, 2. 149.

Vastu, variant of Babhru, son of Romapáda, 4. 67.

Vastu-bhúta, what, in philosophy, 2. 309.

Vastudeva (?), variant of Devavat, son of Akrúra, 4. 96.

Vastunába (?), variant of Vasu-dána, son of Brihadratha, 4. 165.

Vasus. Sons of Dharma and Devi, 2. 21. Sons of Dharma and Vasu, 2. 22. Eight, and their names, 2. 23. Their chief, Pávaka, 2. 85. Their descendants, 2. 23. See also 1. 121, 141, 142; 2. 29; 3. 13, 15, 123, 158; 4. 111, 249, 258, 272, 293; 5. 2, 100, 143, 234, 247, 388.

Vasus, variant of Viswas, 5. 143.

Vasu, the same as Apaspati, son of Uttánapáda, 1. 159.

Vasu, son of Vatsara, son of Dhruva, 1. 178.

Vasu, ruler over the realm of Vasu, and son of Hirańyaretas, king of Kusa-dwípa, 2. 197.

Vasu, a Rishi in the ninth Manwantara, 3. 25.

Vasu, one of the Viswe devas, 3. 189, 190, 191, 192.

Vasu, son of Bhútajyotis, 3. 335.

Vasu, son of Purúravas, son of Budha, 4. 13.

Vasu, son of Kusa, 4. 15.

Vasu, son of Jamadagni, 4. 20.

Vasu, son of Vasudeva, son of Súra, 4. 111.

Vasu, son of Kritaka, son of Chyavana, 4. 149.

Vasu, son of Krishńa and Satyá, 5. 79.

Vasu, daughter of Daksha, and wife of Dharma, 2. 21, 22.

Vasu, a region in Kusa-dwípa, 2. 197.

Vasu, a certain ray of the sun, 5. 191. And see 2. 297, 298.

Vasu (??), variant of Tamsu, 4. 130.

Vasubhŕidyána, son of Vasishťha, 1. 155.

Vasudáman, variant of Vasudána, son of Bŕihadratha, 4. 165.

Vasudána, a king named in the Revá-máhátmya, 2. 151.

Vasudána, ruler over the kingdom of Vasudána, and son of Hiraṅyaretas, king of Kuśa-dwípa, 2. 197.

Vasudána, son of Bŕihadratha, son of Tigma, 4. 165.

Vasudána, a region in Kuśa-dwípa, 2. 197.

Vasudeva, son of S'úra, son of Devamídhusha, 4. 100, 101. Marries the seven daughters of A'huka, 4. 98. Becomes father of Kŕishńa or Vishńu, 4. 268, 269. Is previously imprisoned, with his wife Devakí, by Kamsa, 4. 259. He burns himself with Kŕishńa's corpse, 5. 154. See also 3. 84; 4. 108, 110, 113, 233, 248, 249, 260, 261; 270, 273, 275, 279, 299, 335, 336, 337; 5. 18, 26, 35, 40, 42, 44, 58, 76, 141, 149, 150. He has the epithet A'nakadundubbi.

Vásudeva, patronym of Kŕishńa or Vishńu, P. 41, 46, 54, 55; 1. 1, 2, 17, 18, 119, 163; 2. 59, &c.; 3. 39, 77, 166, 205, 312; 4. 81, 82, 83, &c., 111; 5. 4, 5, 16, 57, 122, 126, &c. &c. One with the three Vedas, and also one with Om, 3. 39. The word etymologized, 1. 2, 17; 5. 213.

Vasudeva, a Kaṅwa king, 4. 192, 193, 194.

Vásudeva, Pauṅdŕaka, an impostor, 5. 121, 124.

Vásudeva, a title, 5. 122, 123, 129.

Vasudevá, variant of Sutárá, daughter of S'waphalka, 4. 95.

Vasujyeshťha, according to the Matsyá-puráńa, son of Púshpamitra, 4. 191.

Vásuki, a serpent, son of Kaśyapa and Kadrú, 1. 142, 143; 2. 74. 210, 211, 285, &c.; 5. 12, 251, 383. King of the Nágas, 2. 86. His abode, in one of the Pátálas, 2. 210, 211.

Vasumanas, son of Rohidaśwa, 3. 284.

Vasumánas, variant of Sumanas, son of Haryaśwa, 3. 284.

Vasumat, variously genealogized, 3. 14, 15, 232.

Vasumat, son of Kŕishńa and Jámbavatí, 5. 79.

Vasumitra, variously genealogized, 4. 191.

Vasundharas, a caste in S'álmaladwípa, 2. 195.

Vasuruchi, a Gandharva, 1. 188.

Vásusomádhi (?), variant of Somápi, son of Sahadeva, 4. 151 (note §).

Vasuśreshťha, variant of Vasujyeshťha, 4. 191.

Vasuvarchas (??) variant of Sudhanwan, son of S'áśwata, 3. 334.

Vaswasanta (??), variant of S'áśwata, son of S'ruts, 3. 334.

Vaswaukasárá, the same as Amarávatí, Indra's city, 2. 240.

Vaswokasárá, a river in India, 2.
121.

Váta, a Rákshasa, 2. 285, &c.

Vata, a tree, the Ficus Indica, 2.
116.

Váta, variant of S'amin, son of
Súra, 4. 99.

Vátadhánas, a people, 2. 167.

Vátajámas (?), a people, 2. 175.

Vátajámaratboragas (?), a people,
2. 175.

Vataka (??), son of Chakora or
Chakorasátakarnin, 4. 198.

Vátápi, son of Hráda, 2, 69.
Called son of Viprachitti, 2.
71.

Vátáyanas, a people, 2. 176.

Vátáyudha (?), variant of Abhayada, 4. 127.

Vatsas, variant of Matsyas, 2.
158.

Vatsa, a Nága, 2. 287; 5. 251.

Vatsa, son of Pratardana, son of
Divodása, 4. 24, 36.

Vatsa, the same as Pratardana,
son of Divodása, 4. 35. (Perhaps this is the Vatsa named
in 4. 40.)

Vatsa, son of some Vatsa, according to the Váyu-purána, 4. 38.

Vatsa, the same as Vatsabhúmi, (?)
4. 38, 39.

Vatsa, son of Uruksbepa, son of
Bŕihatkshaṇa, 4. 167.

Vatsa, a region in India, 2. 158.

Vatsa (??), variant of Vatsahanu,
4. 141.

Vatsabálaka, son of Súra, son of
Devamíd'husha, 4. 101, 113,

Vatsabhúmi, variously genealogized, 4. 37-39.

Vatsahanu, son of Senajit, son of
Viswajit, 4. 141.

Vatsaka, son of Súra, son of
Devamíd'husha, 4. 101.

Vatsandbamaka (??), variant of
Vatsabálaka, 4. 101.

Vatsaprí, son of Bhalandana, 3.
241, 242.

Vatsapríti, the same as Vatsaprí,
3. 241, 242.

Vatsara, son of Dhruva, son of
Uttánapáda, 1. 178.

Vatsára, sprung from Kaśyapa,
son of Marichi, 3. 15.

Vatsara, a certain cyclic year, 2.
255.

Vatsarája, 'king of Vatsa,' intending Udayana, 2. 158; 4. 163.

Vatsaśrí (??), variant of Vatsaprí,
3. 242.

Vatsavat (??), variant of Vatsabálaka, 4. 113.

Vatsavŕiddha (??), variant of Vatsavyúha, 4. 167.

Vatsavyúha, variously genealogized, 4. 167.

Vátsya, disciple of S'ákalya, and
promulgator of the Rig-veda, 3.
46.

Vátsya, promulgator of the White
Yajur-veda, 3. 57.

Vátsyáyana, the same as Kautilya,
4. 186.

Váyavíya-purána = Váyu-purána,
P. 35, 36.

Váyavya, the same as Swáti, an
asterism, 2. 277.

Váyu, 'wind.' Produced from the
rudiment of touch, produces the
rudiment of form, 1. 35, 36.
As a god, P. 3, 35, 37, 38, 86;

1. 180; 2. 79, 80; 3, 118; 4. 159. Is king of the Gandharvas, 2. 86. Kŕíshńa sends him on an errand to Indra, 5. 45, 46. A form of Vishńu, in Sálmala-dwípa, 2. 194. His city, as a Lokapála, 2. 112, 118.

Vayuna, son of Kŕíśáśwa, 2. 29.

Váyu-puráńa, analysis of it, &c., P. 7, 17, 18, 24, 26, 35, 86, 87, 89; 1. 121; 5. 308.

Váyuputra, patronym of Hanumat, 1. 117.

Vedas. Their main scope, P. 1, &c. Their extent, 3. 63. Typified by Om, 1. 1, 2. Their various parts produced from various parts of Brahmá's body, 1: 84–86. Divisions and promulgators of them, &c. &c., 3. 33-63. Division of one original Veda into the four Vedas, 3. 31, 33. The original Veda a composition containing one hundred thousand stanzas, 3. 40.

Vedá, a river in India, 2. 145.

Vedabáhu, son of Pulastya, 1. 155.

Vedabáhu, a Ŕishi in the fifth Manwantara, 3. 10.

Vedadarśa, disciple of Sumantu, and teacher of the Atharvaveda, 3. 61, 62.

Vedagarbhá, a female form of Vishńu, 4. 262, 265.

Vedaká, an Apsaras, 2. 82.

Vedamitra, another name of Sákalya, promulgator of the Rig-veda, 3. 45.

Vedaná, 'torture,' daughter of

Anŕita, and wife of Raurava, 1. 112.

Vedángas, 'sciences dependent on the Vedas.' These, six in number, are enumerated in 3. 67. See also 3. 174; 5. 2.

Vedánta, a system of philosophy, P. 41, 94; 1. 172, 199; 2. 6, 95; 4. 253, 256; 5. 4, 200.

Vedánta-paribháshá, a Vedánta treatise, quoted, 2. 337.

Vedasiní, a river in India, 2. 131, 145, 146.

Vedaśira, son of Kŕíśáśwa, 2. 29.

Vedaśiras, son of Márkańdeya, 1. 152, 155.

Vedaśiras, son of Prána, son of Dhátŕi, 1. 200.

Vedaśiras, according to the Bhágavata-puráńa, a Ŕishi in the fifth Manwantara, 3. 10.

Vedaśiras, a Muni who became master of Pátála, and who aided in transmitting the Vishńu-puráńa (identical with some Vedaśiras before mentioned?), 5. 251.

Vedaśiras (who?), 3. 3, 17.

Vedasmŕitá, a river in India (one with the Vedasmŕiti?), 2. 144, 340.

Vedasmŕiti, a river in India (now called the Beos?), 2. 130, 131, 339, 340.

Vedasparśa, disciple of Kabandha, and promulgator of the Atharva-veda, 3. 61.

Vedaśrí, a Ŕishi in the fifth Manwantara, 3. 10.

Vedaśrutas, according to the Bha-

gavata-puráña, a class of gods in the third Manwantara, 3. 6.

Vedáśwá, a river in India, 2. 151.

Vedavainásiká, a river in India, 2. 145, 146.

Vedavatí, an Apsaras, 2. 82.

Vedavatí, a river in India, 2. 144, 146, 339.

Vedavit, 'a Bráhman who understands the meaning of the text of the Vedas,' 3. 174, 175.

Vedavyása, 3. 31, 33, 41; 5. 180. See Vyása.

Vedha, equivalent to one hundred Truťis, 1. 48.

Vedhaka, a hell, 2. 218.

Vedhas, another name of Brahmá, 1. 83, 100; 3. 56.

Vediká, what, in architecture, 5. 31.

Vegasáras, a people, 2. 179.

Vegavat, son of Bandhumat, 3. 245.

Vegavat, son of Kŕishńa and Satyá, 5. 79.

Vegavatí, a river in India (now called the Vyki), 2. 155.

Vegavatyas, a class of Apsarases, 2. 75, 82.

Vegetables, creation of, and kinds of, 1. 70.

Vegipúyavaha (??), variant of Púyavaha, 2. 218.

Velá, daughter of Meru, and wife of Samudra, 1. 157.

Vena, son of Anga, son of Úru, P. 42 (where correct the spelling); 1. 177, &c. See Veńa (??).

Vena, Vyása of the twenty-second Dwápara age, 3. 35. See Rájaśravas. See Veńa (??):

Vena (??), (who ?), 3. 70.

Veńá, a river in India, 2. 150.

Vena, variant of Prámśu, son of Vaivaswata, 3. 232.

Veńa (??), variant of Vena, son of Anga, and of the Vyása, respectively, P. 42; 3. 35.

Veńá, variant of Pará, a river, 2. 147.

Veńí, a river in India, 2. 150.

Venkas, a people, 2. 104, 105.

Venkaťas (??), variant of Venkas, 2. 104.

Venkaťa (??), a country, 2. 104.

Venkaťa, a hill in India, 2. 141.

Venkaťa Adhwarin, a modern author, referred to, 2. 134.

Venkaťádri, the temple of, in the Deccan, P. 34.

Veńu, son of Vaivaswata, the Manu, 3. 232.

Veńu, a Yádava king, variously genealogized, 4. 53, 54.

Veńuhaya, variant of Veńu, the Yádava king, 4. 53.

Veńuhotra, according to the Bhágavata - puráña, son of Dhŕishťaketu, son of Satyaketu, 4. 37–39.

Veńuhotŕi (??), variant of Veńuhotra, 4. 37.

Veńuká, variant of Renuká or Dheńuká, the river so called, 2. 199.

Veńumat, ruler over the kingdom of Veńumat, and son of Jyotishmat, king of Kuśa-dwípa, 2. 195.

Veńumat, a division of Kuśa-dwípa, 2. 195.

Vetála, his devotion to Deví, P. 90.

Vetálabhaṭṭa, an author, referred to the court of king Vikramáditya, P. 8.

Vetasiní (⁇), variant of Vedavatí, the river so called, 2. 145.

Vetravatí, Vetrávatí, the river now popularly called the Betwa, 2. 131, 143, 147, 340.

Vetravatí (⁇), variant of Chandrabhágá, 2. 147.

Veṭṭahaya (⁇), variant of Veńu, the Yádava king, 4. 53.

Vibhá, the same as Vibhávarí, 2. 240.

Vibhása, one of the seven suns, 5. 191.

Vibhávarí, Soma's city, where situated, 2. 240. Etymology of the word, 2. 342.

Vibhávasu, a Dánava, son of Kaśyapa, son of Maríchi, 2. 70.

Vibhávasu, 'fire,' 5. 197.

Vibhávasu (?), variant of Vibháss, 5. 191.

Vibhíshaṇa, a Rákshasa, according to the Bhágavata-puráńa, son of Viśravas, son of Pulastya, 1. 154.

Vibhrája, son of Sukṛiti, son of Pṛithu, 4. 141.

Vibhu, a transformation of Vishńu, when he appeared as son of Vedaśiras and Tushitá, 3. 17.

Vibhu, Indra in the fifth Manwantara, 3. 9.

Vibhu, son of Prastáva, 2. 107.

Vibhu, variously genealogized, 4. 37, 38.

Vibhu, variant of Vipra, son of Śrutanjaya, 4. 174.

Vibhúti, 'superhuman or divine power or dignity,' &c. &c., 2. 89; 3. 251; 4. 256.

Vibhúti, variant of Ativibhúti, (?) 3. 243.

Vibudha, son of Kṛita (?) or Kṛiti, son of Kírttiratha, 3. 331.

Vichakshus (⁇), variant of Nichakru, 4. 163, 164.

Vicháru (⁇), variant of Busheńa, son of Kṛishńa, 5. 78.

Vichitra, son of Ruchya, the Manu, 3. 28.

Vichitrá, variant of Pavitrá, a river in India, 2. 148.

Vichitravírya, son of Śántanu, 4. 157, 158.

Vidagdha, promulgator of the White Yajur-veda, 3. 57.

Vidáman (⁇), variant of Anenas, son of Áyus, 4. 30.

Vidarbhas, a people, 2. 164; 5. 69.

Vidarbhas, variant of Sunayas, 2. 181.

Vidarbha, a king, father of Keśiní, 3. 297.

Vidarbha, son of Jyámagha, 4. 64, 66.

Vidarbha, a country, now called Berar, P. 107; 2. 144, 145, 157, 171, 173; 3. 285; 4. 112, 134; 5. 69–71.

Viddhisára (⁇), variant of Bimbisára, 4. 180.

Videhas, a people, 2. 165.

Videha, a country, 3. 221, 330; 4. 64, 84, 344.

Vidahá (?), a city (?), 2. 341.

Videśa (?), a country, 4. 213. See Vidiśa.

Vidhátri, 'Brahmá, as protector,' 5. 15.

Vidhátri, son of Bhrigu, 1. 118, 152, 157; 2. 307; 3. 118.

Vidhátri, the same as Vishńu, or an epithet of him, 5. 11 (where "Brahmá," in the text, must be wrong), 214.

Vidhideva (??), son of Vasudeva, son of Súra, 4. 110.

Vidhisára (??), variant of Bimbisára, 4. 180.

Vidhriti, 'a holy ordinance,' 2. 338.

Vidhriti (??), variant of Dhyushi-táswa, 3. 322, 323.

Vidbhu (??), variant of Vipra, son of of Srutanjaya, 4. 174.

Vidiśa (?), Vidiśá (?), a country, 3. 221; 4. 191, 213. See Vaidiśá.

Vidiśá, a river in India, perhaps that now popularly called the Bess, 2. 150.

Vidisára (??), variant of Bimbisára, 4. 180.

Vidmisára (??), variant of Bimbisára, 4. 180, 181, 186.

Vidruma, a mountain in Kuśa-dwípa, 2. 196.

Vidula, son of Durgama (?), son of Dhrita, 4. 119.

Vidupa, son of Durgama (?), son of Dhrita, 4. 119.

Vidura, son of Krishńadwaipá-yana, P. 41; 4. 158.

Vidúratha (who?), father of Su-nandá, 3. 242.

Vidúratha, a king (who?), 3. 268; 4. 153; 5. 70.

Vidúratha, sprung from Púru, son of Jahnu, 4. 24.

Vidúratha, son of Bhajamána, 4. 99.

Vidúratha, son of Suratha, son of Jahnu, 4. 153.

Vidúratha (??), variant of Viprithu, son of Chitraka, 4. 96.

Vidut (??), a Veda of the Magas, 5. 383.

Vidyás, certain branches of know-ledge, of four kinds, particular-ized, 1. 148.

Vidyádharas, 'a kind of demigods,' 1. 82, 122; 5. 246.

Vidyádharís, 'a kind of demigod-desses,' 1. 135.

Vidyávatí, an Apsaras, 2. 82.

Vidyudambhá (??), variant of Vi-dyudambhas, 2. 196.

Vidyudambhas, a river in Kuśa-dwípa, 2. 196.

Vidyudushńá (?), variant of Vid-yudambhas, 2. 196.

Vidyudwarńá (??), an Apsaras, 2. 82.

Vidyut, a Rákshasa, 2, 285, &c.

Vidyutparńá, an Apsaras, 2. 81, 82.

Vihangamas, a class of gods in the eleventh Manwantara, 3. 26.

Vijáti, according to the Linga-puráńa, son of Nahusha, son of Áyus, 4. 46.

Vijayas, a people, 2. 166.

Vijaya, variously genealogized, 3. 289.

Vijaya, son of Jaya, 3. 335.

Vijaya, son of Purúravas, son of Budha, 4. 13, 14.

Vijaya, son of Jaya or Vijaya, 4. 43, 44. (Perhaps this is the same as Vijaya, son of Jaya, named above. The doubt here may begin as far back as Ane-

nas; for, by Aneuas, son of Kshemári, and Anenas, son of Áyus, one and the same person may be intended.)

Vijaya, variously genealogized, 4. 125, 126.

Vijaya, an Andhra king, son of Yajnaśrí, &c., 4. 199, 201.

Vijaya, son of Krishńa and Jámbavatí, 5. 79.

Vijayá, daughter of Daksha, and wife of Krisáśwa, 2. 29, 337; 3. 82.

Vijayá, wife of Sahadeva, son of Dasra, 4. 159.

Vijayanagara, a city in Southern India, P. 34.

Vijitáśwa, the same as Antardhána, son of Prithu, 1. 192.

Vijnána, 'internal sensation or intelligence,' 3. 210, 218; 5. 204.

Vijnáneśwara, a commentator on Yájnavalkya, 3. 102, 187.

Vikala, a measure of time, equivalent to six Práńas, 1. 48.

Vikala (?), variant of Vikriti, son of Jímúta, 4. 68.

Vikala (?), variant of Ivilaka, or Apílaka, 4. 196.

Vikalpas, variant of Vikalyas, 2. 178.

Vikalpa, what, in Vaidik literature, 3. 62, 69.

Vikalpa, what, in philosophy, 4. 241.

Vikalyas, a people, 2. 178.

Vikarńi (?), variant of Chakoraśátakarńin, 4. 197.

Vikartri, 'transformer,' 5. 90.

Vikáśa, what, in philosophy, 1. 29.

Vikeśí, wife of Sarva, the Rudra, and mother of Lohitánga, 1. 117; 2. 259.

Vikhanas, father of Vasira, 3. 337.

Vikramáditya, King, son of Gardabhila, P. 7–9; 1. 61, 62; 5. 337, 392. (Perhaps two persons are intended, and one of them fictitious.)

Vikramorvaśí, the, a drama, referred to, 2. 287; 4. 5.

Vikránta, a Prajápati, according to the Váyu-puráńa, 1. 102.

Vikrishna (?), variant of Gaurakrishńa, 4. 200.

Vikrita, son of Daksha, the Prajápati, 1. 103.

Vikriti, son of Jímúta, son of Vyoman, 4. 68.

Vikriti, what, in philosophy, 1. 76.

Vikukshi, surnamed Saśáda, son of Ikshwáku, 3. 259–261, 297.

Vikuńthá, wife of Subhra, and mother of Vishńu, 3. 17; 4. 278.

Vilohita, variant of Vimohana, 2. 214 (where correct the spelling).

Vilomaka (?), variant of Viloman, 4. 97.

Viloman, a Yádava king, variously genealogized, 4. 97.

Vilwisára (?), variant of Bimbisára, 4. 181.

Vimala, son of Sudyumna, son of Vaivaswata, 3. 237.

Vimati (?), variant of Vinśati, 3. 260.

Vimochaní, a river in Sálmaladwípa, 2. 194.

Vimoha, the same as Vimohana, 2. 217.

Vimohana, a certain hell, 2. 214. See the last.

Vimśa, variously genealogized, 3. 242, 243.

Vimśaja, a certain king, 4. 212.

Vimśati, son of Ikshwáku, 3. 260.

Vimukti, what, in theology, 5. 242.

Viná, a river in India, 2. 148.

Vinadí, a river in India, 2. 150.

Vinata, son of Sudyumna, son of Vaivaswata, 3. 237.

Vinatá, daughter of Daksha, and wife of Kaśyapa, otherwise called Tárksha, P. 83 ; 2. 26, 28, 73 ; 3. 298.

Vinatáśwa, son of Sudyumna, son of Vaivaswata, 3. 237.

Vinaya, 'prudence,' son of Dharma and Kriyá, 1. 110.

Vinaya, son of Sudyumna, son of Vaivaswata, 3. 237.

Vinda, son of Jayasena, the Ávantya, 4. 103 ; 5. 82.

Vindhusára (??), variant of Bimbisára, 4. 181.

Vindhyas, a race, 4. 213-215.

Vindhya, a mountain-range in Central India, P. 55, 107 ; 1. 181 ; 2. 113, 127, 128, 130, 141, 339 ; 3. 240, 260, 319 ; 4. 59, 77, 219, 221 ; 5. 387.

Vindhyachulikas (as, probably, the name should be written, and not Vindhyachulukas, Vindhyachulakas, or the like), a people, 2. 179.

Vindhyamauleyas, a people mentioned in the Márkańdeya-puráńa, 2. 180.

Vindhyamúlikas, variant of Vindhyachulikas, 2. 179.

Vindhyapálakas, variant of Vindhyachulikas, 2. 179.

Vindhyaśakti, a certain king, 4. 210, 212, 213.

Vindhyasena (?), variant of Bimbisára, 4. 180.

Vindhyavásiní, a place near Mirzapore, on the Ganges, 4, 262.

Viníta, son of Pulastya, according to the Váyu-puráńa, 1. 155.

Vipápá, a river in India, 2. 143, 153, 340.

Vipápá, variant of Vipáśá, a river in Plaksha-dwípa, 2. 192.

Vipápman (?), variant of Anenas, son of Áyus, 4. 30.

Viparyaya, what, in philosophy, 1. 69.

Vipáś, a river in India, 2. 121. (This is the ancient name of the Vipáśá.)

Vipáśá, a river in India, the Byásá or Beas, popularly so called, 2. 143, 144, 169 ; 3. 170 ; 4. 118. (It is identified with the Hyphasis or Bibasis. And see the last article.)

Vipáśá, a river in Plaksha-dwípa, 2. 192.

Vipaśchit, Indra in the second Manwantara, 3. 3.

Viplava, 'disappearance,' 3. 29.

Vipra, son of Slishti, 1. 177.

Vipra, son of Srutanjaya, 4. 174.

Viprachitti, son of Kaśyapa and Danu, 1. 145, 148 ; 2. 30, 55, 70, 71 ; 5. 87. King of the Dánavas, 2. 86.

Viprachitti, an Apsaras, 2. 81, 83, 291.

Viprarshi, the same as Brahmarshi, 5. 121.

Viprishta, according to the Bhágavata-puráńa, son of Vasudeva, son of Súra, 4. 111.

Viprithu, son of Chitraka, 4. 96; 5. 148.

Vipula, son of Vasudeva, son of Súra, 4. 109.

Vipula, a mountain serving as buttress to Mount Meru, to the west, 2. 111, 115.

Vipura, what, in philosophy, 1. 31, 32.

Víras, according to the Bhágavata-puráńa, a class of gods in the fourth Manwantara, 3. 7.

Víra, son of Swáyambhuva, 1. 108.

Víra, son of Gŕinjima (?), 4. 113.

Víra, according to the Bhágavata-puráńa, son of Kŕishńa and Kálindí, 5. 79.

Víra, according to the Bhágavata-puráńa, son of Kŕishńa and Nágnajití or Satyá, 5. 79.

Vírá, a river in India, 2. 148.

Víra (?), variant of Vimśa, son of Kahnpa, 3. 242.

Vírabhadra, created by Maheśwara or Śiva, is a subordinate of the goddess Deví, 1. 121, 128, 130, &c.; 4. 339. He mauls the gods and goddesses cruelly, 1. 131. See Pinákadhŕik.

Virádha, a Rákshasa slain by Ráma, 3. 316.

Vírahotras, variant of Vítihotras, 4. 58.

Vírahotra, variant of Vítihotra, 4. 57.

Viráj, ' Vishńu, as the first male,' ' Brahmá, the creator,' &c., 1. 59, 105, &c., 170, 172; 2. 229, 342; 3. 159.

Viráj, son of Nara, son of Gaya, 2. 107.

Virajas, according to the Bhágavata-puráńa, a class of gods in the eighth Manwantara, 3. 24. (On Viraja, as a corruption, see 2. 107, note †.)

Virája, the same as Brahmá, 3. 159.

Virája, a Prajápati, 3. 158, 159.

Viraja, son of Twashtŕi, 2. 107.

Viraja, father of Sudhámau, 2. 262.

Viraja, according to the Bhágavata-puráńa, disciple of Játúkarńya, 3. 48.

Virajá, wife of Nahusha, son of Áyus, 3. 164; 4. 45.

Virajá, mind-born daughter of the Ájyapas, 3. 164.

Viraja-loka, according to the Váyu-puráńa, a region tenanted by the Agnishwáttas, 3. 160.

Virajas, one of the saints called Kumáras, 1. 79.

Virajas, son of Paurńamása, son of Maríchi, 1. 153; 2. 262. See Vairája.

Virajas, son of Vasishtha, the Prajápati, 1. 155.

Virajas, a Rishi in the sixth Manwantara, 3. 12.

Virajas, son of Sávarńi, Manu of the eighth Manwantara, 3. 24.

Virajaska, in the Bhágavata-puráńa, instead of Virajas, son of Sávarńi, 3. 24.

Víraka, according to the Bhága-vata-puráńa, a Rishi in the sixth Manwantara, 3. 14.

Virańa, (who?), father of Push-karińí or Vírańí, 1. 178.

Vírańa, a patriarch, father of Asik-ní, 2. 12, &c. For his identity with Panchajana, see 2. 15.

Vírańa (?!), variant of Viraňin, 3. 57.

Víranagara, a city lying on the river Devíká, 2. 330.

Vírańí, daughter (?!) of some Víraňa, 1. 178. See Pushkariń, her other name.

Víraňin, a promulgator of the White Yajur-veda, 3. 57.

Virankará, a river in India, 2. 149.

Víraratha, variant of Bahuratha, 4. 144.

Vírásana, a certain posture, in the Yoga philosophy, 3. 140; 5. 230.

Vírasena, father of a Nala, 3. 304.

Víravatí, a river in India, 2. 149.

Víravrata, according to the Bhá-gavata-puráńa, son of Madhu, son of Bindumat, 2. 107.

Víriňa (?!), variant of Varuńa, ancestor of Pushkariń, 1. 179.

Virochana, a Daitya, son of Prah-láda, 1. 188; 2. 69; 3. 19, 23; 4. 123, 250; 5. 6.

Viruddhas, a class of gods in the tenth Manwantara, 3. 25.

Virúpa, son of Ambarísha, son of Nábhága, 3. 257.

Virúpáksha, a Rudra, 2. 25.

Virúpáksha, a Dánava, son of Kaśyapa, son of Marichi, 2. 70.

Víryadharas, a caste in Śálmala-dwípa, 2. 195.

Víryavat (?!), variant of Dharmin, son of Bŕihadrája, 4. 169.

Víryavat (?), variant of Vipra, son of Śrutanjaya, 4. 174.

Viś, the same as Vaiśya, 8. 86.

Viśada (?!), variant of Víśwajit, son of Jayadratha, 4. 140.

Viśákha, son of Kumára, son of Agni, 2. 23; 4. 283.

Viśákhá, an asterism, 2. 256, &c.; 3. 167.

Viśákhadhúpa (?), Viśákhapúpa (?), variants of Viśákharúpa (?). 4. 179.

Viśákharúpa (?), son of Pálaka, son of Pradyotana, 4. 179.

Viśákhasúpa (?), Viśákhayúpa (?), variants of Viśákharúpa (?), 4. 179.

Viśála, son of Tŕińabindu, son of Budha, 3. 243, 244, 246.

Viśálá, an Apsaras, 2. 82,

Viśálá, a name of Ujjayiní, 3. 221, 246.

Viśamana (?!), variant of Viśasana, 2. 214.

Viśasana, a certain hell, 2. 214, 215, 218.

Vishámsu (?!), variant of Rushad-gu, 4. 61.

Vishńu, a god of the first order. The same as Brahma, Íśwara, spirit; the cause of creation, preservation, and destruction; the parent of nature, and the material of the universe; the origin, end, and substance of the world, 1. 3–11. His nature, 1. 13, &c. Four forms of him,

1: 17, &c. ; 2. 88. The same
with Brahmá, Vishńu, and Siva,
as creator, preserver, and destroyer, respectively, 1. 41–43.
He is all that is, with particulars, 5. 247, 248. He is one
with Brahma, or supreme spirit,
2. 236. He is the asylum of
all spirit and spirits, 5. 237.
His energy encompasses the
universe, 2. 232, &c. Particulars of its immanence, 2. 294,
&c. He is the same as Áditya,
the Sun, 3. 18. Forms of him
in the four ages of the world,
3. 31. 32. Forms of him worshipped in different Varshas, 2.
125. He sleeps on the serpent
Sesha, in the midst of the ocean,
5. 195. His world or station,
where, 2. 230, 270. His orna-
ments and cognizances, 2. 94.
Is incarnate as Krishńa and
Balabhadra, 4. 258, 259. Is
combined, in all forms, with
Sri, or Lakshmi, &c., 1. 118–
120. Is worshipped in the
form of Váyu, or Wind, by the
inhabitants of Sálmala-dwípa,
2. 194. Is embodied in every
Vyása, 3. 33. Is disguised under
the form of Buddha, for the destruction of the Daityas, 5. 378.
Remembrance of him is the best
expiation, 2. 222, 223. How his
true worshippers are recognis-
able, 3. 76. He is hymned by Pri-
thiví, or Earth, 1. 59–61. He is
lauded by the gods, 1. 139, 140;
4. 251–256. He is praised by
Dhruva, 1.169–173. Is hymned
by the Prachetasas, 1. 196–198.
Is praised by Akrúra, 5. 13–16.
General laudation of him, clos-
ing the Vishńu-puráńa, 5. 254,
255. He is worshipped by Prahláda, 2. 36. The gods pray to
him, 3. 201–205. He directs
the gods to churn the ocean, 1.
142. He deceives the Daityas
and the Dánavas, assisting him
therein, 1. 143. Again he deceives the Daityas, 3. 206 : and
see Máyámoha and 5. 378, referred to already. Various
names of him, Achyuta, Ananta,
Govinda, Hrishikesa, Kesava,
Mádhava, Yajnesa, &c., 2. 313.
He has a thousand names or
epithets, 1. 5, 41. The word
Vishńu expounded and etymologized, 1. 4, 5 ; 3. 19. Besides
the names specified above,
Vishńu is called Bhagavat,
Bhútesa, Hari, Ísa, Janárdana,
Mahídhara, Makhesa, Murári,
Nara, Náráyańa, Purusha, Pu-
rushottama, Sárngadhanwan,
Sárngin, Satya, Satyasena,
Sauri, Swadhá, Swáhá, Trivi-
krama, Tushita, Vaikuńtha,
Vibhu, Vidhátri, Viswabhávana,
Viswarúpa, Yajna, Yajurmúrti,
Yajnapati, Yajnapurńa, Yujna-
purusha, Yajnárádhya, Yajnes-
wara, &c. &c.

Vishńu, an Áditya, 2. 27, 285, &c.
Chief of the Ádit. 2. 85.
Vishńu, a Rishi in the eleventh
Manwantara, 3. 26.
Vishńu (?), variant of Dhrishta,
son of Vaivaswata, 3. 13.

Vishńubhá, the same as S'ravańa, an asterism, 2. 276.

Vishńudharma, a composition, quoted, 2. 222.

Vishńudharmottara, a composition, quoted, 3. 339.

Vishńugupta, the same as Kautilya, 4. 186.

Vishńu-loka, the site of, 2. 230. And see Vishńupada.

Vishńupada, the station of Vishńu,' its situation, 2. 270. It is represented as being a mountain, or as situated on one, in 4. 124 (note 1). And see Vishńuloka.

Vishńu-puráńa. Size of it, P. 24, 34, 35; 1. 9. Analysis of it, P. 92, &c. Its approximate age, P. 112. Its origin and extent, 3. 66. Merit of hearing it, 5. 246, &c. How communicated, 5. 250, &c. Its characteristics, &c., 5. 264, 272, 273, &c. &c. And see Vaishńava-puráńa.

Vishńuvŕiddhas, a race sprung from Vishńuvŕiddha, 3. 284.

Vishńuvŕiddha, son of Sambhúti, son of Purukutsa, according to the Linga-puráńa, 3. 284.

Vishńuyaśas, a Bráhman in whose family Kalki is to be born, 4. 229.

Vishtaráśwa (?), variant of Viśwagáśwa (rightly, Vishwagaśwa), 3. 263.

Vishwagjyotis, eldest of the hundred sons of S'atajit, son of Raja, 2. 107.

Viśoka, a Kumára, 1. 79.

Viśoká, 'exemption alike from infirmity and from grief,' 1. 91.

Viśránta, a king named in the Márkańd'eya-puráńa, 3. 11.

Viśravas, son of Pulastya, the Prajápati, 1. 10, 154; 3. 68, 246.

Viśruta, according to the Bhágavata-puráńa, incarnation of the Vasus, and son of Vasudeva, son of S'úra, 4. 111.

Viśruta (?), variant of S'ruta, son of Bhagíratha, 3. 303.

Viśruta (?), variant of Vibudha, 3. 332.

Viśrutavat, son of Mahaswat, 3. 325.

Vistára, 'diameter,' 2. 206.

Viśuddhas (?), variant of Viruddhas, the gods so called, 3. 25.

Viśwas (?), a class of subordinate gods, 3. 14; 5. 101, 143. See Viśwe devas.

Viśwá, daughter of Daksha, and wife of Dharma, 2. 21. Mother of the Viśwe devas, 2. 21; 3. 191.

Viśwabhávana; a title of the god Vishńu, its import, &c., 1. 1–3.

Viśwabhávana, a Kumára, 1. 79.

Viśwáchí, an Apsaras, 2. 75, 81–83, 285, 288, 291, 293; 4. 48.

Viśwadevas, intending Viśwe devas, which see, and also 3. 178 (note ‖).

Viśwadhára, ruler over the realm of Viśwadhara, and son of Medhátithi, sovereign of S'ákadwípa, 2. 200.

Viśwadhára, a division of S'ákadwípa, 2. 200.

Viśwaga (??), variant of Viśwa-gaśwa (rightly, Vishwagaśwa), 3. 263.

Viśwagandhi (??), variant of Viśwa-gaśwa (rightly, Vishwagaśwa), 3. 263.

Viśwagaśwa (rightly, Vishwagaś-wa), son of Prithu, son of Anenas, 3. 263.

Viśwagata (??), variant of Viśwa-gaśwa (rightly, Vishwagaśwa), 3. 263.

Viśwa-gochara, what, in philo-sophy, 5. 234.

Viśwaguńádarśa, the, a modern Sanskrit composition, referred to, 2. 134.

Viśwajit, son of Jayadratha, son of Bŕihatkarman, 4. 140.

Viśwajit, son of Satyajit, son of Sunítá, 4. 176.

Viśwajit (?), variant of Juname-jaya, son of Dŕidharatha, 4. 126.

Viśwaka (??), variant of Viśwa-gaśwa (rightly, Vishwagaśwa), 3. 263.

Viśwakarman, the architect of the gods, son of Prabhása, the Vasu, 1. 145 ; 2. 24 ; 3. 70, 253, 272 ; 5. 344, 345. (A Viśwakarman, this, or some other, is named in 3. 20, &c.)

Viśwakarman (who?), father of Bárhishmatí, according to the Bhágavata-puráńa, 2. 100.

Viśwakarman, 'wind,' 2. 83.

Viśwakarman, a certain ray of the sun, 2. 297, 298 ; 5. 191.

Viśwakáryo, a certain ray of the sun, 2. 298.

Viśwaksena (rightly, Vishwak-

sena), Manu of the fourteenth Manwantara, according to some Puráńas, 3. 25.

Viśwakseua (rightly, Vishwak-sena), son of Brahmadátta, 4. 142 ; 5. 158.

Viśwamahat, according to the Váyu-puráńa, son of Viśwakar-man, and husband of Yaśodá, mind-born daughter of the Upa-hútas, 3. 163.

Viśwámitra, son of Gádhi, 3. 16 ; 4. 18. His descendants, 4. 25, &c. His elder sons cursed to become progenitors of most abject races, as Andhrás, &c., 2. 170. A Rájarshi, or royal Rishi, 3. 68. He figures as Rishi in the current Manwan-tara, 3. 13. President over a month, 2. 285, &c. He is changed into a crane, by a curse, 3. 288. He raises Tri-śanku to heaven, 3. 285-287. He induces Kámadhenu, the cow, to produce certain nations for him, the Pahlavas, Śakas, &c., 3. 339. His variance with Vasishťha, P. 39, 56, 108 ; 1. 7 ; 3. 306 ; 4. 22. His Tírtha, 2. 150.. See also 3. 15, 315 ; 4. 19, 22, 39, 51, 138 ; 5. 141.

Viśwámitrá, a river in India, 2. 150.

Viśwananda, a mind-born son of Brahmá, 1. 79.

Viswara, a technicality of the Yoga philosophy, 1. 32.

Viśwarúpa, 'universal substance,' &c., an epithet of Vishńu, 1. 42 ; 4. 257.

Viswarúpa, self-born son of Twashtri, the Rudra, 2. 24.

Viswarúpa (??), variant of Virúpa, son of Ambarisha, 3. 257.

Viswarúpadhara, rendered by "universal," 4. 257 (note *).

Viswarúpin, rendered by "who is the substance of all things," 5. 103.

Viswasaha, variously genealogized, 5. 311, 314.

Viswasaha, son of Dhyushitáswa, 3. 323; 5. 391.

Viswasáhwan (??), variant of Visrutavát, 3. 325; 5. 391.

Viswasarman, father of Viswamahat, according to the Váyu-puráña, 3. 163 (note ||).

Viswasphání, Viswaspháráni (??), Viswaspháti (??), variants of Viswasphatika, 4. 217.

Viswasphatika, a king in Magadhá, 4. 216; 5. 392.

Viswasphíni (??), Viswasphúrji (??), variants of Viswasphatika, 4. 217.

Viswasphúrti (??), variant of Viswasphatika, 4. 217, 219, 222.

Viswátman, rendered by "universal spirit," 5. 201.

Viswatryarchas, a certain ray of the sun, 2. 297; 5. 191 (where correct Viswavyarchás).

Viswavada, a Veda of the Magas, 5. 383. (It has been identified with the Vísparad of the Zoroastrians.)

Viswávasu, two Gandharvas so called, 1. 122, 144, 190; 2. 285, &c.; 4. 7.

Viswávasu, one of the Viswe devas, 3. 192.

Viswávasu, son of Jamadagni, 4. 20.

Viswávasu, son of Purúravas, son of Budha, 4. 13.

Viswavyachas (??), or "Sun" (??), 2. 83. (Error for Viswavar-chas?)

Viswáyus, son of Purúravas, son of Búdha, 4. 13.

Viswe, 5. 101 (note *). See Viswe devas.

Viswe devas (not Viswadevas: see 3. 178, note ||), certain gods. Sons of Dharma and Viswá, 2. 21, 22. Specified as five, ten, twelve, &c., by various Puráñas, 2. 22; 3. 189-192. Eight personages, and the Aswins, named together in the Ríg-veda, are considered as Viswe devas, 3. 179. Daily offerings to them, 2. 22; 3. 179. They are worshipped at Sráddhas, 3. 158, 178. See also 1. 141, 142; 3. 15, 87, 113, 149, 154, 179-181, 185, 186, 188; 5. 247. It is vaguely rendered "all the gods," in 3. 118, 119, 182; and see 3. 185, text and note ‡. See, further, Vaiswadeva, Vaiswadevika, Viswas, Viswadevas, and Viswe.

Viswesá, the same as Viswá, in two Puráñas, 2. 21.

Viswesá, a philosophical term, 1. 31.

Vitá, what, as variously explained, 2. 104.

Vítahavya, son of Sunaya, son of Rita, 3. 335.

Vîtahavya, (who ?), a king of the Haihayas, who became a Bráhman, 4. 40.

Vîtahotras, a dynasty named with the Bríhadrathas, 4. 178.

Vîtahotra (?), variant of Vainahotra, 4. 38.

Vîtahotra (?), variant of Vîtihotra, 4. 57.

Vîtala, a Pátála, or underworld, 2. 209.

Vîtamaya (?), variant of Abhayada, 4. 127.

Vîtaśokha, a town in Saililá'vatí, 2. 165.

Vîtastá, a river, the Jhelam or Hydaspes, 2. 121, 14¼, 339; 4. 118.

Vitatha, successor of some Bharata, 4. 38.

Vitatha, the same as Bharadwája, son of Bríhaspati, 4. 134-136, 139.

Vîthí, 'a triad of asterisms,' 2. 267, &c. The Vîthís are sons of Bhrigu, 2. 276, 337.

Vîtihotras, a tribe of Haihayas dwelling near the Vindhya mountains, 4. 58, 59.

Vîtihotras, a dynasty comprehending twenty kings, 4. 184.

Vîtihotra, according to the Bhágavata-puráña, son of Priyavrata, and once king of Pushkara-dwípa, 2. 100, 203.

Vîtihotra, son of Indrasenâ, son of Púrva, 3. 335.

Vîtihotra, son of Sukumára, 4. 37.

Vîtihotra, son of Tálajangha, son of Jayadhwaja, 4. 57.

Vîtrishñâ, a river in Sálmaladwípa, 2. 194.

Vivádabhangárñava, a very modern digest of law, referred to, 3. 103.

Vivâhu, a mind-born son of Brahmá, 1. 79.

Vivaswat, 'the Sun,' son of Kaśyapa and Aditi, 3. 20, 230, 231. Called son of Brahmá, 3. 343: and see 3. 297, note ‡, throughout. Is called, in the Váyu-puráña, a Prajápati, 1. 109. Yama is his son, 5. 48. Is reckoned an Áditya, 2. 27, 259, 285, &c.; 3. 56, 116. Is counted among the Lokapálas, and, as such, has a city near Mount Meru, 2, 118. See Vaivaswata, the Manu, his son.

Vivaswat (?), variant of Havishmat, 3. 14.

Viveka, what, in philosophy, 5. 210.

Viviktanáman, ruler over the kingdom of Viviktanáman, and son of Hiráñyaretas, sovereign of Kuśa-dwípa, 2. 197.

Viviktanáman, a region in Kuśadwípa, 2. 197.

Vivilaka (?), Vivilika (?), variants of Ivílaka, 4. 196.

Viviṁśas, a caste in Plakshadwípa, 2. 193.

Viviṁśa, son of Viṁśa, 3. 243.

Viviṁśati, in the Bhágavata-puráña, instead of Viviṁśa, 3. 243.

Viyati, Viyáti (?), son of Nahusha, son of Áyus, 4. 45, 46.

Vod'hu, son of Brahmá, in Swetadwípa, 2. 200.

Vraja, son of Havirdhána, 1. 193.

Vraja, a district in India, 4. 276.

281, 282, 287–289, 296, 306, 308, 312, 316, 321–323, 326, 331, 335, 342 ; 5. 11, 64, 68.

Vrata, son of Chákshusha, the Manu, 1. 178.

Vrata, an observance of a specific . kind, P. 63, 64, 82, 84, 99.

Vrata (?), variant of Darva, 4. 121.

Vratacharyá, translated by "the diligent observance of self-denial," 5. 181.

Vrateyu, son of Raudráśwa, 4. 128, 129.

Vriddha-chánakya, the, an ancient composition, referred te, 4. 42.

Vriddha Garga, an astronomer, 2. 255.

Vriddhakarman, variant of Viéwa-saha, 3. 314.

Vriddhaśarman (who ?), 3. 164.

Vriddhaśarman, son of Ilavila, 3. 311, 314.

Vriddhaśarman, a Kárúsha king, 4. 103.

Vriddhaśarman (?), variant of Kshattravriddha, son of Áyus, 4. 30.

Vriddhi-śráddha, 'a sacrifice on an accession of prosperity,' &c., 3. 99, 147, 149.

Vrijinavat (?), Vrijinivat (?), Vrijínivat (?), variants of Vrijinivat, 4. 61.

Vrijinívat, son of Kroshtu, 4. 61.

Vrikas, a people, 2. 179.

Vrika, according to the Bhága-vata-puráña, son of Prithu, son of Vena, 1. 192.

Vrika, son of Ruruka, 3. 289.

Vrika, according to the Bhága-

vata-puráña, son of Devamí-dhusha,. son of Súra, 4. 101.

Vrika, son of Krishña and Mitra-vindá, 5. 79. But son of Krish-ña and Mádrí, 5. 107.

Vrikadevá, daughter of· Devaka, son of Áhuka, and wife of Vasu-deva, son of Súra, 4. 98.

Vrikadevi (?), variant of Vrika-devá, 4. 110.

Vrikala, són of Slishti, 1. 177.

Vrikatejas, son of Slishti, 1. 177.

Vrikshas (?), variant of Krishñas, the name of a caste in Sálmala-dwípa, 2. 194.

Vrindávana, a certain famous forest, P. 22, 66, 110; 4. 246, 282, 283, 286, 325, 329, 335, 339 ; 5. 65, 285, 345.

Vrisha, Indra of the eleventh Manwantara, 3. 26.

Vrisha, according to the Linga-puráña, son of Nriga or Na-bhaga, 3. 335.

Vrisha, son of Bharata, son of Tálajangha, 4. 57.

Vrisha, according to the Hari-vaṃśa, son of Vrishasena, 4. 126.

Vrisha, son of Krishña and Ká-lindá, 5, 79.

Vrisha, son of Krishña and Satyá, 5, 79.

Vrisha, a horse of the Moon, 2. 299.

Vrisha (?), variant of Vrika, son of Vijaya, 3. 289.

Vrisha (?), variant of Vrishaña, son of Súrasena, 4. 57.

Vrisha (?), variant of Vrishñi, son of Krikaña, 4. 72.

Vrishabha, king of kine, 2. 85.

Vrishabhá, a river in India, 2. 152, 340.

Vrishabhá, the same as Árshabhí, 2. 276.

Vrishabha, the older word for Ŕishabha, the mountain so called, 2. 340.

Vrishabba (¶), variant of Vrishaṇa, son of Arjuna, 4. 57.

Vrishabha (?), variant of Ŕishabha, son of Kuśágra, 4. 150.

Vrishadarbhas, a people sprung from Vrishadarbha, 4. 121.

Vrishadarbha, son of Sibi, son of Uśínara, 4. 121.

Vrishadevá (?), variant of Vrikadevá, 4. 98.

Vrishaká, a river in India, 2. 154.

Vrishakáhwayá (?), a river in India, 2. 154.

Vrishákapi, a Rudra, 2. 24, 25.

Vrishalí, definition of, 3. 176.

Vrishaṇa, son of Arjuna, son of Kritavírya, 4. 57.

Vrishaṇa (?), according to some authorities, son of Madhu, 4. 58. (The better reading seems to be Vrishṇi.)

Vrishaparvan, a Dánava, son of Kaśyapa, son of Maŕichi, 2. 70; 4. 46, 47, 132.

Vrishasá, variant of Vrishaká, 2. 154.

Vrishasena, son of Karṇa, 4. 126.

Vrishṇis, a people, 2. 159; 5. 150, 159.

Vrishṇis, a family sprung from Vrishṇi, son of Madhu, 4. 58.

Vrishṇi, son of Madhu, 4. 58; 5. 56, 110, 163.

Vrishṇi, son of Kunti, son of Kratha, 4. 68.

Vrishṇi, son of Satwata, 4. 71, 73, 74, 93, 116.

Vrishṇi, son of Bhajamána, son of Satwata, 4. 72.

Vrishṇi, son of Anamitra, 4. 94.

Vrishṇi (?), variant of Vishṇu, the Ŕishi so called, 3. 26.

Vrishṇi (?), variant of Vrishaṇa, son of Arjuna, 4. 57.

Vrishṇi (?), variant of Prishṇi, 4. 94.

Vrishṇi (?), variant of Vrishṭa, son of. Kukura, 4. 97.

Vrishṇimat, son of Suchiratha, 4. 164.

Vrishṭa, son of Kukura, 4. 97.

Vrishṭadharma, variant of Drishṭasárman, 4. 96.

Vrishṭi (?), variant of Vrishṭa, son of Kukura, 4. 97.

Vrishṭimat (?), variant of Vrishṇimat, 4. 164.

Vrita (?), variant of Vrishṇi, son of Kunti, 4. 68.

Vrita (?), variant of Mridura, 4. 96.

Vrita (?), variant of Dhrita, son of Dharma, 4. 119.

Vritaka (?), variant of Vrika, son of Ruruka, 3. 289.

Vriteyu (?), variant of Ghriteyu, 4. 129.

Vritra, an Asura or demon slain by Indra, P. 40, 56; 2. 79; 4. 258; 5. 354.

Vritraghní, a river in India, 2. 155.

Vritrahan, an epithetical designation of Indra, 5. 354.

Vṛitraripu, an epithetical designation of Indra, 4. 258.

Vṛitti, variant of Dhṛiti, wife of the Rudra Manu, 1. 117.

Vyádhi, 'disease,' son of Mṛityu, 1. 112.

Vyághra, a Rákshasa, 2. 285, &c.

Vyághraśweta, variant of Vyághra, 2. 292.

Vyághrívan (?), variant of Vaprivan, 3. 34.

Vyáhṛitis, three certain mystical terms so called, 3. 38, 39.

Vyákaraña, 'grammar,' an Anga of the Vedas, 3. 67.

Vyakta, what, in philosophy, P. 94; 1. 15, 19.

Vyála, the term defined, 3. 138.

Vyámas, a class of Pitṛis, allotted to the lowest castes, 3. 163, 339.

Vyaṁśa, son of Víprachitti, 2. 71.

Vyangala (?), variant of Varánga, 4. 211.

Vyanjana, 'pot-herbs and the like,' 3. 181.

Vyápin, what, in philosophy, 1. 201.

Vyápta (?), variant of Vyoman, son of Daśárha, 4. 68.

Vyáptimátra, what, in philosophy, 2. 91.

Vyása. The generic name of a transformation of Vishṇu, and arranger of the Vedas, in every Dwápara age, 3. 33. The sixth Vyása, a Rishi, son of Puráśara and Satyavatí, in the current Dwapara age, especially so called, P. 17; 3. 23; 4. 150, 158: see Bádaráyaña, Dwaipáyana, and

Kṛishṇadwaipáyana. Of his son, Suka, P. 40, 46; 4. 142: and see Suka. His conjectured time, 4. 232. The twenty-eighth Vyásas, their names, &c., 3. 33-37. The present Vyása communicates the Kriyá-yogasára to Jaimini, P. 33. He distributes the Veda, P. 39; 3. 43. He teaches the Bhágavata-puráña to Suka, P. 46. He arranges the Vedas, Itihásas, and Puráñas, P. 98; 3. 41, 42. He gives an account of the Magas to Sámba, 5. 383, 384. See also 4. 161, 162; 5. 160-162, 167, 180, 181, 184, 278.

Vyása-gítá, the, a part of the Kúrma-puráña, P. 79.

Vyása-sútra, the, quoted, 3. 224.

Vyashṭí, mystical explanation of, 5. 215.

Vyatala (??), variant of Atala, 2. 209.

Vyatipáta, Vyalípáta, what, in astrological terminology, 3. 163, 169.

Vyavasáya, 'perseverance,' son of Dharma, the Prajápati, 1. 110.

Vyaya, what, in philosophy, 1. 27.

Vyoma (?), variant of Vyoman, son of Daśárha, 4. 68.

Vyoman, son of Daśárha, 4. 68.

Vyoman, the same as Ákáśa, 5. 254. And see Kha.

Vyomin, a horse of the Moon, 2. 299.

Vyúha, the technicality explained, 5. 16.

Vyúkas (?), variant of Sakas, 2. 179.

Vyushta, son of Pushpárna, 1. 178.

Vyushti, part of the day, 2. 249.

War. Between the gods and the demons, 3. 201. Between the same, in the Tretá age, 3. 261. Between the gods and the Daityas, an account of Tárá's being abducted by Soma, 4. 3.

Water. Produced from the rudiment of taste, producing the rudiment of smell, &c., 1. 35, 36. Why the waters are called Nárá, 1. 56.

Wife, due qualifications required in a wife, 3. 101-105.

Wind or air. See Váyu.

Wine from the Kadamba-tree, 5. 66.

World, the. Its dimensions, 2. 205, 206. The destruction of it, 5. 190, &c.

Wrestling, modes of, 5. 36-38.

Yádavas. A tribe descended from Yadu, son of Yayáti, 4. 58. They become very numerous, 4. 114. They go to Prabhása, 5. 146, 147. There, Krishna and Dáruka excepted, they are destroyed, 5. 149. See also P. 12, 43; 2. 159; 4. 59, 65, 77, 78, &c., 87, 88, &c., 113, &c., 246, 271, 280, 335, 337; 5. 34, 45, 46, 50, 52-56, 70, 84, 86, 105, 112, 123, 130, 131, 138, 140, &c. &c., 382. And see Yadus.

Yadus, a people, 4. 237; 5. 64. See Yádavas.

Yadu, son of Yayáti, 4. 46. He is king of the south, 4. 49. His descendants, 4. 52, &c., 3. 289, 319; 4. 47, &c., 61, 247; 5. 44, 46, 53, 56, 58, 63, 112, 131, 137, &c. &c., 382.

Yadu, according to the Mahábhárata, son of Vasu, son of Kritaka, 4. 149.

Yadu (??), variant of Turvasu, 4. 116.

Yadudbra (??), variant of Mahámuni, a Rishi, 3. 11.

Yadu-nandana, an epithet of Akrúra, 5. 5.

Yajna, 'sacrifice,' son of Ruchi, 1. 108. He marries his twin sister, Dakshiná, 'donation to a Bráhman,' 1. 108. Is personified as sacrifice, and is decapitated, 1. 131. Furnished with the head of a deer, he is transformed, by Brahmá, into the constellation Mrigasiras, 1. 132. The principal kinds of Yajnas or sacrifices, 3. 40, 93, 112-114.

Yajna, a form of Vishnu, 3. 15, 16.

Yajna, son of Anantaka, 4. 63.

Yajnabáhu, son of Priyavrata, and king of Sálmala-dwípa, 2. 100, 195.

Yajnahotra, son of Auttami, and a Rishi in the third Manwantara, according to the Bhágavata-puráňa, 3. 7.

Yajnakrita, son of Vijaya, son of Sanjaya, 4. 44.

Yajnamúrti, 'the form or personification of sacrifice,' an epithet of Vishnu, 1. 61.

Yajnapati, an epithet of Vishńu, 1. 60 ; 5. 177.

Yajnápeta, a Rákshasa, 2. 285, &c.

Yajna-puñs, ' the male of sacrifice,' an epithet of Vishńu, 5. 200.

Yajnapurusha, ' the male or soul of sacrifice,' an epithet of Vishńu, 1. 61, 163 (note *), 180, 181 ; 2. 136 ; 3. 237 ; 4. 14 ; 5. 2, 4.

Yajnárádhya, ' who is to be propitiated by sacrifice,' a title of Vishńu, 1. 61.

Yajnaśarman (??), variant of Kshattravŕiddha, 4. 30.

Yajnaśrí, son of Śivaskandha, &c., 4. 198, 201, 203.

Yajnaśrísátakarńí, variant of Yajnaśrí, 4. 198, 202.

Yajnaśrísátakarńika, variant of Yajnaśrí, 4. 201.

Yajnaśrísátakarńin, variant of Yajnaśrí, 4. 198.

Yájnavalkyas, Kauśika Bráhmans, 4. 28.

Yájnavalkya, an ancient writer on law, referred to, P. 60. See Yájnavalkya-smŕiti.

Yájnavalkya, disciple of Báshkali, and promulgator of the Rig-veda, 3. 44. He defeats Śákalya in a disputation, and the latter thereupon dies, 3. 45.

Yájnavalkya, a Ŕishi, son of Brahmaráta, disciple of Vaiśampáyana, early promulgator of the White Yajur-veda, &c., 3. 52, 53, 323, 324. He propitiates the Sun, in order to recover possession of the lost texts of the Yajur-veda, and to a favourable result, 3. 55-57. He has a dispute with Vaiśampáyana, 4. 162.

Yájnavalkya, a writer on the Yoga philosophy, quoted, or referred to, 5. 228, 230.

Yájnavalkya-smŕiti, the, a code of law, referred to, or quoted, &c., 2. 343 ; 3. 89, 90, 99, 101, 102, 104, 112, 126, 148, 151, 169, 173, 177, 178, 184, 187, 338.

Yajnaváma, son of Parvasa, 1. 153, 155.

Yajna-vidyá, rendered "knowledge or performance of religious rites," 1. 148.

Yajneśa, ' lord of sacrifice,' an epithet or title of Vishńu, 1. 124 (note †) ; 2. 313. And see Yajneśwara.

Yajneśwara, ' lord of sacrifice,' an epithetical designation of Vishńu, 3. 183 ; 5. 200, 253. And see Yajneśa and the synonymous Makheśa.

Yajnopeta, variant of Yajnápeta, a Rákshasa, 2. 292, 293.

Yajur-veda, the. Its origin from Brahmá's southern mouth, 1. 84. It was the original Veda, 3. 43. Its composition, and the division of it into four Vedas, 3. 43. The Saṃhitás and teachers of it, 3. 52-57. The Taittiríya, or Black Yajur, Veda, 3, 54 ; 4. 162. The Vájasanayi, or White Yajur, Veda, 3. 57 ; 4. 162. See also 1. 171 ; 5. 200. And see Yajus.

Yajus, equivalent to Yajur-veda, 3. 57, &c. Etymology of the word, 3. 43, 44.

Yajus (?), variant of Mahámuni, a Rishi, 3. 11.

Yajwin, correctly, 'sacrificing priest,' 2. 136.

Yaktillomana, a people, 2. 166.

Yakshas, a sort of gods. Their origin from Brahmá, 1. 83. Sprung from Kaśyapa and Khasá, 2. 75. Their king, Kubera, 1. 122; 3. 86. Twelve of them named, 2. 285–289. Etymology of the word, 1. 83. See also 1. 82, 188; 2. 284; 3. 116, 119, 203; 4. 52, 250, 323; 5. 59, 94, 234, 236, 246, 247, 251. And see Grámańís, a synonym of Yakshas, and also 3. 255, (note *). (In 4. 266, Yakshas is vaguely represented by "fiends.")

Yaksha, son of Kaśyapa, son of Marichi, and, by one account, progenitor of the Yakshas, 2. 75.

Yaksha, son of S'waphalka, 4. 95.

Yakshman, consumption personified (?), 3. 119.

Yámas, a class of gods in the Manwantara of Swáyambhuva, sons of Yajna and Dakshiná, twins, 1. 109, 166; 3. 2 (where correct the spelling); 5. 390. They reside in Mahar-loka, 2. 227.

Yama, son of Vivaswat and Sanjná, 3. 20. God of hell, 2. 216; 3. 21. King of the Pitris, 2. 85. He obtains the rank of Lokapála, 2. 118; 3. 21. His city, Samyamaní, where, 2. 12,

118, 239, 240. It is visited by Krishńa, 5. 48. His place in the Siśumára, 2. 308. Is presiding deity over Bharaní, the asterism, 2. 337. He bears a club, which, in combat, Krishńa, with his own, knocks down and breaks, 5. 100. On another occasion, Vírabhadra breaks it, 1. 131. He reviles Chháyá, and would kick her; she curses him with sores and worms in the leg; his father gives him a cock to eat the worms, &c., 3. 21. See also 1. 119, 142, 180; 2. 34; 4. 133, 241, 258; 5. 15, 207. How men may free themselves from subjection to him, 3. 74, &c. Yama has the epithets of Antaka, Dharmarája, Pretarája, Sráddhadeva, which see. (In 3. 34, the Translator wrongly identifies Mrityu with him.)

Yama, an ancient lawgiver, quoted, or referred to, 3. 96, 100.

Yama (who?), father of Iliná, 4. 131.

Yama, the term, as used in ethics, defined, 3. 77; 5. 222, 227, 230, 240.

Yáma, 'a watch of the day or night,' 1. 48.

Yama (?), variant of Dama, son of Narishyanta, 3. 336.

Yamadútas, Kauśika Bráhmans, 4. 28.

Yama-dwípa, an island, probably fabulous, 2. 129.

Yama-gítá, a passage in the Vishńu-puráńa, so called, 3. 79.

Yamakoti, a city in Bhadráśwa, 2. 207. See the two next names following.

Yamakotipattana, the same as Yamakoti, 2. 111.

Yamakoṭipuri, the same as Yamakoti, 2. 113.

Yámalas, an heretical sect, P. 80; 5. 286, 287, 375, 380.

Yámí, Yámí, 'night,' daughter of Dakṣha, and wife of Dharma, 2. 21, 23, 337.

Yamí, daughter of Vivaswat and Sanjná, 3. 20. See Yamuná, intending the same.

Yáminí, daughter of Dakṣha, and wife of Kaśyapa, son of Maríchi, 2. 28.

Yámunas, a people, 2. 171.

Yámuna, a mountain named in the Rámáyaṇa, 2. 171.

Yamuná, daughter of Vivaswat and Sanjná, and one with the river now popularly called the Jumna, 3. 20; 5. 82. Kṛishṇa's compulsion with her, 5. 65–68, 130. She meets him at Indraprastha, and claims him as husband, 5. 82. See also 1. 165; 2. 121, 142, 148, 171; 3. 257; 4. 40, 269, 286–288, 295, 322, 327; 5. 11, 17, 249. Other names of the Yamuná are Kálindí and Tápí.

Yámya, Yámyá, the same as Bharaṇí, the asterism, 2. 265, 266, 277, 337.

Yantramáti (??), son of Swátisheṇa, 4. 202.

Yaśas, 'reputation,' son of Dharma, 1. 111.

Yáska, an ancient author, quoted, or referred to, 2. 121; 3. 18, 46, 48, 54; 5. 178.

Yaśodá, mind-born daughter of the Upahútas, certain Pitṛis, and wife of Viśwamahat, 3. 163, 164.

Yaśodá, wife of Nanda, the cowherd who fosters Kṛishṇa, 4. 111. She brings forth Yoganidrá, who is changed for Kṛishṇa, 4. 270. See also 4. 261, 265, 276, 279, 280, 288–290, 296, 335.

Yaśodeví, wife of Bṛihanmanas, son of Bṛihadbhánu, 4. 125.

Yaśodhara, son of Kṛishṇa and Rukmiṇí, 4. 112.

Yaśodhará, wife of Sahishṇu, son of Pulaha, 1. 155.

Yaśonandi, a king named in the Bhágavata-puráṇa, 4. 211.

Yátaná, 'torture,' daughter of Mṛityu, 1. 111.

Yathá-sankhyá, a rhetorical figure of speech, exemplified, 5. 191.

Yati, Yáti (??), son of Nahusha, son of Áyus and Prabhá, 4. 45, 46.

Yati, 'one who practises self-constraint,' 1. 155; 3. 177; 5. 200, 230.

Yatidharman (??), variant of Dṛisha-táśarman, 4. 96.

Yátrá-śráddha, 'a Śráddha held by a person going on a journey,' 3. 147.

Yátudhánas, a sort of demons, sprung from Kaśyapa and Surasá, 2. 74. Twelve of them enumerated, 2. 291, 292, where they are made one with Rá-

kahasas. See also 2. 284; 3.
183, 196. .

Yaudheyas, a people founded by
Nriga, son of Uśinara, 4. 121.

Yaudheya, son of Yudhishṭhira,
4. 159.

Yaudheya, a kingdom named in
the Váyu-puráňa, 4. 122.

Yaudheyí, wife of Yudhishṭhira,
4. 159.

Yauvanáśwa, patronym of Ambarísha, 3. 280, 281; 5. 391.

Yavakshá, a river in India, 2. 151.

Yavanas, a people, or peoples,
sprung from Turvasu, 4. 117.
Identified with the Ionians or
Greeks, &c., 2. 130, 162, 181;
3. 292. Dwelling to the west,
of Bharatavarsha, 2. 129. Kings
of their race, 4. 203, 206, 208,
209, 211. Sagara opposes them,
3. 291. He makes them shave
their heads entirely, 3. 294.
Characterized as " wise and pre-
eminently brave," 2. 339. Pushpamitra engages with them on
the Indus, 4. 191. See also 2.
182, 184; 3. 290, 295; 5. 53-
58.

Yavana, an Asura, the same as
Kálayavana, 5. 54.

Yavanáśwa (??), variant of Yuvanáśwa, 3. 263.

Yavayasa, ruler over the realm of
Yavayasa, and son of Idhmajihwa, king of Plaksha-dwípa,
2. 193.

Yavayasa, a region in Plaksha-
dwípa, 2. 193.

Yavínara, son of Dwimíḍha, son
of Bhallátá, 4. 142.

Yavínara (??), variant of Pravíra,
son of Haryaśwa, 4. 144.

Yavíynaí, ' a very young woman,
3. 102.

Yayáti, son of Nahusha, son of
Ambaríaha, 3. 314; 4. 1. 45-
53, 117, 120, 240; 5. 45.

Yayu, a horse of the Moon, 2. 299.

Year. Of mortals, 1. 49. Of the
gods, 1. 49. Of the Rishis, 1.
49 (note 1). Of Dhruva, 1. 49.
(note 1). Of Brahmá, 1. 53.
Of a Manu, 1. 54. Years of
five kinds, namely, Saṁvatsara,
Parivatsara, Idwatsara, Anuvatsara, and Vatsara. 2. 254, 255.

Yoga, ' contemplative devotion,
resulting in mystical union.'
Personified as son of Dharma,
1. 111. How Yoga is effected,
2. 92, 93. Some particulars
regarding it, 1. 164. The Yoga
philosophy, 3. 325; 4. 253.
Certain terms of the Yoga philosophy, 2. 90. The practice explained at length, 5. 225, &c.
&c. Etymology of the term, 5.
226. See also P. 14, 29, 38,
43, 70, 79, 81, 89; 1. 163;
2. 61, 270, 328; 3. 323; 5.
216, &c. &c. And see Pátanjala and Patanjali.

Yogácháras, a Bauddha sect, 3.
210.

Yoga-gámin, rendered by "endowed with magic power," 5. 110.

Yoganidrá, ' personified delusion.'
Sprung from Vishńu, 4. 260.
His ministress, 4. 111. Her
exploits, as Durgá, 4. 261. She
is born of Yaśodá, 4. 264. Her

further proceedings, mockery of Kaṁsa, and disappearance, 4. 269–271. And see 5. 195, text and note **. Other names of Yoganidrá are Mahámáyá and Nidrá; and she is called Ambiká, Áryá, Bhadrá, Bhadrakálí, Durgá, Kshemankarí (or Kshemakarí), Kshemyá, Vedagarbhá, also, 4. 262.

Yogasiddhá, sister of Bṛihaspati, son of Angiras, and wife of Prabhása, a Vasu, 2. 24.

Yoga-tárá, the term defined, 3. 167.

Yoga-yuj, 'a novice in the practice of Yoga,' 5. 228, 234, 237.

Yogin, 'a performer of Yoga.' How he attains final liberation, 2. 89, &c. Yogins of two classes, the novice and the adept, 5. 228. See also P. 38; 1. 154; 2. 271; 3. 175, 180, 188; 4. 306, 307; 5. 4, 57, 61, &c., 200, 231, 233, 241, 253, 291.

Yokhalu (?), variant of Gokhalu, 3. 46.

Yonarája, a king named in an old Hindu inscription, 2. 181.

Yoní, a river in Sálmala-dwípa, 2. 194.

Yoni-śástras, certain scriptures so called, 5. 287 (where correct the spelling), 288.

Yudakas (?), variant of Padukas, 4. 221.

Yuddha, according to the Váyu-puráṇa, son of Ugrasena, son of Áhuka, 4. 99.

Yuddhamushṭi, son of Ugrasena, son of Áhuka, 4. 99.

Yuddhaṛishṭi (?), variant of Yuddhamushṭi, 4. 99.

Yudhájit, variously genealogized, 4. 73, 74, 94.

Yudhájita (?), variant of Yudhájit, 4. 94.

Yudhishṭhira, son of Páṇḍu and Pṛithá, 4. 101, 102. His children, 4. 159. See also P. 65 (where correct the spelling); 4. 113, 232, 234, 241, 321; 5. 134, 167.

Yuga, 'cycle.' One of five years, 2. 255. The Maháyuga, its length, 1. 50. The four Yugas termed Kṛita, Tretá, Dwápara, and Kali, their duration, &c., 1. 49, &c.

Yuga, a measure of spatial length, 'four cubits,' 3. 144 (note *).

Yugádya, the term defined, 3. 168.

Yugandharas, variant of Dhurandharas, 2. 162.

Yugandhara, son of Túñi, 4. 93.

Yukta, a Ṛishi in the fourteenth Manwantara, 8. 29.

Yuvanáśwa, son of Árdra, son of Viśwagaśwa (rightly, Vishwagaśwa), 3. 263.

Yuvanáśwa, variously genealogized, 3. 265–268, 280–282, 297; 4. 14. (Possibly, two persons are intended.)

Yuyudhan (?), variant of Sudhanwan, son of Sáśwata, 3. 334.

Yuyudhána, son of Satyaka, son of Sini, 4. 93; 5. 148. See Sátyaki.

Zoroaster and the Magas or Magi, 5. 383.

ON CERTAIN ERRATA, &c.

WITH few exceptions, it is only of proper names that account is taken in what follows. Moreover, it is not professed that the illustrations of the points treated of are by any means exhaustive.

Professor Wilson, in the work here edited, usually employed *ri* to represent equally a vowel and the combination of the Nágarí symbols for *r* and *i*. To represent the former, I have substituted *ṛi*. Again, where, in his translettering, he did not entirely ignore *visarga*,[1] he allowed a simple *h* to stand for it. I have preferred *ḥ*. A third alteration which I have introduced consists in denoting *anusvára*, followed by a nasal, a sibilant, *y*, or *h*, by *ṁ*,—used elsewhere, also,—and not by *n*.

As to accents and diacritical marks, I have supplied many thousands which before were wanting. Of the former I have, besides, removed a great many which were intrusive, and not a few of the latter, as well.[1] Further, in Atáviśikharas (*sic*),[2] for Aṭaviśikharas, 2. 169, and in Vyushtá (*sic*), for Vyushṭi, 2. 249, the dash belonging to a consonant was shifted to the vowel following it; while in Játahásini (*sic*), for Jálahásini, 4. 112, and in Srijávaña (*sic*),[3] for Srijavána, 1. 152, the accent of a vowel was transferred to a consonant.

---

[1] For instances where he so ignores it, see the middle of p. 261, *infra*.

[2] This is intended to indicate, that the word which it follows is recognized as containing some deviation from accuracy over and above that for which it is topically adduced. Thus, in Atáviśikharas, the first *i* is unaccented.

In Professor Wilson's own Index, we have Aṭiviśikharas, in which, compared with the name as given in his text, one mistake is redressed, one is added, and one is repeated.

That Index, while silently amending a host of minor faults, originates perhaps an equal number, if not even more.

[3] Srijávaña is the still more erroneous form which Professor Wilson inserts in his Index.

Numerous errors which I have rectified may be traceable, as many of those just adverted to are unquestionably traceable, to the indistinct way in which Professor Wilson wrote certain letters, to his momentary forgetfulness, or else to his negligence in correcting the press.

His *a* and *u* were, I conjecture, often much alike.[1] If so, we may see why we find Anavinda, for Anuvinda, 4. 103 ; Dhúti (*sic*),[2] for what he would optionally have written Dhátá (my Dhátri), 2. 27 ; Kroshtí, 4. 53 ;[3] Maṅidhanu (*sic*), for Maṅidhána, 4. 221 ; Nichakra, for Nichakru, 4. 163 ; Nyurvuda (*sic*), for Nyarbuda, 5. 188 ; Punnagas, for Pannagas, 5. 94 ; Puru (*sic*), for Pura, 4. 109 ;[4] Purajit, for Purujit, 3. 334 ; Ritudhámá (*sic*),[5] for Ritadháman, 3. 27 ; S'atrujit (*sic*), for Sattrájita, 5. 81 ; Sulomadhi, for Salomadhi, 4. 199 ; Suvarṅi (*sic*), for Sávarṅi, 3. 64 ; Vipritha (*sic*), for Viprithu, 4. 96.[6]

His *n* and *r* must sometimes have closely resembled each other. Hence, presumably, Animejaya, for Arimejaya, 4. 148 ;[7] Anjuna, for Arjuna, 3. 326 ; Sanyáti (*sic*), for Saryáti, 3. 13 ;[8] S'aryáti, for what he would have written Sanyáti (my Samyáti), 4. 46.[9]

Confusion between a manuscript *a* and *o* may be the ground, in part, or wholly, of Ároga, for Ároga, 5. 191 ; Kulindápatyakas, for Kulindopatyakas, 2. 176 ; Tapa-loka, for Tapo-loka, 1. 98.[10]

If his written *a* and *i* were very similar,—the dot over the latter being not seldom omitted,—we have only to suppose, additionally, that, at the press, one was taken for the other, and an error in each of the

---

[1] His Index to the *Vishṅu-puráña* authorises one to be pretty positive on this point.

[2] This is referred to again at pp. 257 and 260, *infra*.

[3] My annotation there does not express my present opinion. I am now disposed to think that Professor Wilson took Kroshṭu to be wrong, and preferred the Kroshṭrí of the *Bhágavata-puráña:* that he wrote, indistinctly, Kroshṭá ; and that the printer mistook this for Kroshṭí. In 4. 61, Kroshṭrí (*sic*), which appears twice, is intended, I surmise, as the scholarly substitute for his former Kroshṭá.

[4] But see the note there. I have assumed that Púru was intended by "Puru."

[5] This is referred to again at p. 259, *infra*.

[6] In his Index, Professor Wilson has amended Anavinda, but has reproduced Nichakra, Solomadhi, and Vipritha. Instead of Dhúti, Maṅidhanu, and Ritudhámá, we there have Dhúti, Manidhána, and Ritudháman, all of them still faulty, as substitutes

[7] Corrected in 5. 391.

[8] See 3. 337.

[9] See note †† there.

[10] All three of these errors, however, are copied into Professor Wilson's Index.

words following is accounted for: Chitrika,[1] for Chitraka, 4. 96; Da-
dbíchí, for Dadhícha, 5. 250; Dakshasávarni (sic), for Dakshasávarṇa,
3. 24; Dharman, for Dharmin, 4. 169; Dhritamatí (sic), for Dhṛitimatí, 2. 152; Divaratha, for Diviratha, 4. 123; Dhútí (sic),[2] for Dhátá
(my Dhátí), 2. 27; Garddhabas (sic), for Gardabhins,[3] 4. 202; Káliká, for Kálaká, 2. 71; Kumári, for Kumárá, 2. 131, 132; Mahá-
nanda, for Mahánandin,[3] 4. 183; Mahishas, for Mahishins,[3] 4. 214;
Naimittaka, for Naimittika, 5. 186; Parvasí, for Parvasá, 1. 153;
Sávarṅí, for Sávarṅa, 3. 27, &c.; S'ílavatí (sic), for S'álávatí, 4. 28;
Sujátí, for Sujáta, 4. 59; Sujátí (sic), for Sujáta, 4. 57; Támráyani
(sic), for Támráyaṅa, 3. 57; Vikuṅťhí, for Vikuṅťhá, 3. 17; Vítihavya,
for Vítahavya, 4. 40 (bis); Vyushťa, for Vyushťí, 2. 249. That the
wrong forms here specified originated as above suggested, is, however,
nothing but theory.[4] In the case—supplementary to the preceding
list,—of Sukhíbala, for Sukhábala, 4. 165, it is pretty evident that
Professor Wilson allowed his choice of lection to be influenced by the
reading of the *Bhágavata-puráṅa*, and by the translation of the *Vishṅu-
puráṅa* which was prepared for him at Calcutta; and his substitutions
for Dakshasávarṇa, Kálaká, Kumárá, and Sávarṇa were, I apprehend,
designed.

Other errors, probably arising from the printer's having taken one
letter, unclearly written, for another, are seen in Amtrasílá,[5] for
Antrasílá, 2. 151; Dhava, for Dhara, 2. 23; Ghaťokkacha, for Gha-
ťotkacha, 4. 159; Gohamukha (sic), for Gokámukha, 2. 141; Játa-
hasiní (sic), for Jálahásiní, 4. 112; Jayatí, for Jagatí, 2. 239; Kakkudwat (sic), for Kakudmat, 2. 194; Kakudwatí, for Kakudmatí, 4. 112;
Kaśyata, for Kaśyapa, 1. 153; Magh, for Mugh, P. 64; Matimara

---

[1] Professor Wilson had Chitraka in 4. 94, and in his Index. However, among
the names here grouped together, only this and one or two others are effectually
set right there.

[2] See, also, what I have said of this at p. 256, *supra*, and at p. 260, *infra*.

[3] Professor Wilson would have written Gardabhís, Mahánandí, and Maháhís,
or else Gardabhís, &c., most probably. I refer to this point at p. 259, *infra*.
He actually had Mahánandí in 4. 182; and it passed into his Index. And there is
Gardhabas, too, which is nothing.

With reference to Mahánandí, see further, note 12 to p. 259, *infra*.

[4] Nevertheless, it is a theory well supported by close inspection of his Index to the
Vishṅu-puráṅa. There, to name one instance out of fifty adducible, he has made
Satrájit—corrupted from Sattrájit, the reading of some Puráṅas for Sattrájita,—
and Satrujit into one word.

[5] This, with Ghaťokkacha and Jayatí, is corrected in Professor Wilson's own
Index; but Dhava and Kaśyata are there, and Gohamukha is further worsened
into Gohamuka.

z

(*sic*), for Matinára,[1] 3. 266; Salapalka (*sic*), for Satapatha, 3. 63; Salpa, for Jalpa, 3. 8; &c. &c.

In a multitude of instances, I have, on good warrant, put a *b* instead of Professor Wilson's *v* or *w*. Alterations have thus been effected of his Kambalavarhish (*sic*), Kokavakas, Kuvera, Nalakúvera (*sic*), Nyurvuda (*sic*), Práchínaverhis (*sic*), Saivas (from Sibi), Saivya, Saivyá, Samvara (*sic*),[2] Sasavindu, Satavaláka, Sauvalyas, Savaláswas, Sivi, Suvala, Trinavindu (*sic*), Ulwana (*sic*),[3] Upavarhana (*sic*), Uttánavarhish (*sic*), Valáka, Valákáswa, Valakrama, Várhadrathas, Várhaspatyas, Varhish (*sic*),[4] Varhishad, Varhishads, Varhishmatí, Váshkala, Vindumatí, Vindusára, Vopadeva, Vrihaspati (*sic*), Vrihat (*sic*), Vrihatí (*sic*), and all names, &c., which he began with Vrihad- (*sic*), Vrihan- (*sic*), and Vrihat- (*sic*). On the other hand, I have changed to *v* *b* in Bajikarana (*sic*),[5] Bárava (*sic*), Chitrabáhá,[6] Gandharba, Gandharbas, Gándharba, Gándharbí, and his *bh* in Mahávishubha.

Lapsing into Sir William Jones's capricious fashion of sometimes denoting the inherent vowel by *e*, he wrote Práchínaverhis (*sic*), for Práchínabarhis, 1. 192, 193; Selu, for Salu, 2. 151, 340;[7] Sherga (*sic*), for Shadja, 2. 329; Súryaverchchas, for Súryavarchas, 2. 289; Vasavertis (*sic*), for Vasávartins, 3. 6; Viswakermá (*sic*), for Viswakarman, 1. 145.

In Bengal, and elsewhere in India, the lingual *d* (*d*) has much of the sound of *r*. Compliance with this corruption is exhibited in his Bárava (*sic*), for Vadává, 4. 110; Dráviras (*sic*), for Drávidas, 2. 177; Dráviras (*sic*),[8] for Dravidas, 3. 295, and 4. 117; Drirhamána (*sic*), for Dridhamána (?), 4. 196; Kahora, for Kahoda, 5. 164; Nárika, for Nádiká, 1. 48; Sherga, (*sic*), for Shadja, 2. 329; Soraai (*sic*),[9] for Shodasin, 1. 85.

Conforming to the old unscientific mode, he generally put -*sh* at the

---

[1] See 5. 390.

[2] According to Professor Wilson's Index, "Sambara," who carried off Pradyumna, differs from "Samvara," son of Kasyapa and Danu. One person, under different names, is thus made into two.

Professor Wilson's Index has Ulwana, which is right as to its nasal letter.

[4] This we had in 4. 169, but Varhis in 1. 192, and in the reference to it in his Index.

[5] Bájikaraña, but still wrong, in Professor Wilson's Index.

[6] In Professor Wilson's Index, Chitrabáhá, importing a fresh error.

[7] It is shown, in 2. 340, that no proper name is intended in the original.

[8] This form appears in Professor Wilson's Index; and so does Nárika, mentioned just below.

[9] This is mentioned again at p. 260, *infra*.

end of substantives, instead of -s. I have altered his Anáyush, Archish, Bhútajyotish, Chakshush,[1] Danáyush, Dridhadhanush (sic), Kambalavarhish (sic), Prachínavarhish (sic),[2] Pulomárchish, Surochish, Swarochish, Uttánavarhish (sic), Varhish (sic),[3] Viswagjyotish (sic), Yajush, &c. &c.

With regard to nouns terminating in -an, his mode of spelling them was not uniform. This is virtually acknowledged by his "Púshá or Púshan," 4. 339, and by his Viswakarmá (sic),[4] 1. 145, and Viswakarmá (sic), 2. 24 (bis), but Viswakarman (sic), 2. 100, and Viswakarman, 2. 298, and 3. 272.[5] The accent of the nominatival form he also omitted frequently. Hence we find Sudhámas (now corrected), 3. 6, 25, but Sudhámana, 3. 28, note °; Sudharmas (now corrected), 3. 24, but Sudharmana, 3. 28; Sukarmas (now corrected), 3. 27, but Sukarmana, 3. 28.[6] I have altered Átmá and Bhútátmá, 1. 3; Haryátmá, 3. 35; Indriyátmá, Paramátmá, and Pradhánátmá, 1. 3; Ritudhámá (sic),[7] 3. 27; and also Parvas, 3. 143, 147; Sudámas, 2. 175; Sudháma, 2. 142; Yakrillomas (sic), 2. 166.

In like manner, he was far from rigid as to nouns ending with -in. He had both Pálin[8] and Pálí in 1. 192; Kesín, 4. 250, &c. &c., but Kesí (sic), 5. 97;[9] Samin,[10] 4. 99, but Sami, 4. 97. I have regularized his Dámís, Sringí (sic), Vaktrayodhí,[11] &c. &c. And here, too, he largely omitted the accent; thus producing such forms, now redressed, as, to specify a few only, Kesi, mentioned just above; Kriti (sic), 4. 149; Mahánandi,[12] 4. 182; Sami, mentioned just above; Saptabhangis

---

[1] In 1. 178, and in Professor Wilson's Index, under Ákúti (rightly, Ákúti).

[2] In 1. 157, and twice in Professor Wilson's Index, though referring to pages where the forms used are Práchínavarhis and Práchínavarhis.

[3] See note 4 to p. 258, supra.

[4] Here, as often below, I copy the form for which I have substituted the correct one.

[5] Further, in his Index, Professor Wilson gives Viswakarmá (sic) as the name of the artist of the gods, and Viswakarman as that of a certain solar ray.

[6] Both Sudhámas and Sudhámans are entered in Professor Wilson's Index, and as if they differed; and so both Sukarmas and Sukarmans; but Sudharmas only.

[7] This has already been referred to at p. 256, supra. In his Index, Professor Wilson has Ritudhámán.

[8] This is the form which he registers in his Index.

[9] Senáni, 2. 25, is correct; but, in his Index, it becomes Senánin, from mistake as to its declension.

[10] Corrupted, in his Index, into Sámin.

[11] In his Index, this is changed into Vaktrayodhi.

[12] Possibly, however, Professor Wilson meant to write thus, complying with the lection of the Bhágavata-purána, and did not intend to suggest the nominative of Mahánandin, namely, Mahánandí.

and Saptavádis, 3. 209 ; Sorasi (for Shoďaśin), 1. 85 ; Sumáli, 1. 188 ;
Syádvádis, 3. 209 ; Vasavertis (sic), 3. 6 ; Yogi, 5. 228, 230, &c.

Instead of the crude form, he had the nominatival, in Dhátá,[1] 1.
118 ; Pratiharttá, 2. 106 ; Vidhátá,[2] 1. 118 : Samrát (sic), and Swarát
(sic), 1. 170 ; Virát (sic),[3] 1. 59, 105, &c., 170, and 2. 107 ; Hanumán,
P. 50, &c. ; Mahán, 1. 117 ; Mályaván, 2. 117, &c. ; Jará, 5. 143, 152 ;
Pumán, 1. 3, 23, &c. ; Samvit (sic),[4] 1. 32 ; Satyavák, 1. 177 ; Swarña-
bhák,[5] 5. 191. Áyushmanta, for Áyushmat, 1. 159, and Havishmantas,[6] for Havishmats, 3. 163, are impossible. They remind one of,
for instance, Hanumanta, which is common, in Hindí poetry, for
Hanumat.

Such of his plurals as Angirasas, Apsarasas, &c., it seemed to me too
bold to disturb, more especially as they were dictated by a fixed prin-
ciple. In my own annotations, and in my Index, however, I have
everywhere written, for example, Angirases and Apsarases ; the singu-
lars of these words being Angiras and Apsaras, not Angirasa and
Apsarasa.

A little heed should have prevented the presentation of solecisms, &c.,
like Ahichchhatra, for Ahichhatra, 2. 161 ; Ávasatthya, for Ávasathya,
5. 115 ; Dadícha, for Dadhícha, 5. 250 ; Dharbaká, for Darbhaka, 4.
182 ; Dhrishťasarman, for Dŕishťaśarman, 4. 95 ; Dhyánajyápyas, for
Dhyánajapyas, 4. 28 ; Drishťaketu,[7] for Dŕishťaketu, 4. 148 ; Gach-
chas, for Gachchhas, 2. 176 ; Garddhabas, for Gardabhins, 4. 202 ;
Garddhabhin, for Gardabhin, 4. 209 ; Gaveduká, for Gavedhuká, 1. 95 ;
Ghritsamada, for Gŕitsamada, 4. 31 ; Ghritsamati, for Gŕitsamati, 4.
136 ; Ghritsatamas, for Gŕitsatamas, 4. 32 ; Gomantha, for Gomanta,
5. 66 ; Hiráñyagarbha, for Hiráñyanábha, 3. 324 ; Kachaníra, for
Kachchhaníra, 2. 286 ; Kachchas, for Kachchhas, 2. 169, 176 ; Kach-

---

[1] How Dhútí came to appear for Dhátá, in 2. 27, has been conjectured at
pp. 256 and 257, supra.
[2] Dhátrí (sic) and Vidhátri (sic) were found in 1. 152.
[3] Properly written, these three words have -j in the nominative case singular.
In 1. 105, Professor Wilson had both Virát (sic) and the correct Viráj ; in 2.
229, the latter. In his Index, he has three articles, instead of one, to-wit, on
Viráj, on Virát, and on Virái. After Viráj, he adds, in brackets, "or Viśáj."
There is no such word.
[4] The right form, in -d, was used in 1. 172.
[5] This, I assume, was before the printer, whose senseless Swamábhák Professor
Wilson not only allowed in his text, but inserted in his Index.
[6] Both Áyushmanta and Havishmantas are in the Index of Professor Wilson.
[7] Dhrishťaketú (sic), in Professor Wilson's Index, where, however, occur Dhri-
dhanemi (sic), and Dhridháśwa (sic), though the names, in his text, contain no h.

chapa, for Kachchhapa, 4. 27, 28 ; Kachchiyas, for Kachchhiyas, 2.
169 ; Kakkudwat, for Kakudmat, 2. 194; Kakutshtha, for Kakutstha,
3. 315 ; Máhibaka, for Máhishaka, 4. 220 ; Medhaśiras, for Medaśiras,
4. 198; Mitravrindá, for Mitravindá, 5. 79 ; Mlechchhas, for Mlechchhas, 1. 182 (bis); Nábhágarishfha, for Nábhágárishťa, 3. 231 ;
Nábhanidishťa, for Nábhánedishťha, 3. 13, 227 ; Navalá, for Naďwalá,
1. 177; Nedishťa, for Nedishťha, 3. 232, 256, 336 ; Niryati, for
Niyati, 1. 152, and 5. 387 ; S'ákhya, for S'ákya, 3. 746; S'ankana, for
S'ankhaña, 3. 314; Saudhodani, for S'auddhodani, 4. 170 ; Savarga,
for Sarvaga (or Sarvavega ?), 3. 27, 227 ; Sudanstra, for Sudamshťra, 4.
100 ; Uchatthya, for Uchathya, 3. 16 ; Utatthya, for Utathya, 3. 16 ;
Uttathya, for Utathya, 1. 154 ; Vávriddhas, for Váchávriddhas, 3. 28 ;
Yajnawalka, for Yájnavalkya, 3. 45 ; Yajnyawalkya, for Yájnavalkya, 5.
228 ; Yuddhamushťhi, for Yuddhamushťi, 4. 99. And due regard for
grammar would have precluded, besides most of the foregoing words,
Adhośiras, for Adhaśiras, 2. 215 ; Antassilá for Antaśśilá, 2. 151 ;
Ápa, for Ápaḥ, 1. 57, 58 ; Dukha, for Duḥkha, 1. 113; Marut-loka,
for Marul-loka, 1. 98 ; Nárá, for Náráḥ, 1. 57, 58 ; Tauava, for Tana-
vaḥ, 1. 57 ; Uchchaiśśravas, for Uchchhaiḥśravas, 1. 147 ; Uchchai-
śravas, for the same, 2. 85.[1]

Most, if not all, of the errors which follow are less susceptible of
arrangement according to subject-matters, than those which are dealt
with above ; and they have, therefore, been disposed alphabetically.
A fair share of them have to do with authors and books quoted by
Professor Wilson, or by myself ; and some of them testify to my own
ignorance or oscitance. Occasionally, where a point is of particular
interest, I have drawn upon, or referred to, the preceding Index,[2] in

---

[1] Of the errors collected in this paragraph, besides that referred to in the last
note, Gomantha, Kakutshtha, Mlechchhas, S'ákhya, and Yuddhamushťhi are corrected in Professor Wilson's Index, which repeats, however, Dharbaka, Gashobas,
Ghritamada, Kachchhas, Kachchhiyas, Mitravrindá, Navalá, Nedishťa, S'ankana,
Vávriddhas, Yajnawalka ; Adhośiras, Ápa, Dukha, Marut-loka, Nárá. Niyati and
Yájnawalkya, there, are half-corrections ; Gardhabas is, as I have said before,
none at all ; and Uchchaiśśravas is as bad.

[2] To take leave of Professor Wilson's own Index, last I may be supposed, by
any one who compares it closely with mine, to be, presumably, wrong, where I do
not reproduce its statements exactly, I annex a sample of specifications from it,
which I have displaced in favour of others, or which I have omitted, with all
deliberateness. Such are: Airávata, king of serpents ; Bharata, son of Vítihotra ;
Bhúri, son of Báhlíka ; Bhúriśravas, son of Báhlíka ; Brahmabali, teacher of the
Sáma-veda ; Dhátrí, son of Vishñu and Lakshmí ; Doshá, wife of Kalpa ; Jyotishmat, king of S'áka-dwipa ; Madhu, killed by Satrughna ; Maruts, sons of Marut-
wati; Nakula, son of Páńdu ; Niśitha, son of Kalpa ; Niyut, wife of Mahán (sic) ;

which, for the rest, abundant inadvertencies of various kinds have already been indicated.

Abhyutthitáéwa, for Dhyushitáéwa, 3. 323.

Adharma, for Dharma, son of Rámachandra, 4. 210.

Adhyushitáéwa, Adhyushitáéwa, for Dhyushitáéwa, 3, 322, 323.

Ahichhatra, for Ahichchhatrá, a city, 2. 341.

Ahikshetra, for Ahikshatra, 2. 161; 4. 145.

Aikshwákava, for Aikshwáka, a dynasty, 4. 171, &c.

Alindayas, for Alindas, 2. 180.

Ambá, for Ámbiká, daughter of a king of the Káśis, 4. 158.

Amitadhwaja, for Mitadhwaja, 3, 333; 5. 217..

Amitrasaha, for Mitrasaha, 3. 305.

Amurttarajasa, for Amúrtarajas, 4. 15.

Amurttaraya, for Múrtaya, 4, 15.

Amúrttaya, for Amúrtaraya, 4. 15.

Aparyantabala, no name, but an epithet, 5. 55.

Arhat, for Árhata, 3. 209 (note 2); 5. 390.

Aripu, for Ripu, son of Yadu, 4. 53.

Krahtísapa, for Krahtíshena, 4. 31.

Arvarívas, for Arvarívat, son of Sávarni, 3. 24.

Áryamat, for Aryaman, an Áditya, 2. 286, 306.

Aśmakríshńa, substituted, from adopting the reading of the Bhágavata-puráńa, for Adhisímakríshńa, 4. 163.

Asmarisárin, for Aśmasárin, 4. 155.

Atimukta (not, as printed, Atimukti), for Avimukta, from mistaking a careless Nágarí v for t, 5, 129.

Avarttana, for Ávartana, 2. 129. See 2, 339.

Áyati, daughter of Meru. See the preceding Index, under Niyati.

Báḱkala, for Báshkala, 3. 44.

Báḱkali, for Báshkali, 3. 44.

Báhu, for Pratibáhu, son of Vajra, 4. 113.

Parameshthin (mistaken for Paramekshu), son of Anu; Pathya, teacher of the Sáma-veda; Prabhá, wife of Kalpa; Pradosha, son of Kalpa; Ribhu, son of Rudra; Ripu and Ripunjaya, sons of Dhruva; Rudráńí, wife of a Rudra; Rudrasávarńi, twelfth Manu; Sahadeva, son of Páńḍu; Śala, son of Báhlíka; Sarpi (sic), wife of Śiva; Sáya, son of Kalpa; Sujáti (error for Sujáta), son of Vitihotra; Sumati, son of Sagara; Taru, son of Dhruva; Tríshńá, son of Mrítyu; Vidhátri, son of Vishńu and Lakshmí; Vipra, son of Dhruva; Vríka, son of Vijaya; Vríkala, son of Dhruva; Vríkatejas, son of Dhruva; Vrísha, son of Vitihotra; Vyushta, son of Kalpa. Vinatá is described as wife of Kaśyapa, and also as wife of Tárksha: Kaśyapa and Tárksha are the same person. And let the reader inspect, though ever so cursorily, the following pages, to the end.

Bahwaśwa, for Badhryaśwa, 4. 145, 146.

Bhairika, for Bhaimarika, 5. 107, where, in note †, the origin of the error is pointed out.

Bhajina, for Bhajin, 4. 71.

Bhayada, for Abhayada, 4. 127.

Bhíras, for A'bhíras, 2. 133, 134.

Brahmá, where the original has Vidhátri, that is to say, Vishńu, 5. 11

Chakshu, for Chakshus, son of Purojánu, 4. 144.

Chakshupa, for Kshupa, 3. 242. *Cha* 'and,' was mistaken for part of a name.

Chákshusha, a gross blunder, in the Bhágavata-purańa, for *cha* ('and') Kshupa, 3. 242.

Champaka, mistaken for *panchama*, 'nfth,' 4. 46.

Champamálini, for Champá *or* Málini, 3. 289; 4. 125.

Chandravijaya, for Chandravijna, 4. 199.

Chedyas, for Chedis, 2. 157,

Chit-sukha-yoni, for Chitsukha Yogin, P. 115; 5. 385.

Dalaya, for Dálbhya, 3. 7.

Dańd'anaya, for Dańd'a *and* Naya, 1. 111; 5. 386.

Dárvan, for Darva, 4. 121.

Devamíd'hush, for Devamíd'husha, son of Vrishni, 4. 73.

Devamíd'hush, for Devamíd'husha, son of Súra, 4. 100.

Dharmadhris, for Dharmadhrik, 4. 95.

Dharmasávarni, for Dharmasávarńika, 3. 26.

Dhátaki (*i.e.*, Dhátakin), for Dhátaki, son of Savana, 2. 201, where see note †, for Dhátaki, the name of a region, left unrepresented.

Dhŕishťu, for Dhŕishńu, 3. 13, 337.

Dhúmaketu, for Dhúmrakesa, 2. 29.

Diśá, for Diśas, 1. 117.

Driptiketu for Díptiketu, son of Dákshasávarńa, 3. 25.

Durvásas, for Daurvásasa, P. 87 (line 2); 1. 199.

Duryáman, for Durgama (?), 4. 119.

Dúshitáśwa, for Dhyushitáśwa, 3. 322, 323.

Gahwaras (?), a people, 2. 187.

Gáńapátas, for Gáńapatas, 5. 280.

Gandhamojaváńá, two names, with the first corrupted, run into one, 4. 95, where see note **.

Gara, for Nara, 4. 121, where see note †, on the probable origin of the error.

Gardabhinas, for Gardabhinas, 4. 203.

Gautama, for Gotama, sprung from Utathya, 8. 16.

Girigahwaras, no name of a people, 2. 186.

Goswalu, for Gokhalu, 3. 46, where see note *, for the origin of the error.

Gotama, for Gautama, the Vyása, 3. 35.

Hari, for Haryá, 3. 17.

Hayagríva, confounded with Haya-
síraha, a form of Vishṇu, P.
86; 5. 2, 3.

Hayaśirá, for Hayaśiras, daughter
of Vṛishaparvan, 2. 70.

Hayaśiras, for Hayaśirá, daughter
of Vaiśwánara, 2. 71 (bis).

Hímáhwa, for Hima, 2. 103.

Jángalas, no such people named
in the Vishṇu-puráṇa, 2. 156,
176.

Jarutkáru, for Játúkarṇa, a Vyása,
3. 36.

Jaṭhara. See the preceding Index.

Jayantapur (sic), for Jayanta, a
city, 3. 331.

Jrimbhiká. See I. 82, note †.

Ka, no wind so called, 4. 304,
where, in note ‖, the origin of
the error is shown.

Kakud, for Kakubh, 2. 21; 5.
388.

Kálíká-puráṇa. See Kálíká-upa-
puráṇa, in the preceding Index.

Kámákshyá, for Kámákhyá, P. 90.

Kambalavarhish, for Kambalabar-
hisha, 4. 97, 100.

Kanaka, for Kanavaka, 4. 113.

Kanárka, for Koṇárka, 5. 311.
See Koṇárka, in the preceding
Index.

Kanwas, for Kanwáyanas. See
the preceding Index.

Kauśala, for Kausalya, 'of Kosala,' 5. 82.

Kharadúshana, for Khara and
Dúshaṇa, 3. 316.

Kodrava, for Koradúsha, 1. 95;
5. 386.

Kritajaya, for Kṛita and Jaya, 4.
27.

Kroshṭí (sic), for Kroshṭu, 4. 53.
Vide supra, p. 256, note 3.

Kroshṭri, for Kroshṭu, 4. 61.
Vide supra, p. 256, note 3.

Kroshṭuki, for Kraushṭuki, 5.
381.

Kshatropakshatra, for Kshattra
and Upakshattra (?), 4. 95.

Kshemí, for Kshemyá, 4. 262.

Kubháṇḍa, for Kumbháṇḍa, 5.
109. Probably there was, instead of m in a conjunct, an
anuswára, dimly written, or
else unnoticed.

Kubjá, no name, but an epithet,
5. 21, 22.

Kukkuras, for Kukuras, 5. 147.

Kukkura, for Kukura, 4. 97; 5.
132.

Kuṇḍinapura. See the preceding
Index.

Kuravas, for Kurus, 4. 184.

Kuru, for Úrva, grandfather of
Jamadagni, 3. 16, 80.

Kuśa, for Úrva, grandfather of
Jamadagni, 3. 16, 80.

Kuśáśwa. See 4. 15, note ⁑

Lakshaná, for Lakshmaná, 5. 83.

Lavana, for Lambana, doubly denotative, 2. 195, where, in note
‡, the origin of the error is de-
monstrated.

Lomaharsha, for Lomaharshaṇa,
3. 64.

Lunation, misuse of the term, P
64; 5. 109, 249.

Madhwat, for Mídhwas, 3. 335.

Madhyama, for Madhya, 5. 188.

Madra, for Madraka, 4. 122,

Mádreyas, no name, 2. 156.

Magadha, for Magadhá, a city (?), 4. 216.

Magadhá, for Magadh_, a country, P. 107; 4. 151; 5. 50 (where, in note ‡, read ‘ Magadhá’).

Magadhá, for the Magadhas, 4. 218, where see note ‡, for the origin of the error.

Mahánandi, 4, 182. *Vide supra*, p. 259, note 12.

Mahándhraka, corrupted from Mahídhraka, 3. 332.

Mahásaila, no proper name (?), 2. 197.

Mahávanyá, no name, 2. 196.

Maitreya, error for Mitrayu, 3. 64, note ||.

Mandahára, for Mandarahariñá, 2. 129.

Manichaka, for Manívaka, from mistaking for *oh* the Nágari *v* carelessly written, 2. 198.

Márshtí, for Márahi, 4. 109.

Márshtímat, for Márshimat, 4. 109.

Maruts, for Marutwats, 2. 21, 22.

Medha, for Medhas, 2. 100; 5. 388.

Medhatíthi, Medhátíthi, for Medhádhfíti, 3. 25, 227, where the origin of the error is pointed out.

Menda, for Mainda, 5. 139. The Translator seems to have been misled by M. Langlois's Mênda.

Meru, substituted, by the Translator, for Sumeru, 1. 129; 5. 387.

Mithilá, not the name of a country, as in some places said to be, 4. 344

Nábhin, for Nábha, variant of Nábhága, 3. 303.

Nujava, for Nahusha, 3. 232.

Nála, error for Tála, a measure so called, 1. 93. A Nágari *t* must have been mistaken for *n*.

Naraka, erroneously substituted for Raurava, 1. 112; 5. 386.

Nirámaya, no name (?), 3. 25. See the preceding Index.

Niryyúha, for Nirvyúha, 5. 31. The Sanskrit corresponded, in the former edition.

Nishatha, for Nisatha, 5. 68.

Niyati, See the preceding Index.

Nrichakshu, for Nrichakshus, 4. 164.

Pabnavas. See the preceding Index, and 2. 187, note §.

Páninas, for Pániñs, 4. 28.

Panéchi, for Panchi (?), 4. 46.

Parájita, for Aparájita, son of Krishña, 5. 81.

Páravas, for Páradas, 3. 290.

Paushyinji, for Paushpinji, 3. 58, 60, 61.

Pippaláyani, for Paippaláyani, 3. 62.

Prájápati, for Prájápatya, a wind so called, 5. 204.

Prastútas (?), for Prastútas, 3. 12.

Pratibimba. See 1. 82, note †.

Prativyoman, for Prativyoma, 4. 167.

Prithurukman, for Prithurukma, 4. 64.

Priyamedhas, for Priyamedha, 4.
140.

Pulomat, for Puloman, 2. 211.

Puraña, for Ápuraña, 5. 251.

Purishin, for Purishí, 1. 85.

Purujit, for Ruchaka, son of Usanas, 4. 63.

Ramya, no name, but an epithet,
2. 199.

Rasalomá, for Rusaná, 4. 117.

Rathínara, for Rathítara, son of
Písbadaswa, son of Virúpa, 3.
258. A Nágarí t was mistaken
for n.

Ratnagarbha Bhatta, for Ratnagarbha Bhattáchárya, 5 385.

Riju, for Rijwáhwa, 5. 382, 385.

Riña, for Riñajya, 3. 35.

Rishikesa, for Hrishíkesa, 4. 278.

Romáñas, for Romans, 2. 176.

Ropáñas, for Ropana, 2. 176.

Rukman, for Rukma, 4. 64.

Rushadru, for Rushadgu, from
reading as dru the Nágarí conjunct letter for dgu.

Saktri, error for Sakti, son of
Vasishtha, 1. 6–8, 155; 3. 35,
36, 306.

Saláká, for Sálákya, 4. 33.

Salu (Salu), no word (for khalu),
2. 151, 340.

Salya, for Sálwa, king of the Saubhas, 5. 70.

Salya, for Sala, son of Somadatta,
5. 134.

Samparáyaña, for Paráyaña, 3. 57.

Sankbapáda, for Sankbapád, the
Lokapála, 1. 155; 2. 86, 263,
338.

Santákhya, for Santaraya, 4. 43.

Santati, for Samnati, 4. 37, perhaps from mistaking a Nágarí
t for n.

Sáranga, for Sárnga, 5. 135.

Sárimejaya, for Arimejaya, 4. 95.

Sarpi, for Sarpis, 2. 109.

Sarpí, for Sarpis, 1. 117 (where
expunge, in note ||, "Sarpí . . .
neuter").

Saru, for Satha, from reading as ru
the Nágarí letter for th, 4. 109.

Sarvapápahará, no name, but an
epithet, 2. 196.

Sasadharman, for Satadhanwan,
4. 190.

Satábhishá (rightly, Satabhishá),
substituted, by the Translator,
for Satabhishaj, 2. 268; 3.
167, 169.

Satadhanu, for Satadhanus, son
of Hrídika, 4. 99.

Satrájit, Sátrajit, for Sattrájita, 4.
74; 5. 148.

Satrujit, for Sattrájita, 5. 81.

Saubhímá, for Subbímá, 5. 83.

Saudattá, for Sudattá, 5. 82, 83.

Saurapátas, for Saurapatas, 5.
280.

Savala, for Savana, son of Priyavrata, 2. 100, where, in note †,
the origin of the error is demon-
strated.

Selu. See Salu.

Simálakarni,   Simalakarni,   for
Srímallakarni, 4. 195, 200.

Sisiráyaña, for Saisiráyaña, 5. 53.
note *.

Sítoda, for Asitoda, 2. 117.

Somasushmápaña, for Saumasushmáyaña, 3. 35.

S'ravanti, error for S'ravaati (noted as such), 3. 264.

S'rivaswani, no name, most probably, 4. 196, 200.

Sthaneswara, for Sthanwiswara, 2. 143 ; 5. 388.

Sudhamana, for Sutramana, 3. 28.

Sudhanush, for Sudhanu, 4. 148.

Sudhanwan, substituted, by the Translator, for S'atadhanwan, 4. 89.

Sudhanwat, for Sudhanwan, 4. 148.

S'udhinandi, for Sushinandi, 4. 211.

Sukumara, substituted, by the Translator, for Sukumaraka, 4. 76, &c.

Sumalin, for Sunaman, 5. 41.

Sumallia, for Sumallikas, 2. 175.

S'unahsephas, for S'unahsepha, 3. 289 ; 4. 25.

Sunanda, for Sunandana, 4. 197.

Supratitha, for Supratika, 4. 168.

S'urabhiras, error of M. Langlois, for S'uras and Abhiras, 2. 133.

Susuma, for Susrama, 4. 175.

Suvithi, for Swarvithi, 5. 388.

Swadha, for Sudha, wife of Vamadeva, 1. 117.

Syala, no name of a person, 5. 53.

Talaka, for Pattalaka, 4. 197, note †.

Tamasitra, for Tambamitra, 5. 250.

Tamrapakshi, for Tamrapaksha, 5. 107.

Tosalaka, for Tosalaka, from mistaking a broken Nagari s for m, 5. 39.

Trayyaruna, for Tryaruna, 3. 65.

Trayyaruna, for Tryaruna, 3. 284, note 1.

Trina, no name, 4. 121.

Triyaruna, for Triyaruni (1), 3. 221, 340.

Udayinbhadraka, for Udayibhadraka, 4. 182.

Ujasi, no name, most probably, 4. 123.

Urddhabahu, for Urdhwabahu, son of Vasishtha, 1. 155.

Urddhabahu, for Urdhwabahu, a Rishi, 3. 10.

Uru, for Urva, grandfather of Jamadagni, 3. 16, 80.

Utsavamanketaa, for Utsavasanketaa, from mistaking a broken Nagari s for m, 2. 179.

Uttarakuru, substituted, by the Translator, for Kuru, 2. 123.

Vahlikas, Vahlikas, See the preceding Index.

Vaideha, for Videha, 3. 330.

Vama Yamachárin, for Vamachárin (1), 5. 326, 392.

Vapra, for Vaprivan, 3. 34.

Vapu, for Vapus, daughter of Daksha, &c., 1. 109, 110.

Varanasi, Varanasi, for Varanasi, &c., 5. 121.

Vasahanu, for Vatashanu, 4. 141.

Vedasira, 2. 29. See the preceding Index, where the words "rightly, Vedasiras" require explaining. The advertent corruption in the Bhágavata-puráná is Vedasira, for which the Translator substituted Vedasiras.

Vibhráfra, for Vibhrája, 4. 141.

Viraja, for Vairâ, 3. 86, 261.

Viswagáśwa. See the preceding Index.

Viswagiyotish, for Vishwagjyotis, 2. 107.

Viswaksena. See the preceding Index.

Viśwaphúrji, for Viśwasphúrji, 4. 217.

Viśwasaba, for Viśwasáhwan, 3. 325 ; 5. 391.

Viśwavyarchas, for Viśwatryarchas, 5. 191, which see in the preceding Index.

Vivinéati, for Vivirhśa, 3. 243.

Vraja, for Vajra, son of Aniruddha, 5. 108.

Vrihadbrája, for Brihadrája, 4. 169.

Vrihadrathantara, for Brihat and Rathantara, 2. 295, 343.

Vrishakáhwá, for Vrishaká, 2. 154.

Vrishaaáhwá, for Vrishaaá, 2 154.

Vyushitáśwa, for Dhyushitáśwa, 3. 322, 323.

Vyutthitáśwa, for Dhyushitáśwa, 3. 322, 323.

Yajnakrit, for Yajnakrita, 4. 44.

Yauni, for Yoni, 2. 194.

Yuyudhána, for Yuyudhan, 3. 334, note †††.

www.ingramcontent.com/pod-product-compliance
Lightning Source LLC
Chambersburg PA
CBHW060614030726
47498CB00005B/1670